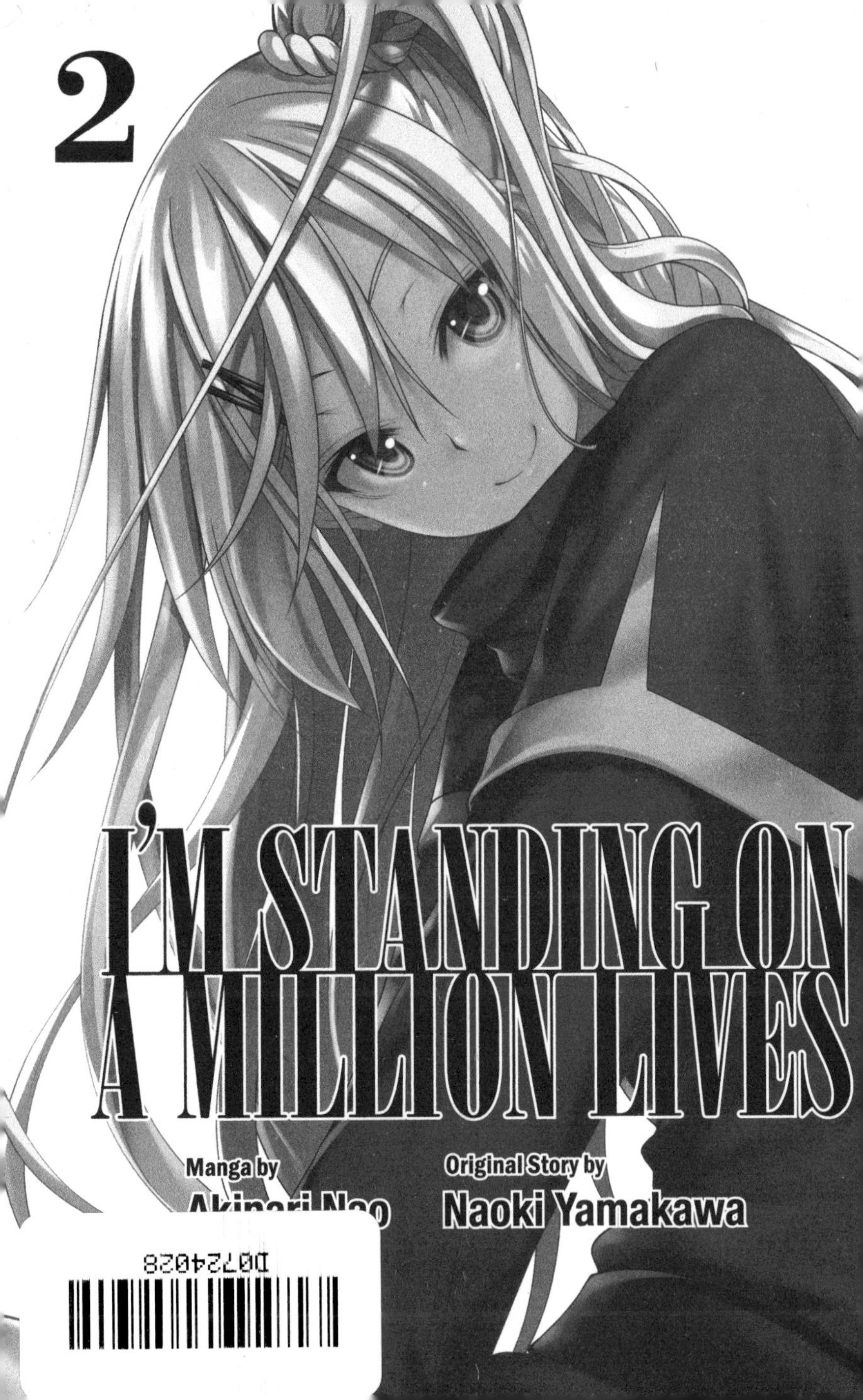
2
I'M STANDING ON A MILLION LIVES
Manga by
Akinari Nao
Original Story by
Naoki Yamakawa

✄ CONTENTS ✄

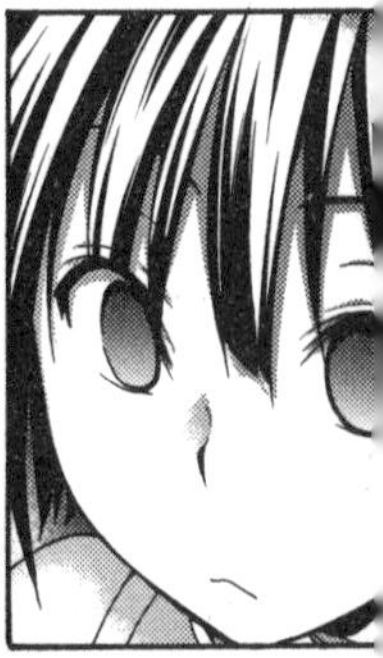

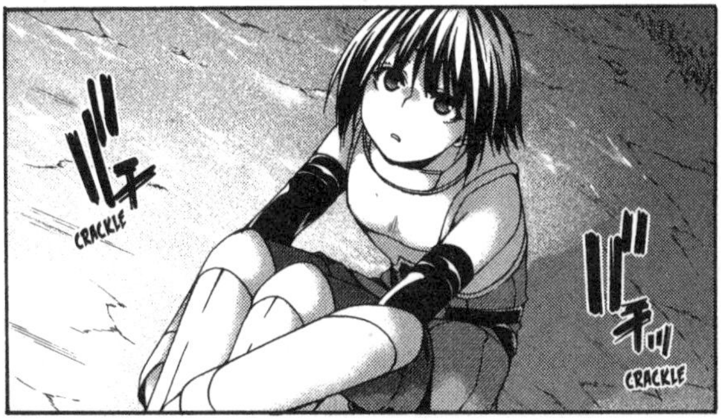
CRACKLE
CRACKLE

#5 The Strength & Meaning of the Sickly Warrior

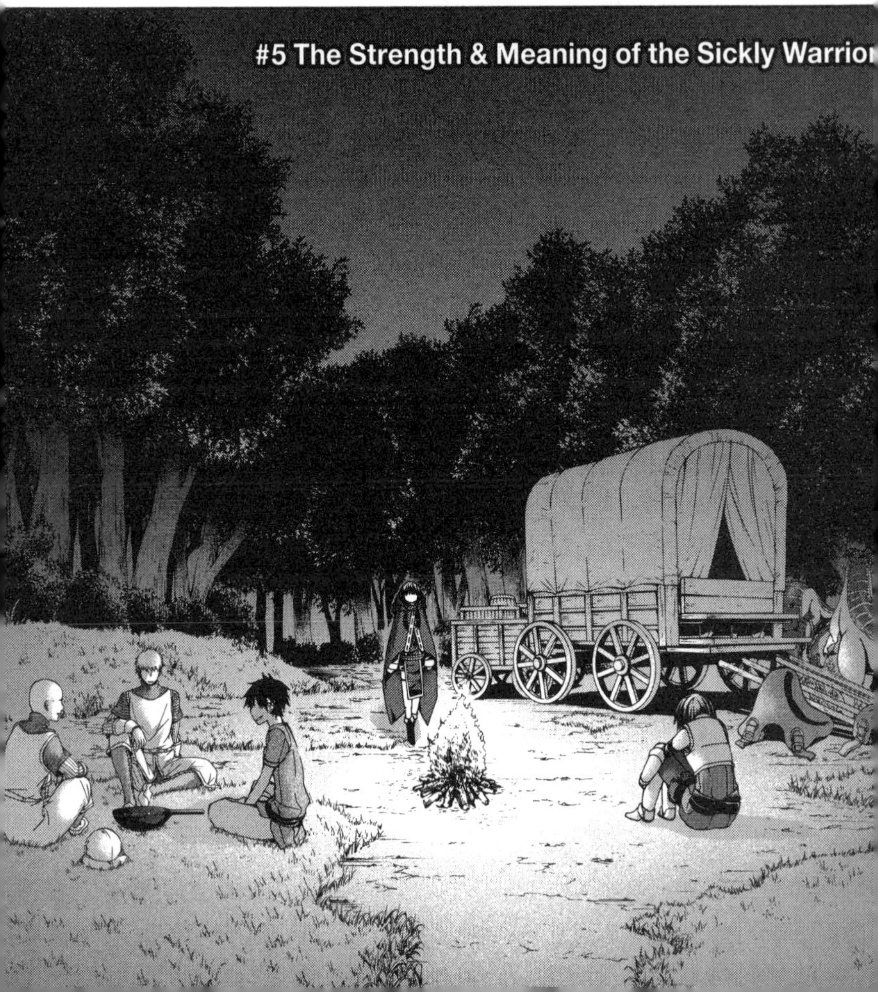

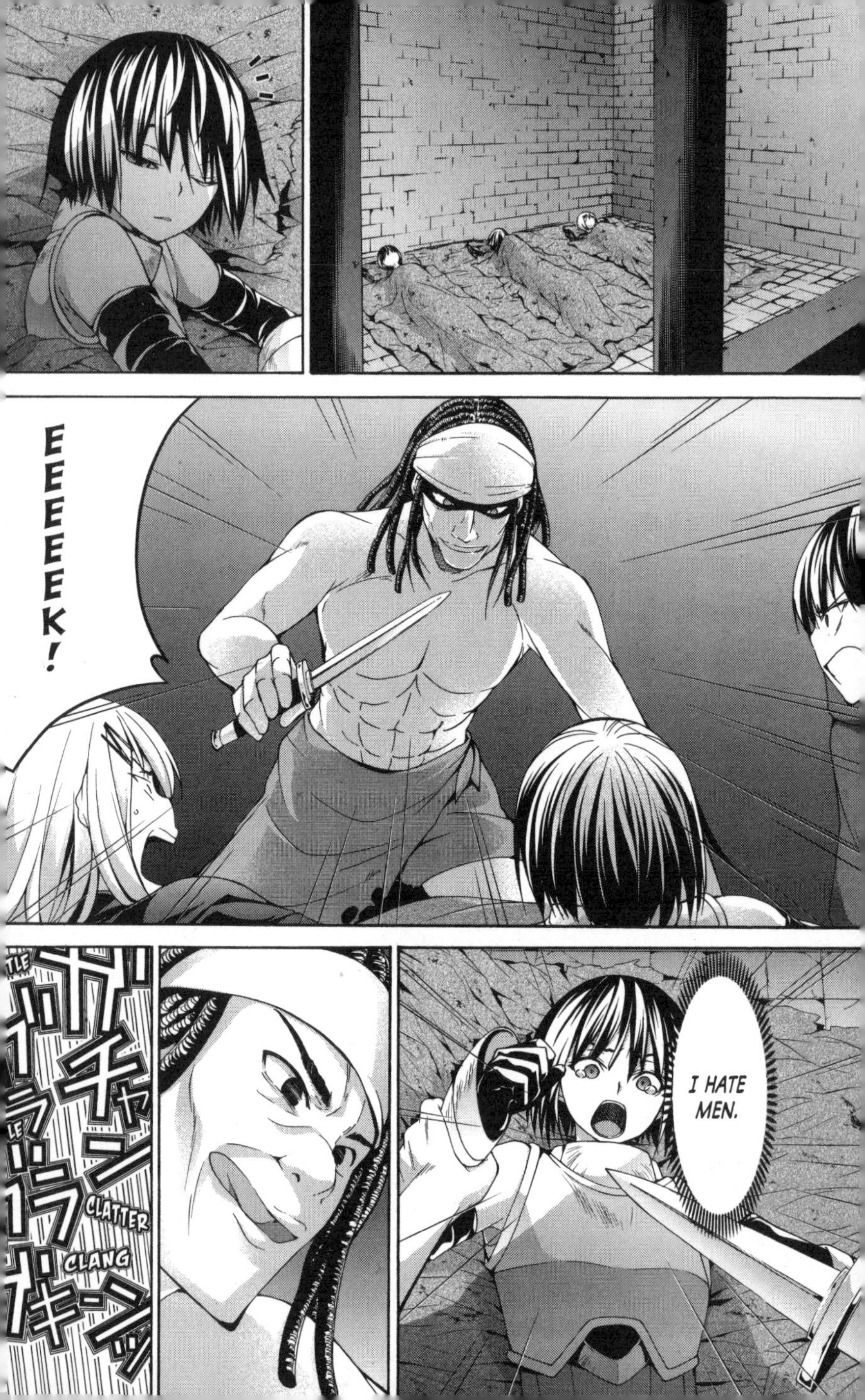
EEEEEEK!
I HATE MEN.
CLATTER
CLANG

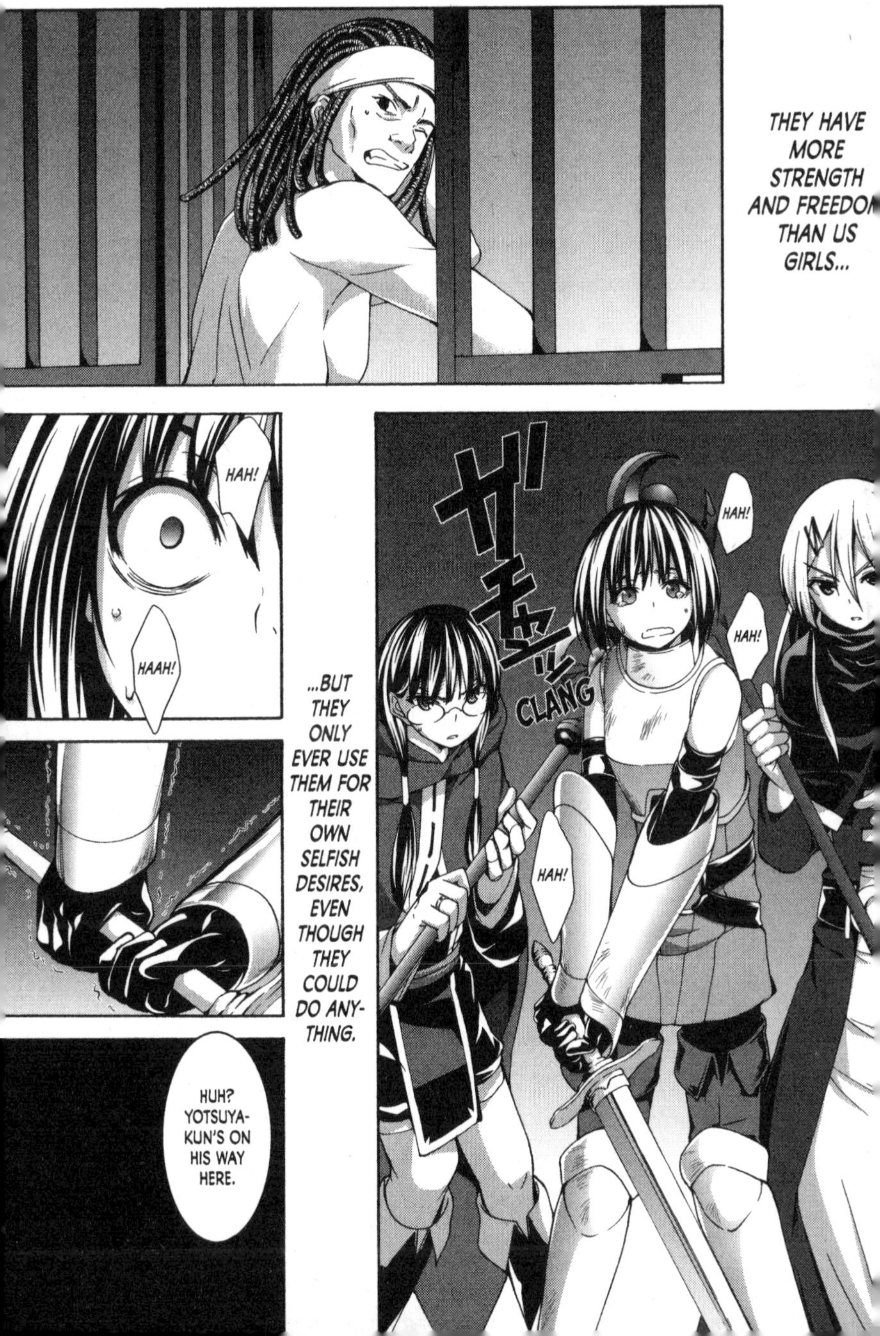
THEY HAVE MORE STRENGTH AND FREEDO THAN US GIRLS...
ガチャッ
CLANG
HAH!
HAH!
...BUT THEY ONLY EVER USE THEM FOR THEIR OWN SELFISH DESIRES, EVEN THOUGH THEY COULD DO ANY-THING.
HAH!
HAH!
HAAH!
HUH? YOTSUYA-KUN'S ON HIS WAY HERE.

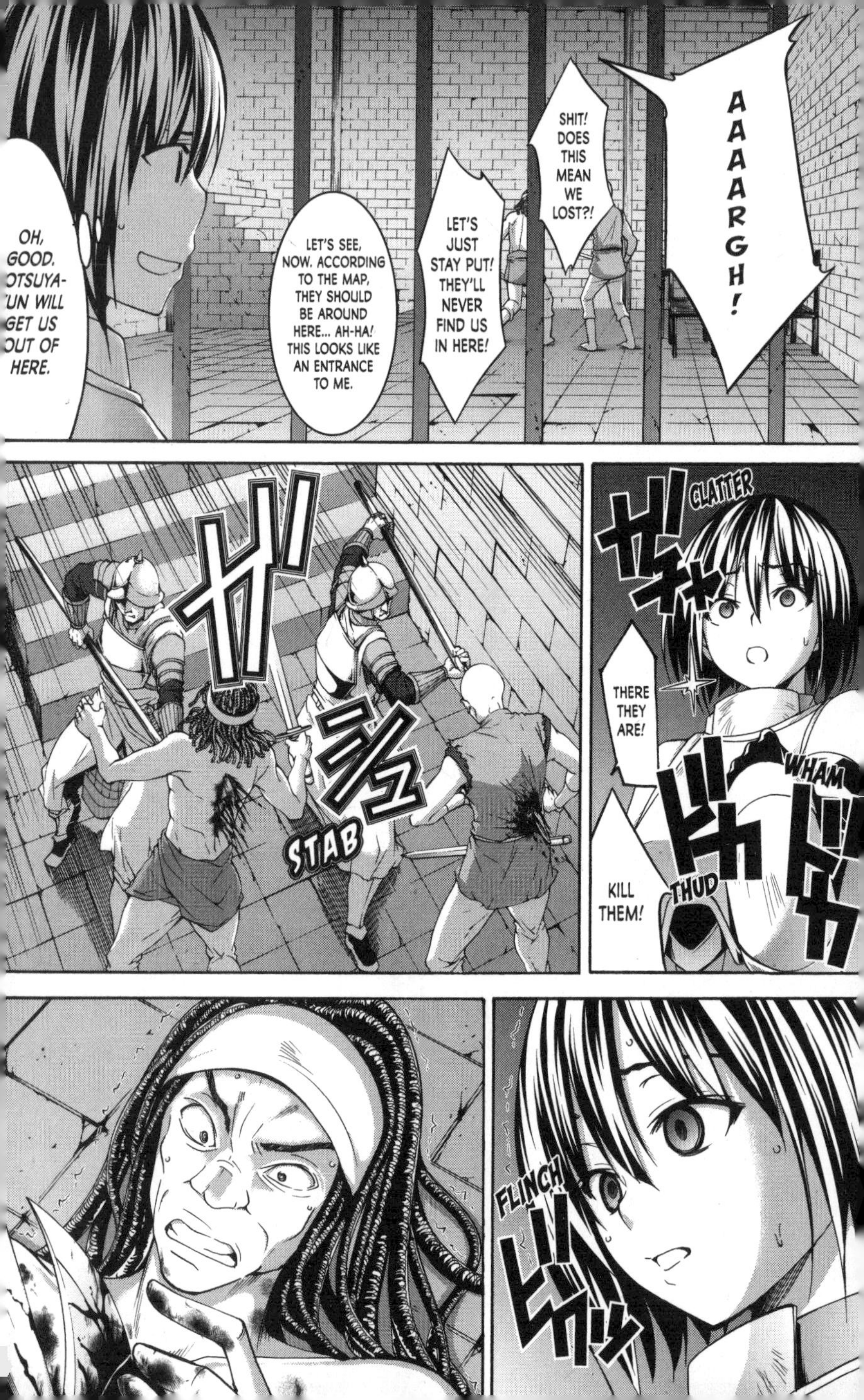
AAAAARGH!
SHIT! DOES THIS MEAN WE LOST?!
LET'S JUST STAY PUT! THEY'LL NEVER FIND US IN HERE!
LET'S SEE, NOW. ACCORDING TO THE MAP, THEY SHOULD BE AROUND HERE... AH-HA! THIS LOOKS LIKE AN ENTRANCE TO ME.
OH, GOOD. OTSUYA-UN WILL GET US OUT OF HERE.
CLATTER
THERE THEY ARE!
WHAM
THUD
KILL THEM!
STAB
FLINCH

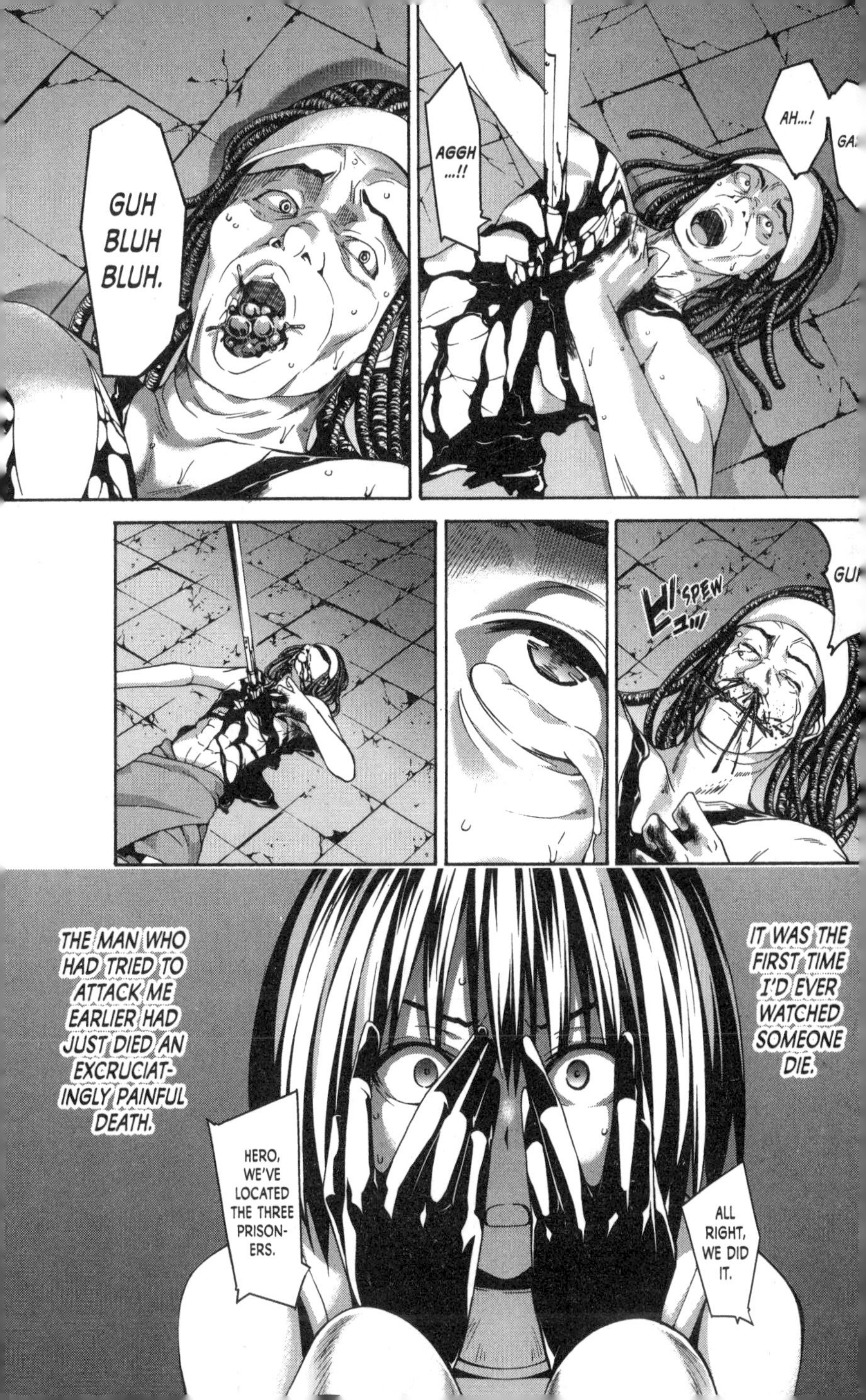
AH...!
AGGH ...!!
GUH BLUH BLUH.
SPEW
IT WAS THE FIRST TIME I'D EVER WATCHED SOMEONE DIE.
THE MAN WHO HAD TRIED TO ATTACK ME EARLIER HAD JUST DIED AN EXCRUCIAT-INGLY PAINFUL DEATH.
HERO, WE'VE LOCATED THE THREE PRISON-ERS.
ALL RIGHT, WE DID IT.

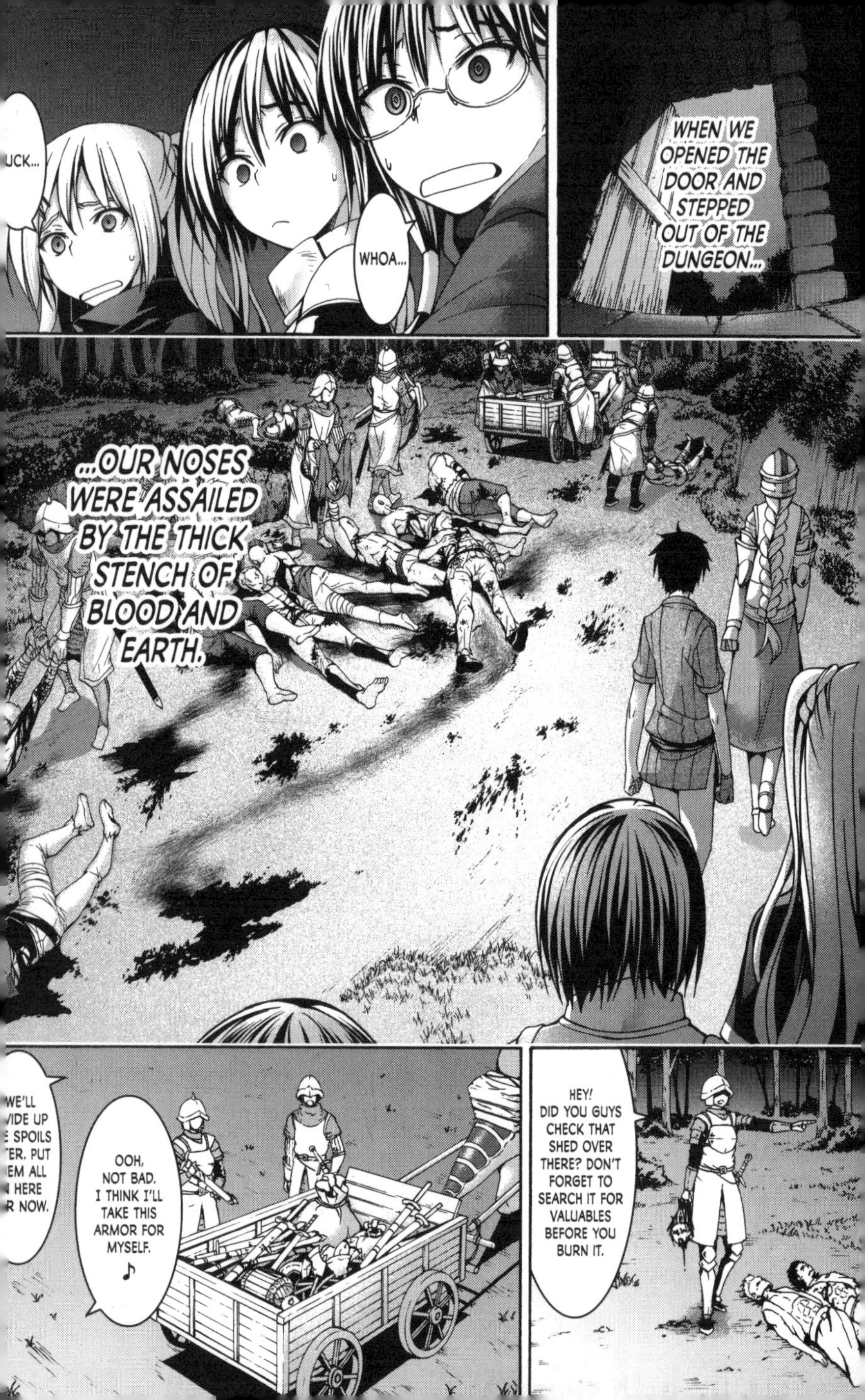
WHEN WE OPENED THE DOOR AND STEPPED OUT OF THE DUNGEON...
WHOA...
UCK...
...OUR NOSES WERE ASSAILED BY THE THICK STENCH OF BLOOD AND EARTH.
HEY! DID YOU GUYS CHECK THAT SHED OVER THERE? DON'T FORGET TO SEARCH IT FOR VALUABLES BEFORE YOU BURN IT.
OOH, NOT BAD. I THINK I'LL TAKE THIS ARMOR FOR MYSELF. ♪
WE'LL VIDE UP E SPOILS TER. PUT EM ALL N HERE R NOW.

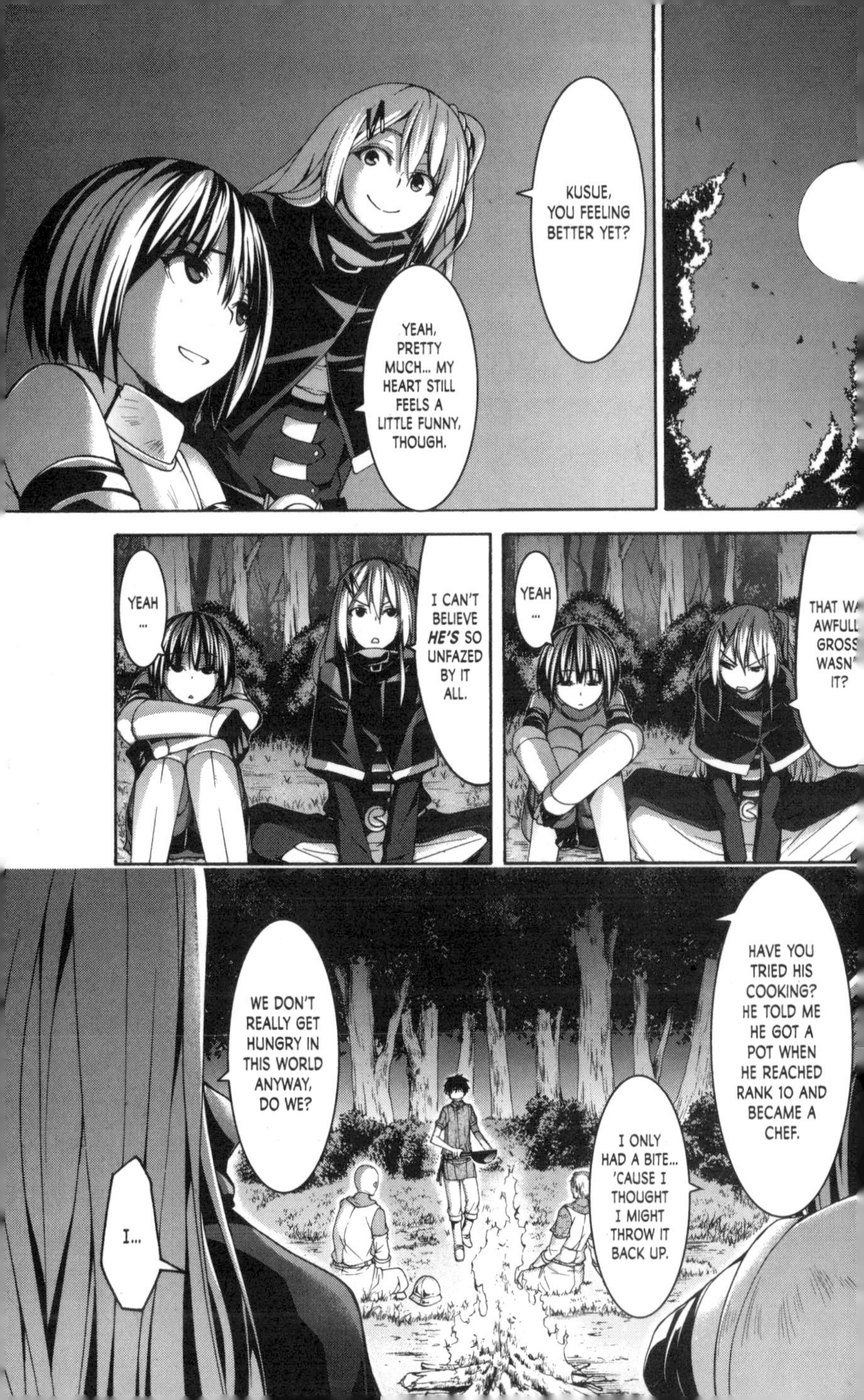

KUSUE, YOU FEELING BETTER YET?
YEAH, PRETTY MUCH... MY HEART STILL FEELS A LITTLE FUNNY, THOUGH.
THAT WA AWFULL GROSS WASN' IT?
YEAH ...
I CAN'T BELIEVE ***HE'S*** SO UNFAZED BY IT ALL.
YEAH ...
HAVE YOU TRIED HIS COOKING? HE TOLD ME HE GOT A POT WHEN HE REACHED RANK 10 AND BECAME A CHEF.
I ONLY HAD A BITE... 'CAUSE I THOUGHT I MIGHT THROW IT BACK UP.
WE DON'T REALLY GET HUNGRY IN THIS WORLD ANYWAY, DO WE?
I...

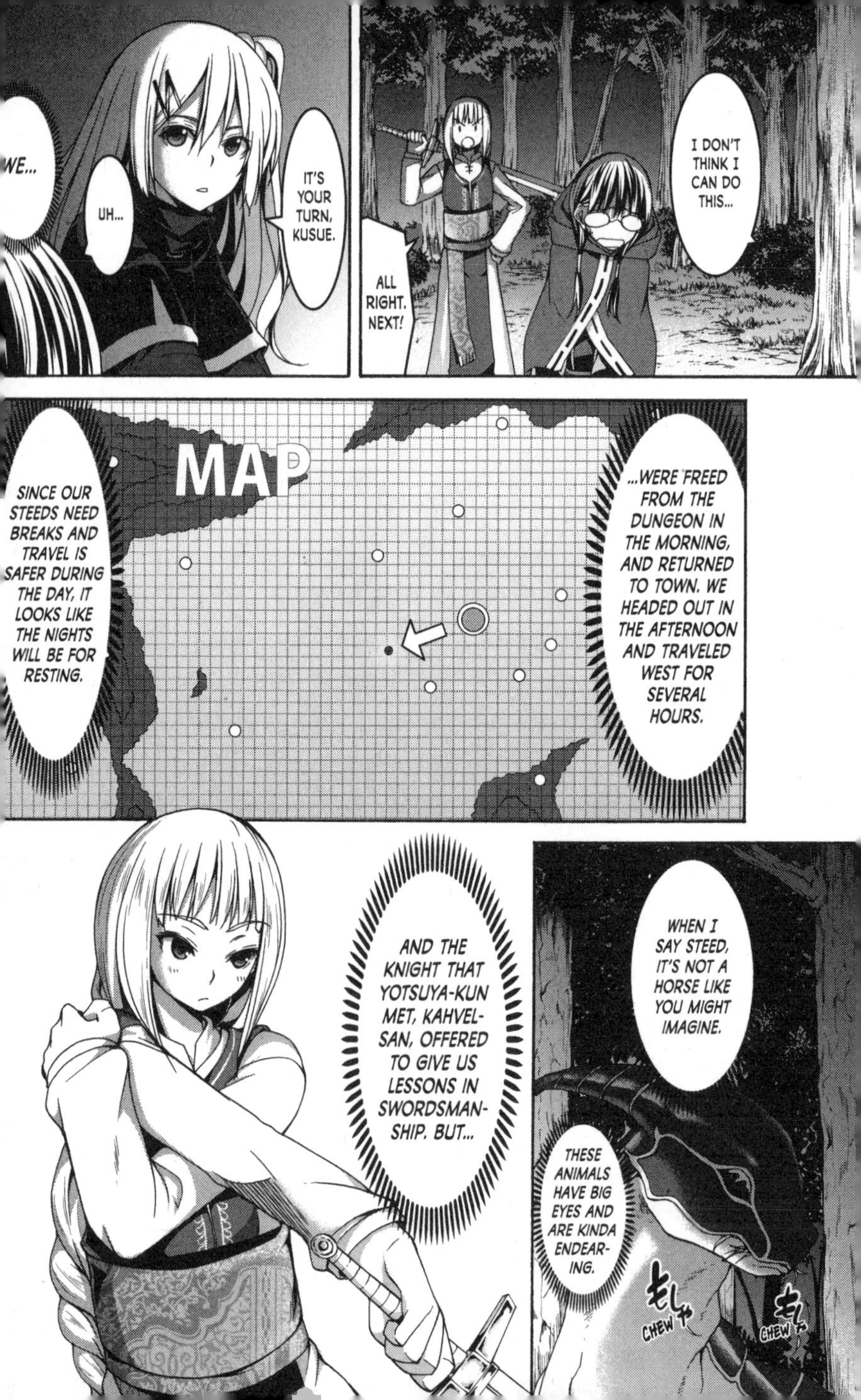
I DON'T THINK I CAN DO THIS...
ALL RIGHT. NEXT!
IT'S YOUR TURN, KUSUE.
UH...
WE...
MAP
...WERE FREED FROM THE DUNGEON IN THE MORNING, AND RETURNED TO TOWN. WE HEADED OUT IN THE AFTERNOON AND TRAVELED WEST FOR SEVERAL HOURS.
SINCE OUR STEEDS NEED BREAKS AND TRAVEL IS SAFER DURING THE DAY, IT LOOKS LIKE THE NIGHTS WILL BE FOR RESTING.
WHEN I SAY STEED, IT'S NOT A HORSE LIKE YOU MIGHT IMAGINE.
THESE ANIMALS HAVE BIG EYES AND ARE KINDA ENDEAR-ING.
CHEW
CHEW
AND THE KNIGHT THAT YOTSUYA-KUN MET, KAHVEL-SAN, OFFERED TO GIVE US LESSONS IN SWORDSMAN-SHIP. BUT...

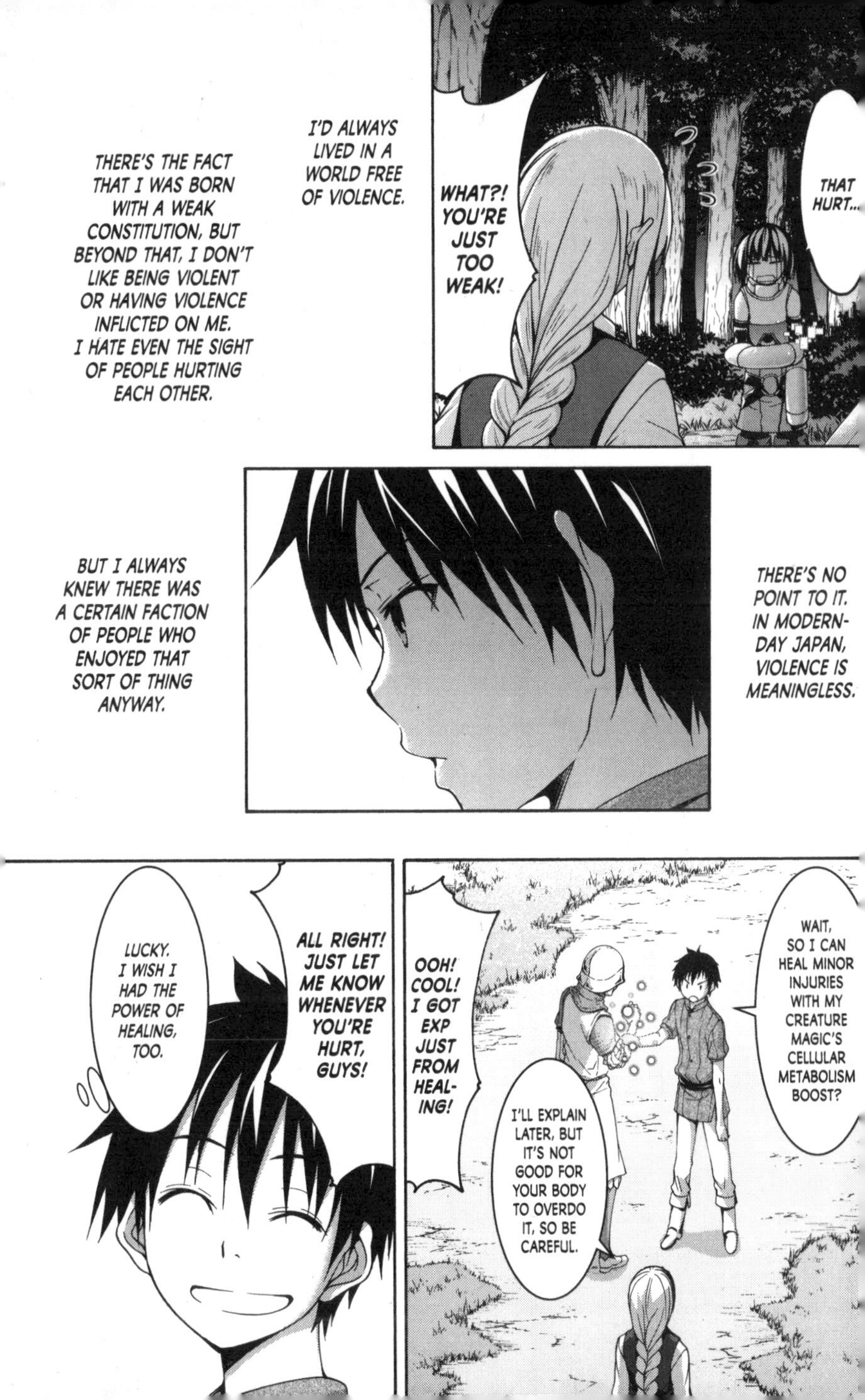
THAT HURT...
WHAT?! YOU'RE JUST TOO WEAK!
I'D ALWAYS LIVED IN A WORLD FREE OF VIOLENCE.
THERE'S THE FACT THAT I WAS BORN WITH A WEAK CONSTITUTION, BUT BEYOND THAT, I DON'T LIKE BEING VIOLENT OR HAVING VIOLENCE INFLICTED ON ME. I HATE EVEN THE SIGHT OF PEOPLE HURTING EACH OTHER.
THERE'S NO POINT TO IT. IN MODERN-DAY JAPAN, VIOLENCE IS MEANINGLESS.
BUT I ALWAYS KNEW THERE WAS A CERTAIN FACTION OF PEOPLE WHO ENJOYED THAT SORT OF THING ANYWAY.
WAIT, SO I CAN HEAL MINOR INJURIES WITH MY CREATURE MAGIC'S CELLULAR METABOLISM BOOST?
I'LL EXPLAIN LATER, BUT IT'S NOT GOOD FOR YOUR BODY TO OVERDO IT, SO BE CAREFUL.
OOH! COOL! I GOT EXP JUST FROM HEAL-ING!
ALL RIGHT! JUST LET ME KNOW WHENEVER YOU'RE HURT, GUYS!
LUCKY. I WISH I HAD THE POWER OF HEALING, TOO.

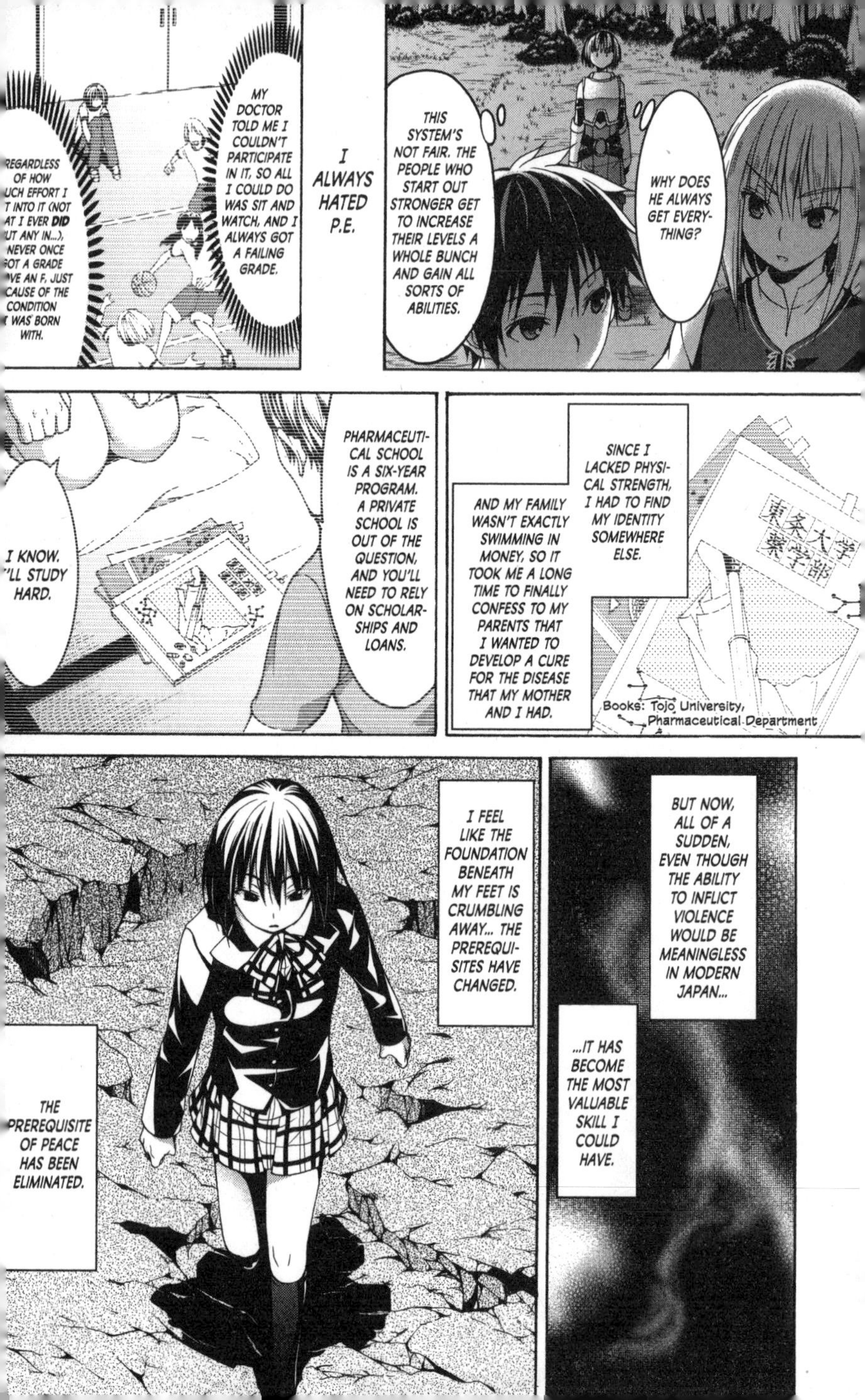

WHY DOES HE ALWAYS GET EVERY-THING?
THIS SYSTEM'S NOT FAIR. THE PEOPLE WHO START OUT STRONGER GET TO INCREASE THEIR LEVELS A WHOLE BUNCH AND GAIN ALL SORTS OF ABILITIES.
I ALWAYS HATED P.E.
MY DOCTOR TOLD ME I COULDN'T PARTICIPATE IN IT, SO ALL I COULD DO WAS SIT AND WATCH, AND I ALWAYS GOT A FAILING GRADE.
REGARDLESS OF HOW UCH EFFORT I T INTO IT (NOT AT I EVER DID UT ANY IN...), NEVER ONCE GOT A GRADE VE AN F, JUST CAUSE OF THE CONDITION WAS BORN WITH.
SINCE I LACKED PHYSI-CAL STRENGTH, I HAD TO FIND MY IDENTITY SOMEWHERE ELSE.
AND MY FAMILY WASN'T EXACTLY SWIMMING IN MONEY, SO IT TOOK ME A LONG TIME TO FINALLY CONFESS TO MY PARENTS THAT I WANTED TO DEVELOP A CURE FOR THE DISEASE THAT MY MOTHER AND I HAD.
東条大学薬学部
Books: Tojo University, Pharmaceutical Department
PHARMACEUTI-CAL SCHOOL IS A SIX-YEAR PROGRAM. A PRIVATE SCHOOL IS OUT OF THE QUESTION, AND YOU'LL NEED TO RELY ON SCHOLAR-SHIPS AND LOANS.
I KNOW. 'LL STUDY HARD.
BUT NOW, ALL OF A SUDDEN, EVEN THOUGH THE ABILITY TO INFLICT VIOLENCE WOULD BE MEANINGLESS IN MODERN JAPAN...
...IT HAS BECOME THE MOST VALUABLE SKILL I COULD HAVE.
I FEEL LIKE THE FOUNDATION BENEATH MY FEET IS CRUMBLING AWAY... THE PREREQUI-SITES HAVE CHANGED.
THE PREREQUISITE OF PEACE HAS BEEN ELIMINATED.

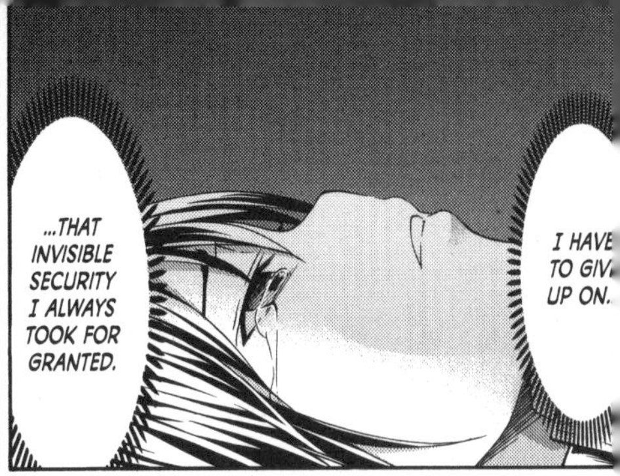
I HAVE TO GIV UP ON.
...THAT INVISIBLE SECURITY I ALWAYS TOOK FOR GRANTED.

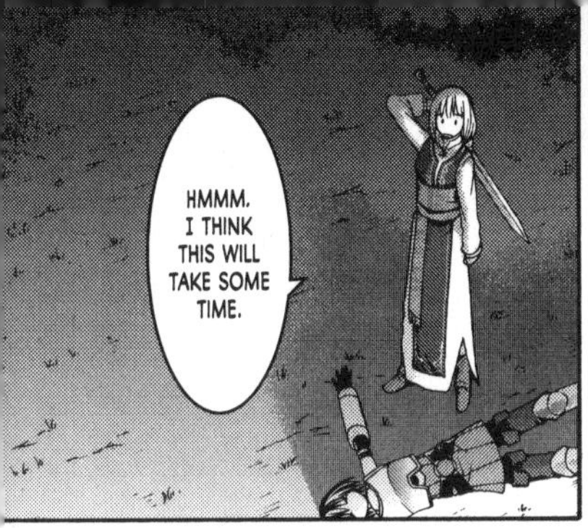
HMMM. I THINK THIS WILL TAKE SOME TIME.

REMAINING TIME: 28 DAYS AND 14 HOURS

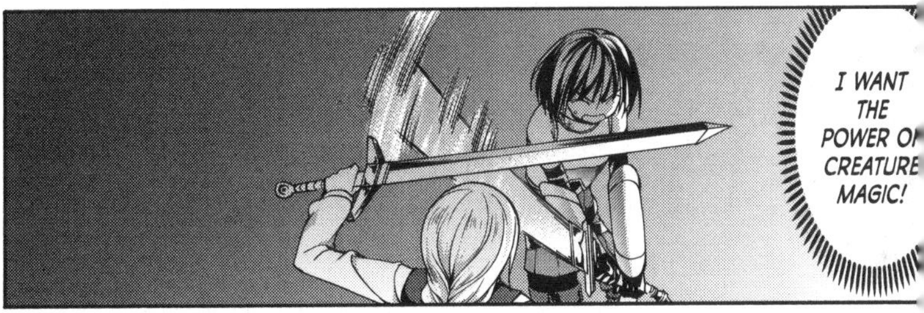
I WANT THE POWER OF CREATURE MAGIC!

REMAINING TIME: 26 DAYS AND 15 HOURS

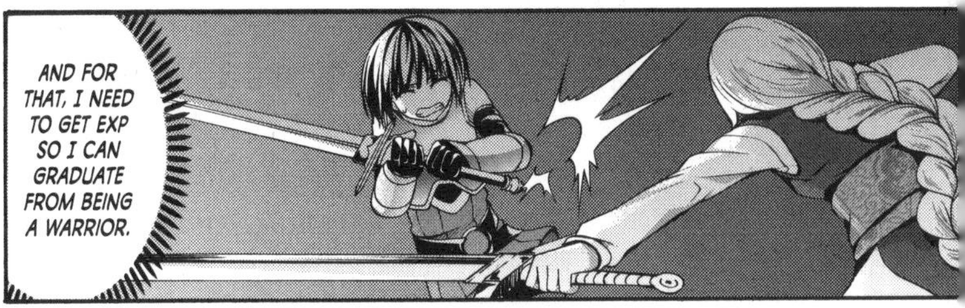
AND FOR THAT, I NEED TO GET EXP SO I CAN GRADUATE FROM BEING A WARRIOR.

REMAINING TIME: 21 DAYS AND 2 HOURS

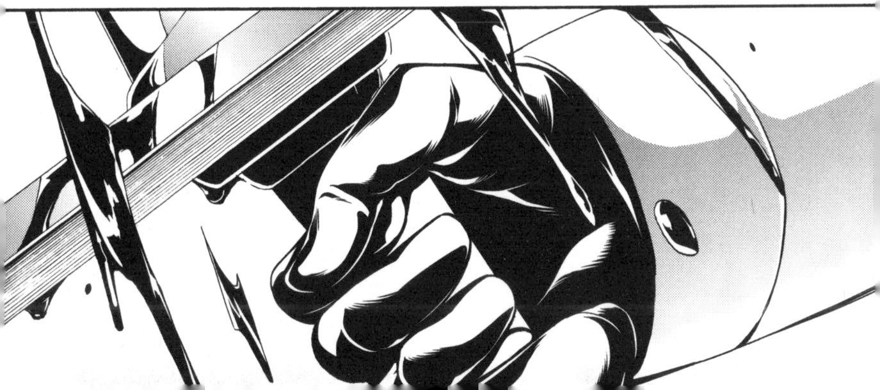

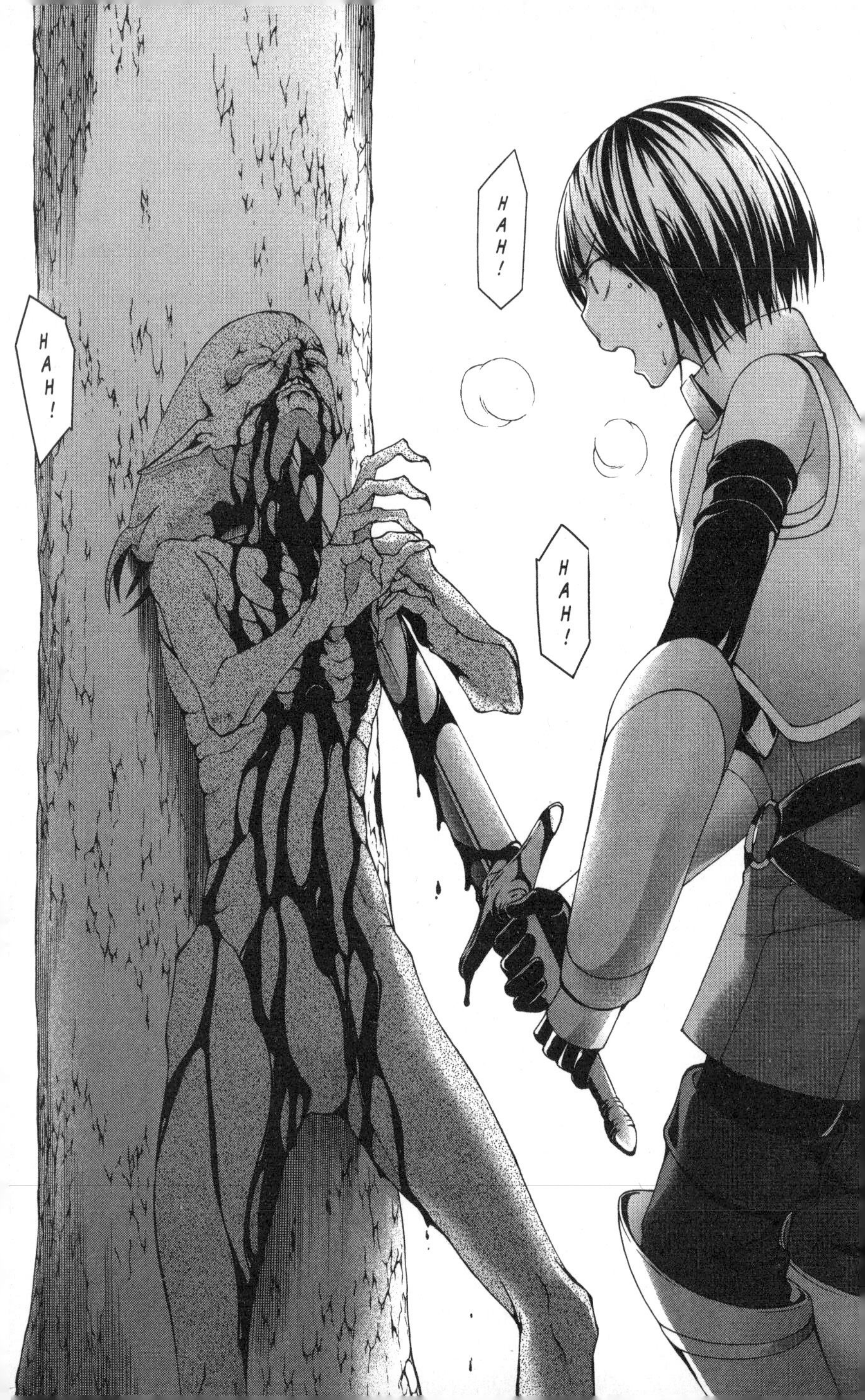
HAH!
HAH!
HAH!

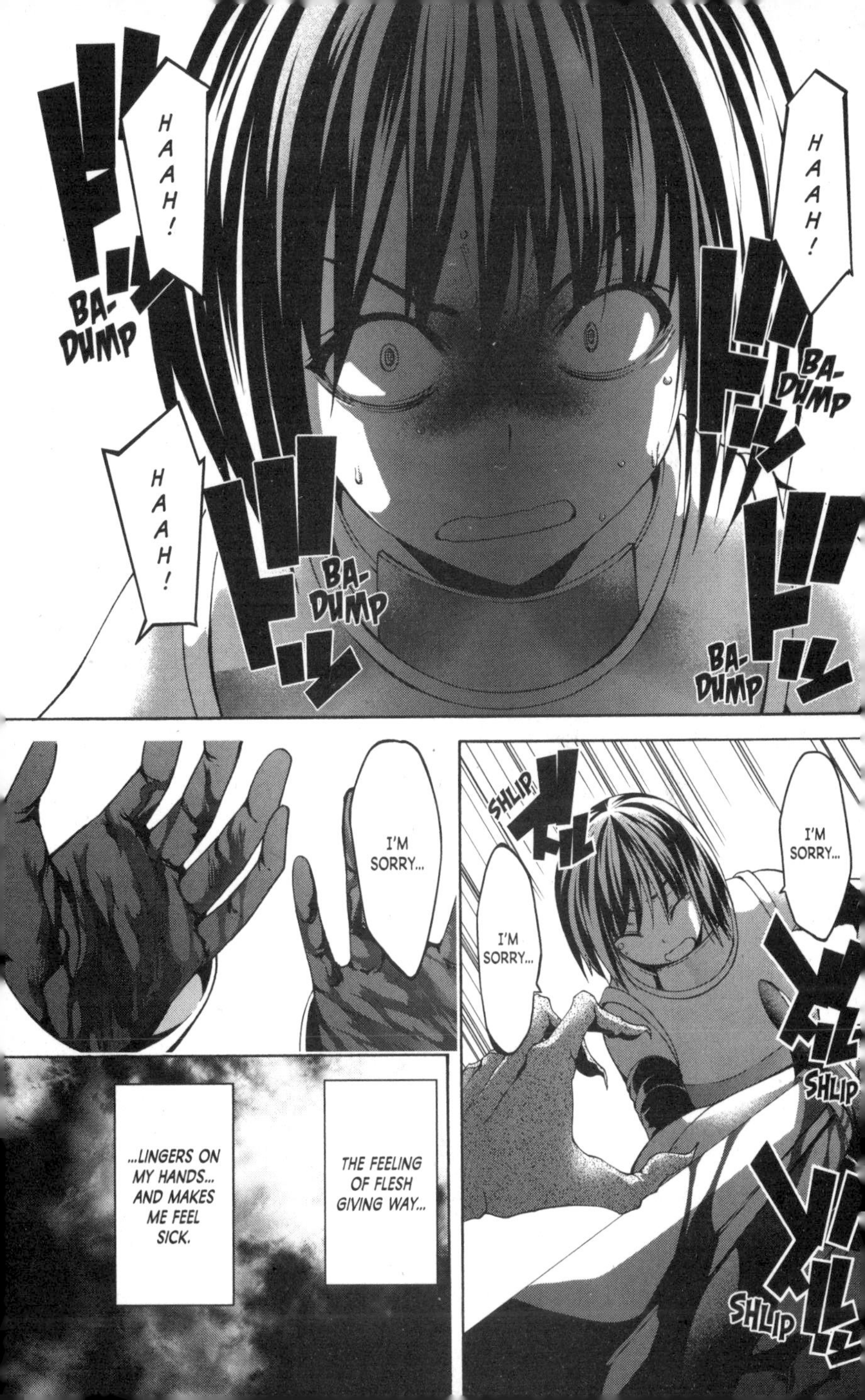
HAAAH!
BA-DUMP
HAAAH!
BA-DUMP
HAAAH!
BA-DUMP
BA-DUMP
SHLIP
I'M SORRY...
I'M SORRY...
SHLIP
SHLIP
I'M SORRY...
THE FEELING OF FLESH GIVING WAY...
...LINGERS ON MY HANDS... AND MAKES ME FEEL SICK.

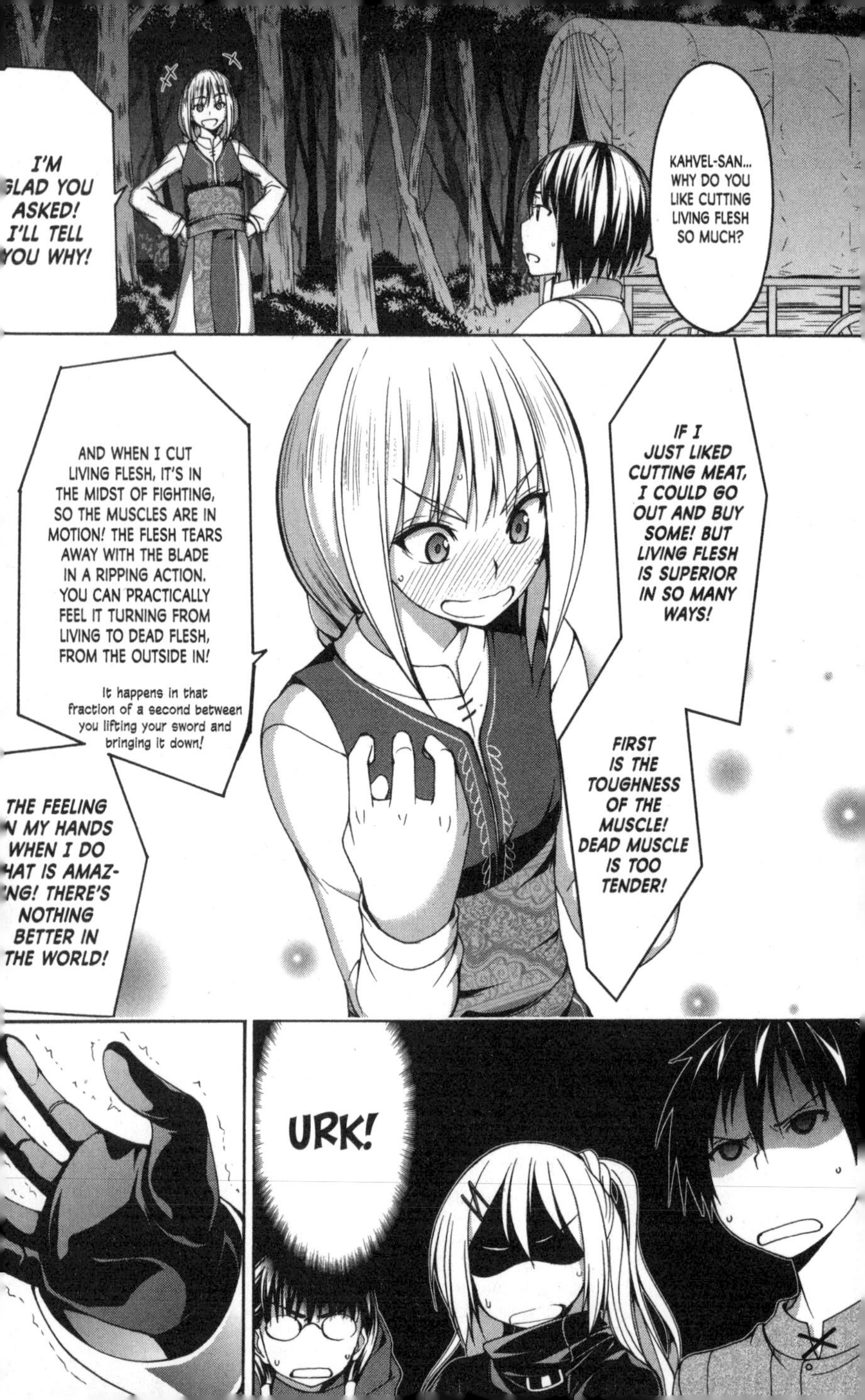
KAHVEL-SAN... WHY DO YOU LIKE CUTTING LIVING FLESH SO MUCH?
I'M GLAD YOU ASKED! I'LL TELL YOU WHY!
IF I JUST LIKED CUTTING MEAT, I COULD GO OUT AND BUY SOME! BUT LIVING FLESH IS SUPERIOR IN SO MANY WAYS!
FIRST IS THE TOUGHNESS OF THE MUSCLE! DEAD MUSCLE IS TOO TENDER!
AND WHEN I CUT LIVING FLESH, IT'S IN THE MIDST OF FIGHTING, SO THE MUSCLES ARE IN MOTION! THE FLESH TEARS AWAY WITH THE BLADE IN A RIPPING ACTION. YOU CAN PRACTICALLY FEEL IT TURNING FROM LIVING TO DEAD FLESH, FROM THE OUTSIDE IN!
It happens in that fraction of a second between you lifting your sword and bringing it down!
THE FEELING IN MY HANDS WHEN I DO THAT IS AMAZ-ING! THERE'S NOTHING BETTER IN THE WORLD!
URK!

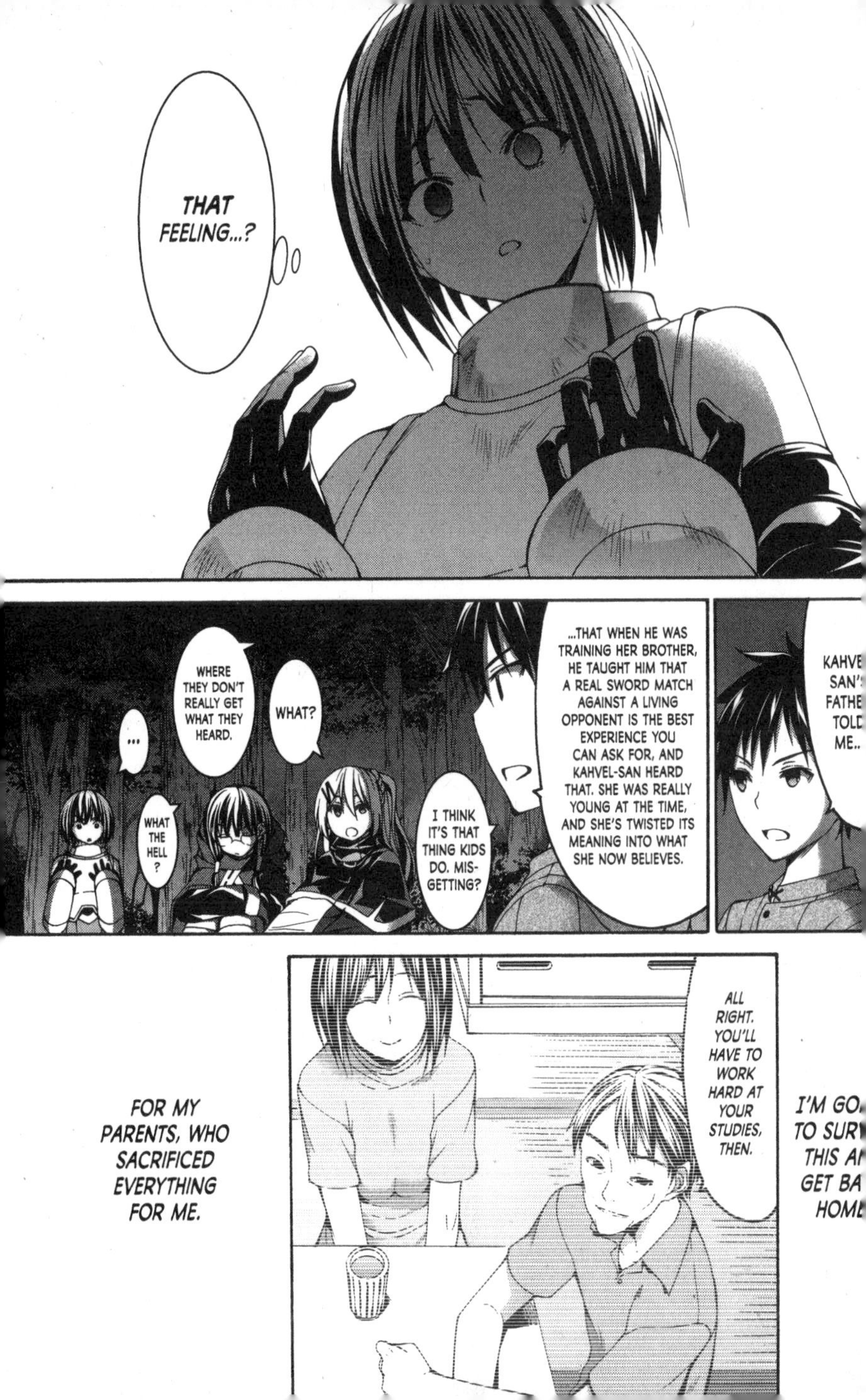
THAT FEELING...?
KAHVE SAN' FATHE TOLD ME..
...THAT WHEN HE WAS TRAINING HER BROTHER, HE TAUGHT HIM THAT A REAL SWORD MATCH AGAINST A LIVING OPPONENT IS THE BEST EXPERIENCE YOU CAN ASK FOR, AND KAHVEL-SAN HEARD THAT. SHE WAS REALLY YOUNG AT THE TIME, AND SHE'S TWISTED ITS MEANING INTO WHAT SHE NOW BELIEVES.
WHAT?
WHERE THEY DON'T REALLY GET WHAT THEY HEARD.
...
I THINK IT'S THAT THING KIDS DO. MIS-GETTING?
WHAT THE HELL?
I'M GO TO SUR THIS A GET BA HOM
ALL RIGHT. YOU'LL HAVE TO WORK HARD AT YOUR STUDIES, THEN.
FOR MY PARENTS, WHO SACRIFICED EVERYTHING FOR ME.

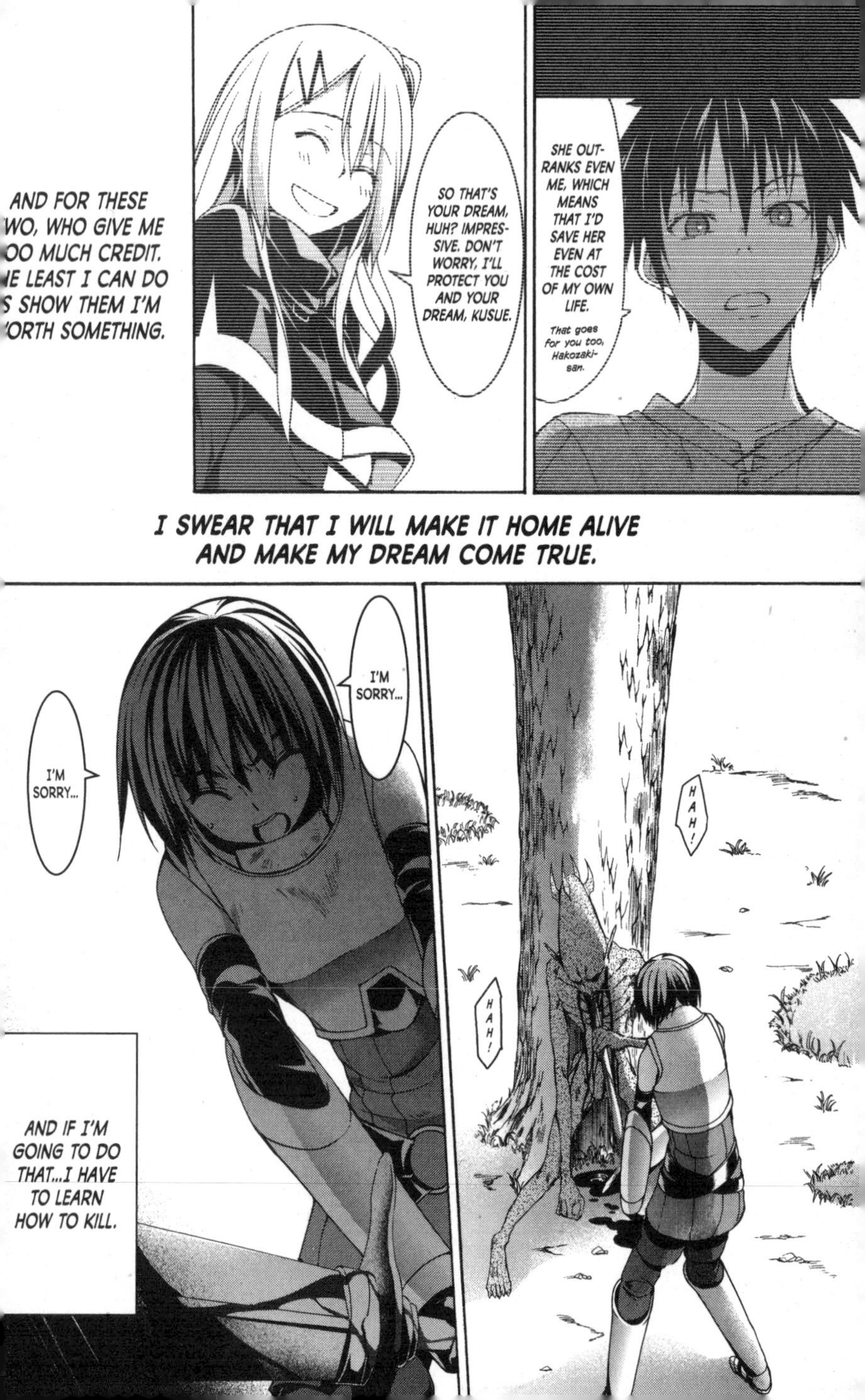
SHE OUT-RANKS EVEN ME, WHICH MEANS THAT I'D SAVE HER EVEN AT THE COST OF MY OWN LIFE.
That goes for you too, Hakozaki-san.
SO THAT'S YOUR DREAM, HUH? IMPRES-SIVE. DON'T WORRY, I'LL PROTECT YOU AND YOUR DREAM, KUSUE.
AND FOR THESE WO, WHO GIVE ME OO MUCH CREDIT. IE LEAST I CAN DO S SHOW THEM I'M ORTH SOMETHING.
I SWEAR THAT I WILL MAKE IT HOME ALIVE AND MAKE MY DREAM COME TRUE.
HAH!
HAH!
I'M SORRY...
I'M SORRY...
AND IF I'M GOING TO DO THAT...I HAVE TO LEARN HOW TO KILL.

REMAINING TIME: 15 DAYS AND 5 HOURS

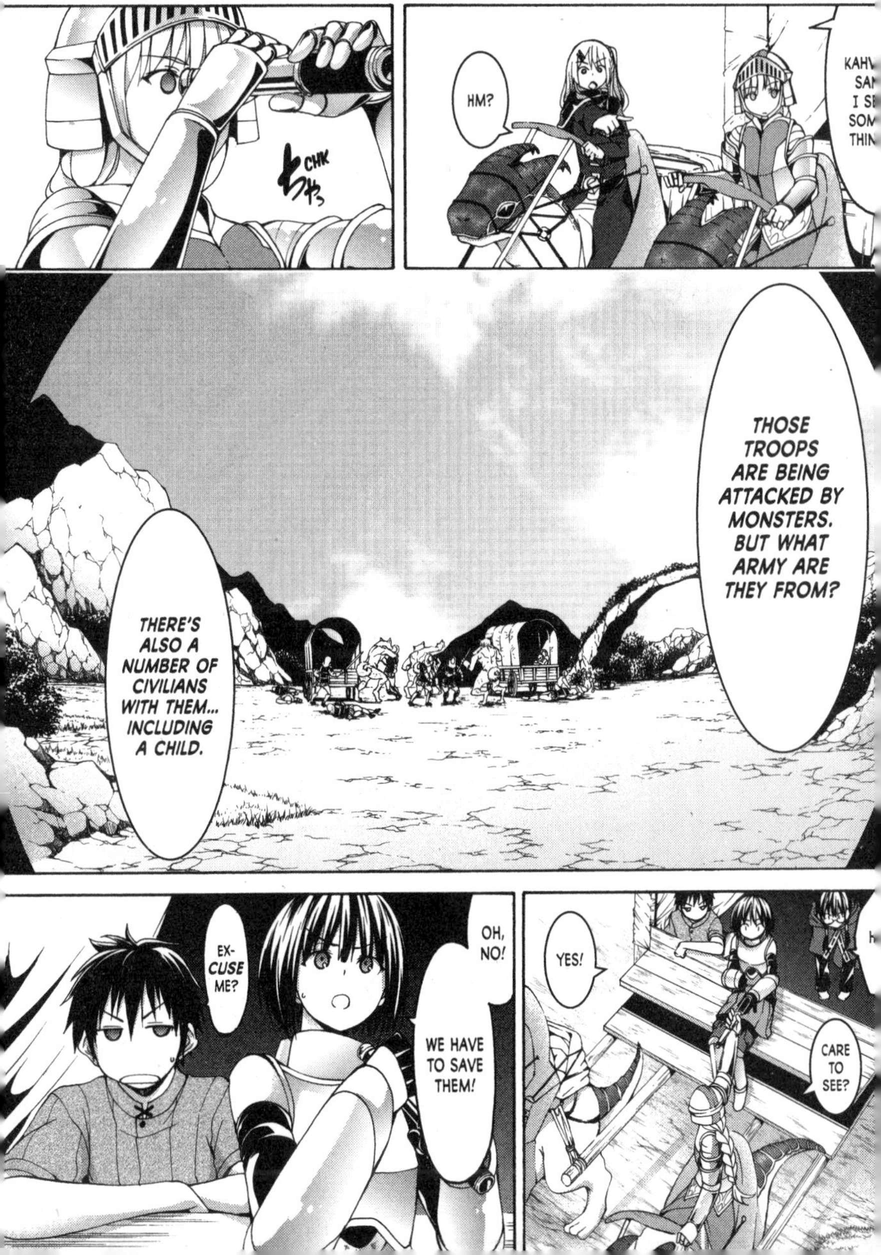
HM?
CHK
THOSE TROOPS ARE BEING ATTACKED BY MONSTERS. BUT WHAT ARMY ARE THEY FROM?
THERE'S ALSO A NUMBER OF CIVILIANS WITH THEM... INCLUDING A CHILD.
CARE TO SEE?
YES!
OH, NO!
WE HAVE TO SAVE THEM!
EX-CUSE ME?

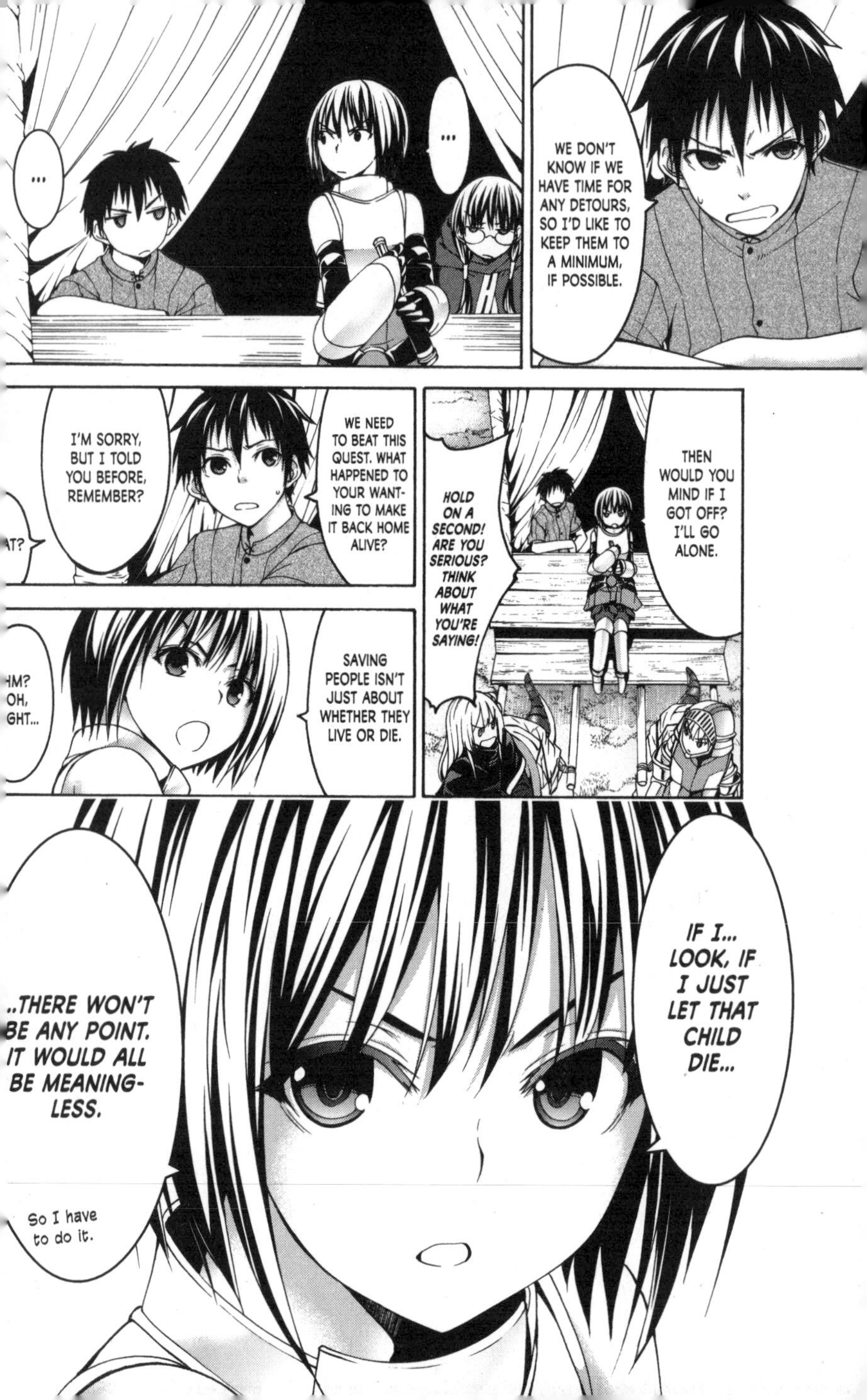
WE DON'T KNOW IF WE HAVE TIME FOR ANY DETOURS, SO I'D LIKE TO KEEP THEM TO A MINIMUM, IF POSSIBLE.
...
...
THEN WOULD YOU MIND IF I GOT OFF? I'LL GO ALONE.
HOLD ON A SECOND! ARE YOU SERIOUS? THINK ABOUT WHAT YOU'RE SAYING!
WE NEED TO BEAT THIS QUEST. WHAT HAPPENED TO YOUR WANT-ING TO MAKE IT BACK HOME ALIVE?
I'M SORRY, BUT I TOLD YOU BEFORE, REMEMBER?
SAVING PEOPLE ISN'T JUST ABOUT WHETHER THEY LIVE OR DIE.
IF I... LOOK, IF I JUST LET THAT CHILD DIE...
..THERE WON'T BE ANY POINT. IT WOULD ALL BE MEANING-LESS.
So I have to do it.

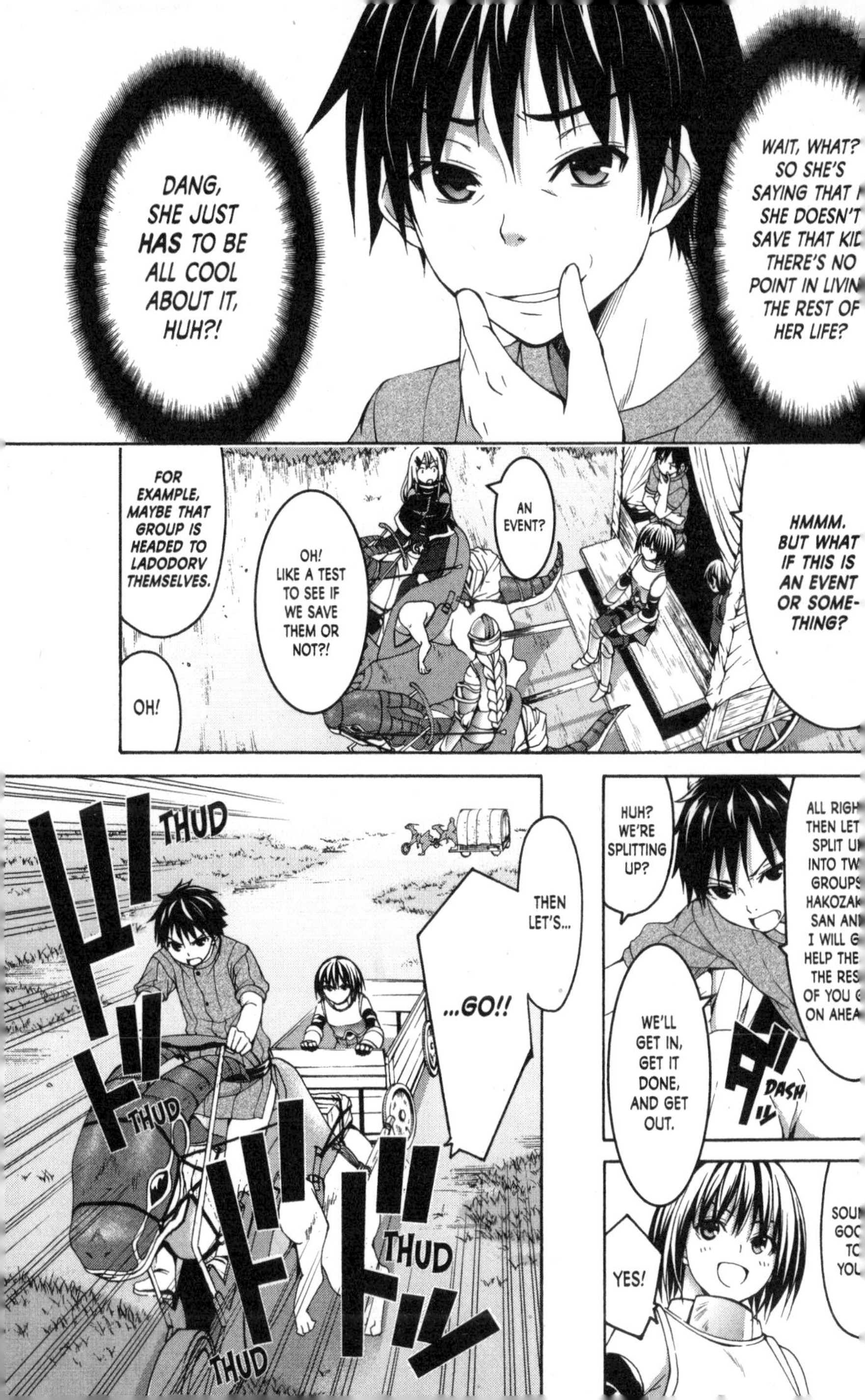

WAIT, WHAT? SO SHE'S SAYING THAT I SHE DOESN'T SAVE THAT KID THERE'S NO POINT IN LIVIN THE REST OF HER LIFE?
DANG, SHE JUST HAS TO BE ALL COOL ABOUT IT, HUH?!
HMMM. BUT WHAT IF THIS IS AN EVENT OR SOME-THING?
AN EVENT?
OH! LIKE A TEST TO SEE IF WE SAVE THEM OR NOT?!
FOR EXAMPLE, MAYBE THAT GROUP IS HEADED TO LADODORV THEMSELVES.
OH!
ALL RIGH THEN LET SPLIT U INTO TW GROUPS HAKOZAK SAN AN I WILL G HELP THE THE RES OF YOU G ON AHEA
HUH? WE'RE SPLITTING UP?
WE'LL GET IN, GET IT DONE, AND GET OUT.
DASH
SOU GOC TO YOU
YES!
THEN LET'S...
...GO!!
THUD
THUD
THUD
THUD

OH, CRAP, THEY'RE ALL HEADING FOR US 'CAUSE WE'RE HEROES!

H... ROES?!

WE'RE HERE! BUT THERE'S HARDLY ANYONE LEFT!

THE INDEX IS CALCULATED BY HOW MANY MEMBERS OF [KINGDOM'S MAIN FORCES (WHICH EQUATES TO THE MARINES, BASICALLY?) IT WOULD TAKE TO HAVE A 50% OR GREATER CHANCE OF DEFEATING THEM. FOR EXAMPLE, OURS WOULD BE...

S = NO CHANCE OF WINNING	**STRONG**
A = 201–∞	
B = 51–200	
C = 11–50	
D = 3–10	
E = 2	
F = 1	
G = < 0.1	**WEAK**

* ASIDE FROM G, ALL OTHERS HAVE BEEN ROUNDED OFF. TECHNICALLY, F IS 0.1–1.5 AND E IS 1.6–2.5.

...IS EXPRESSED IN EIGHT TIERS, FROM G TO S.

DANGER LEVEL...

KOBOLDS?! ALL THREE OF THEM ARE STRONGER THAN A SOLDIER!

MAN-BEAST **MERI KOBOLD**
KOBOLD SPECIES
DANGER LEVEL: E-

IN SHORT, THOSE BEASTS ARE STRONGER THAN THE TWO OF US PUT TOGETHER!

WE'LL KEEP THEM BUSY, SO YOU GUYS COVER US FROM BEHIND!

DASH

...PROBABLY SOMETHING LIKE THIS. OF COURSE, YOU CAN'T PUT A NUMBER ON COMBAT STRENGTH, SO IT'S JUST A ROUGH ESTIMATE. AND THE PLUSES AND MINUSES ARE TO ADJUST THE VALUE DEPENDING ON WHAT KIND OF OPPONENT WE'RE GOING UP AGAINST.

ME:	0.7+/-?	(=F)
KAHVEL:	1.4+/-?	(=F+)
SHINDO:	0.5+/-?	(=F-)
TOKITATE:	0.3+/-?	
HAKOZAKI:	0.3+/-?	

KAHVEL-SAN'S TWO LACKEYS THAT JOINED US FOR THE TRIP: 0.8+/-?

● THIS INCLUDES EQUIPMENT, MAGIC, COMBAT STYLE, AND COMBAT KNOWLEDGE.

YOU GO IT!

CLANG

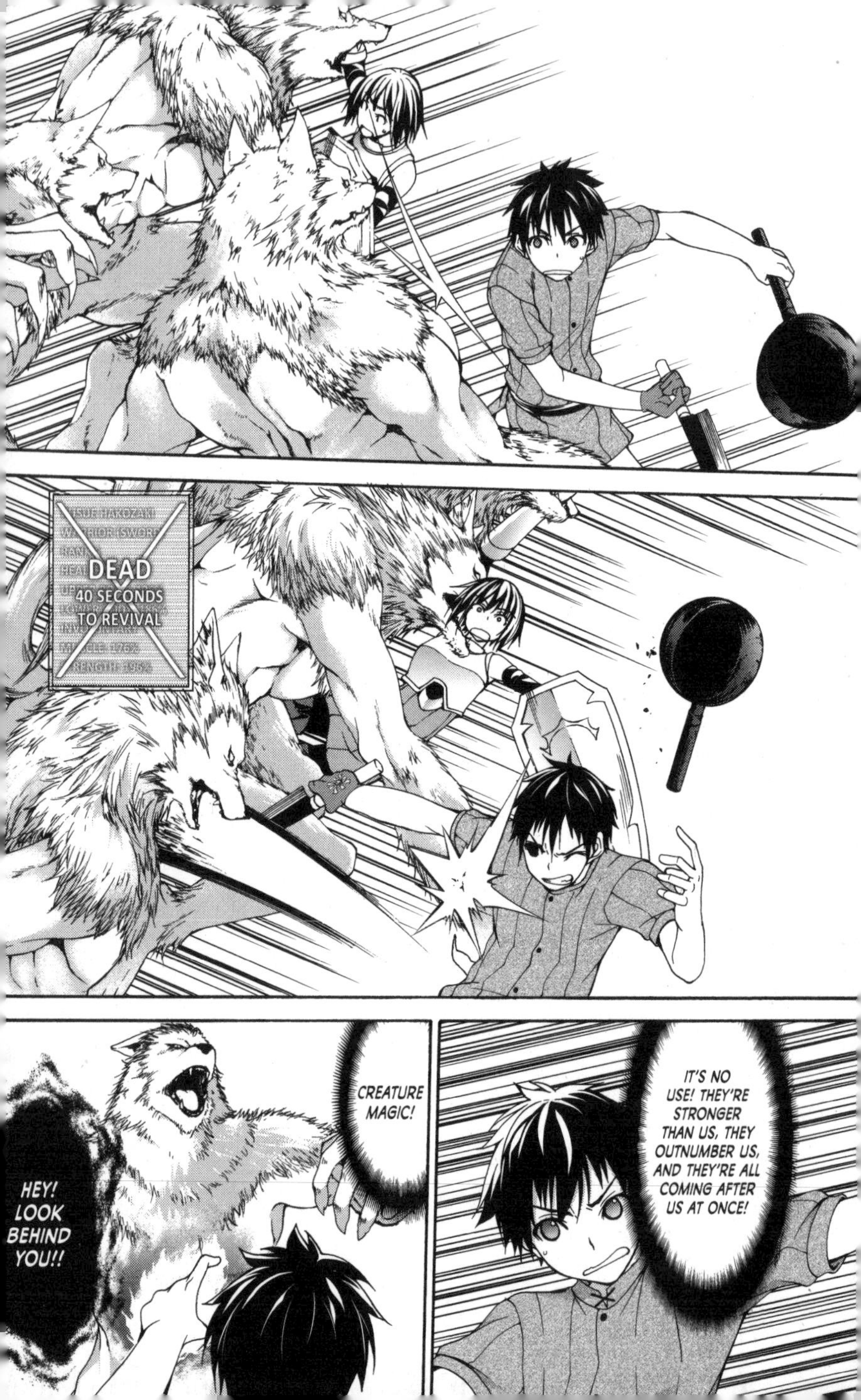
DEAD
40 SECONDS TO REVIVAL
IT'S NO USE! THEY'RE STRONGER THAN US, THEY OUTNUMBER US, AND THEY'RE ALL COMING AFTER US AT ONCE!
CREATURE MAGIC!
HEY! LOOK BEHIND YOU!!

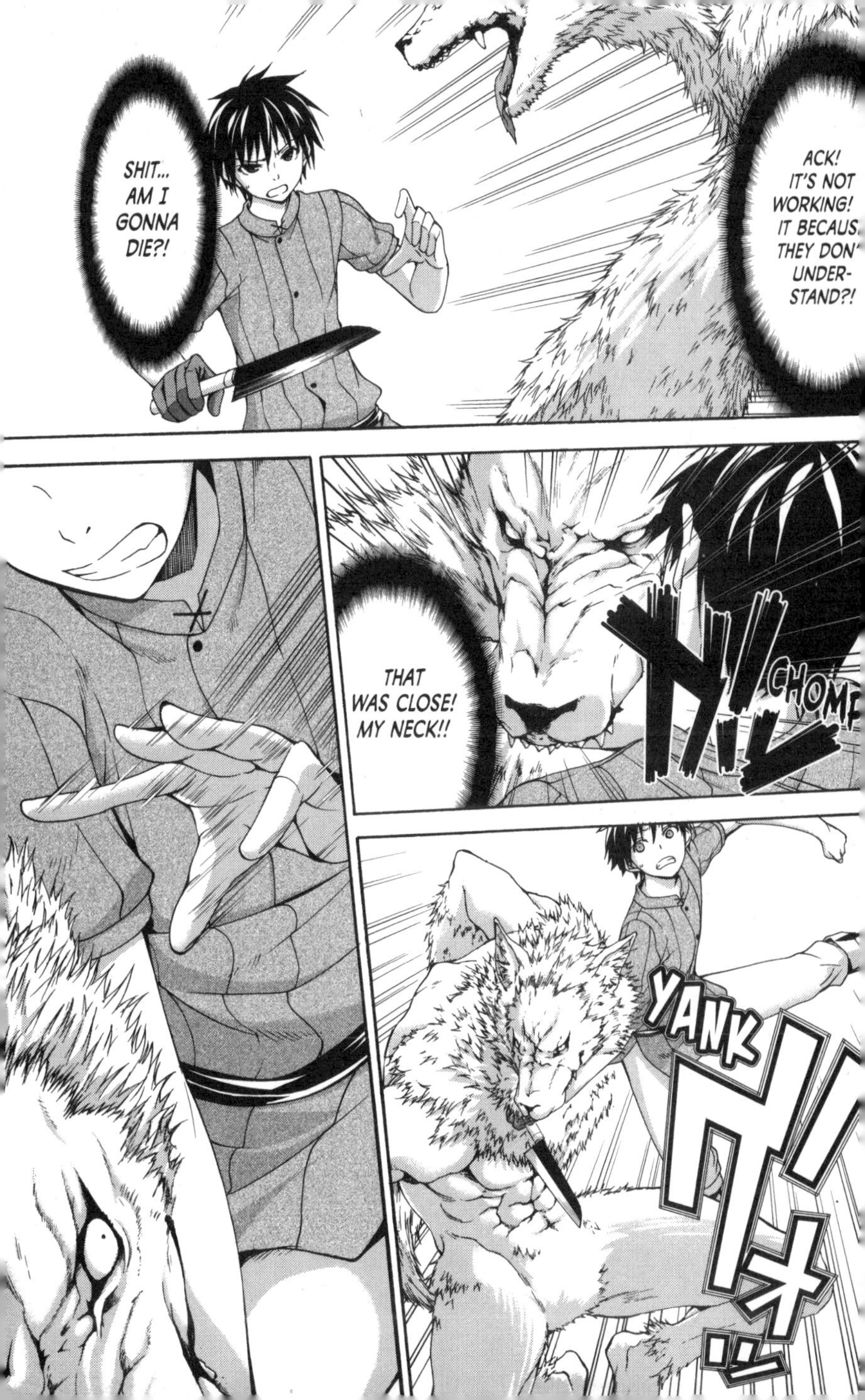
ACK! IT'S NOT WORKING! IT BECAUS THEY DON' UNDERSTAND?!
SHIT... AM I GONNA DIE?!
CHOMP
THAT WAS CLOSE! MY NECK!!
YANK

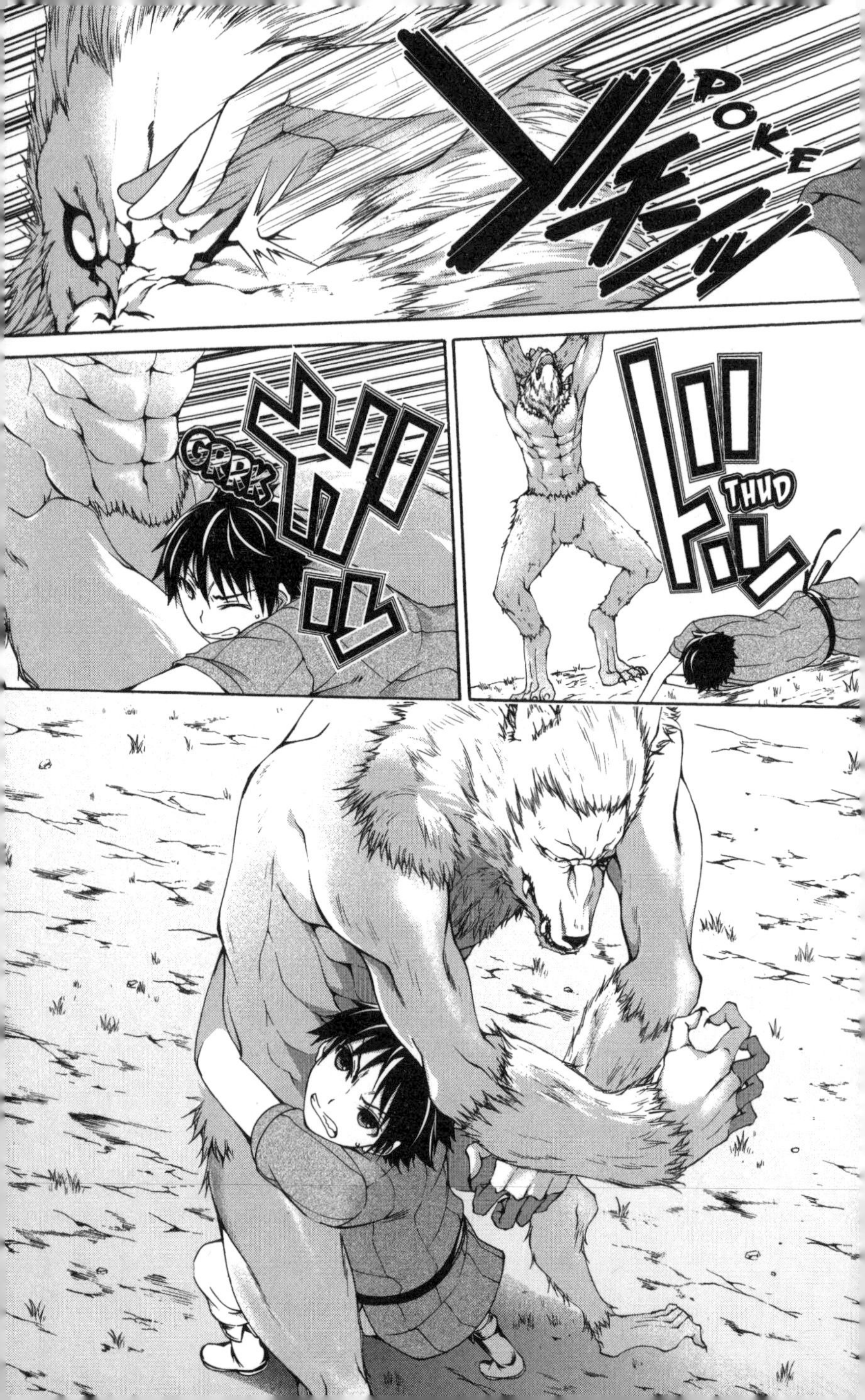
POKE
THUD
GRRK

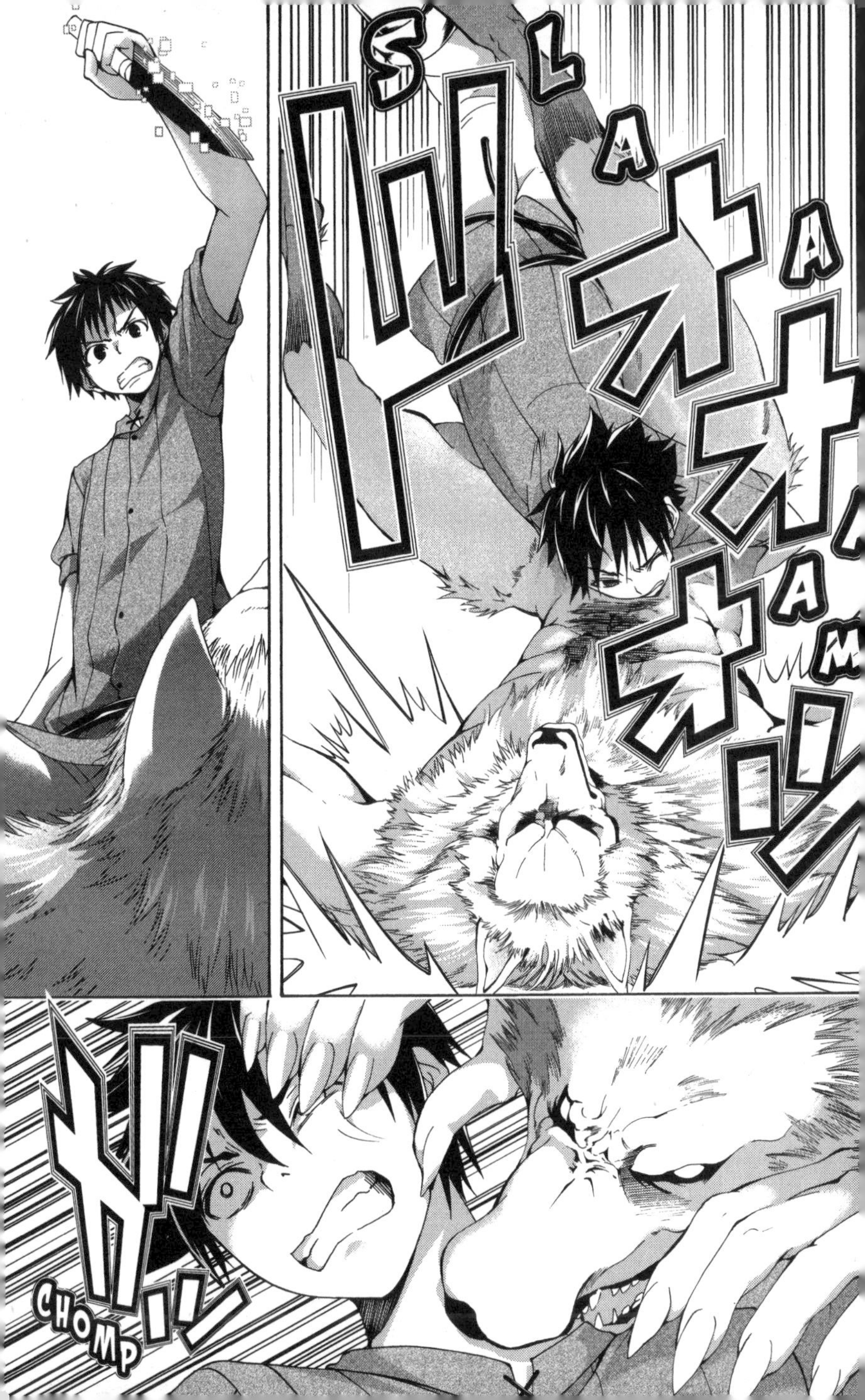
SLAAAAM
CHOMP

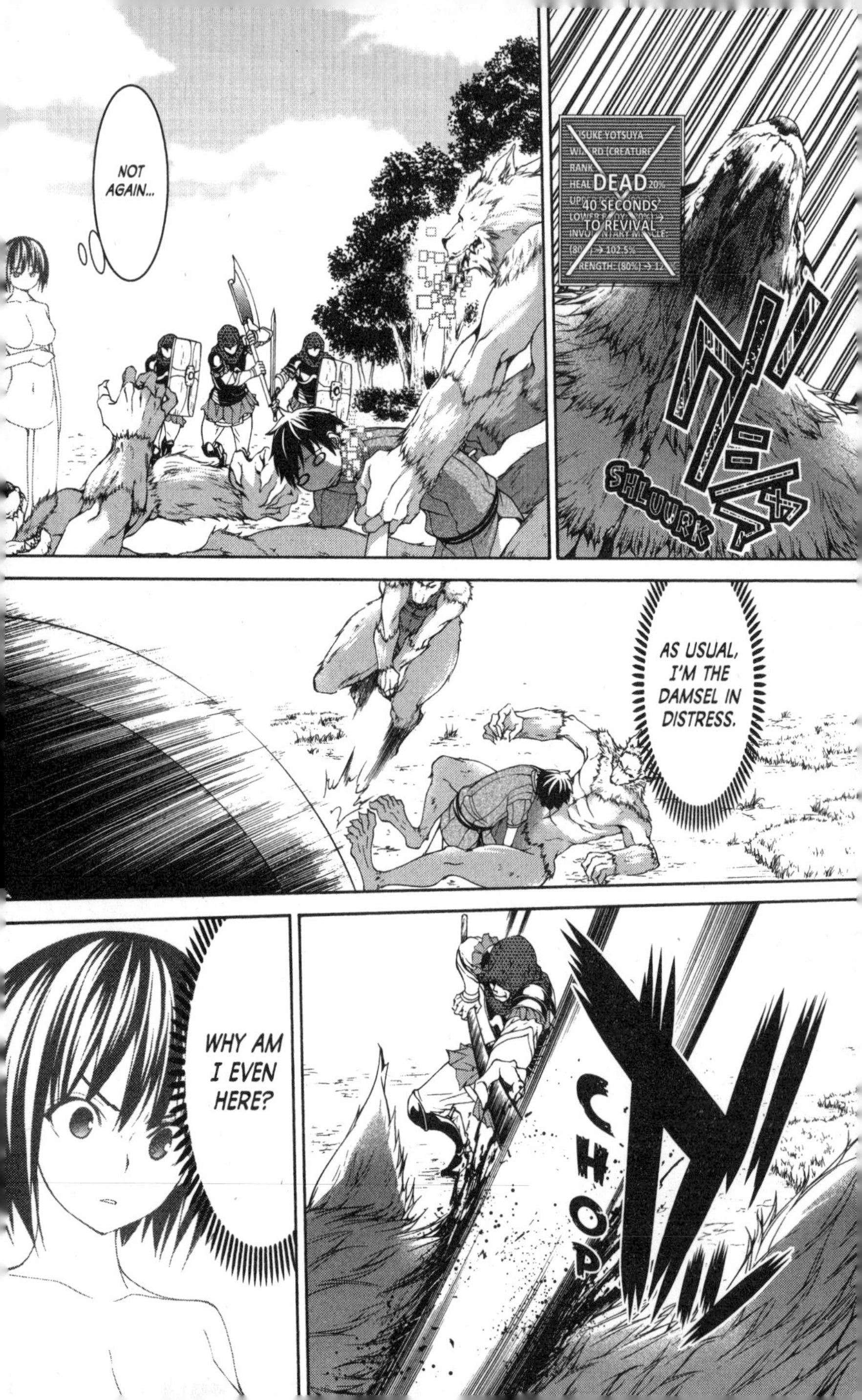
DEAD
40 SECONDS TO REVIVAL
SHLUURK
NOT AGAIN...
AS USUAL, I'M THE DAMSEL IN DISTRESS.
CHOP
WHY AM I EVEN HERE?

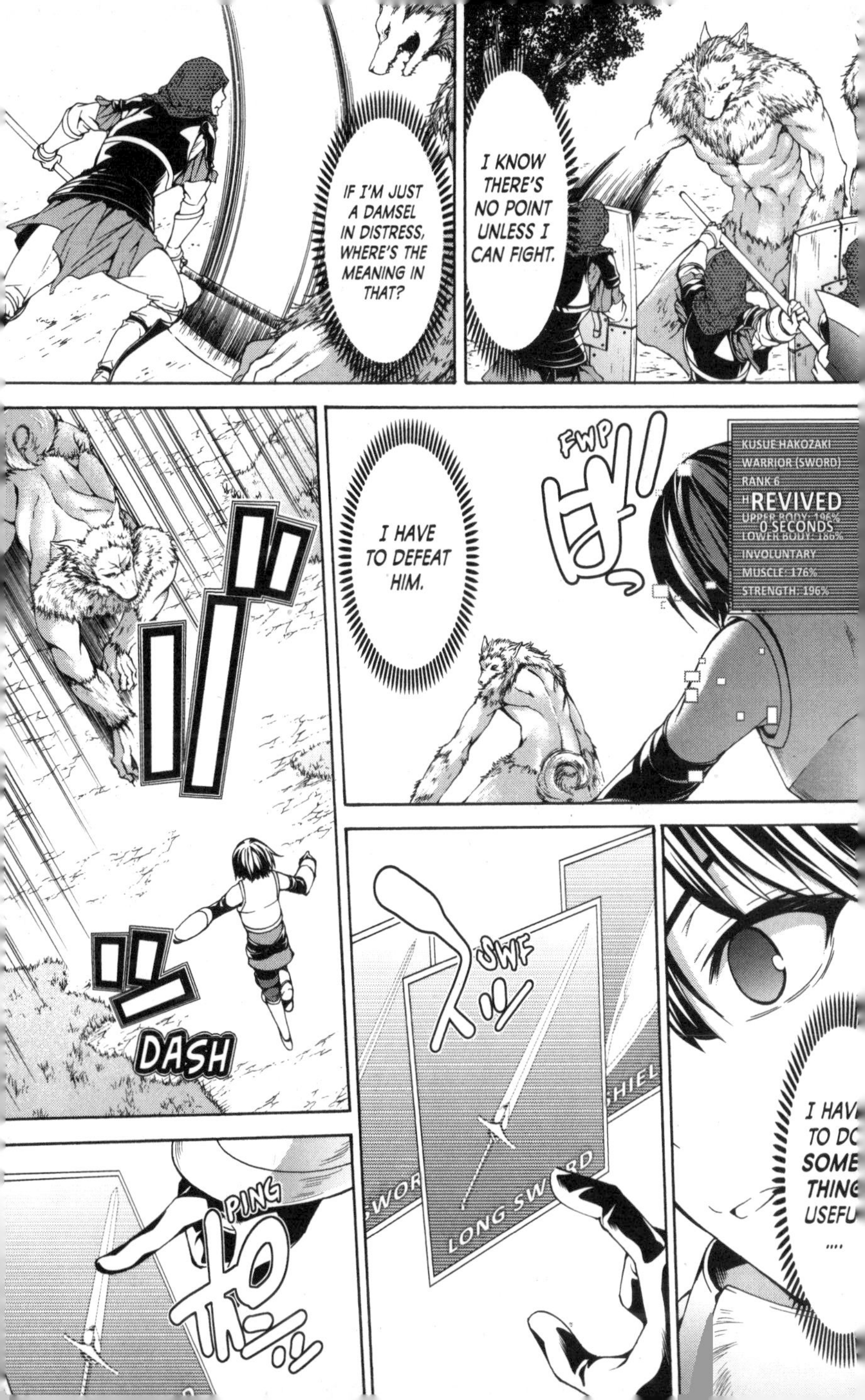

I KNOW THERE'S NO POINT UNLESS I CAN FIGHT.
IF I'M JUST A DAMSEL IN DISTRESS, WHERE'S THE MEANING IN THAT?
FWP
KUSUE HAKOZAKI
WARRIOR (SWORD)
RANK 6
REVIVED
0 SECONDS
UPPER BODY: 196%
LOWER BODY: 186%
INVOLUNTARY
MUSCLE: 176%
STRENGTH: 196%
I HAVE TO DEFEAT HIM.
DASH
I HAV TO DO SOME THING USEFU ....
SWF
LONG SWORD
SWOR
SHIEL
PING

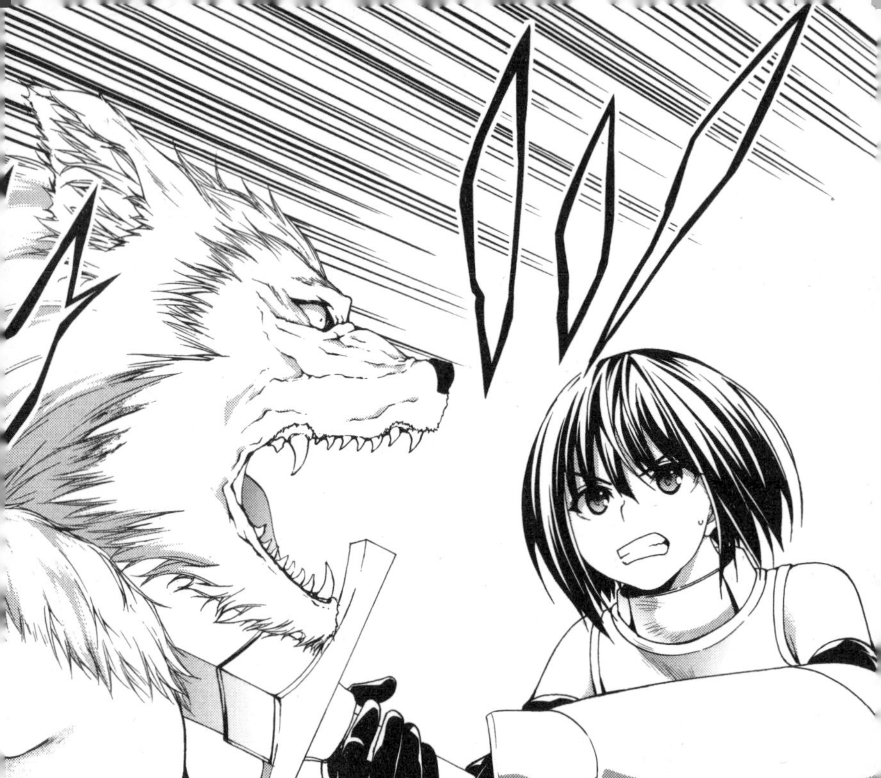

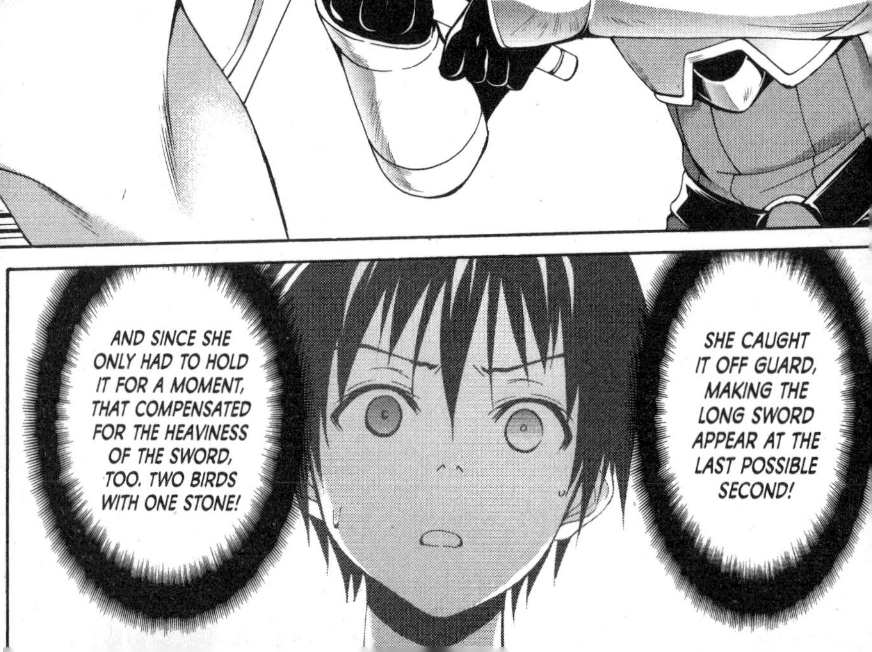
SHE CAUGHT IT OFF GUARD, MAKING THE LONG SWORD APPEAR AT THE LAST POSSIBLE SECOND!
AND SINCE SHE ONLY HAD TO HOLD IT FOR A MOMENT, THAT COMPENSATED FOR THE HEAVINESS OF THE SWORD, TOO. TWO BIRDS WITH ONE STONE!

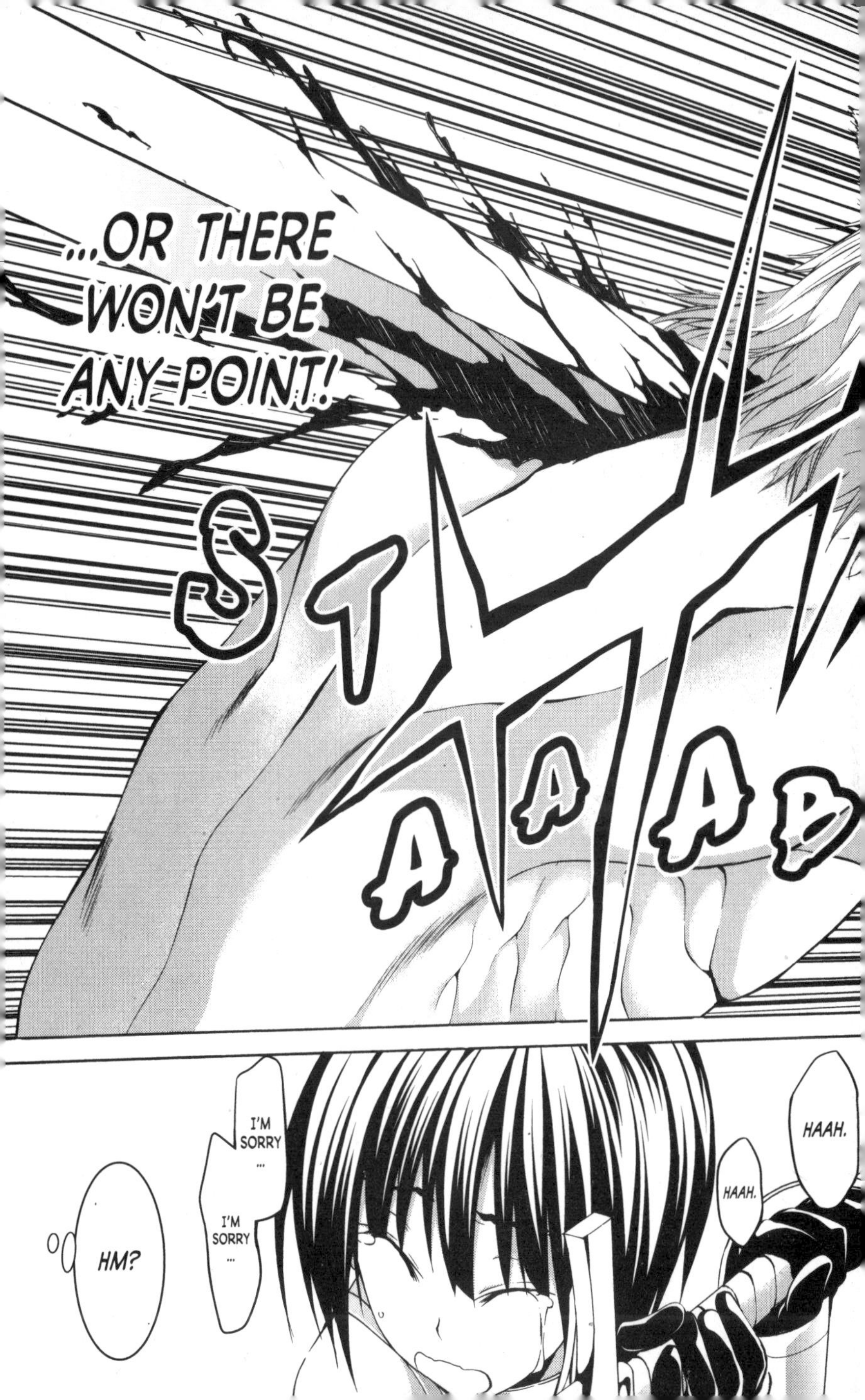
...OR THERE WON'T BE ANY POINT!
STAAAB
HAAH.
HAAH.
I'M SORRY ...
I'M SORRY ...
HM?

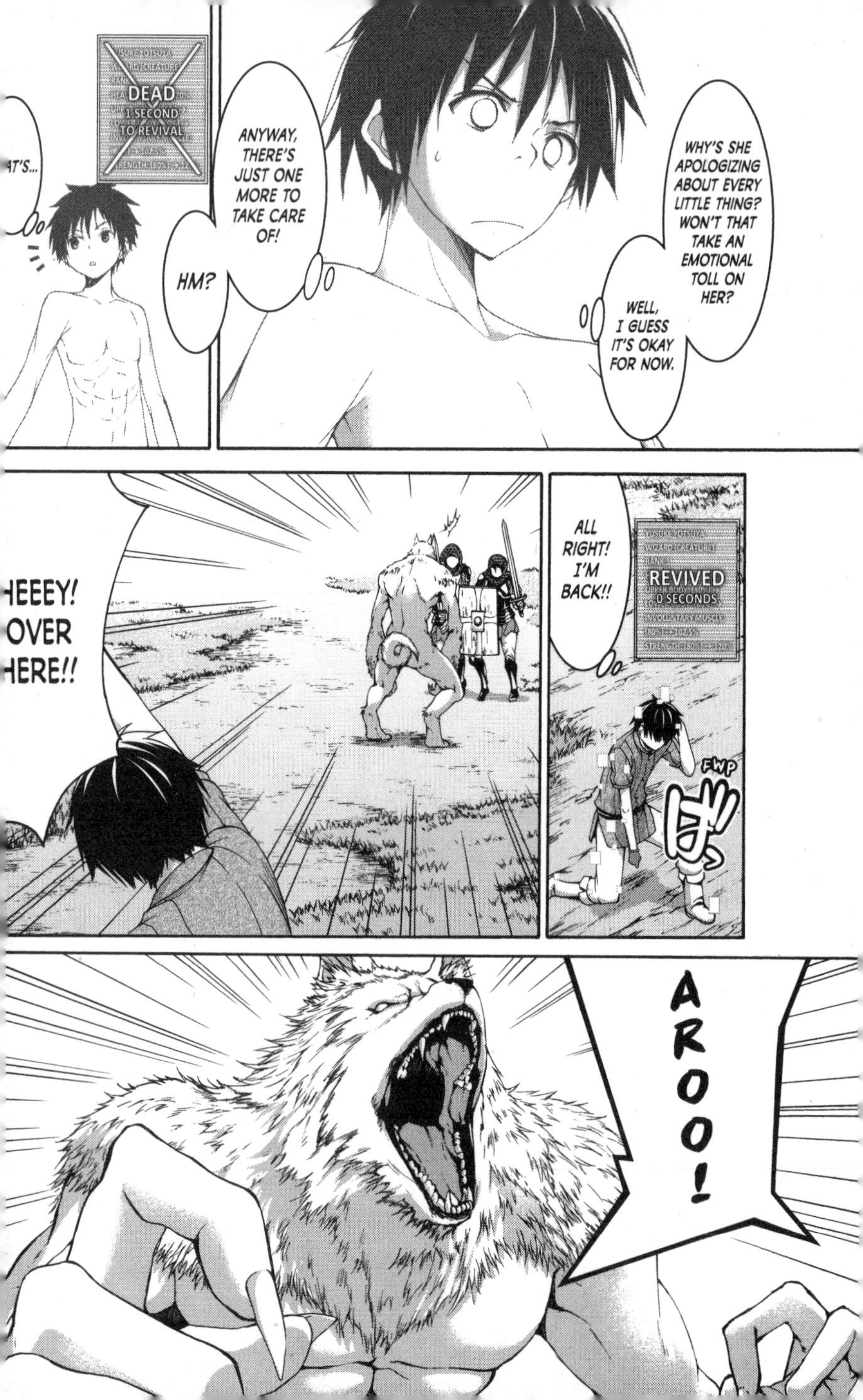
WHY'S SHE APOLOGIZING ABOUT EVERY LITTLE THING? WON'T THAT TAKE AN EMOTIONAL TOLL ON HER?
WELL, I GUESS IT'S OKAY FOR NOW.
ANYWAY, THERE'S JUST ONE MORE TO TAKE CARE OF!
HM?
DEAD
1 SECOND TO REVIVAL
AT'S...
ALL RIGHT! I'M BACK!!
YUSUKE YOTSUYA
WIZARD (CREATURE)
RANK 1
REVIVED
0 SECONDS
INVOLUNTARY MUSCLE
FWP
HEEEY! OVER HERE!!
AROOO!

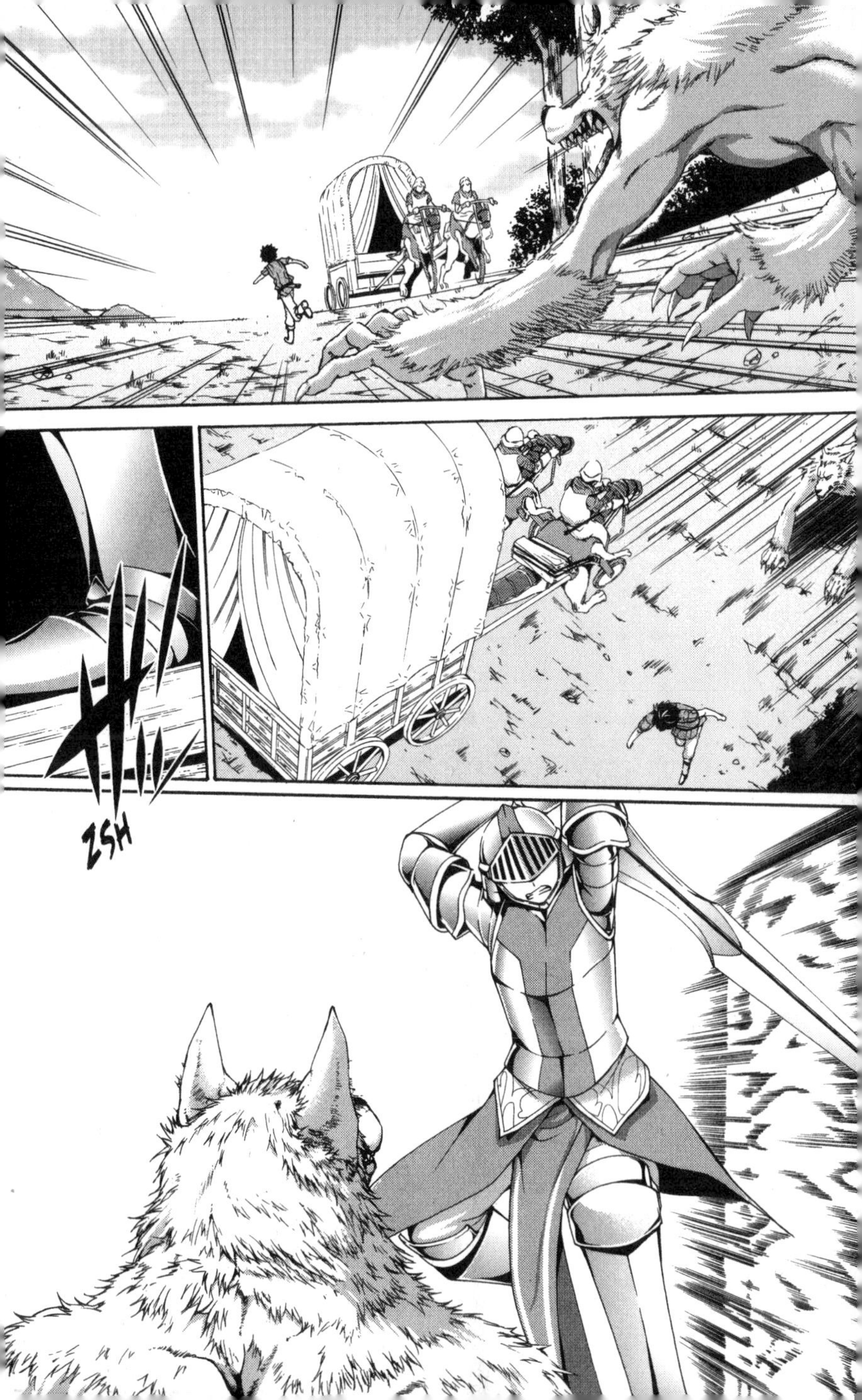
ZSH

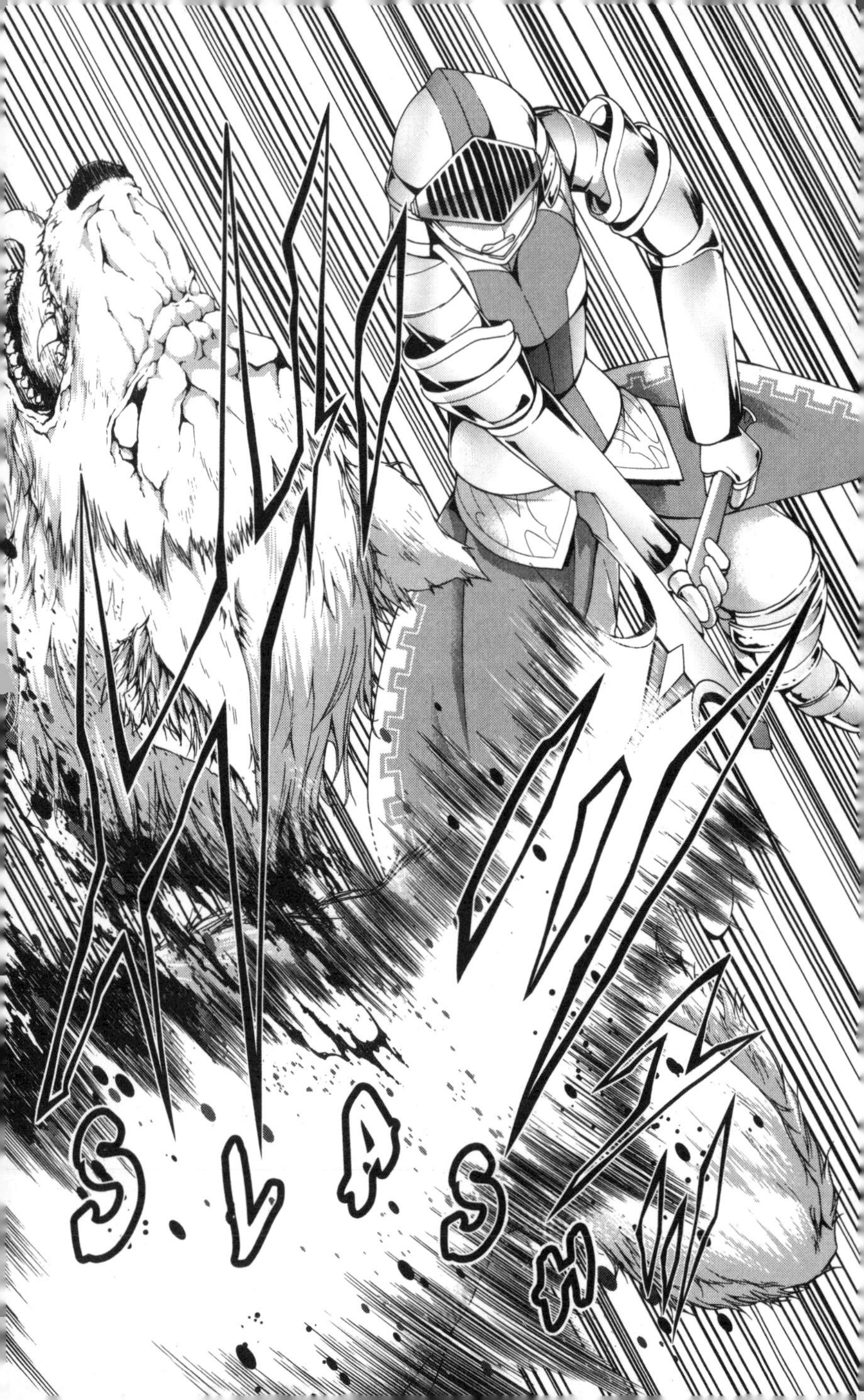
SLASH

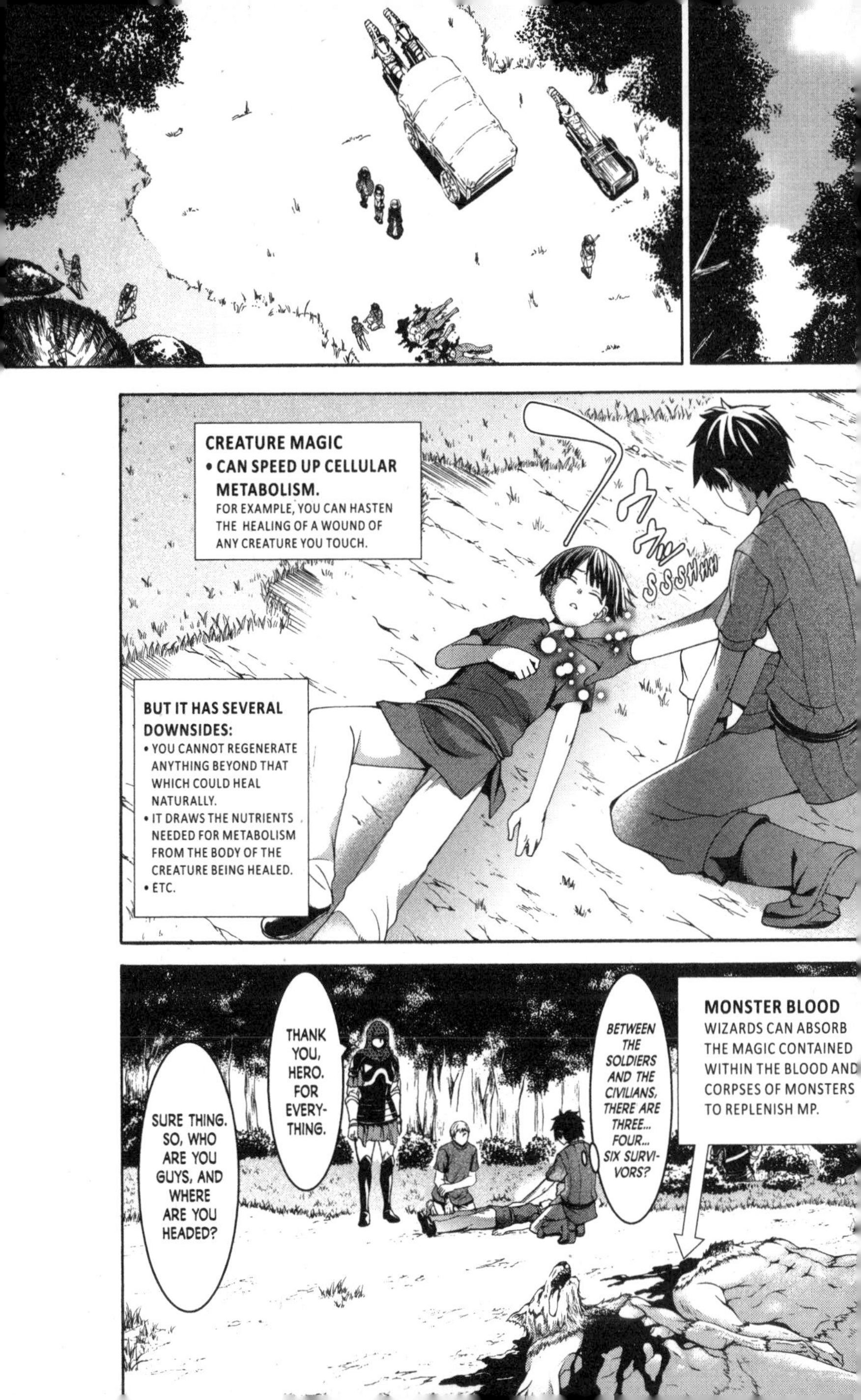
CREATURE MAGIC
• CAN SPEED UP CELLULAR METABOLISM. FOR EXAMPLE, YOU CAN HASTEN THE HEALING OF A WOUND OF ANY CREATURE YOU TOUCH.
SSSHHH
BUT IT HAS SEVERAL DOWNSIDES:
• YOU CANNOT REGENERATE ANYTHING BEYOND THAT WHICH COULD HEAL NATURALLY.
• IT DRAWS THE NUTRIENTS NEEDED FOR METABOLISM FROM THE BODY OF THE CREATURE BEING HEALED.
• ETC.
MONSTER BLOOD WIZARDS CAN ABSORB THE MAGIC CONTAINED WITHIN THE BLOOD AND CORPSES OF MONSTERS TO REPLENISH MP.
BETWEEN THE SOLDIERS AND THE CIVILIANS, THERE ARE THREE... FOUR... SIX SURVIVORS?
THANK YOU, HERO. FOR EVERYTHING.
SURE THING. SO, WHO ARE YOU GUYS, AND WHERE ARE YOU HEADED?

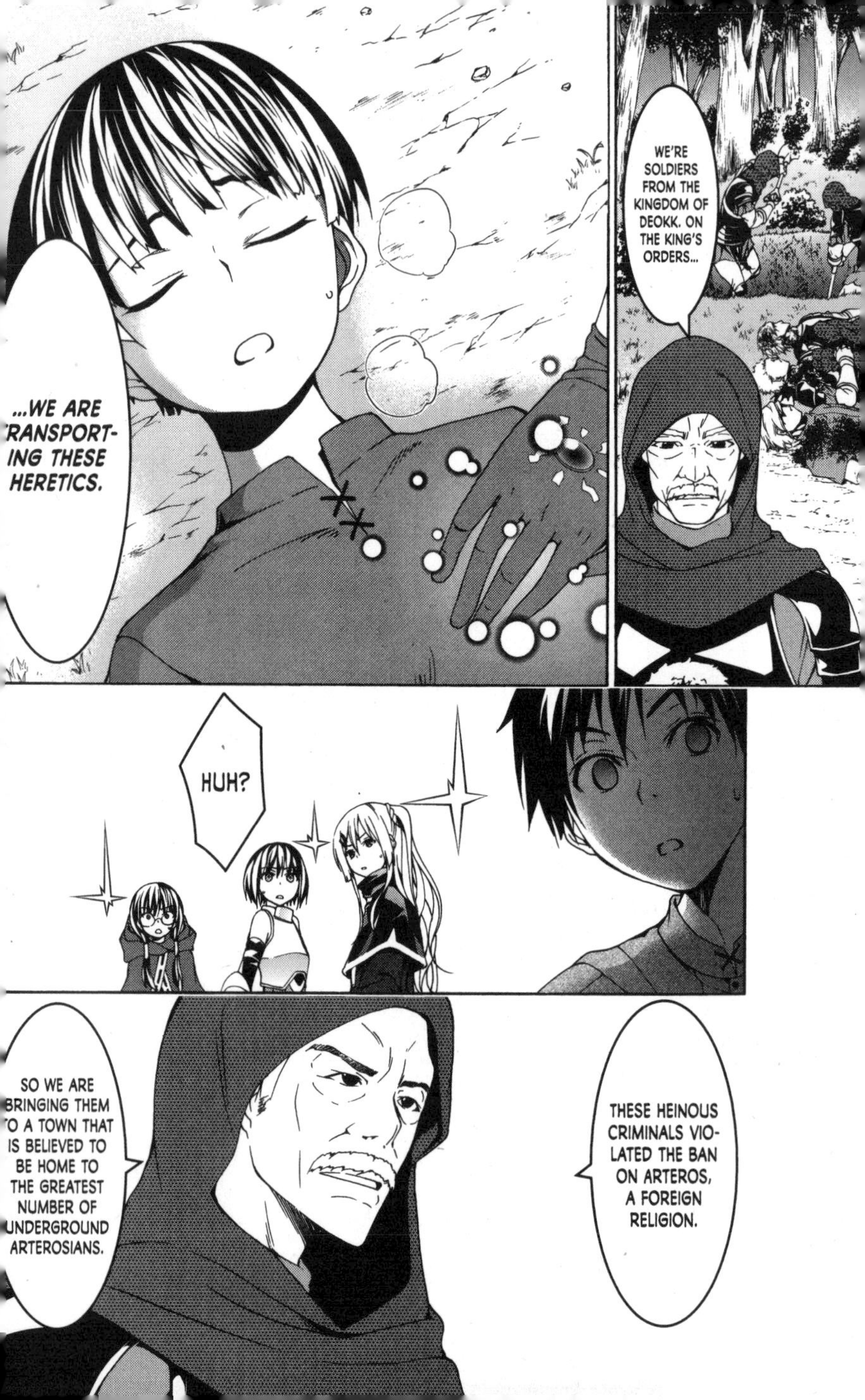
WE'RE SOLDIERS FROM THE KINGDOM OF DEOKK. ON THE KING'S ORDERS...
...WE ARE TRANSPORTING THESE HERETICS.
HUH?
THESE HEINOUS CRIMINALS VIOLATED THE BAN ON ARTEROS, A FOREIGN RELIGION.
SO WE ARE BRINGING THEM TO A TOWN THAT IS BELIEVED TO BE HOME TO THE GREATEST NUMBER OF UNDERGROUND ARTEROSIANS.

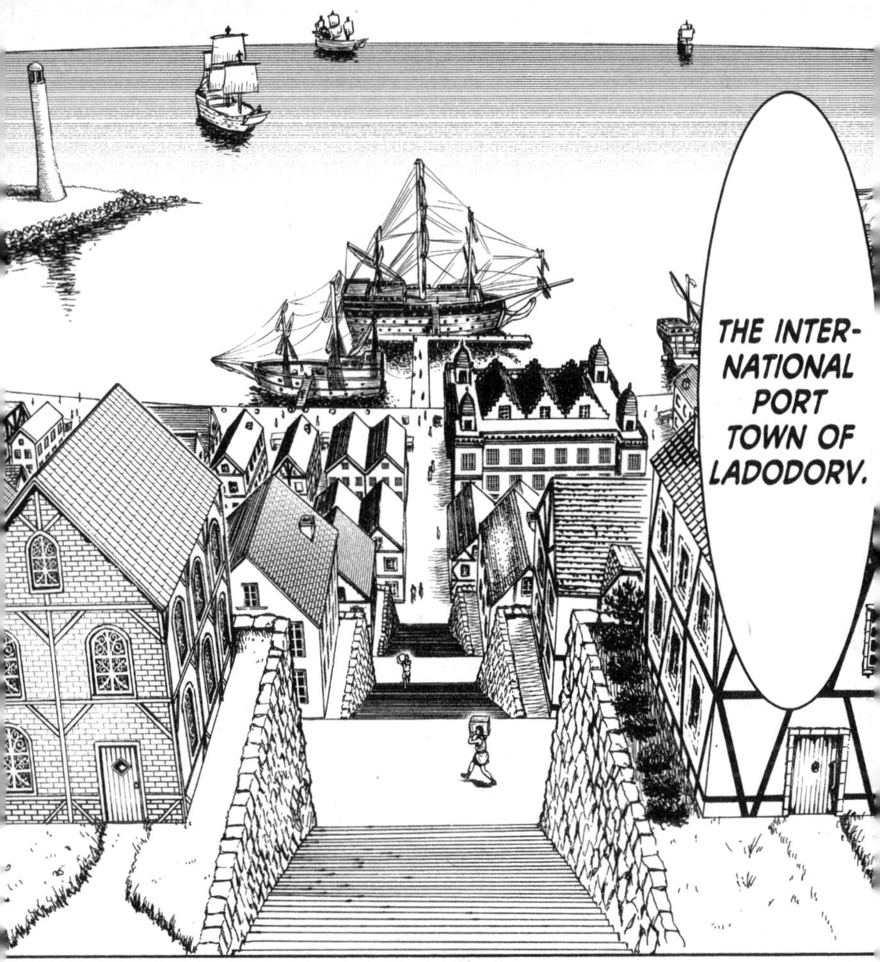
THE INTER-NATIONAL PORT TOWN OF LADODORV.

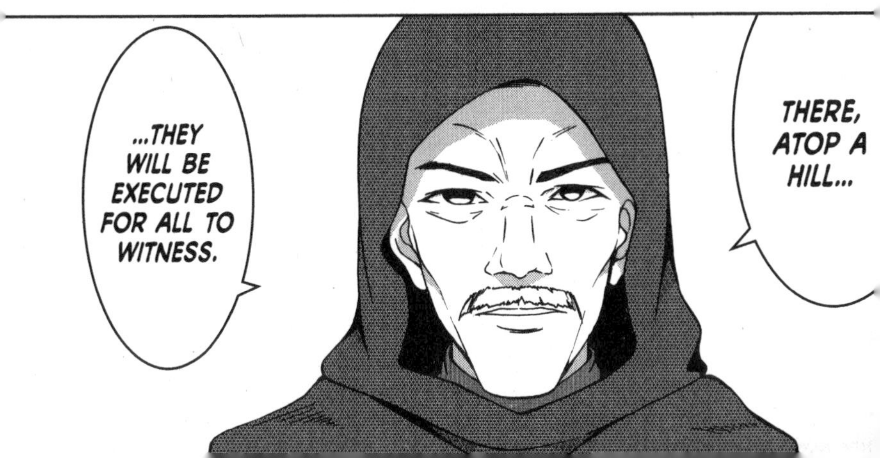
THERE, ATOP A HILL...
...THEY WILL BE EXECUTED FOR ALL TO WITNESS.

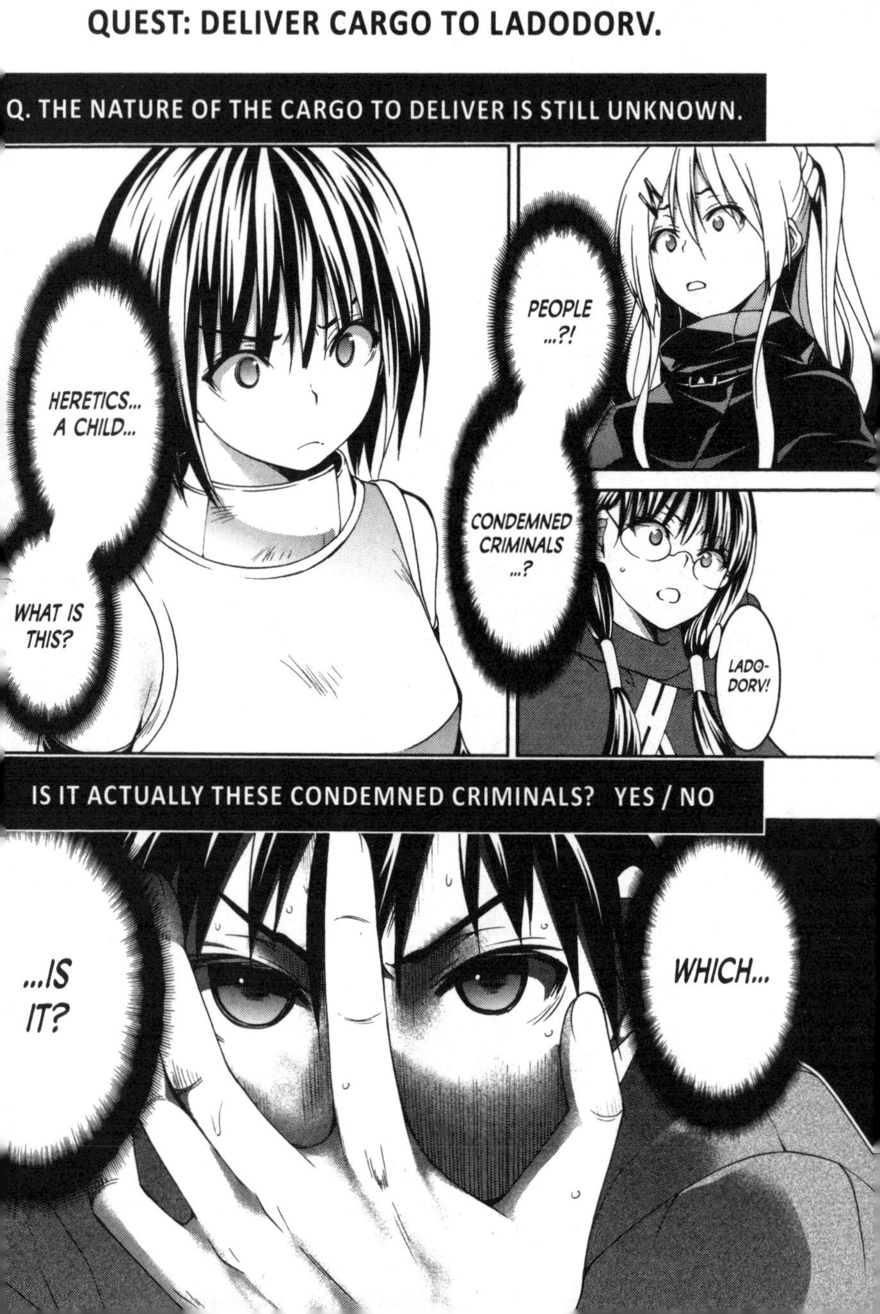
QUEST: DELIVER CARGO TO LADODORV.
Q. THE NATURE OF THE CARGO TO DELIVER IS STILL UNKNOWN.
PEOPLE ...?!
CONDEMNED CRIMINALS ...?
LADO-DORV!
HERETICS... A CHILD...
WHAT IS THIS?
IS IT ACTUALLY THESE CONDEMNED CRIMINALS? YES / NO
WHICH...
...IS IT?

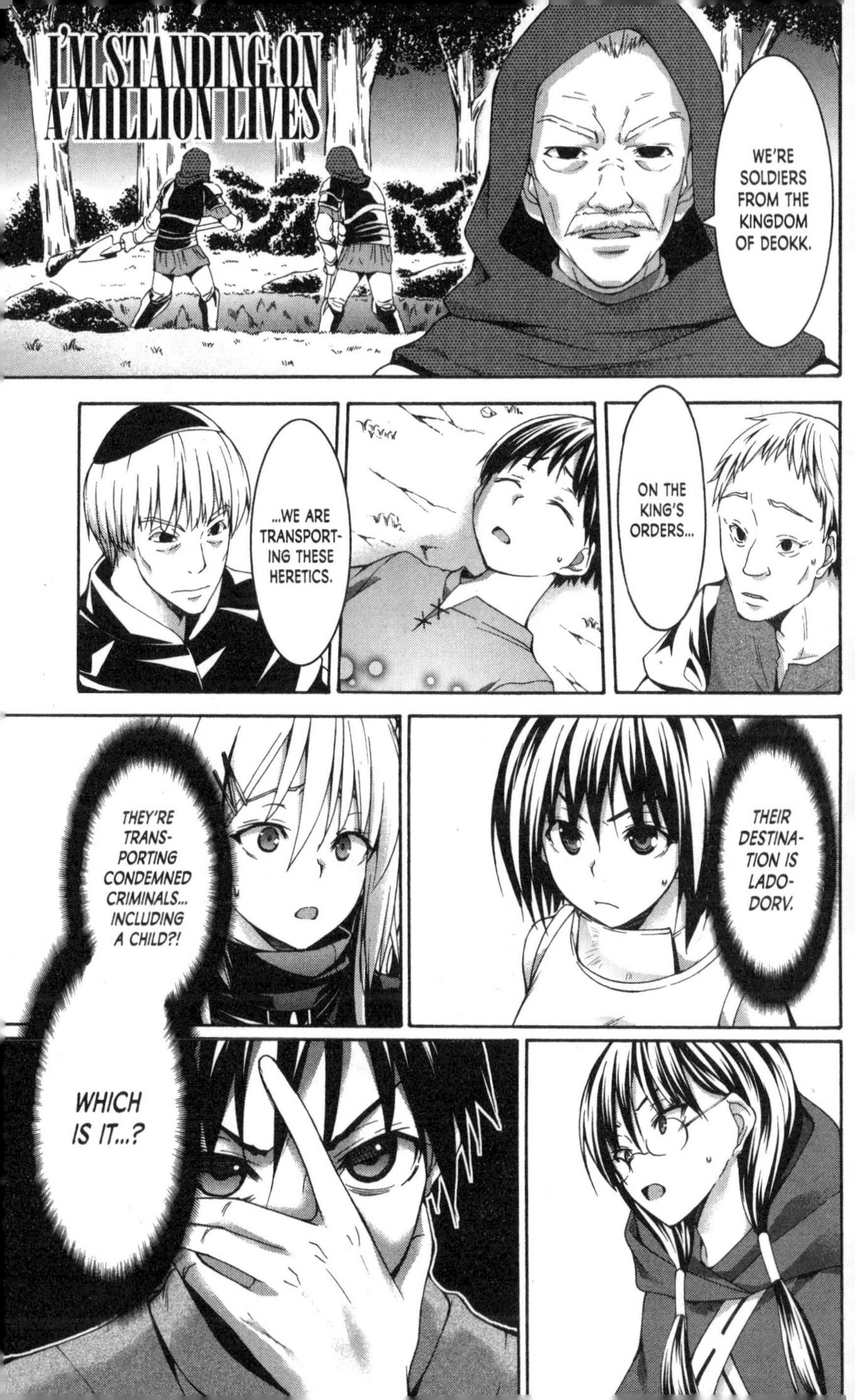
I'M STANDING ON A MILLION LIVES
WE'RE SOLDIERS FROM THE KINGDOM OF DEOKK.
ON THE KING'S ORDERS...
...WE ARE TRANSPORTING THESE HERETICS.
THEIR DESTINATION IS LADODORV.
THEY'RE TRANSPORTING CONDEMNED CRIMINALS... INCLUDING A CHILD?!
WHICH IS IT...?

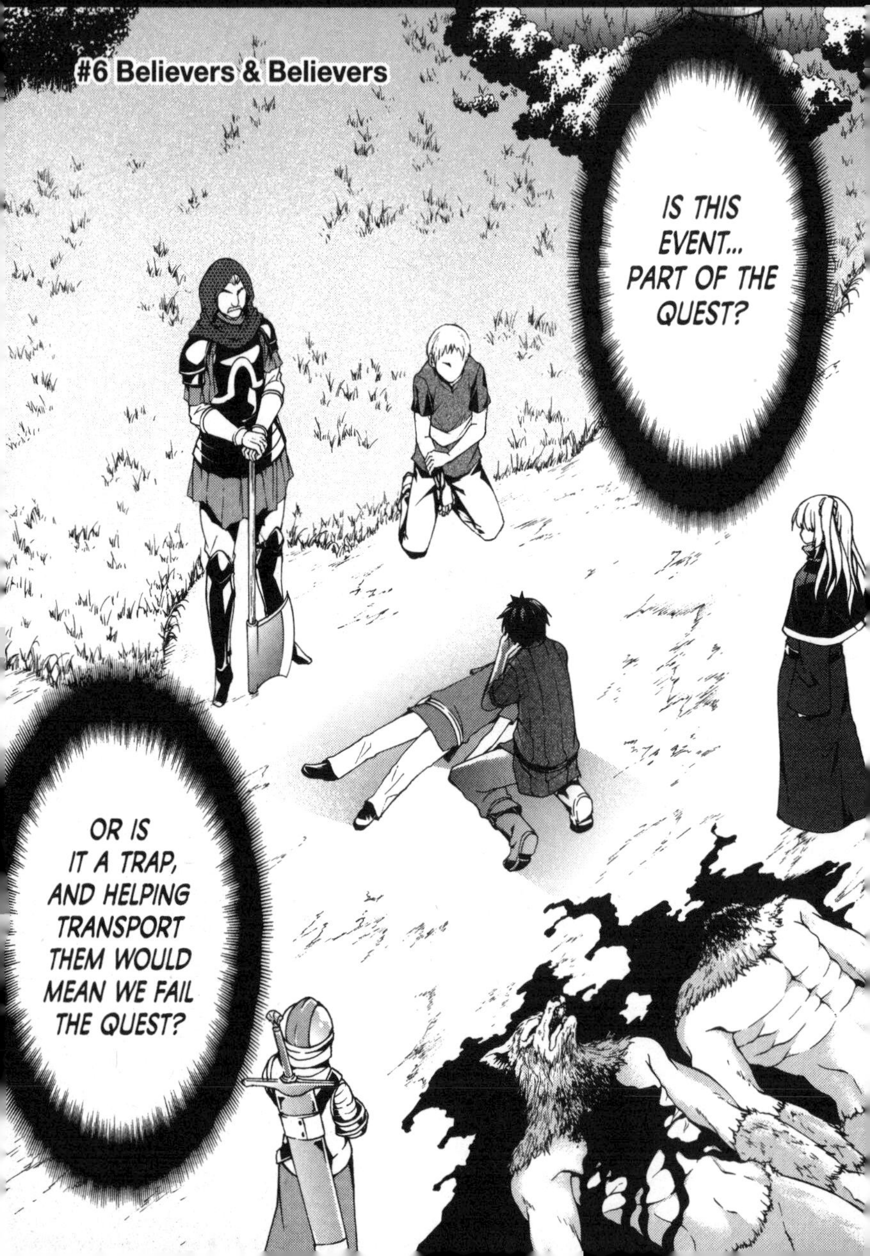
#6 Believers & Believers
IS THIS EVENT... PART OF THE QUEST?
OR IS IT A TRAP, AND HELPING TRANSPORT THEM WOULD MEAN WE FAIL THE QUEST?

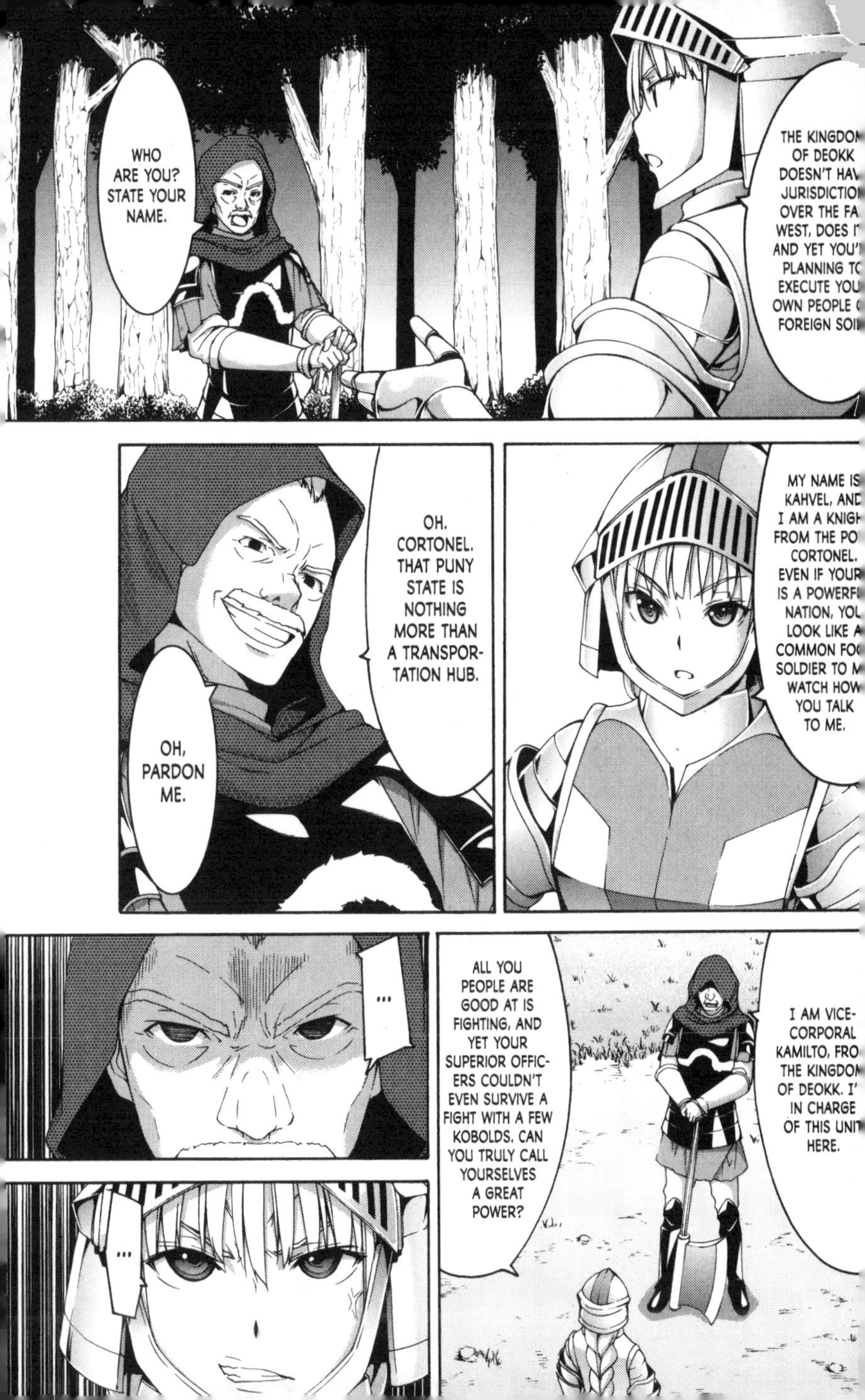
THE KINGDO OF DEOKK DOESN'T HAV JURISDICTIO OVER THE FA WEST, DOES I AND YET YOU' PLANNING TO EXECUTE YOU OWN PEOPLE (FOREIGN SOI
WHO ARE YOU? STATE YOUR NAME.
MY NAME IS KAHVEL, AND I AM A KNIGH FROM THE PO CORTONEL. EVEN IF YOUR IS A POWERF NATION, YO LOOK LIKE A COMMON FO SOLDIER TO M WATCH HOW YOU TALK TO ME.
OH. CORTONEL. THAT PUNY STATE IS NOTHING MORE THAN A TRANSPORTATION HUB.
OH, PARDON ME.
I AM VICE-CORPORAL KAMILTO, FRO THE KINGDO OF DEOKK. I' IN CHARGE OF THIS UNI HERE.
ALL YOU PEOPLE ARE GOOD AT IS FIGHTING, AND YET YOUR SUPERIOR OFFICERS COULDN'T EVEN SURVIVE A FIGHT WITH A FEW KOBOLDS. CAN YOU TRULY CALL YOURSELVES A GREAT POWER?
...
...

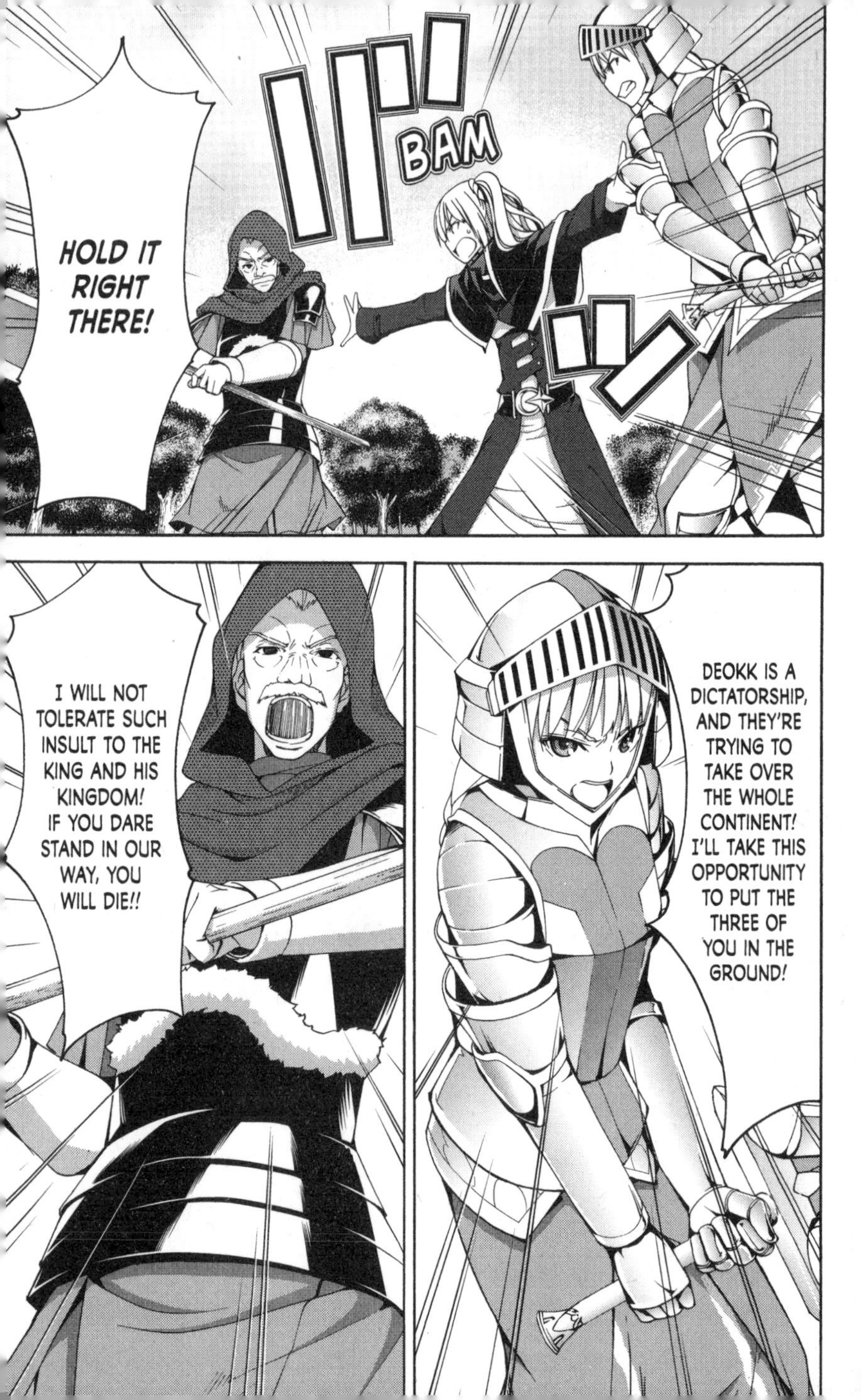
BAM
HOLD IT RIGHT THERE!
DEOKK IS A DICTATORSHIP, AND THEY'RE TRYING TO TAKE OVER THE WHOLE CONTINENT! I'LL TAKE THIS OPPORTUNITY TO PUT THE THREE OF YOU IN THE GROUND!
I WILL NOT TOLERATE SUCH INSULT TO THE KING AND HIS KINGDOM! IF YOU DARE STAND IN OUR WAY, YOU WILL DIE!!

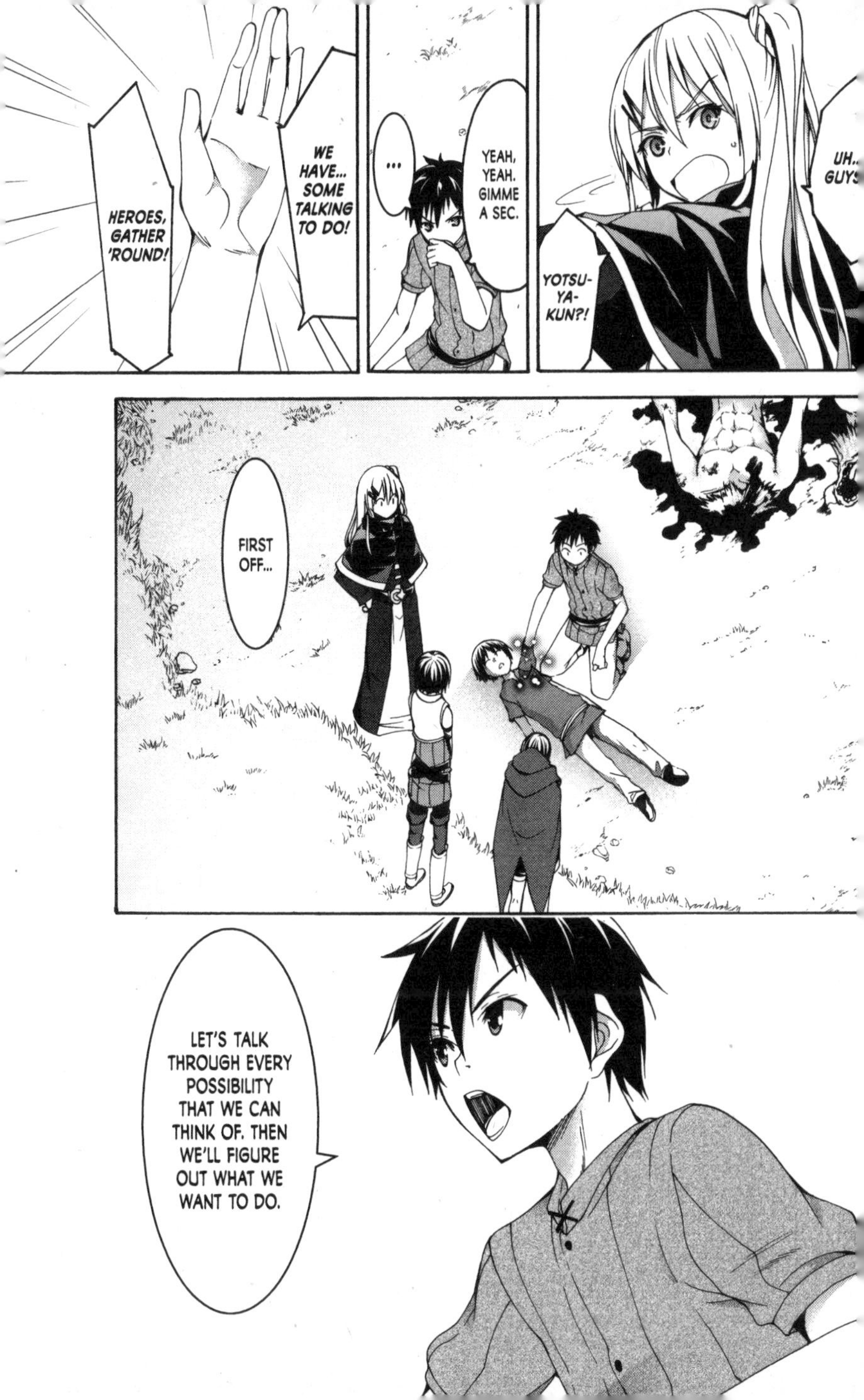
UH.. GUYS
YOTSU-YA-KUN?!
YEAH, YEAH. GIMME A SEC.
...
WE HAVE... SOME TALKING TO DO!
HEROES, GATHER 'ROUND!
FIRST OFF...
LET'S TALK THROUGH EVERY POSSIBILITY THAT WE CAN THINK OF. THEN WE'LL FIGURE OUT WHAT WE WANT TO DO.

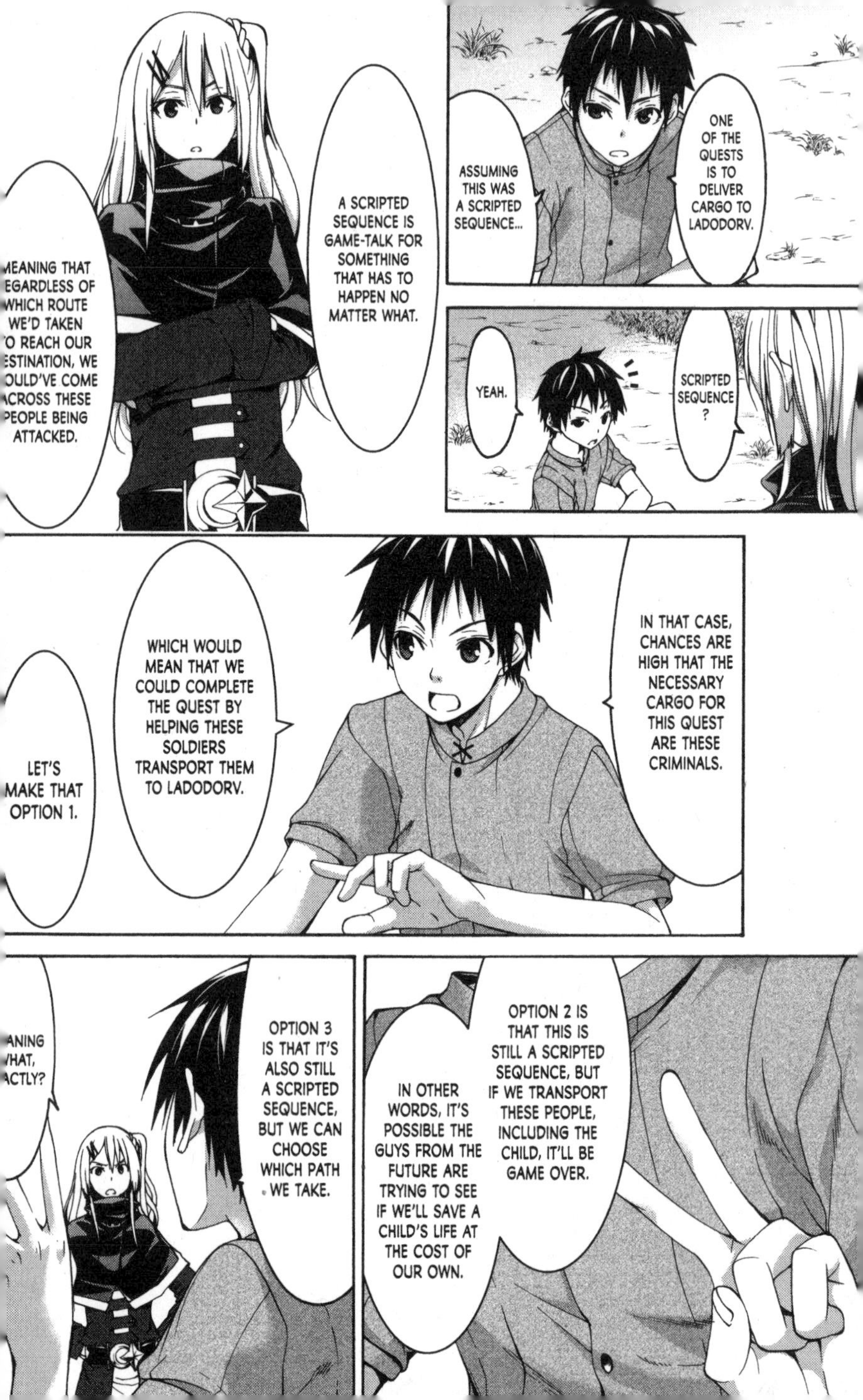
ONE OF THE QUESTS IS TO DELIVER CARGO TO LADODORV.
ASSUMING THIS WAS A SCRIPTED SEQUENCE...
SCRIPTED SEQUENCE ?
YEAH.
A SCRIPTED SEQUENCE IS GAME-TALK FOR SOMETHING THAT HAS TO HAPPEN NO MATTER WHAT.
MEANING THAT EGARDLESS OF WHICH ROUTE WE'D TAKEN O REACH OUR ESTINATION, WE OULD'VE COME ACROSS THESE PEOPLE BEING ATTACKED.
IN THAT CASE, CHANCES ARE HIGH THAT THE NECESSARY CARGO FOR THIS QUEST ARE THESE CRIMINALS.
WHICH WOULD MEAN THAT WE COULD COMPLETE THE QUEST BY HELPING THESE SOLDIERS TRANSPORT THEM TO LADODORV.
LET'S MAKE THAT OPTION 1.
OPTION 2 IS THAT THIS IS STILL A SCRIPTED SEQUENCE, BUT IF WE TRANSPORT THESE PEOPLE, INCLUDING THE CHILD, IT'LL BE GAME OVER.
IN OTHER WORDS, IT'S POSSIBLE THE GUYS FROM THE FUTURE ARE TRYING TO SEE IF WE'LL SAVE A CHILD'S LIFE AT THE COST OF OUR OWN.
OPTION 3 IS THAT IT'S ALSO STILL A SCRIPTED SEQUENCE, BUT WE CAN CHOOSE WHICH PATH WE TAKE.
ANING HAT, ACTLY?

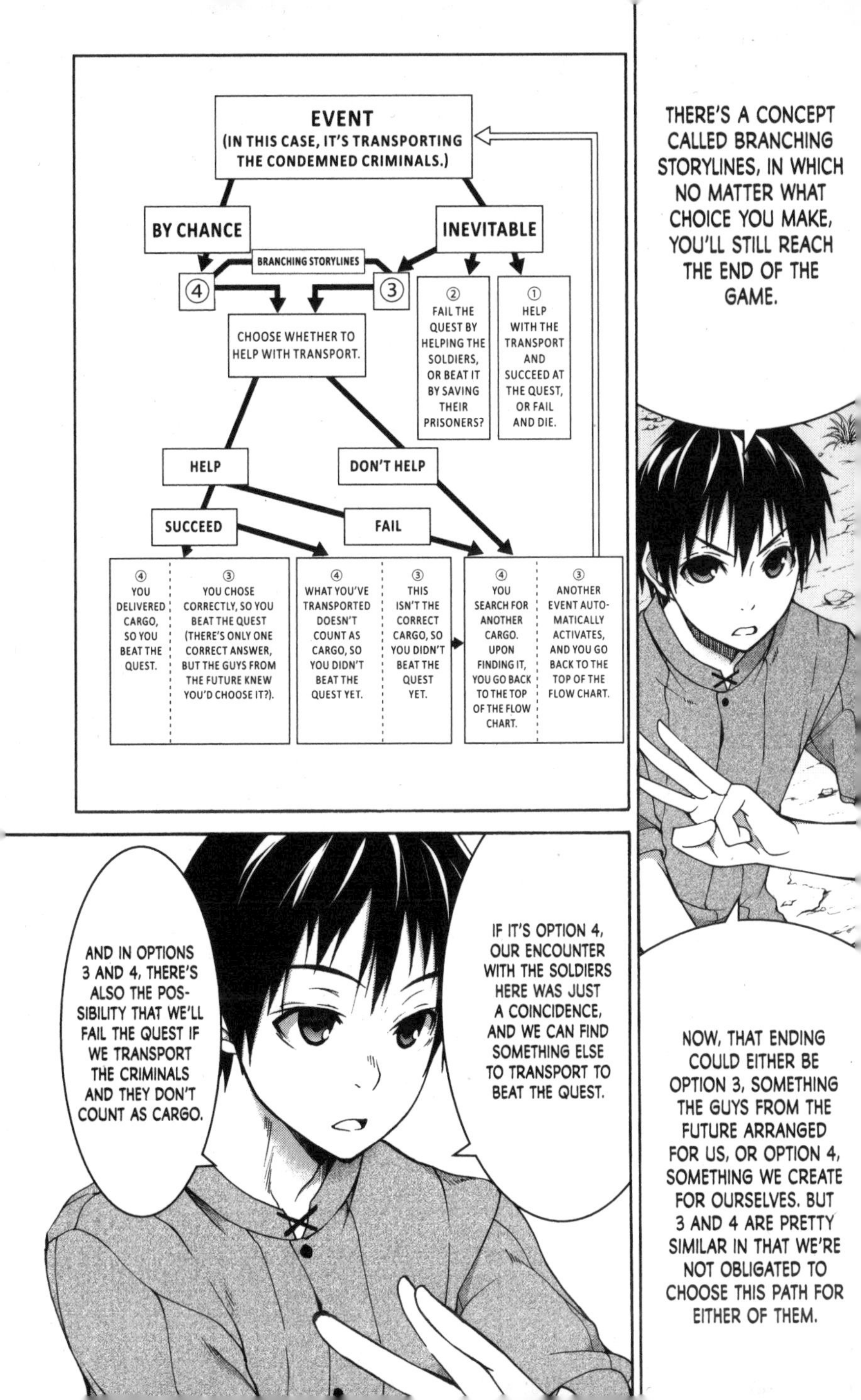
THERE'S A CONCEPT CALLED BRANCHING STORYLINES, IN WHICH NO MATTER WHAT CHOICE YOU MAKE, YOU'LL STILL REACH THE END OF THE GAME.
NOW, THAT ENDING COULD EITHER BE OPTION 3, SOMETHING THE GUYS FROM THE FUTURE ARRANGED FOR US, OR OPTION 4, SOMETHING WE CREATE FOR OURSELVES. BUT 3 AND 4 ARE PRETTY SIMILAR IN THAT WE'RE NOT OBLIGATED TO CHOOSE THIS PATH FOR EITHER OF THEM.
EVENT (IN THIS CASE, IT'S TRANSPORTING THE CONDEMNED CRIMINALS.)
BY CHANCE
INEVITABLE
BRANCHING STORYLINES
④
③
② FAIL THE QUEST BY HELPING THE SOLDIERS, OR BEAT IT BY SAVING THEIR PRISONERS?
① HELP WITH THE TRANSPORT AND SUCCEED AT THE QUEST, OR FAIL AND DIE.
CHOOSE WHETHER TO HELP WITH TRANSPORT.
HELP
DON'T HELP
SUCCEED
FAIL
④ YOU DELIVERED CARGO, SO YOU BEAT THE QUEST.
③ YOU CHOSE CORRECTLY, SO YOU BEAT THE QUEST (THERE'S ONLY ONE CORRECT ANSWER, BUT THE GUYS FROM THE FUTURE KNEW YOU'D CHOOSE IT?).
④ WHAT YOU'VE TRANSPORTED DOESN'T COUNT AS CARGO, SO YOU DIDN'T BEAT THE QUEST YET.
③ THIS ISN'T THE CORRECT CARGO, SO YOU DIDN'T BEAT THE QUEST YET.
④ YOU SEARCH FOR ANOTHER CARGO. UPON FINDING IT, YOU GO BACK TO THE TOP OF THE FLOW CHART.
③ ANOTHER EVENT AUTOMATICALLY ACTIVATES, AND YOU GO BACK TO THE TOP OF THE FLOW CHART.
IF IT'S OPTION 4, OUR ENCOUNTER WITH THE SOLDIERS HERE WAS JUST A COINCIDENCE, AND WE CAN FIND SOMETHING ELSE TO TRANSPORT TO BEAT THE QUEST.
AND IN OPTIONS 3 AND 4, THERE'S ALSO THE POSSIBILITY THAT WE'LL FAIL THE QUEST IF WE TRANSPORT THE CRIMINALS AND THEY DON'T COUNT AS CARGO.

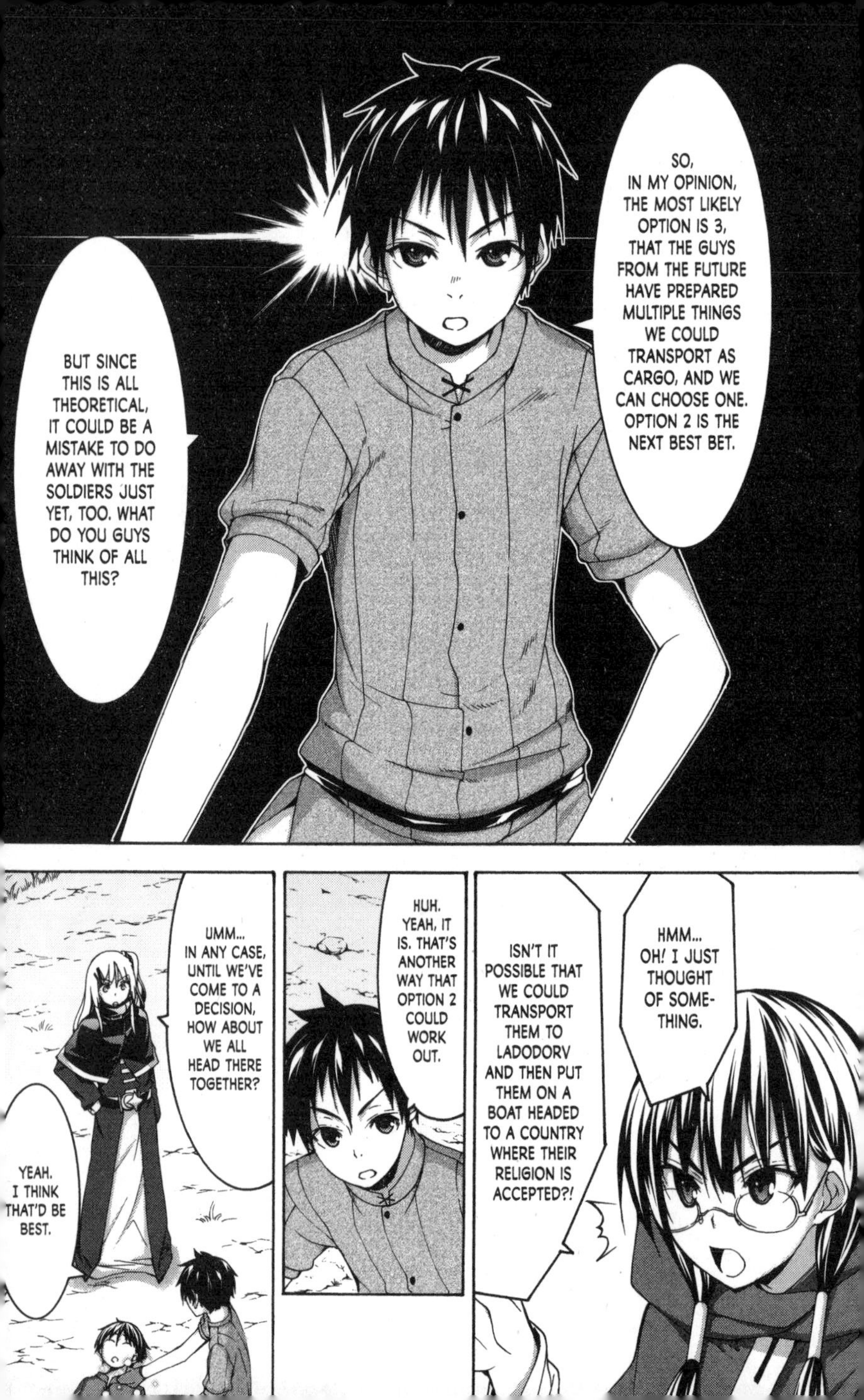
SO, IN MY OPINION, THE MOST LIKELY OPTION IS 3, THAT THE GUYS FROM THE FUTURE HAVE PREPARED MULTIPLE THINGS WE COULD TRANSPORT AS CARGO, AND WE CAN CHOOSE ONE. OPTION 2 IS THE NEXT BEST BET.
BUT SINCE THIS IS ALL THEORETICAL, IT COULD BE A MISTAKE TO DO AWAY WITH THE SOLDIERS JUST YET, TOO. WHAT DO YOU GUYS THINK OF ALL THIS?
HMM... OH! I JUST THOUGHT OF SOME-THING.
ISN'T IT POSSIBLE THAT WE COULD TRANSPORT THEM TO LADODORV AND THEN PUT THEM ON A BOAT HEADED TO A COUNTRY WHERE THEIR RELIGION IS ACCEPTED?!
HUH. YEAH, IT IS. THAT'S ANOTHER WAY THAT OPTION 2 COULD WORK OUT.
UMM... IN ANY CASE, UNTIL WE'VE COME TO A DECISION, HOW ABOUT WE ALL HEAD THERE TOGETHER?
YEAH. I THINK THAT'D BE BEST.

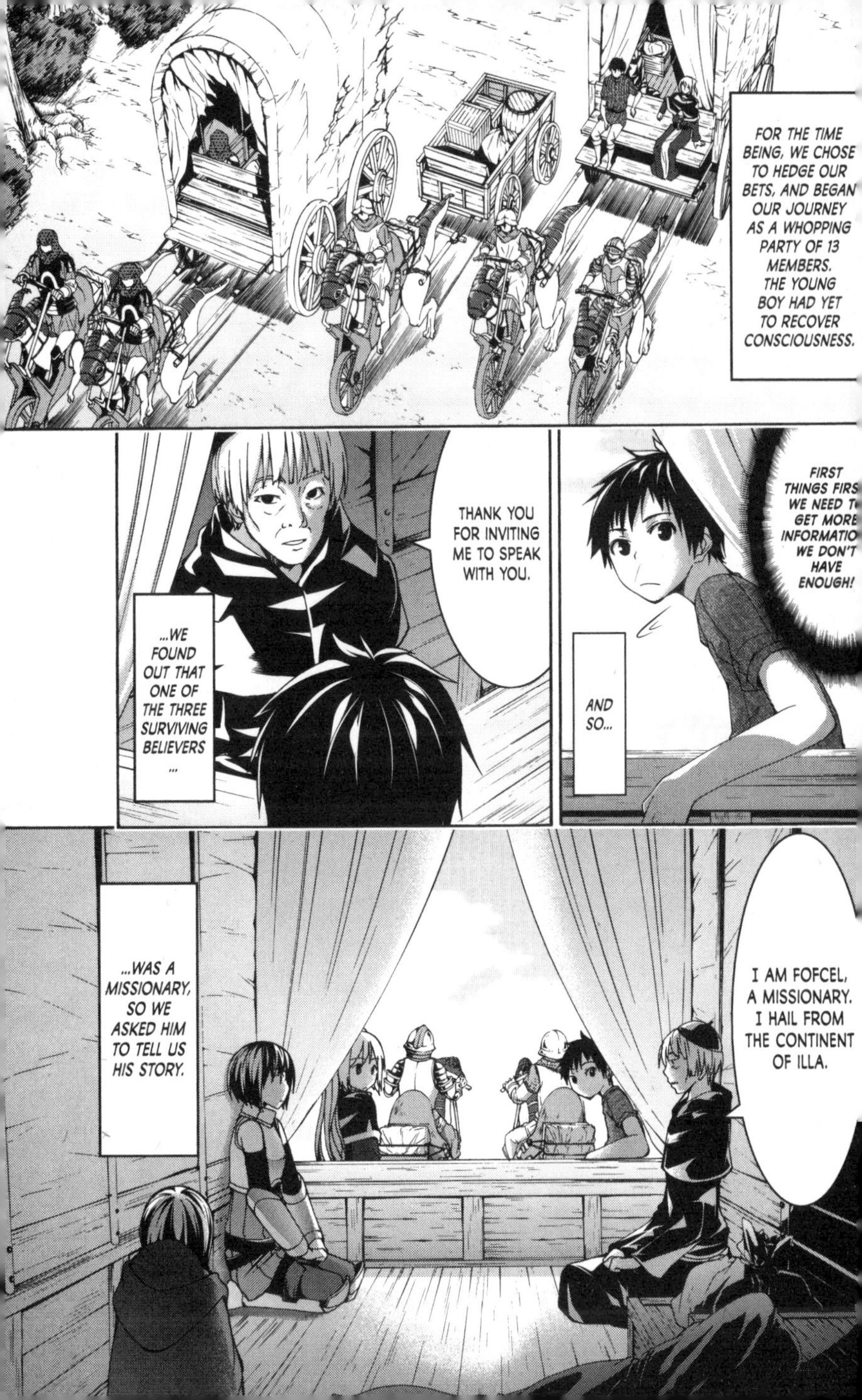
FOR THE TIME BEING, WE CHOSE TO HEDGE OUR BETS, AND BEGAN OUR JOURNEY AS A WHOPPING PARTY OF 13 MEMBERS. THE YOUNG BOY HAD YET TO RECOVER CONSCIOUSNESS.
FIRST THINGS FIRS WE NEED T GET MORE INFORMATIO WE DON'T HAVE ENOUGH!
AND SO...
THANK YOU FOR INVITING ME TO SPEAK WITH YOU.
...WE FOUND OUT THAT ONE OF THE THREE SURVIVING BELIEVERS ...
I AM FOFCEL, A MISSIONARY. I HAIL FROM THE CONTINENT OF ILLA.
...WAS A MISSIONARY, SO WE ASKED HIM TO TELL US HIS STORY.

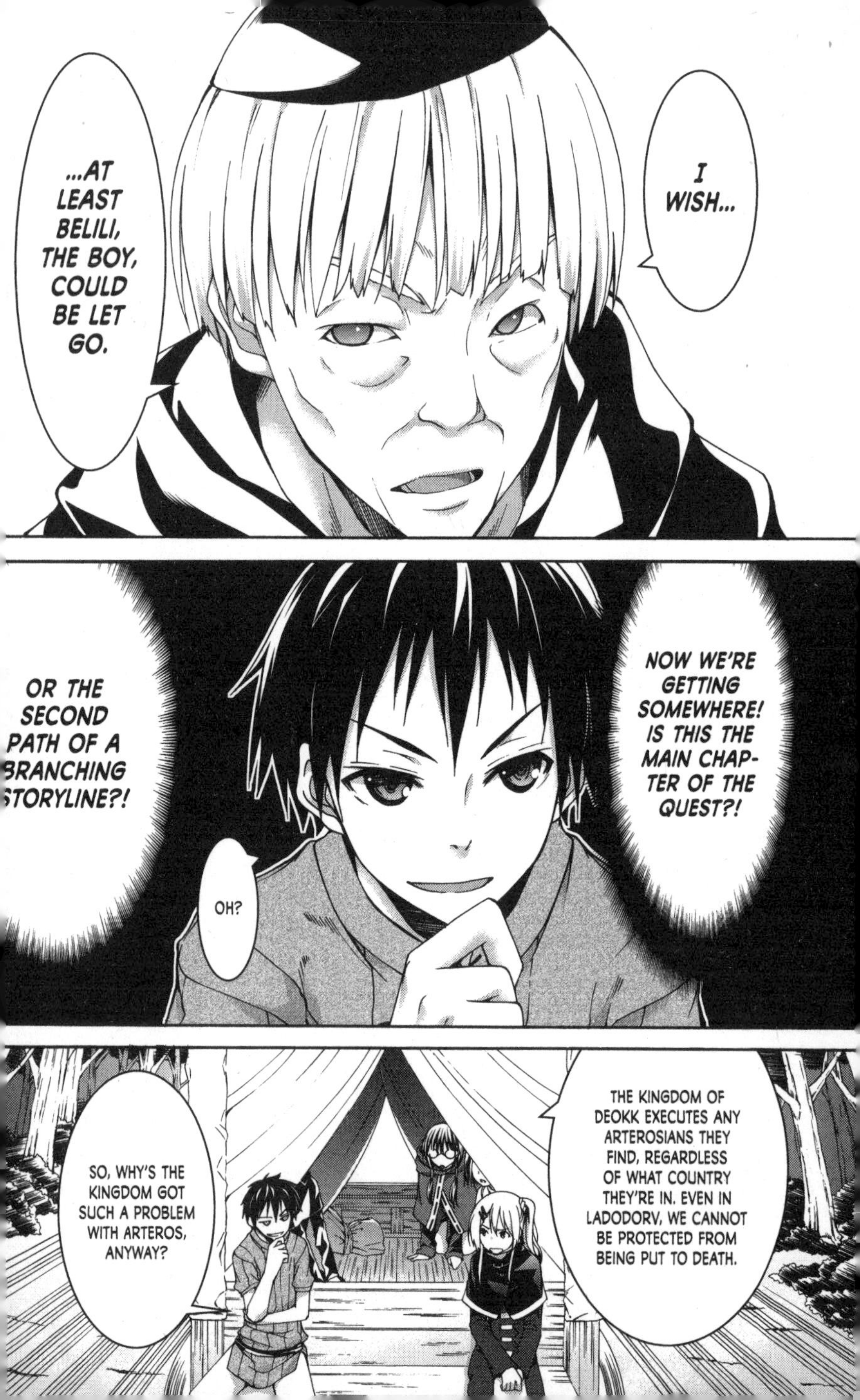
I WISH...
...AT LEAST BELILI, THE BOY, COULD BE LET GO.
NOW WE'RE GETTING SOMEWHERE! IS THIS THE MAIN CHAPTER OF THE QUEST?!
OR THE SECOND PATH OF A BRANCHING STORYLINE?!
OH?
THE KINGDOM OF DEOKK EXECUTES ANY ARTEROSIANS THEY FIND, REGARDLESS OF WHAT COUNTRY THEY'RE IN. EVEN IN LADODORV, WE CANNOT BE PROTECTED FROM BEING PUT TO DEATH.
SO, WHY'S THE KINGDOM GOT SUCH A PROBLEM WITH ARTEROS, ANYWAY?

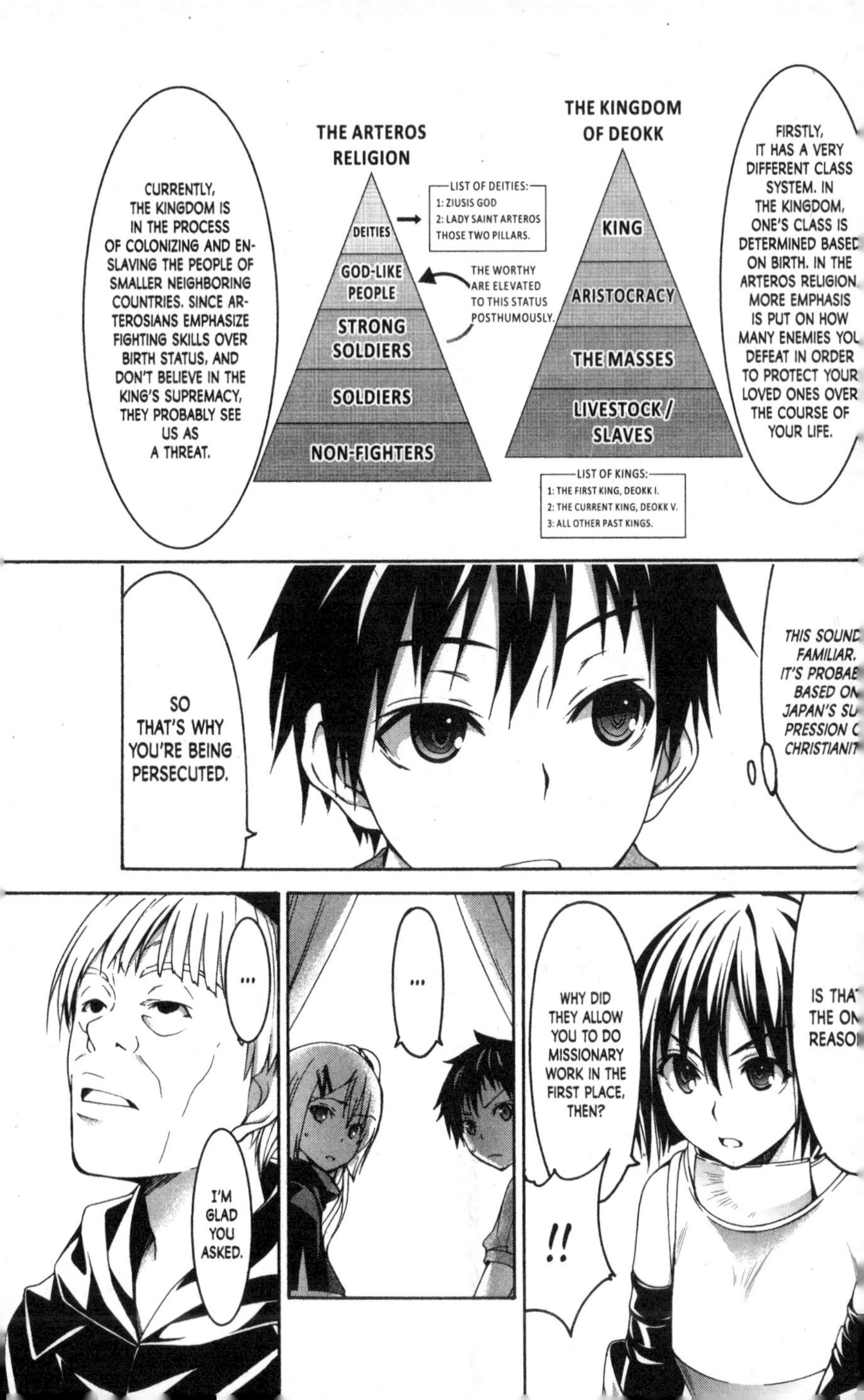

FIRSTLY, IT HAS A VERY DIFFERENT CLASS SYSTEM. IN THE KINGDOM, ONE'S CLASS IS DETERMINED BASED ON BIRTH. IN THE ARTEROS RELIGION, MORE EMPHASIS IS PUT ON HOW MANY ENEMIES YOU DEFEAT IN ORDER TO PROTECT YOUR LOVED ONES OVER THE COURSE OF YOUR LIFE.
THE KINGDOM OF DEOKK
KING
ARISTOCRACY
THE MASSES
LIVESTOCK / SLAVES
LIST OF KINGS:
1: THE FIRST KING, DEOKK I.
2: THE CURRENT KING, DEOKK V.
3: ALL OTHER PAST KINGS.
THE ARTEROS RELIGION
DEITIES
GOD-LIKE PEOPLE
STRONG SOLDIERS
SOLDIERS
NON-FIGHTERS
LIST OF DEITIES:
1: ZIUSIS GOD
2: LADY SAINT ARTEROS
THOSE TWO PILLARS.
THE WORTHY ARE ELEVATED TO THIS STATUS POSTHUMOUSLY.
CURRENTLY, THE KINGDOM IS IN THE PROCESS OF COLONIZING AND ENSLAVING THE PEOPLE OF SMALLER NEIGHBORING COUNTRIES. SINCE ARTEROSIANS EMPHASIZE FIGHTING SKILLS OVER BIRTH STATUS, AND DON'T BELIEVE IN THE KING'S SUPREMACY, THEY PROBABLY SEE US AS A THREAT.
THIS SOUND FAMILIAR. IT'S PROBAB BASED ON JAPAN'S SU PRESSION C CHRISTIANIT
SO THAT'S WHY YOU'RE BEING PERSECUTED.
IS THA THE ON REASO
WHY DID THEY ALLOW YOU TO DO MISSIONARY WORK IN THE FIRST PLACE, THEN?
!!
...
...
I'M GLAD YOU ASKED.

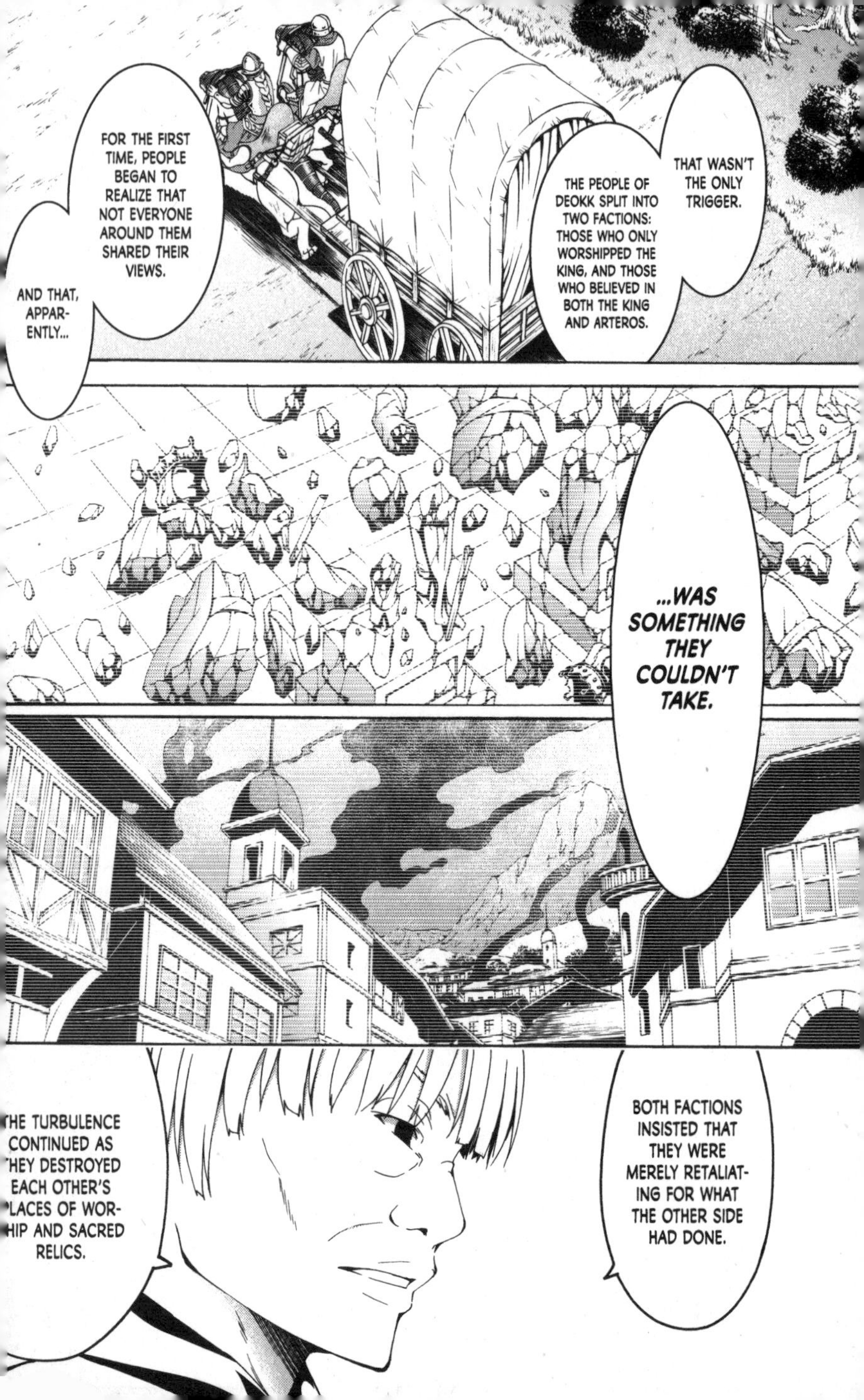
THAT WASN'T THE ONLY TRIGGER.
THE PEOPLE OF DEOKK SPLIT INTO TWO FACTIONS: THOSE WHO ONLY WORSHIPPED THE KING, AND THOSE WHO BELIEVED IN BOTH THE KING AND ARTEROS.
FOR THE FIRST TIME, PEOPLE BEGAN TO REALIZE THAT NOT EVERYONE AROUND THEM SHARED THEIR VIEWS.
AND THAT, APPARENTLY...
...WAS SOMETHING THEY COULDN'T TAKE.
BOTH FACTIONS INSISTED THAT THEY WERE MERELY RETALIATING FOR WHAT THE OTHER SIDE HAD DONE.
THE TURBULENCE CONTINUED AS THEY DESTROYED EACH OTHER'S PLACES OF WORSHIP AND SACRED RELICS.

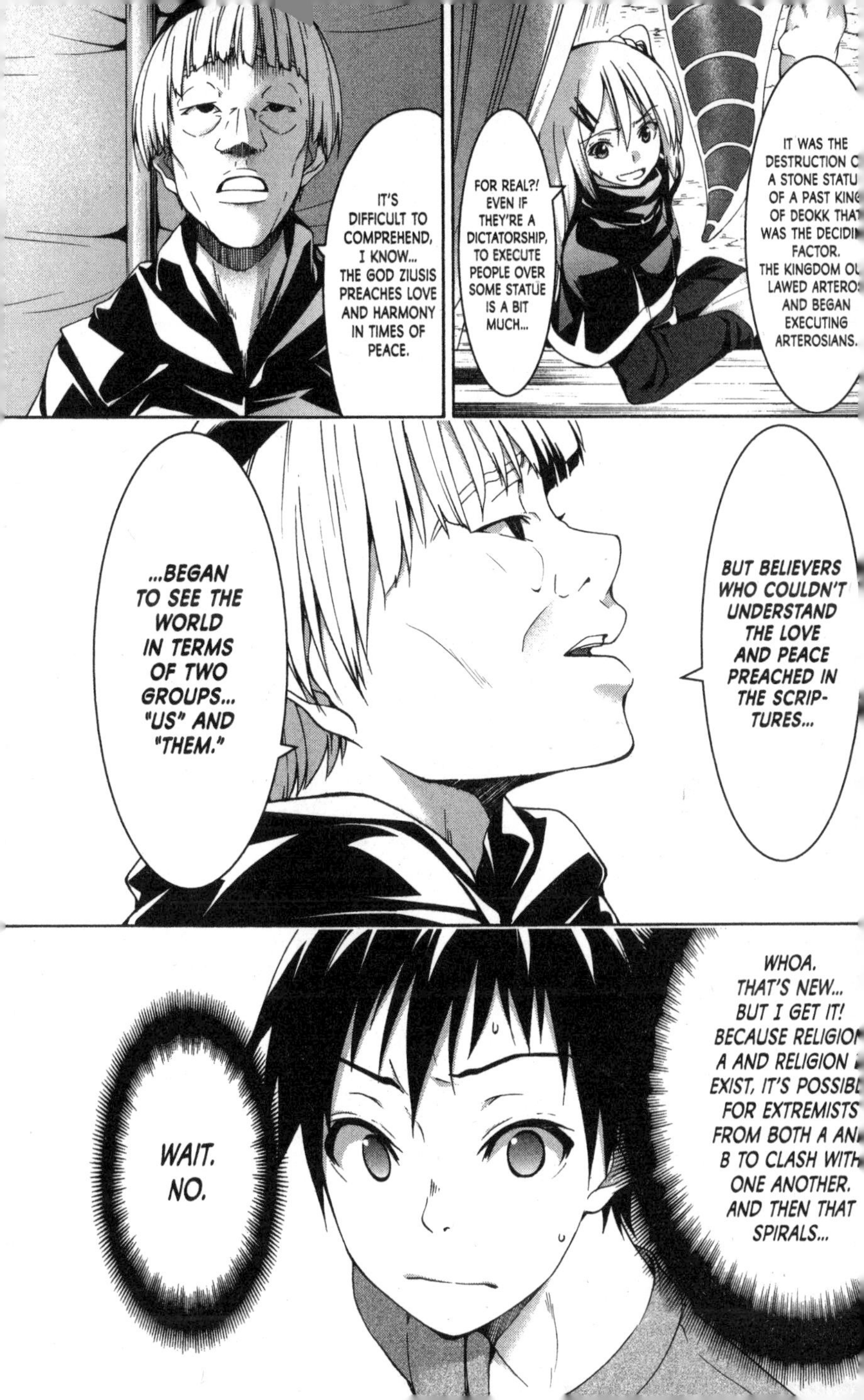
IT WAS THE DESTRUCTION O A STONE STATU OF A PAST KING OF DEOKK THAT WAS THE DECIDI FACTOR. THE KINGDOM OU LAWED ARTEROS AND BEGAN EXECUTING ARTEROSIANS.
FOR REAL?! EVEN IF THEY'RE A DICTATORSHIP, TO EXECUTE PEOPLE OVER SOME STATUE IS A BIT MUCH...
IT'S DIFFICULT TO COMPREHEND, I KNOW... THE GOD ZIUSIS PREACHES LOVE AND HARMONY IN TIMES OF PEACE.
BUT BELIEVERS WHO COULDN'T UNDERSTAND THE LOVE AND PEACE PREACHED IN THE SCRIP-TURES...
...BEGAN TO SEE THE WORLD IN TERMS OF TWO GROUPS... "US" AND "THEM."
WHOA. THAT'S NEW... BUT I GET IT! BECAUSE RELIGIO A AND RELIGION EXIST, IT'S POSSIB FOR EXTREMISTS FROM BOTH A AN B TO CLASH WITH ONE ANOTHER. AND THEN THAT SPIRALS...
WAIT. NO.

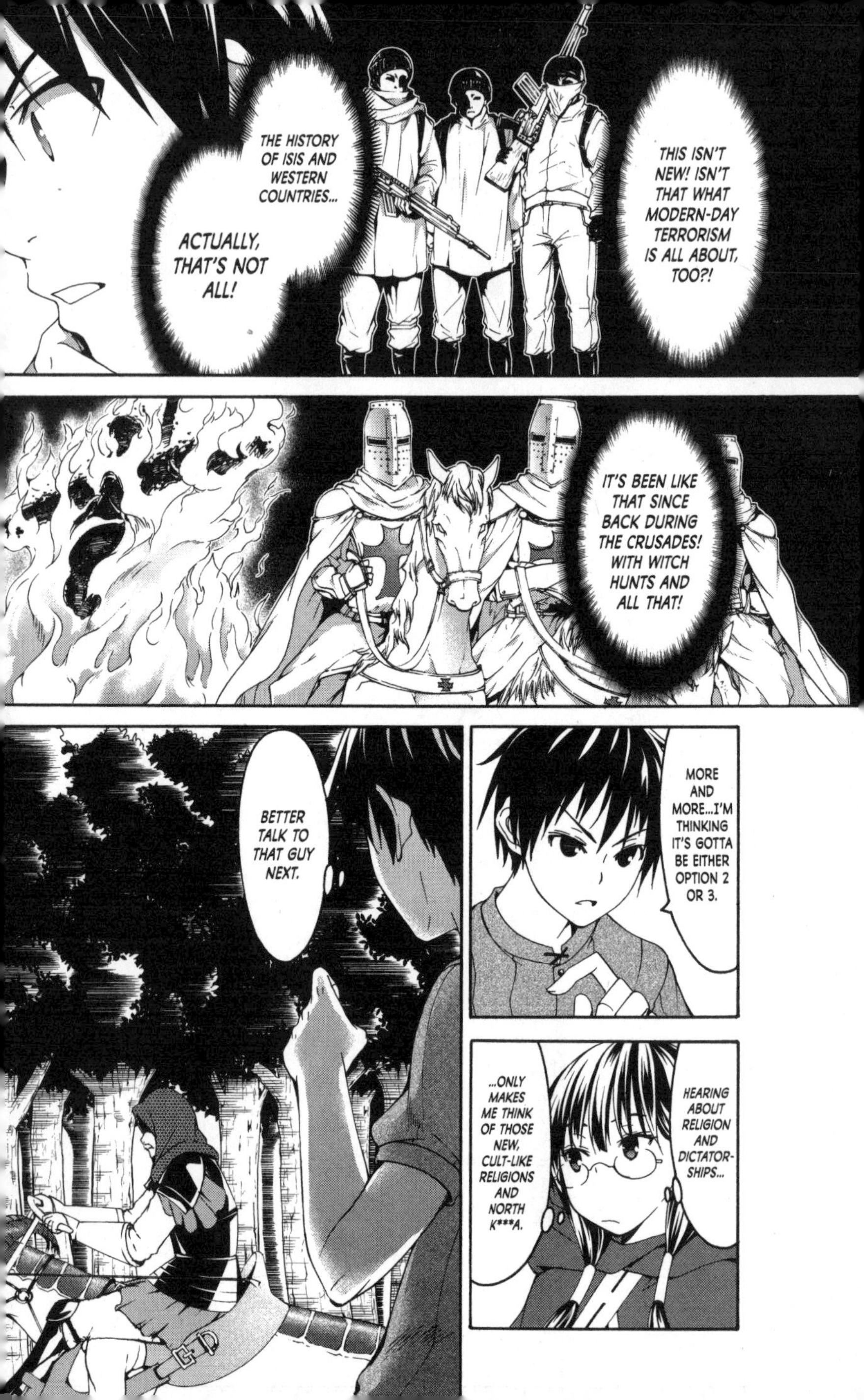
THIS ISN'T NEW! ISN'T THAT WHAT MODERN-DAY TERRORISM IS ALL ABOUT, TOO?!
THE HISTORY OF ISIS AND WESTERN COUNTRIES...
ACTUALLY, THAT'S NOT ALL!
IT'S BEEN LIKE THAT SINCE BACK DURING THE CRUSADES! WITH WITCH HUNTS AND ALL THAT!
MORE AND MORE...I'M THINKING IT'S GOTTA BE EITHER OPTION 2 OR 3.
HEARING ABOUT RELIGION AND DICTATOR-SHIPS...
...ONLY MAKES ME THINK OF THOSE NEW, CULT-LIKE RELIGIONS AND NORTH K***A.
BETTER TALK TO THAT GUY NEXT.

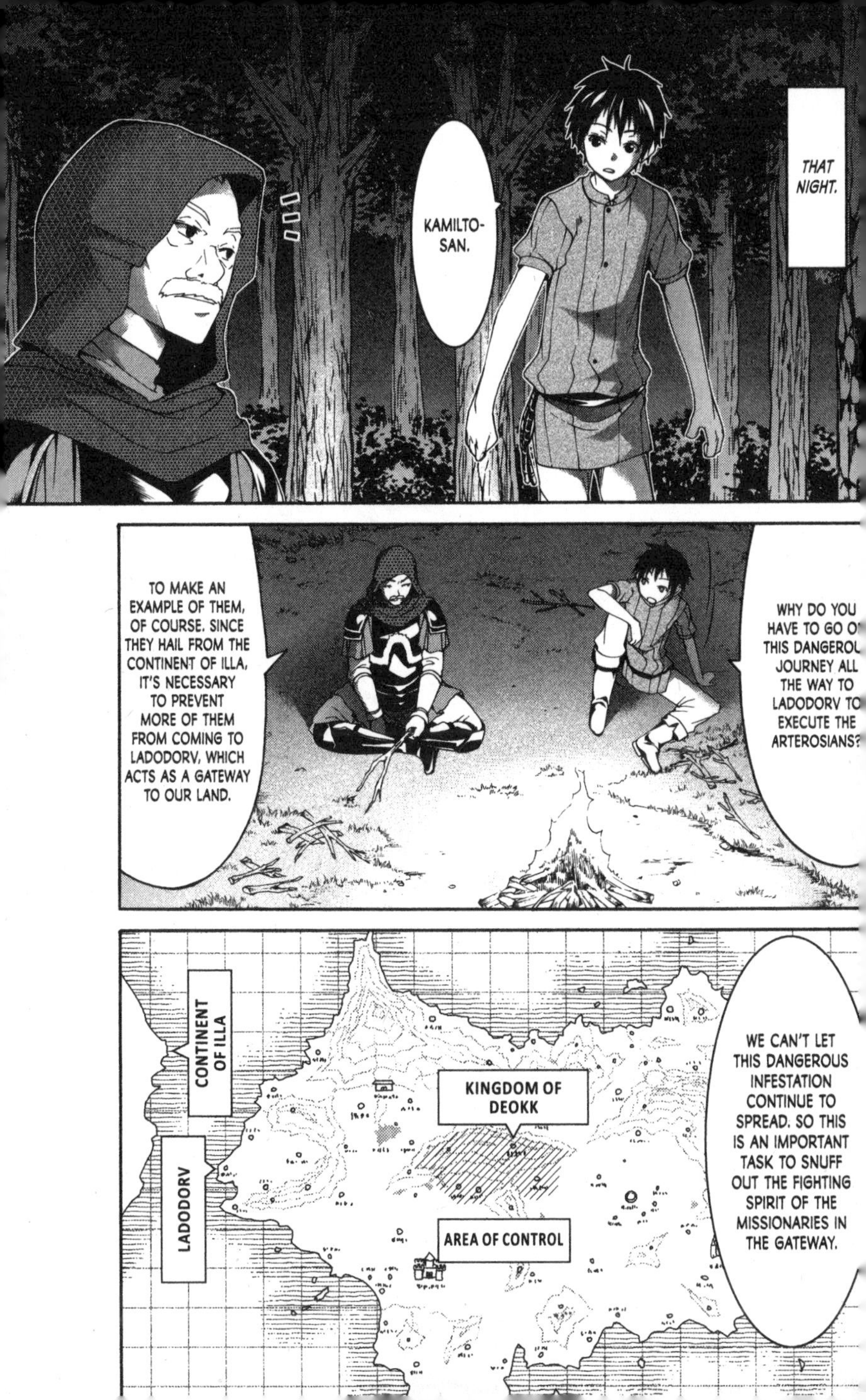
THAT NIGHT.
KAMILTO-SAN.
WHY DO YOU HAVE TO GO O THIS DANGEROU JOURNEY ALL THE WAY TO LADODORV TO EXECUTE THE ARTEROSIANS?
TO MAKE AN EXAMPLE OF THEM, OF COURSE. SINCE THEY HAIL FROM THE CONTINENT OF ILLA, IT'S NECESSARY TO PREVENT MORE OF THEM FROM COMING TO LADODORV, WHICH ACTS AS A GATEWAY TO OUR LAND.
WE CAN'T LET THIS DANGEROUS INFESTATION CONTINUE TO SPREAD. SO THIS IS AN IMPORTANT TASK TO SNUFF OUT THE FIGHTING SPIRIT OF THE MISSIONARIES IN THE GATEWAY.
KINGDOM OF DEOKK
AREA OF CONTROL
CONTINENT OF ILLA
LADODORV

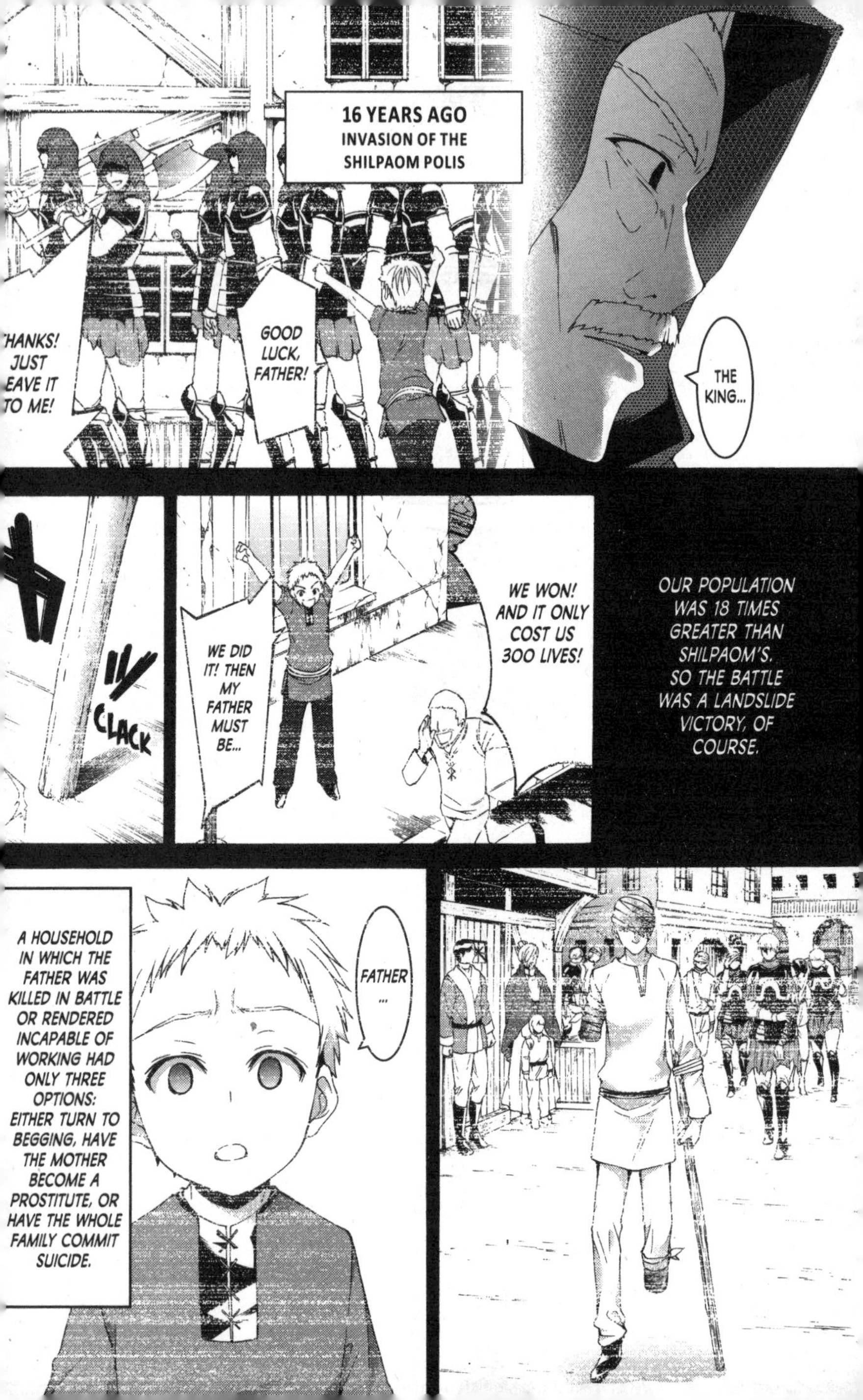
THE KING...
16 YEARS AGO
INVASION OF THE SHILPAOM POLIS
GOOD LUCK, FATHER!
HANKS! JUST EAVE IT TO ME!
OUR POPULATION WAS 18 TIMES GREATER THAN SHILPAOM'S, SO THE BATTLE WAS A LANDSLIDE VICTORY, OF COURSE.
WE WON! AND IT ONLY COST US 300 LIVES!
WE DID IT! THEN MY FATHER MUST BE...
CLACK
FATHER...
A HOUSEHOLD IN WHICH THE FATHER WAS KILLED IN BATTLE OR RENDERED INCAPABLE OF WORKING HAD ONLY THREE OPTIONS: EITHER TURN TO BEGGING, HAVE THE MOTHER BECOME A PROSTITUTE, OR HAVE THE WHOLE FAMILY COMMIT SUICIDE.

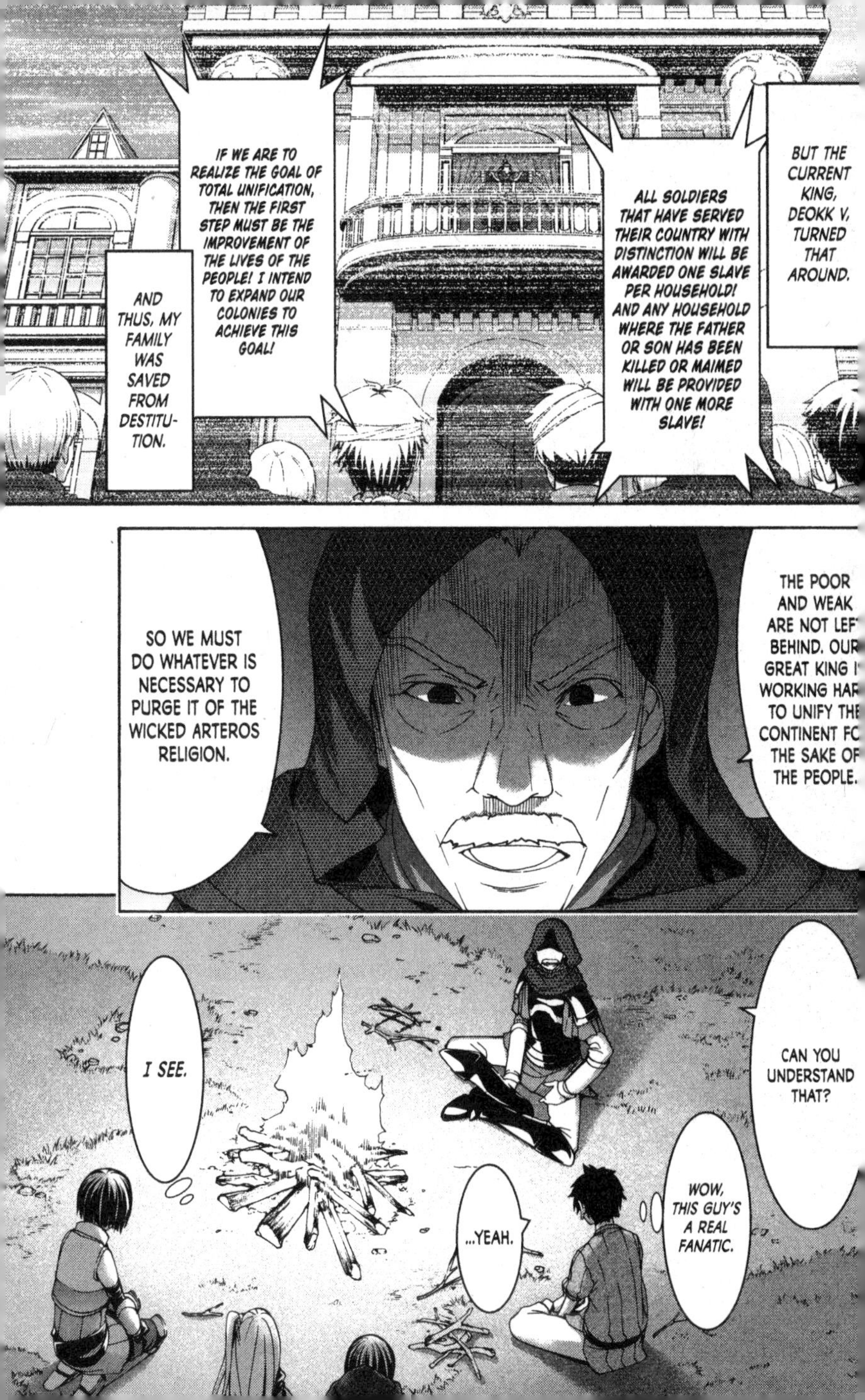
BUT THE CURRENT KING, DEOKK V, TURNED THAT AROUND.
IF WE ARE TO REALIZE THE GOAL OF TOTAL UNIFICATION, THEN THE FIRST STEP MUST BE THE IMPROVEMENT OF THE LIVES OF THE PEOPLE! I INTEND TO EXPAND OUR COLONIES TO ACHIEVE THIS GOAL!
ALL SOLDIERS THAT HAVE SERVED THEIR COUNTRY WITH DISTINCTION WILL BE AWARDED ONE SLAVE PER HOUSEHOLD! AND ANY HOUSEHOLD WHERE THE FATHER OR SON HAS BEEN KILLED OR MAIMED WILL BE PROVIDED WITH ONE MORE SLAVE!
AND THUS, MY FAMILY WAS SAVED FROM DESTITU-TION.
THE POOR AND WEAK ARE NOT LEF BEHIND. OUR GREAT KING I WORKING HAR TO UNIFY THE CONTINENT FO THE SAKE OF THE PEOPLE.
SO WE MUST DO WHATEVER IS NECESSARY TO PURGE IT OF THE WICKED ARTEROS RELIGION.
CAN YOU UNDERSTAND THAT?
WOW, THIS GUY'S A REAL FANATIC.
...YEAH.
I SEE.

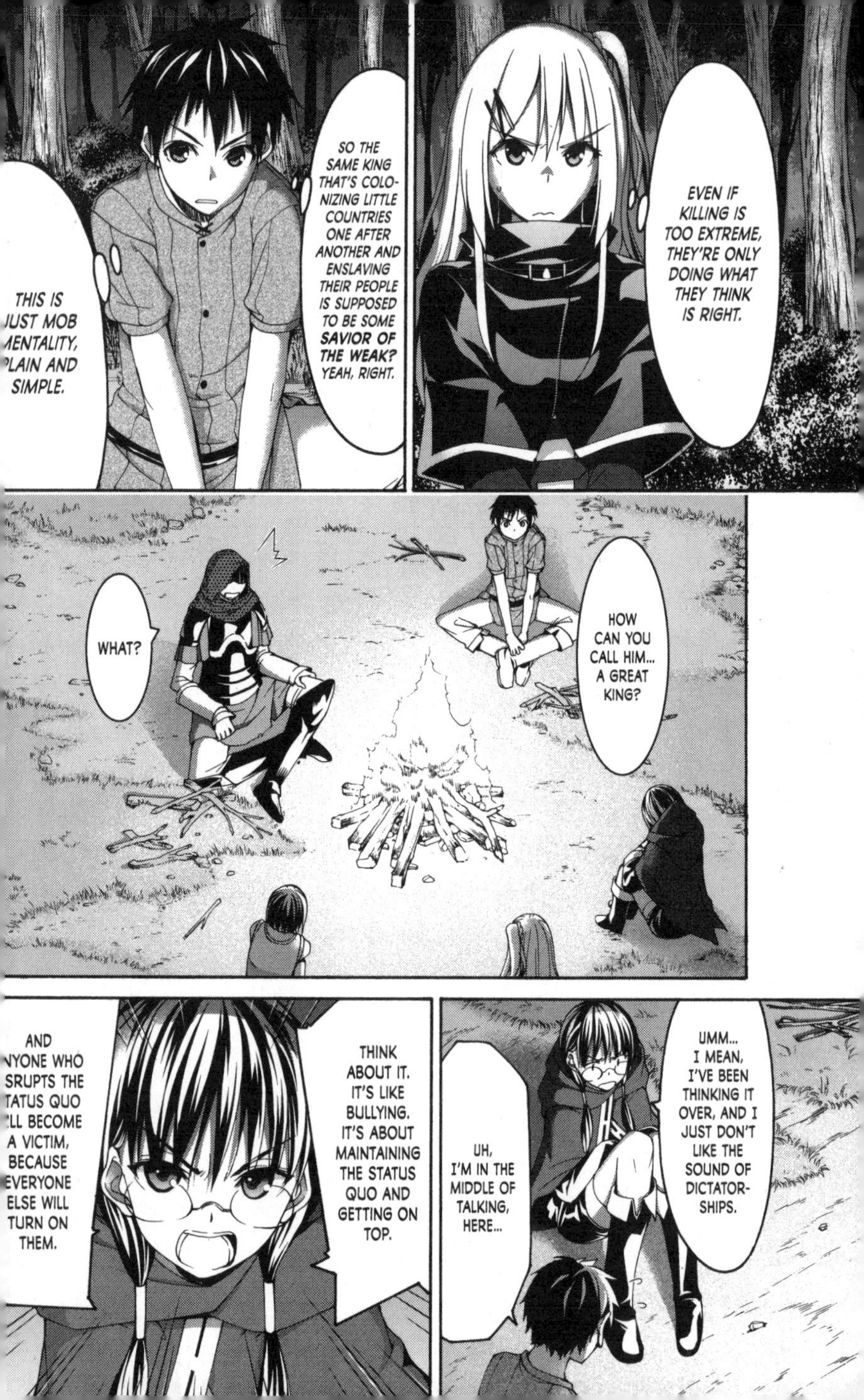
EVEN IF KILLING IS TOO EXTREME, THEY'RE ONLY DOING WHAT THEY THINK IS RIGHT.
SO THE SAME KING THAT'S COLO-NIZING LITTLE COUNTRIES ONE AFTER ANOTHER AND ENSLAVING THEIR PEOPLE IS SUPPOSED TO BE SOME **SAVIOR OF THE WEAK?** YEAH, RIGHT.
THIS IS UST MOB IENTALITY, LAIN AND SIMPLE.
HOW CAN YOU CALL HIM... A GREAT KING?
WHAT?
UMM... I MEAN, I'VE BEEN THINKING IT OVER, AND I JUST DON'T LIKE THE SOUND OF DICTATOR-SHIPS.
UH, I'M IN THE MIDDLE OF TALKING, HERE...
THINK ABOUT IT. IT'S LIKE BULLYING. IT'S ABOUT MAINTAINING THE STATUS QUO AND GETTING ON TOP.
AND NYONE WHO SRUPTS THE TATUS QUO 'LL BECOME A VICTIM, BECAUSE EVERYONE ELSE WILL TURN ON THEM.

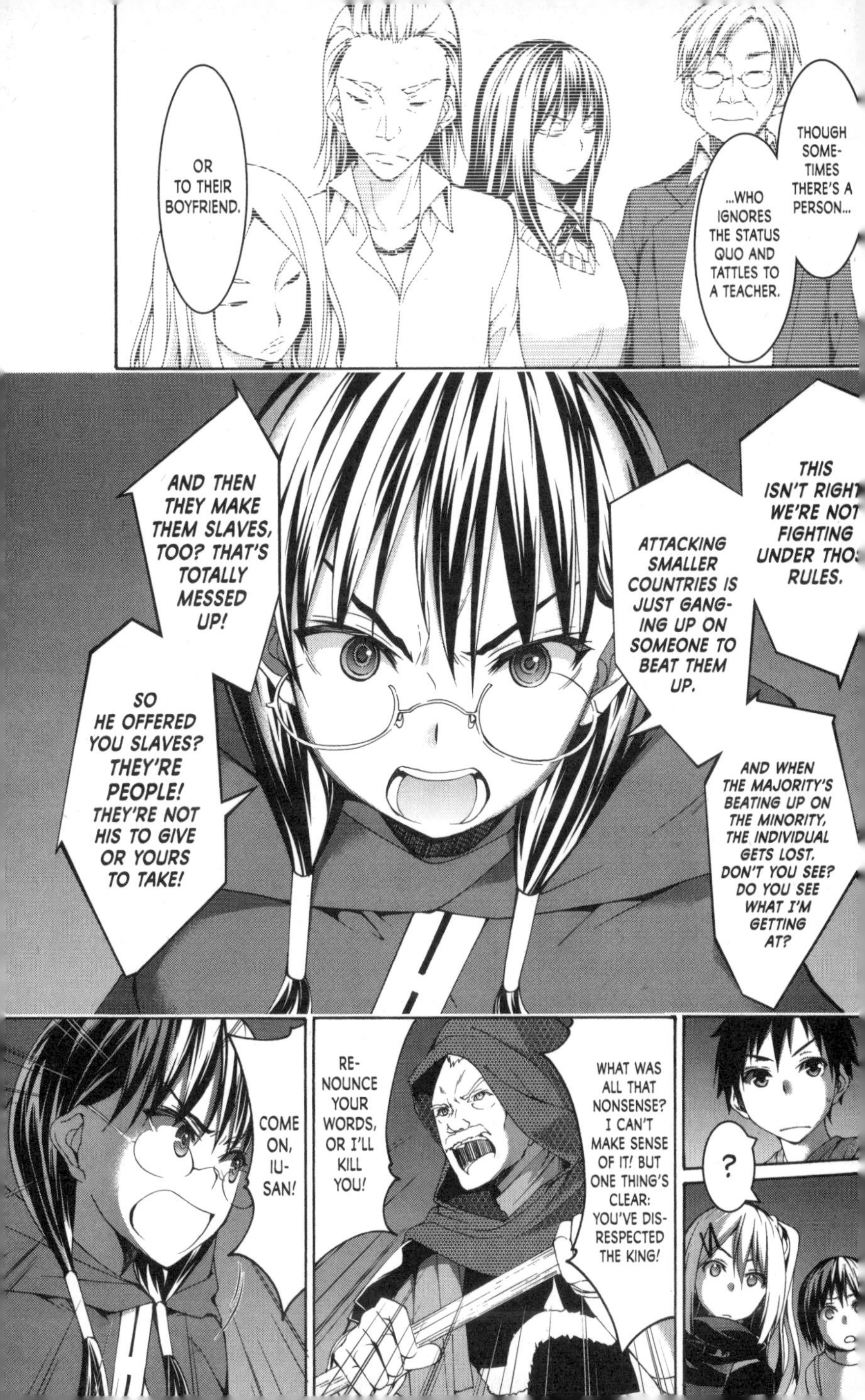
THOUGH SOMETIMES THERE'S A PERSON...
...WHO IGNORES THE STATUS QUO AND TATTLES TO A TEACHER.
OR TO THEIR BOYFRIEND.
THIS ISN'T RIGHT WE'RE NOT FIGHTING UNDER THOS RULES.
ATTACKING SMALLER COUNTRIES IS JUST GANGING UP ON SOMEONE TO BEAT THEM UP.
AND WHEN THE MAJORITY'S BEATING UP ON THE MINORITY, THE INDIVIDUAL GETS LOST. DON'T YOU SEE? DO YOU SEE WHAT I'M GETTING AT?
AND THEN THEY MAKE THEM SLAVES, TOO? THAT'S TOTALLY MESSED UP!
SO HE OFFERED YOU SLAVES? THEY'RE PEOPLE! THEY'RE NOT HIS TO GIVE OR YOURS TO TAKE!
?
WHAT WAS ALL THAT NONSENSE? I CAN'T MAKE SENSE OF IT! BUT ONE THING'S CLEAR: YOU'VE DISRESPECTED THE KING!
RENOUNCE YOUR WORDS, OR I'LL KILL YOU!
COME ON, IU-SAN!

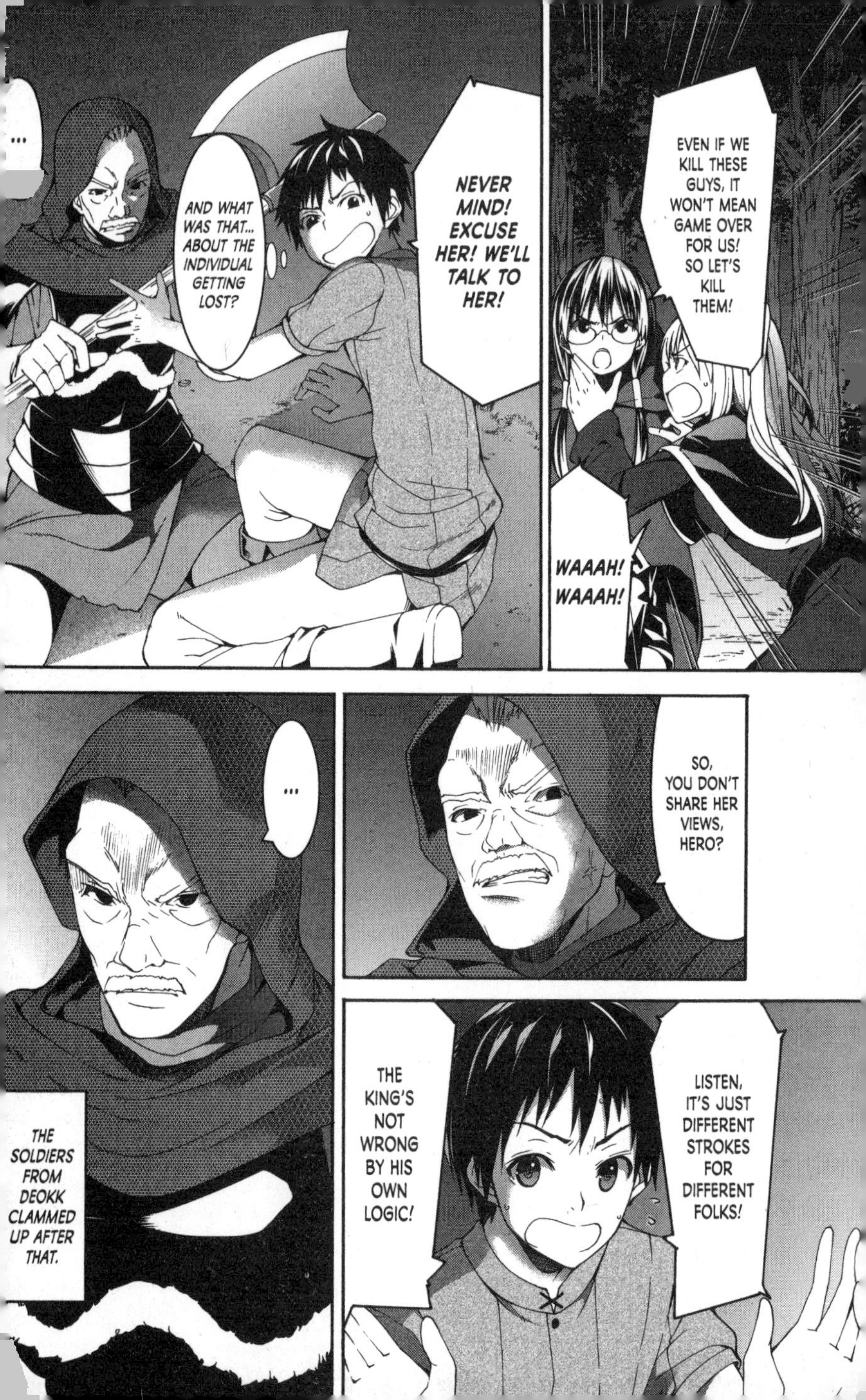
EVEN IF WE KILL THESE GUYS, IT WON'T MEAN GAME OVER FOR US! SO LET'S KILL THEM!
WAAAH! WAAAH!
NEVER MIND! EXCUSE HER! WE'LL TALK TO HER!
AND WHAT WAS THAT... ABOUT THE INDIVIDUAL GETTING LOST?
...
SO, YOU DON'T SHARE HER VIEWS, HERO?
LISTEN, IT'S JUST DIFFERENT STROKES FOR DIFFERENT FOLKS!
THE KING'S NOT WRONG BY HIS OWN LOGIC!
...
THE SOLDIERS FROM DEOKK CLAMMED UP AFTER THAT.

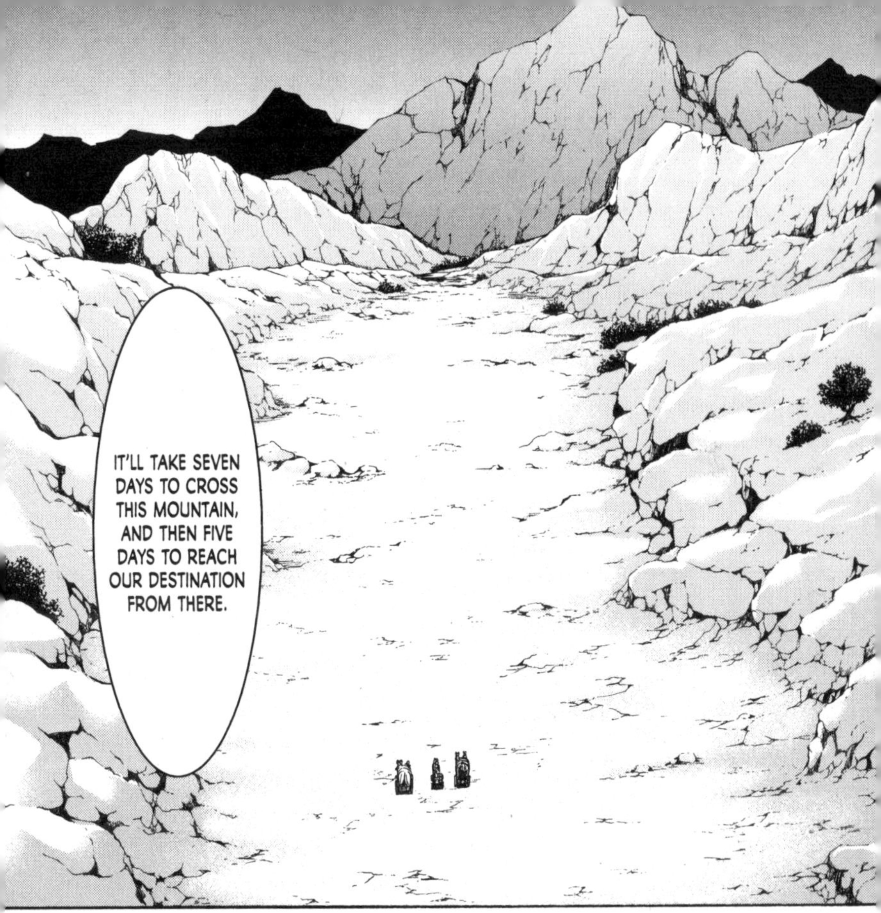
IT'LL TAKE SEVEN DAYS TO CROSS THIS MOUNTAIN, AND THEN FIVE DAYS TO REACH OUR DESTINATION FROM THERE.

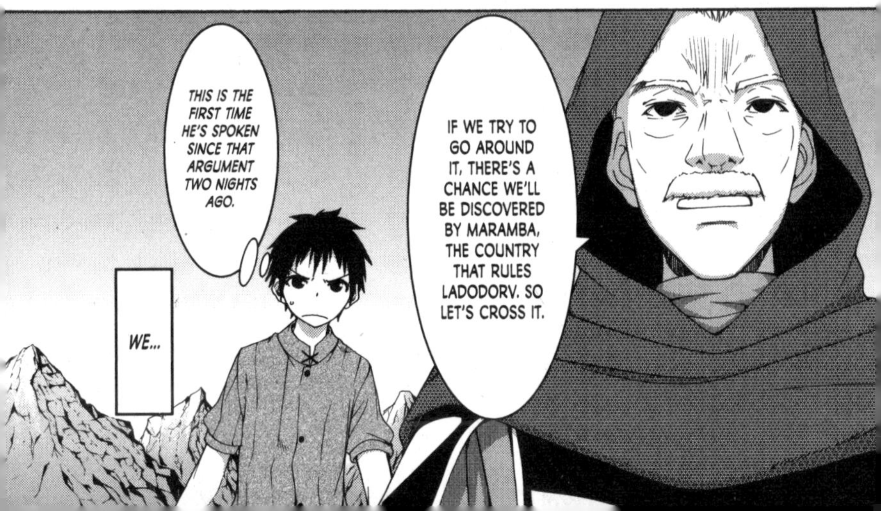
IF WE TRY TO GO AROUND IT, THERE'S A CHANCE WE'LL BE DISCOVERED BY MARAMBA, THE COUNTRY THAT RULES LADODORV. SO LET'S CROSS IT.
THIS IS THE FIRST TIME HE'S SPOKEN SINCE THAT ARGUMENT TWO NIGHTS AGO.
WE...

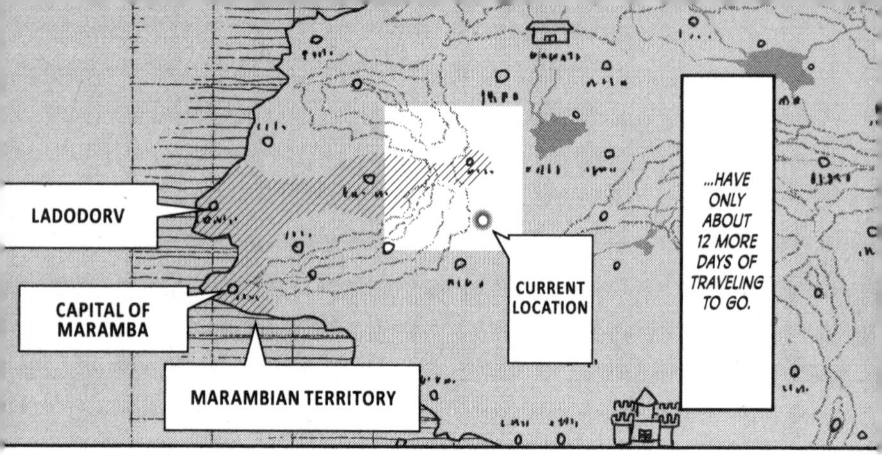
...HAVE ONLY ABOUT 12 MORE DAYS OF TRAVELING TO GO.
CURRENT LOCATION
LADODORV
CAPITAL OF MARAMBA
MARAMBIAN TERRITORY

REMAINING TIME: 13 DAYS AND 6 HOURS

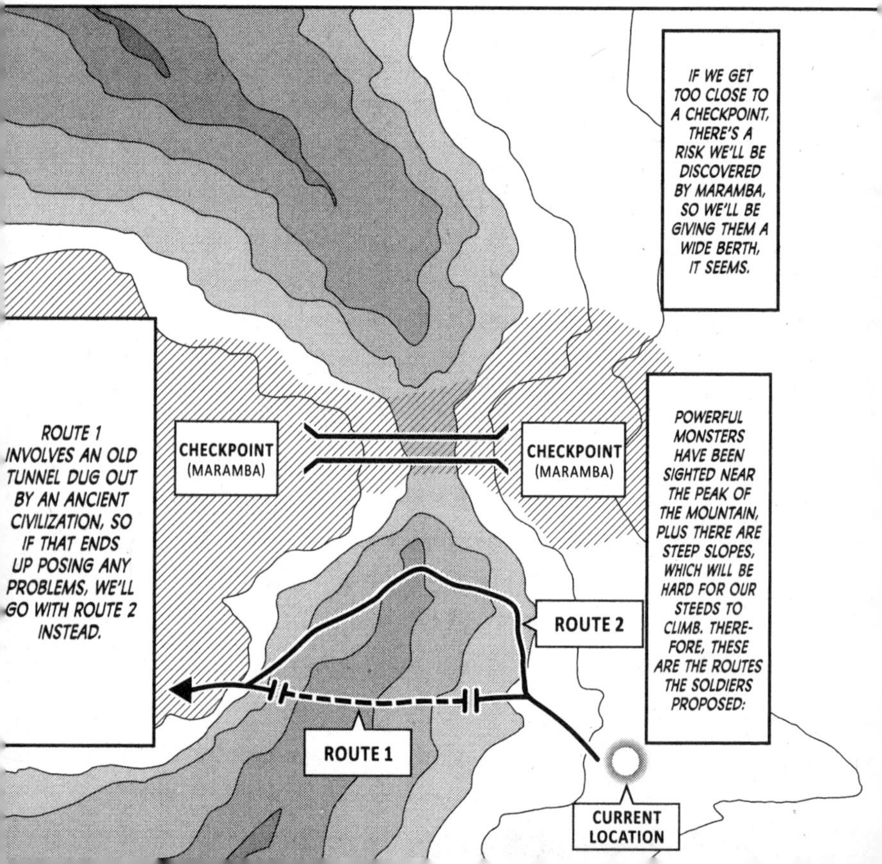
IF WE GET TOO CLOSE TO A CHECKPOINT, THERE'S A RISK WE'LL BE DISCOVERED BY MARAMBA, SO WE'LL BE GIVING THEM A WIDE BERTH, IT SEEMS.
POWERFUL MONSTERS HAVE BEEN SIGHTED NEAR THE PEAK OF THE MOUNTAIN, PLUS THERE ARE STEEP SLOPES, WHICH WILL BE HARD FOR OUR STEEDS TO CLIMB. THERE-FORE, THESE ARE THE ROUTES THE SOLDIERS PROPOSED:
CHECKPOINT (MARAMBA)
CHECKPOINT (MARAMBA)
ROUTE 2
CURRENT LOCATION
ROUTE 1
ROUTE 1 INVOLVES AN OLD TUNNEL DUG OUT BY AN ANCIENT CIVILIZATION, SO IF THAT ENDS UP POSING ANY PROBLEMS, WE'LL GO WITH ROUTE 2 INSTEAD.

REMAINING TIME: 11 DAYS AND 20 HOURS

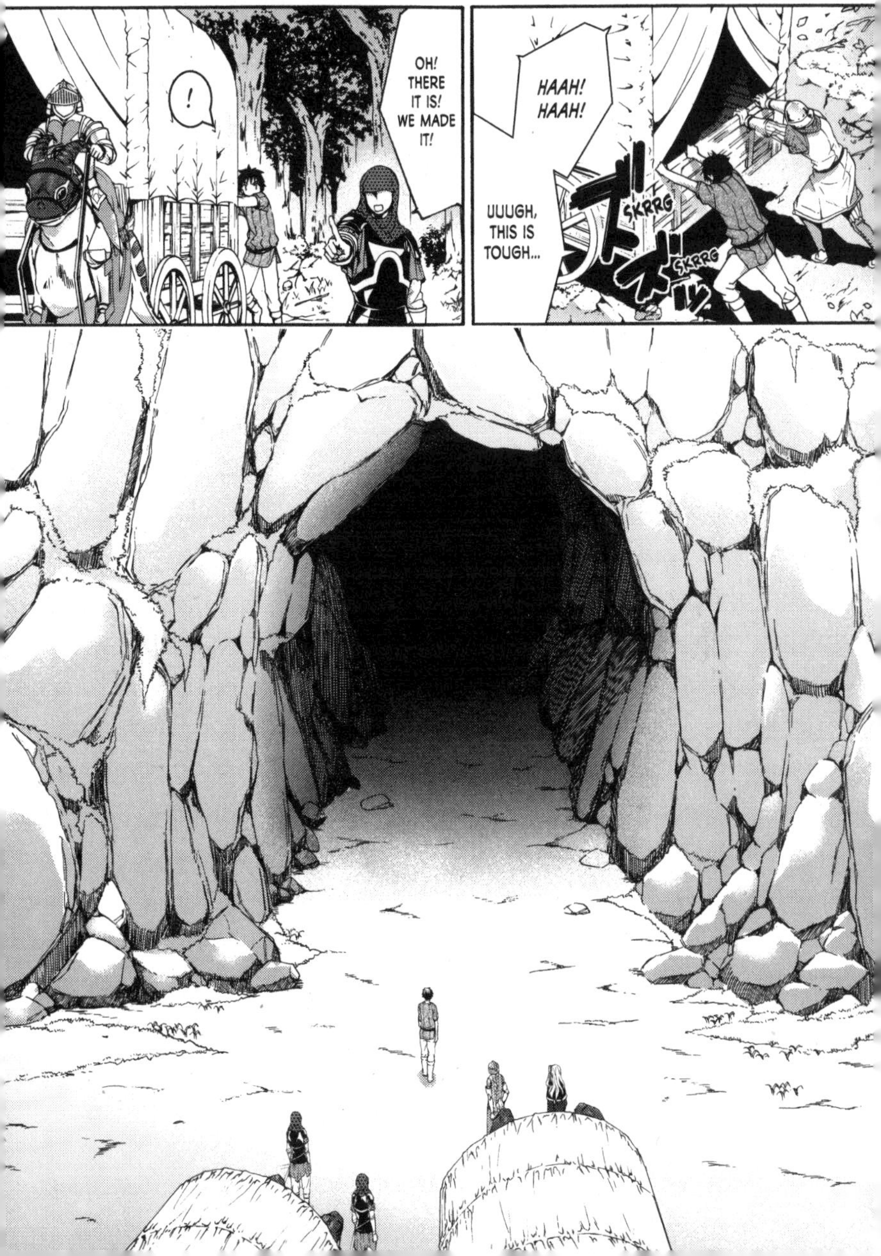
HAAH! HAAH!
UUUGH, THIS IS TOUGH...
SKRRG
SKRRG
OH! THERE IT IS! WE MADE IT!
!

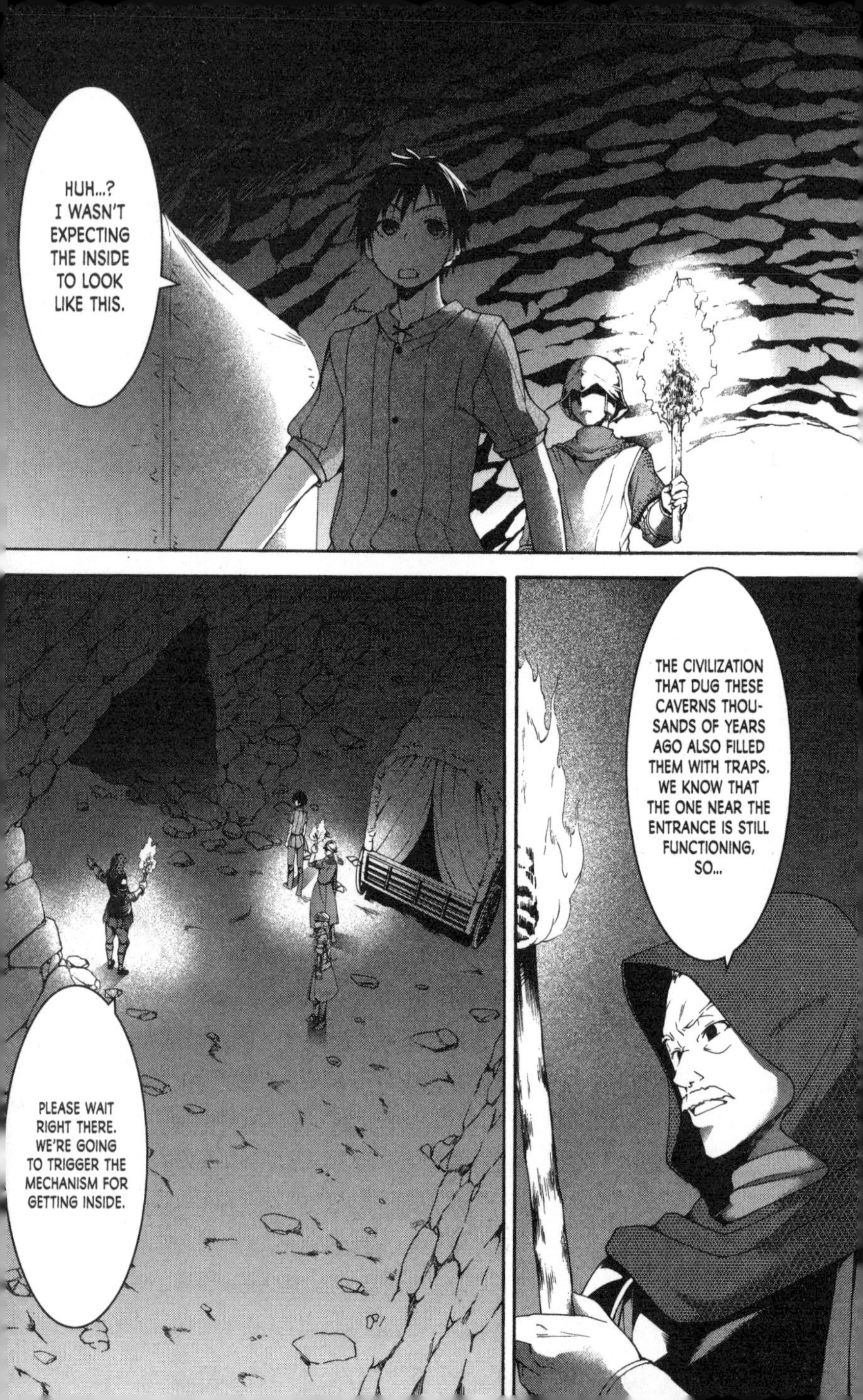
HUH...? I WASN'T EXPECTING THE INSIDE TO LOOK LIKE THIS.
THE CIVILIZATION THAT DUG THESE CAVERNS THOU-SANDS OF YEARS AGO ALSO FILLED THEM WITH TRAPS. WE KNOW THAT THE ONE NEAR THE ENTRANCE IS STILL FUNCTIONING, SO...
PLEASE WAIT RIGHT THERE. WE'RE GOING TO TRIGGER THE MECHANISM FOR GETTING INSIDE.

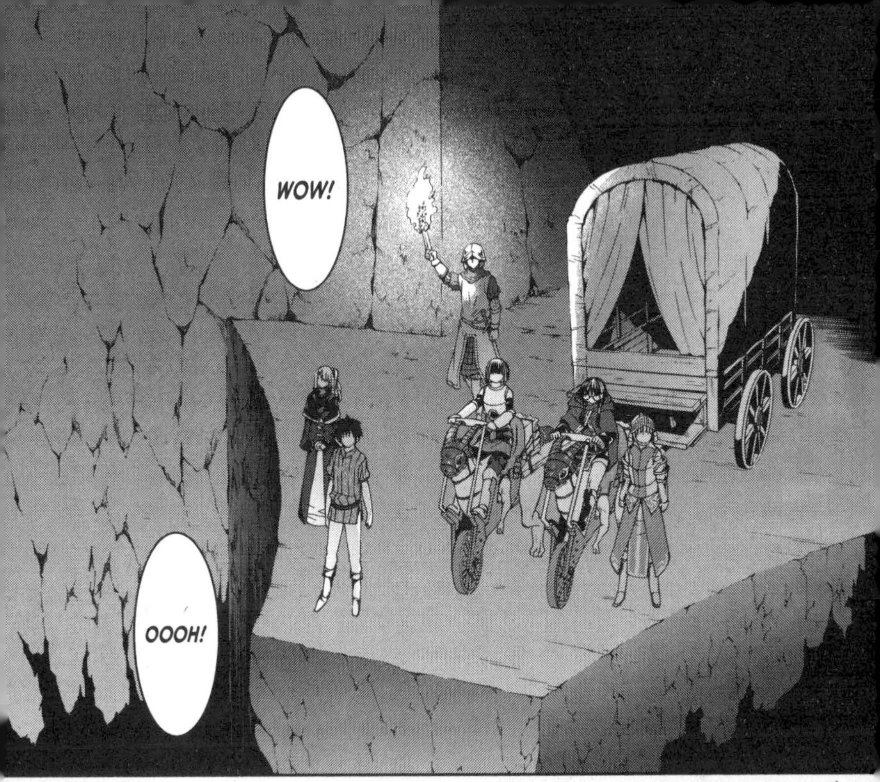
WOW!
OOOH!

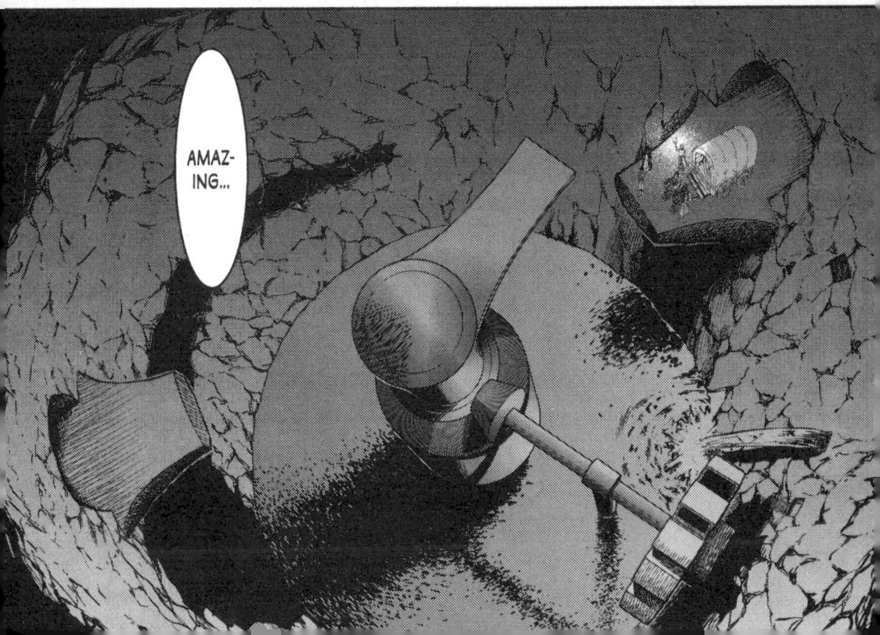
AMAZ-ING...

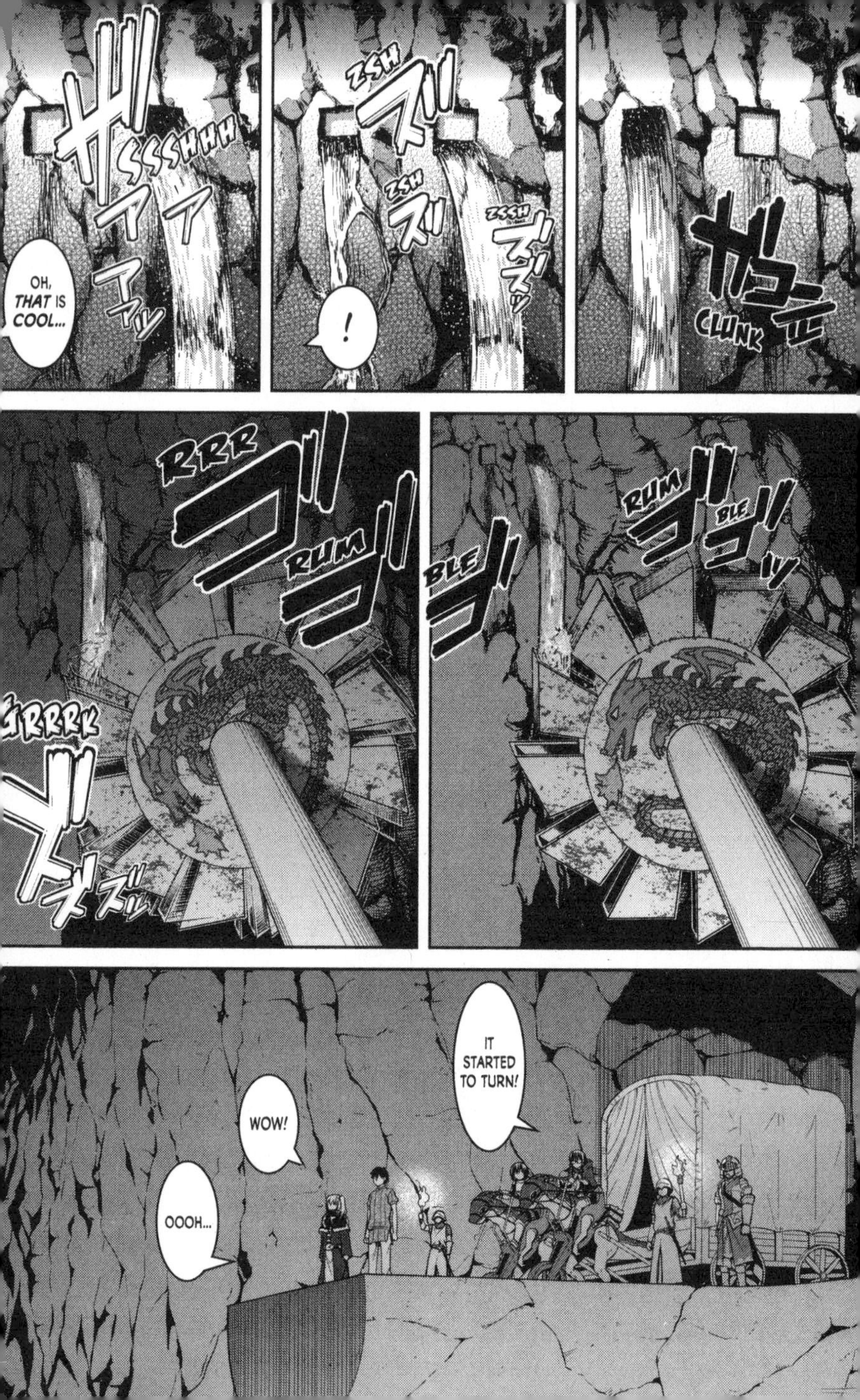
CLUNK
ZSH
ZSH
ZSH
!
SSSSHHH
OH, *THAT* IS COOL...
RUM
BLE
RRR
RUM
BLE
GRRRK
IT STARTED TO TURN!
WOW!
OOOH...

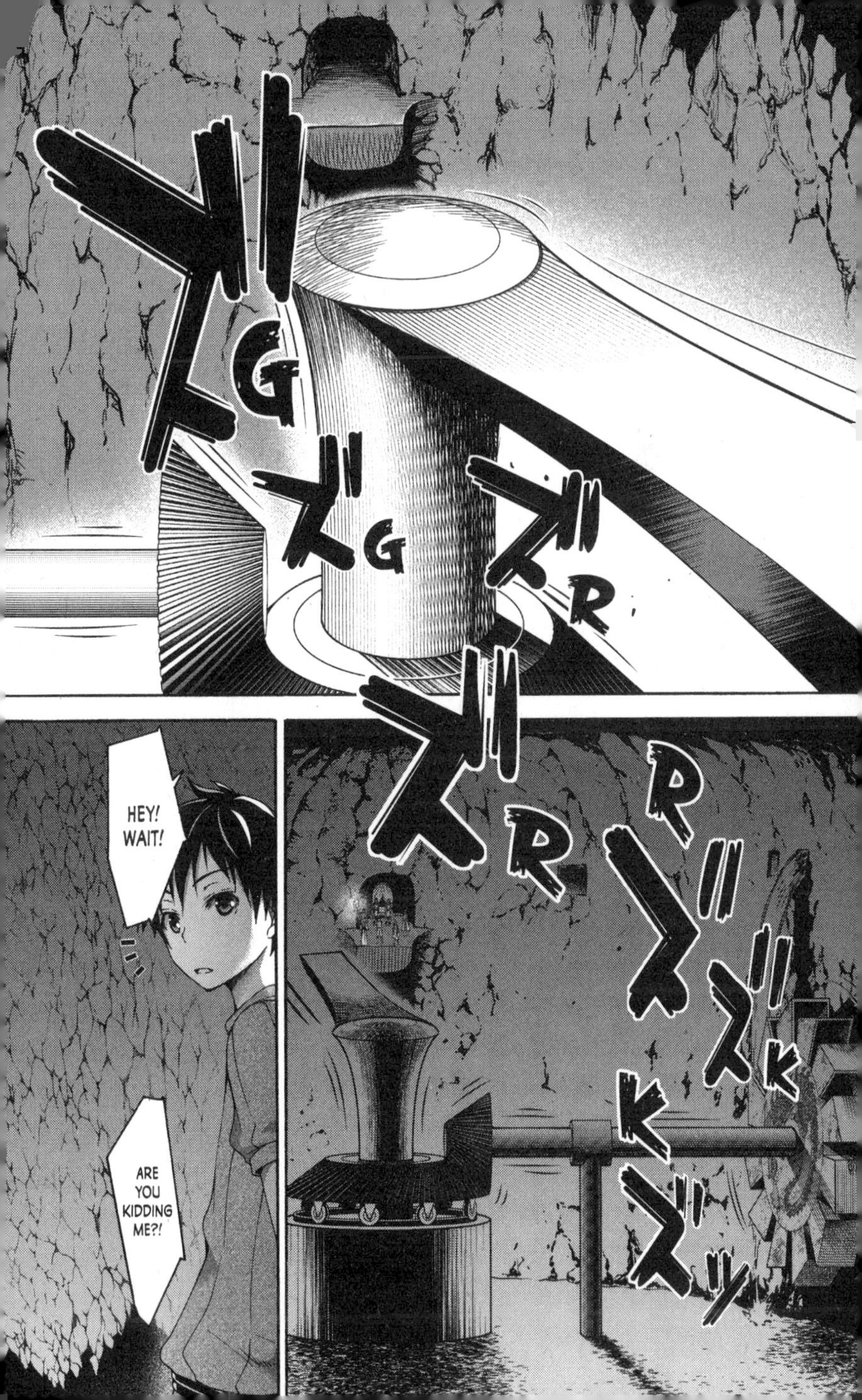
G
G
R
R
R
K
K
HEY! WAIT!
ARE YOU KIDDING ME?!

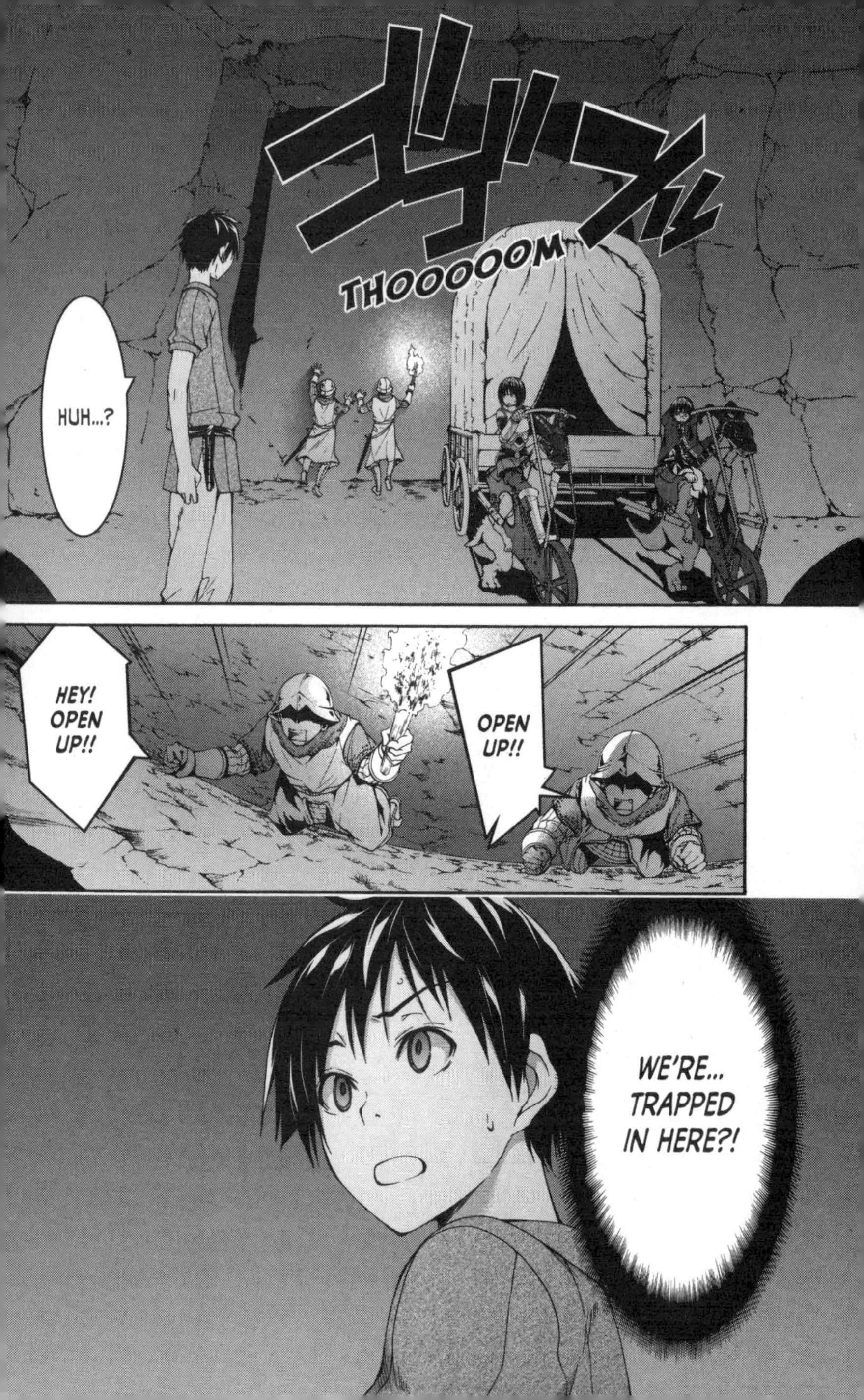
THOOOOOM
HUH...?
OPEN UP!!
HEY! OPEN UP!!
WE'RE... TRAPPED IN HERE?!

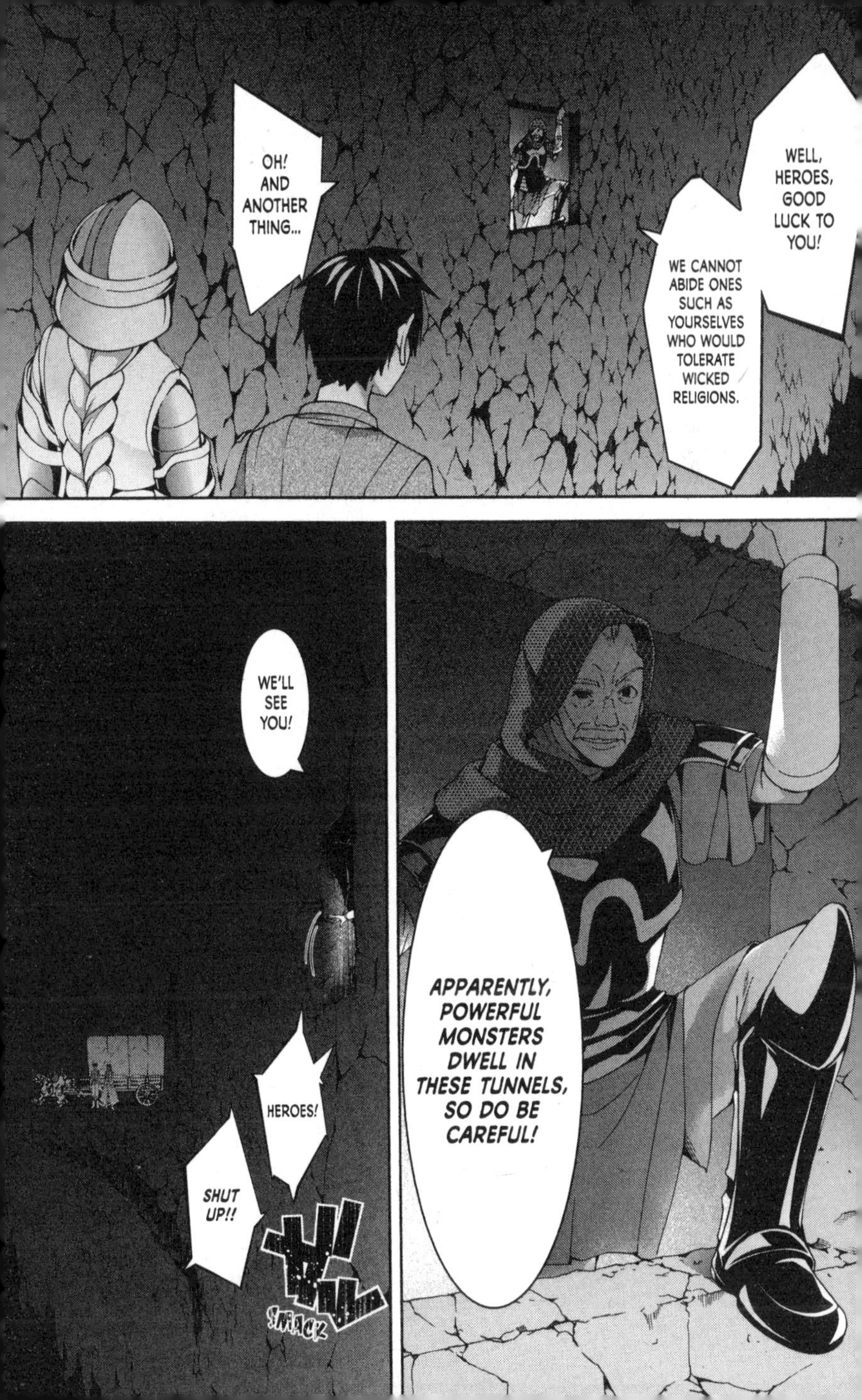
WELL, HEROES, GOOD LUCK TO YOU!
WE CANNOT ABIDE ONES SUCH AS YOURSELVES WHO WOULD TOLERATE WICKED RELIGIONS.
OH! AND ANOTHER THING...
APPARENTLY, POWERFUL MONSTERS DWELL IN THESE TUNNELS, SO DO BE CAREFUL!
WE'LL SEE YOU!
HEROES!
SHUT UP!!
SMACK

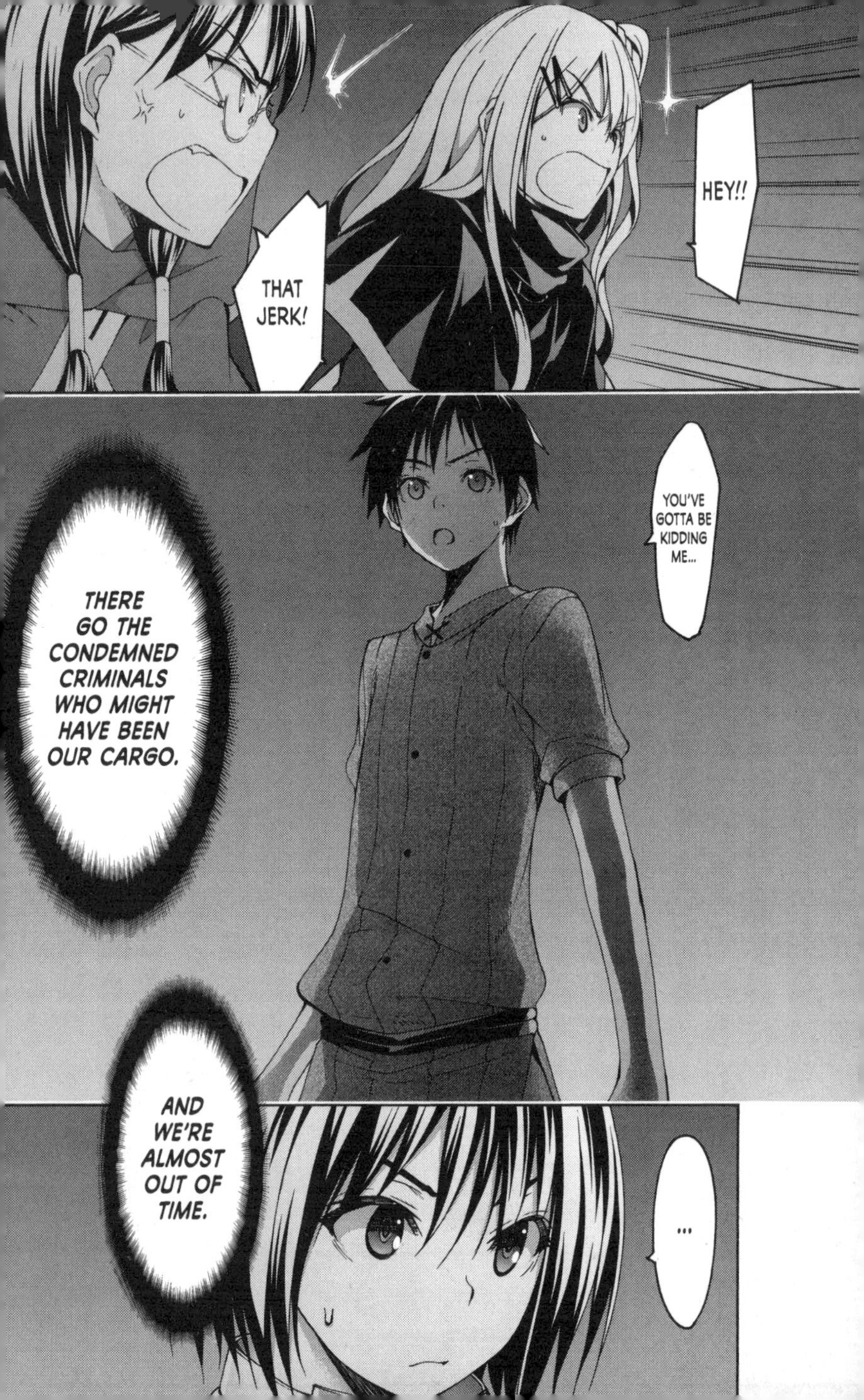
HEY!!
THAT JERK!
YOU'VE GOTTA BE KIDDING ME...
THERE GO THE CONDEMNED CRIMINALS WHO MIGHT HAVE BEEN OUR CARGO.
...
AND WE'RE ALMOST OUT OF TIME.

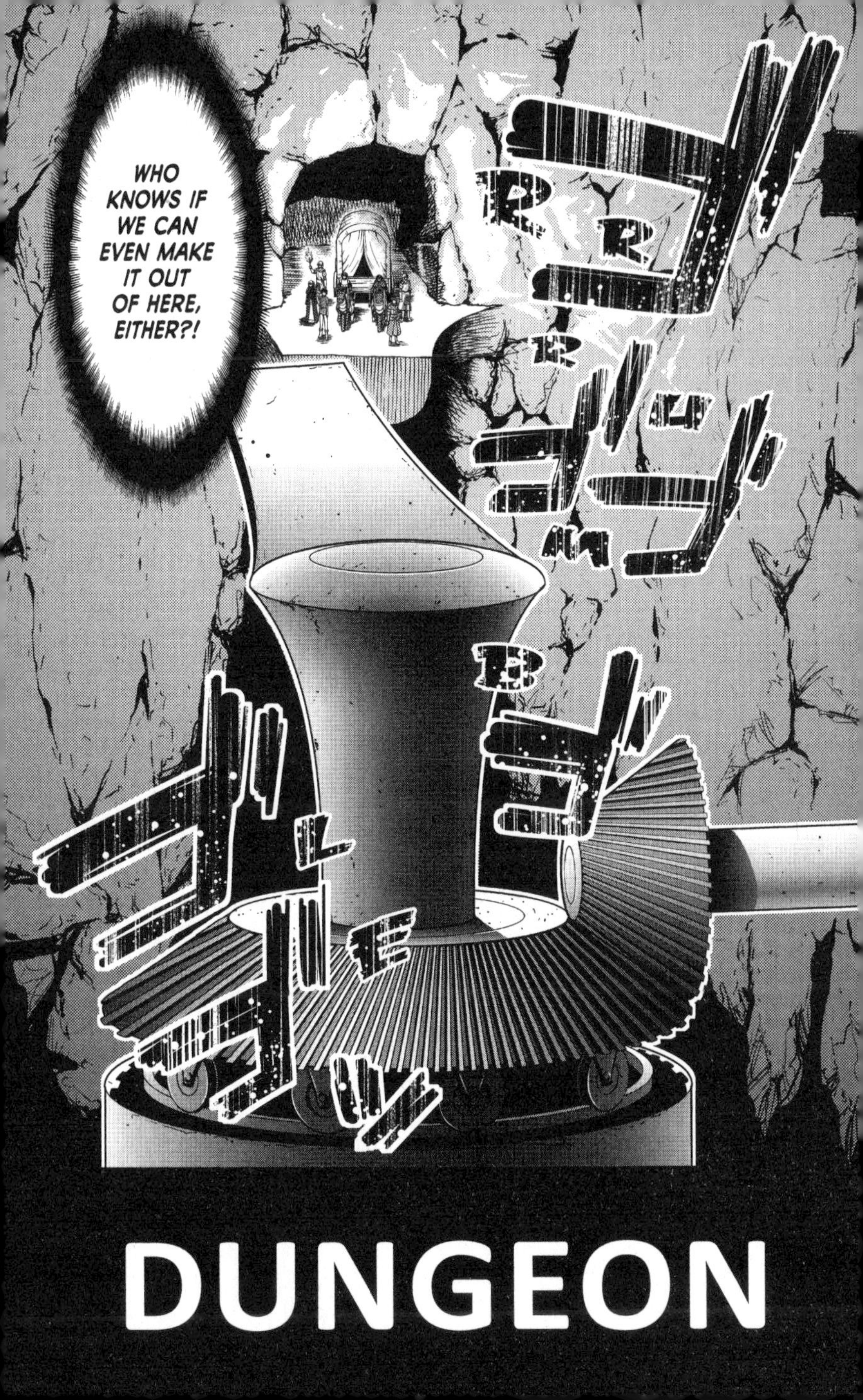
WHO KNOWS IF WE CAN EVEN MAKE IT OUT OF HERE, EITHER?!
DUNGEON

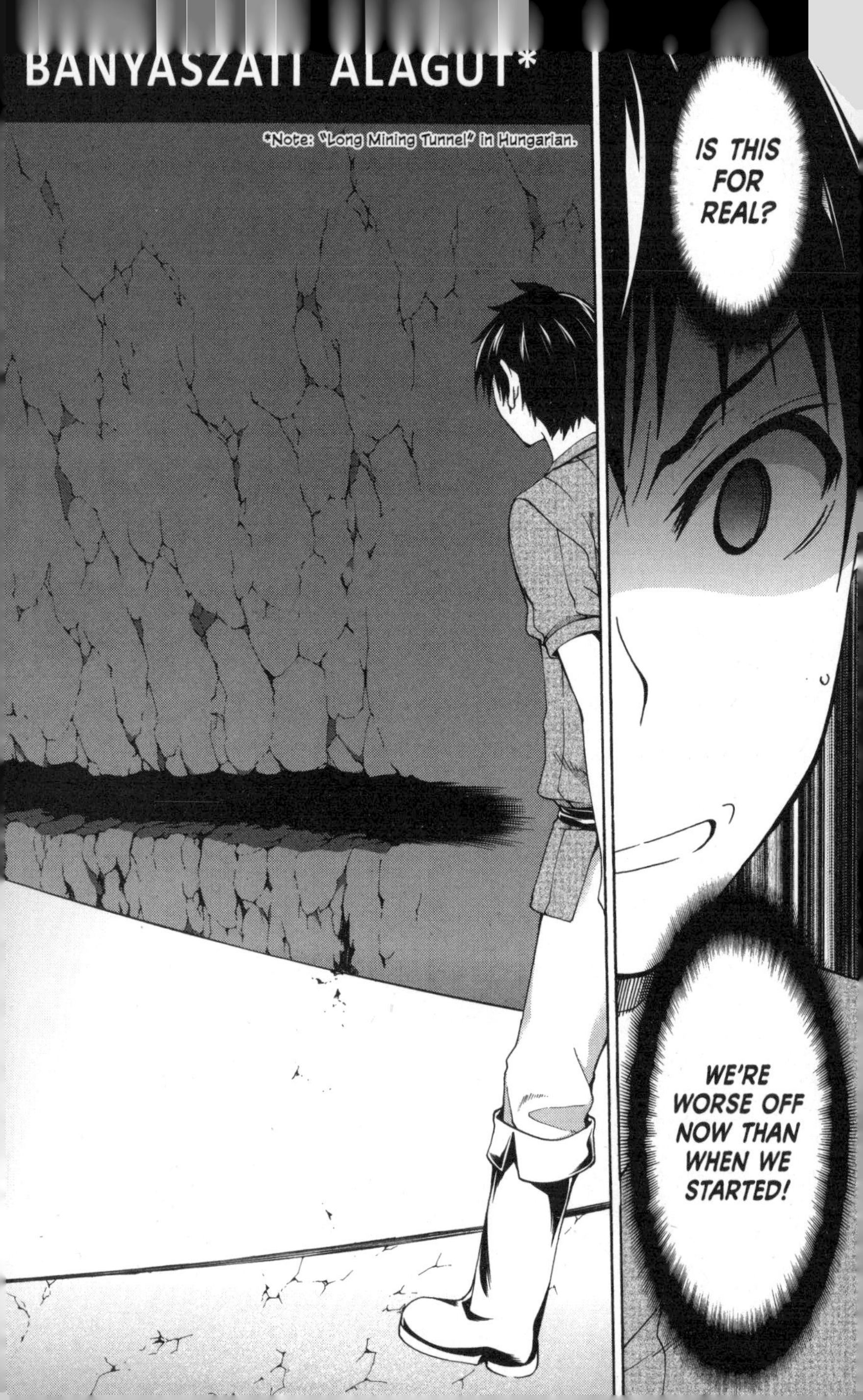
IS THIS FOR REAL?
WE'RE WORSE OFF NOW THAN WHEN WE STARTED!
BANYASZATI ALAGUT*
*Note: "Long Mining Tunnel" in Hungarian.

THE ANCIENTS' CAVE HOSSZU

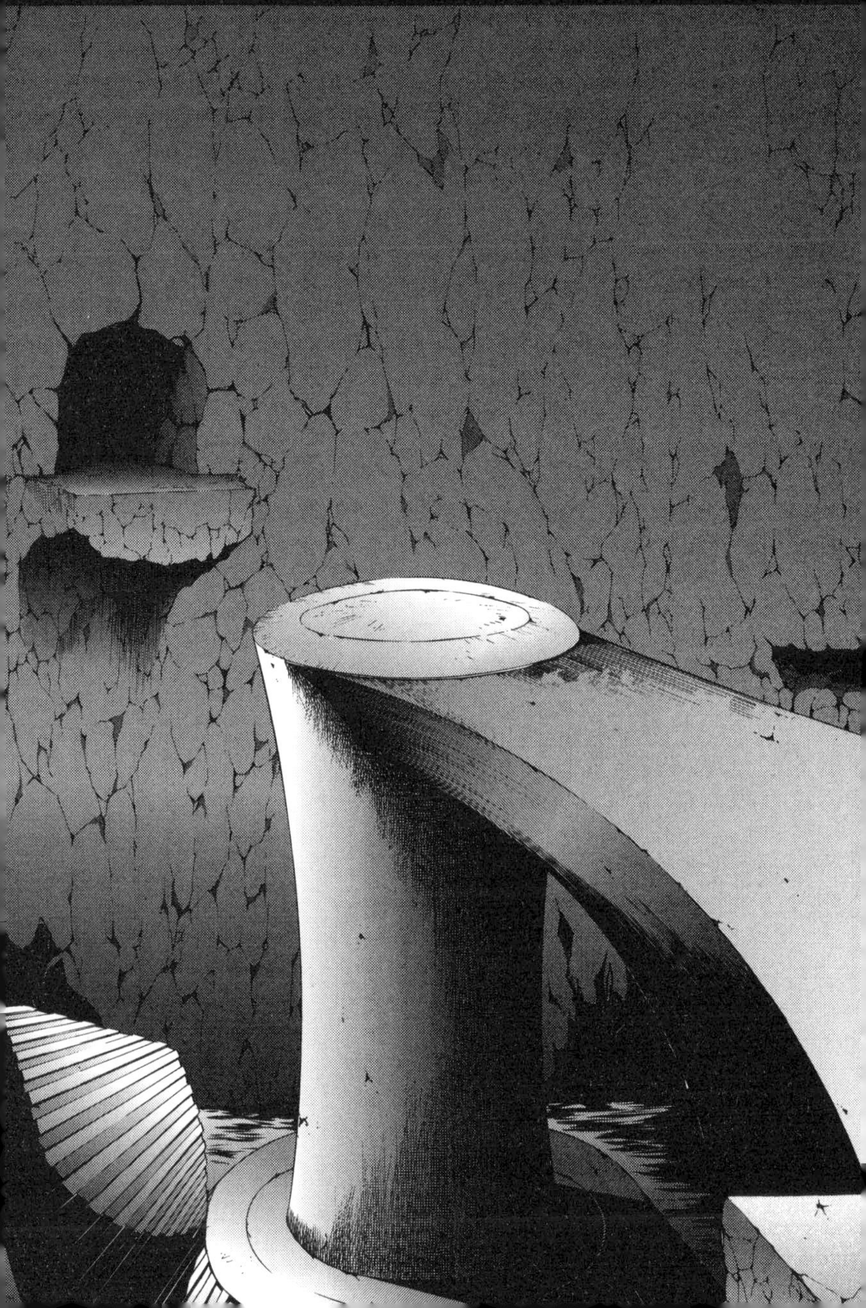

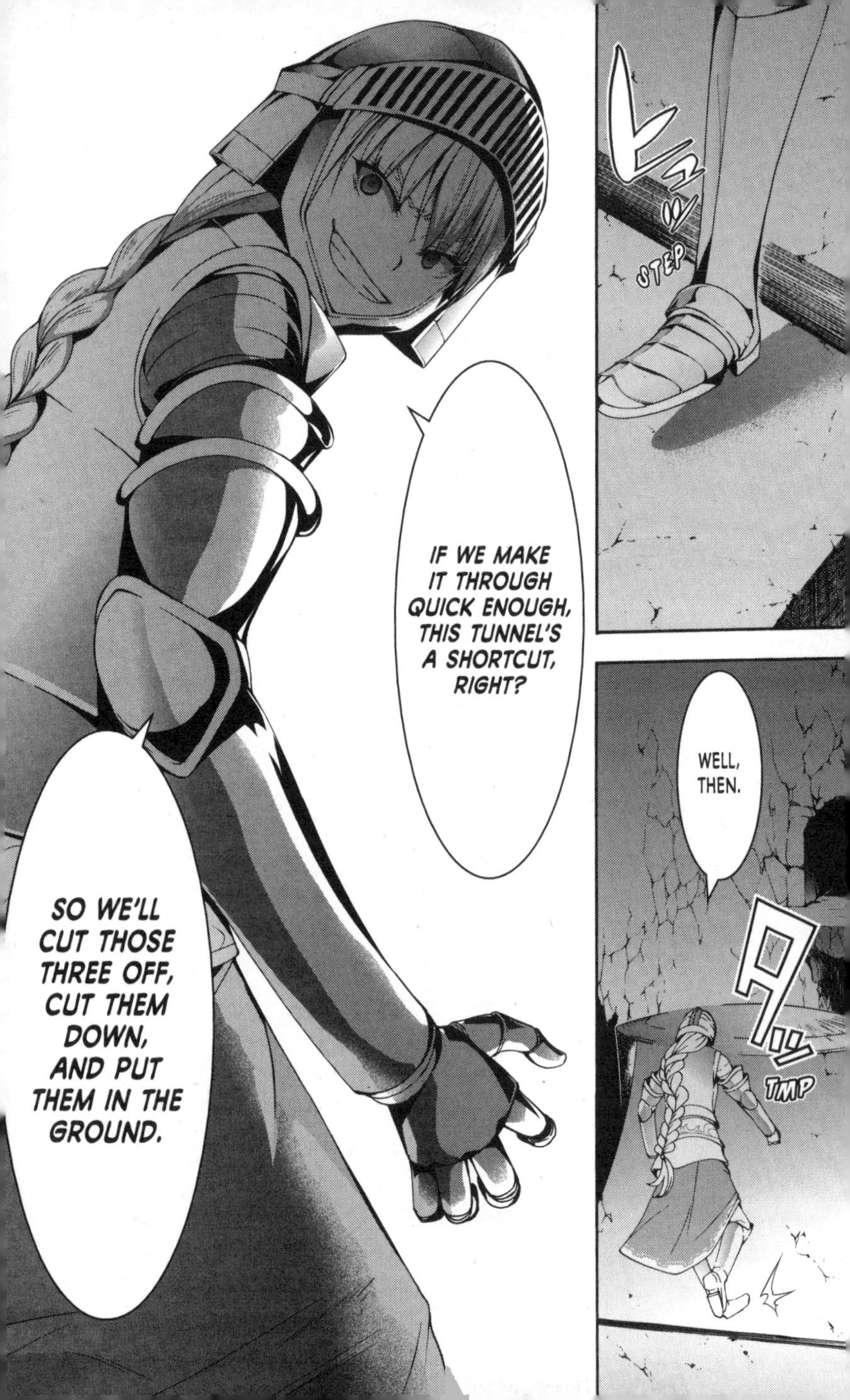
STEP
WELL, THEN.
TMP
IF WE MAKE IT THROUGH QUICK ENOUGH, THIS TUNNEL'S A SHORTCUT, RIGHT?
SO WE'LL CUT THOSE THREE OFF, CUT THEM DOWN, AND PUT THEM IN THE GROUND.

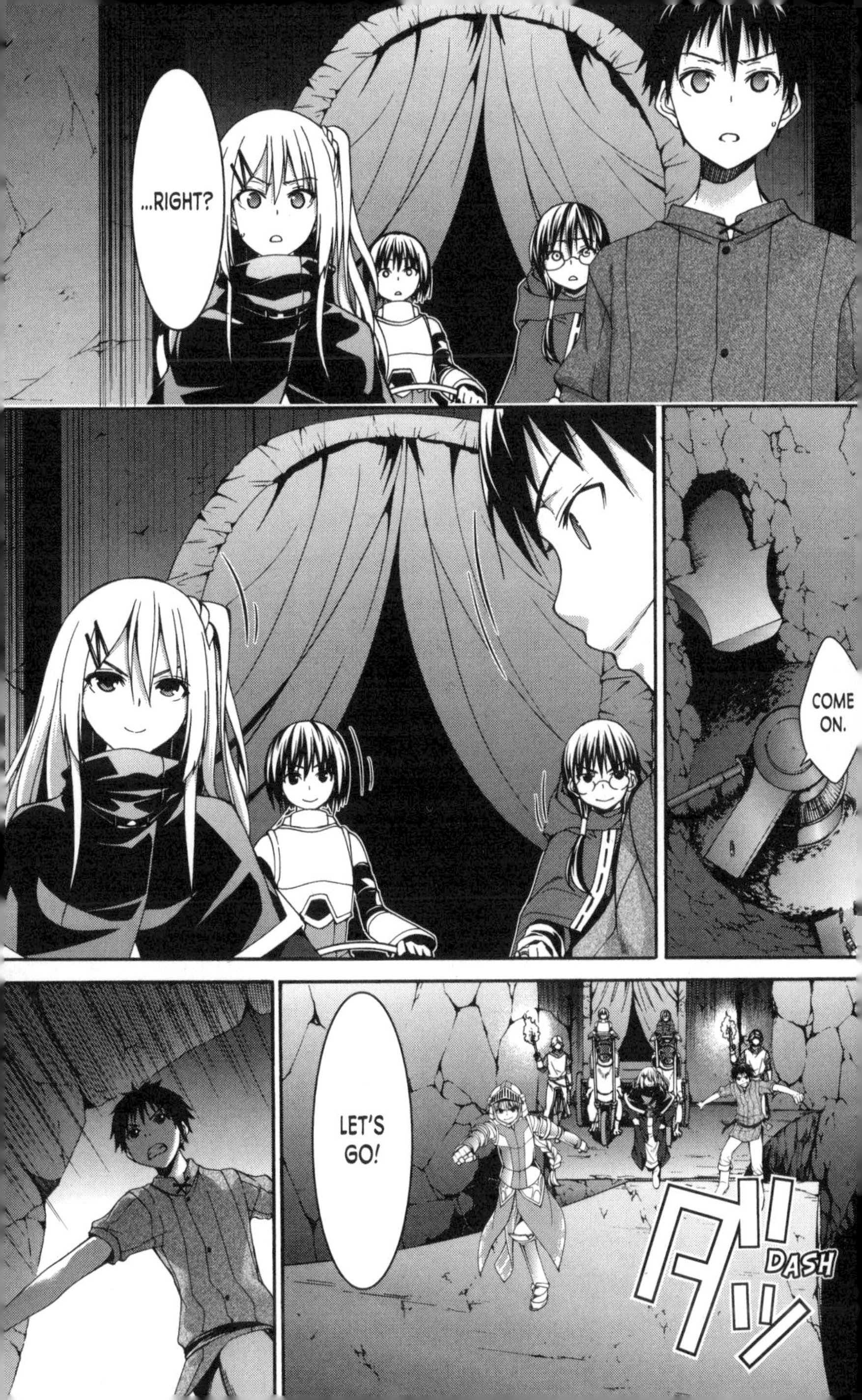
...RIGHT?
COME ON.
LET'S GO!
ダッ
DASH

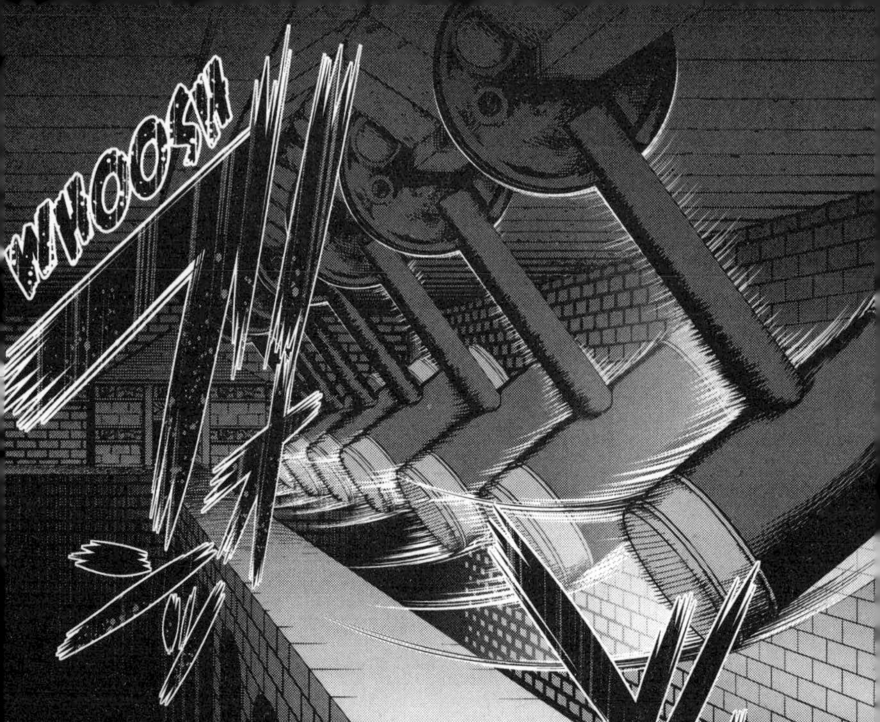
WHOOSH
WHOOSH
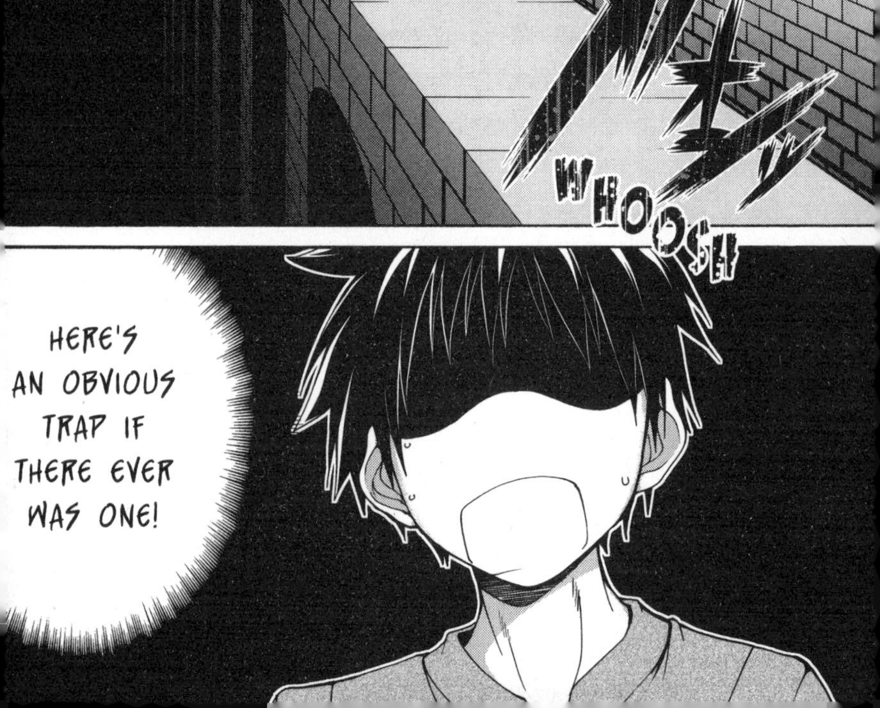
HERE'S AN OBVIOUS TRAP IF THERE EVER WAS ONE!

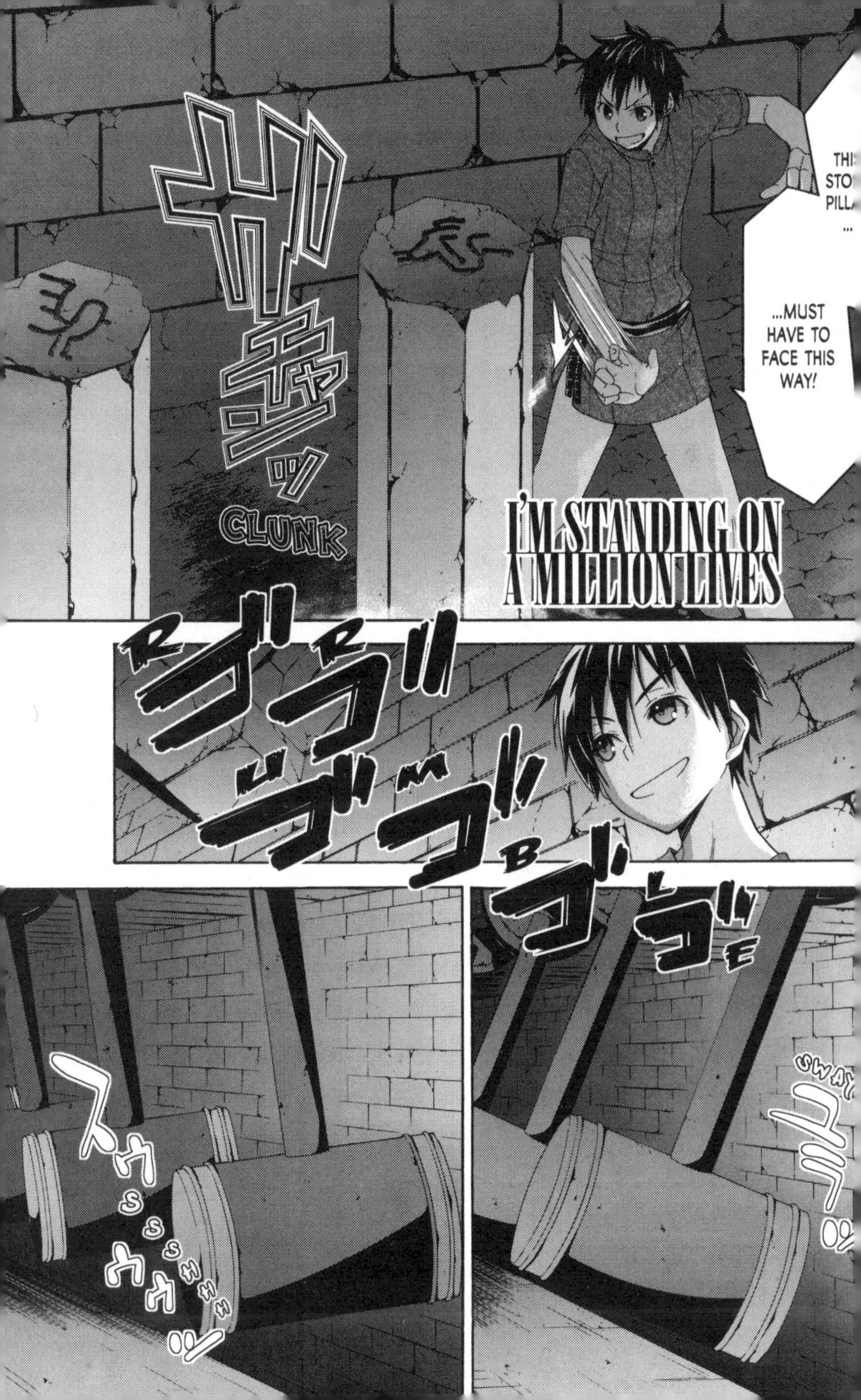
THI STO PILL ...
...MUST HAVE TO FACE THIS WAY!
CLUNK
I'M STANDING ON A MILLION LIVES
RRUMBLE
SWAY
SSSHHH

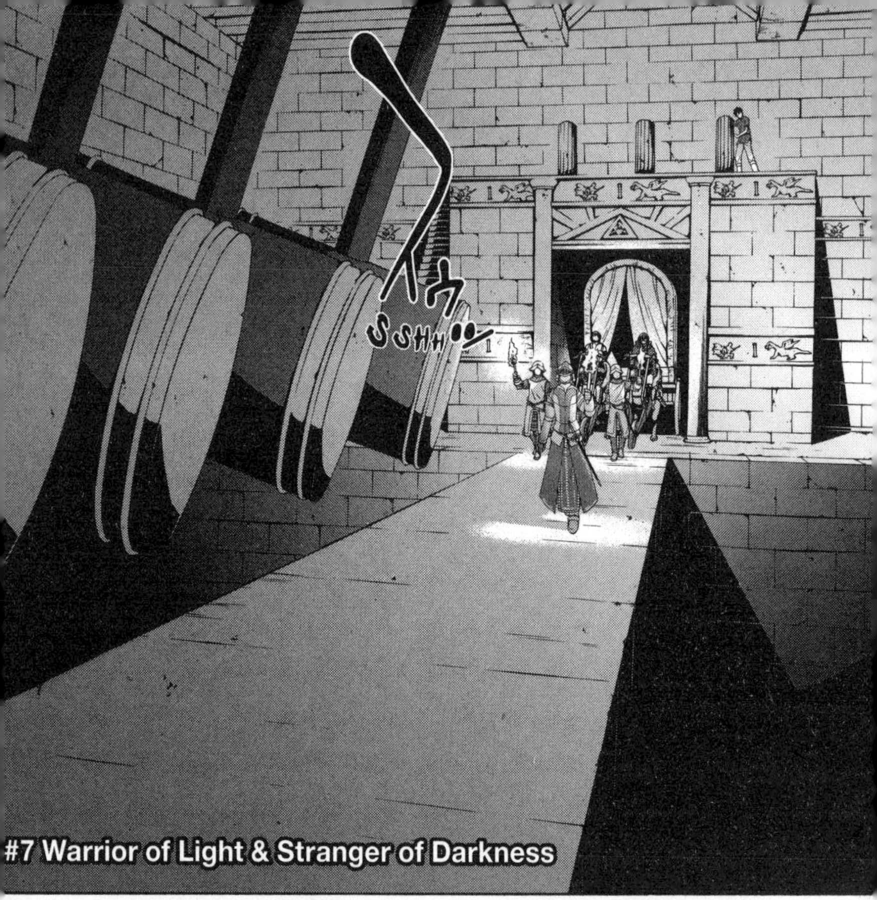
SSHHOO

#7 Warrior of Light & Stranger of Darkness

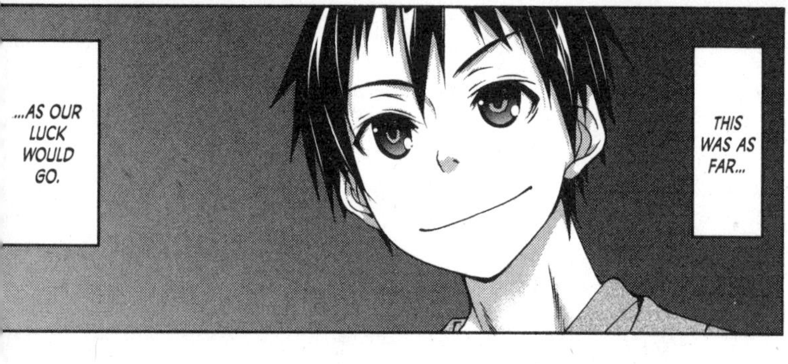
THIS WAS AS FAR...
...AS OUR LUCK WOULD GO.

QUEST REMAINING TIME: 11 DAYS AND 14 HOURS

QUEST REMAINING TIME: 10 DAYS AND 23 HOURS

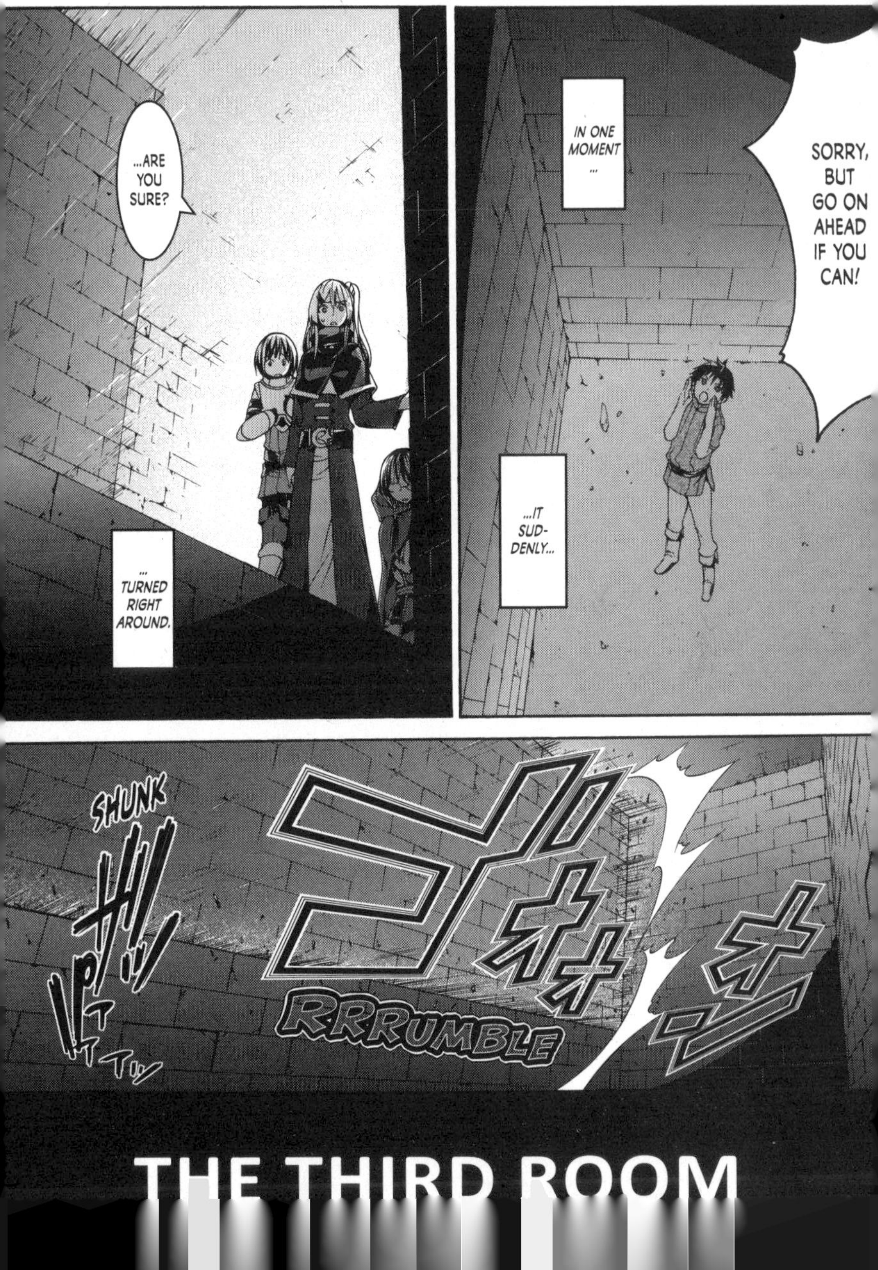
SORRY, BUT GO ON AHEAD IF YOU CAN!
IN ONE MOMENT ...
...IT SUDDENLY...
...ARE YOU SURE?
... TURNED RIGHT AROUND.
RRRUMBLE
SHUNK
THE THIRD ROOM

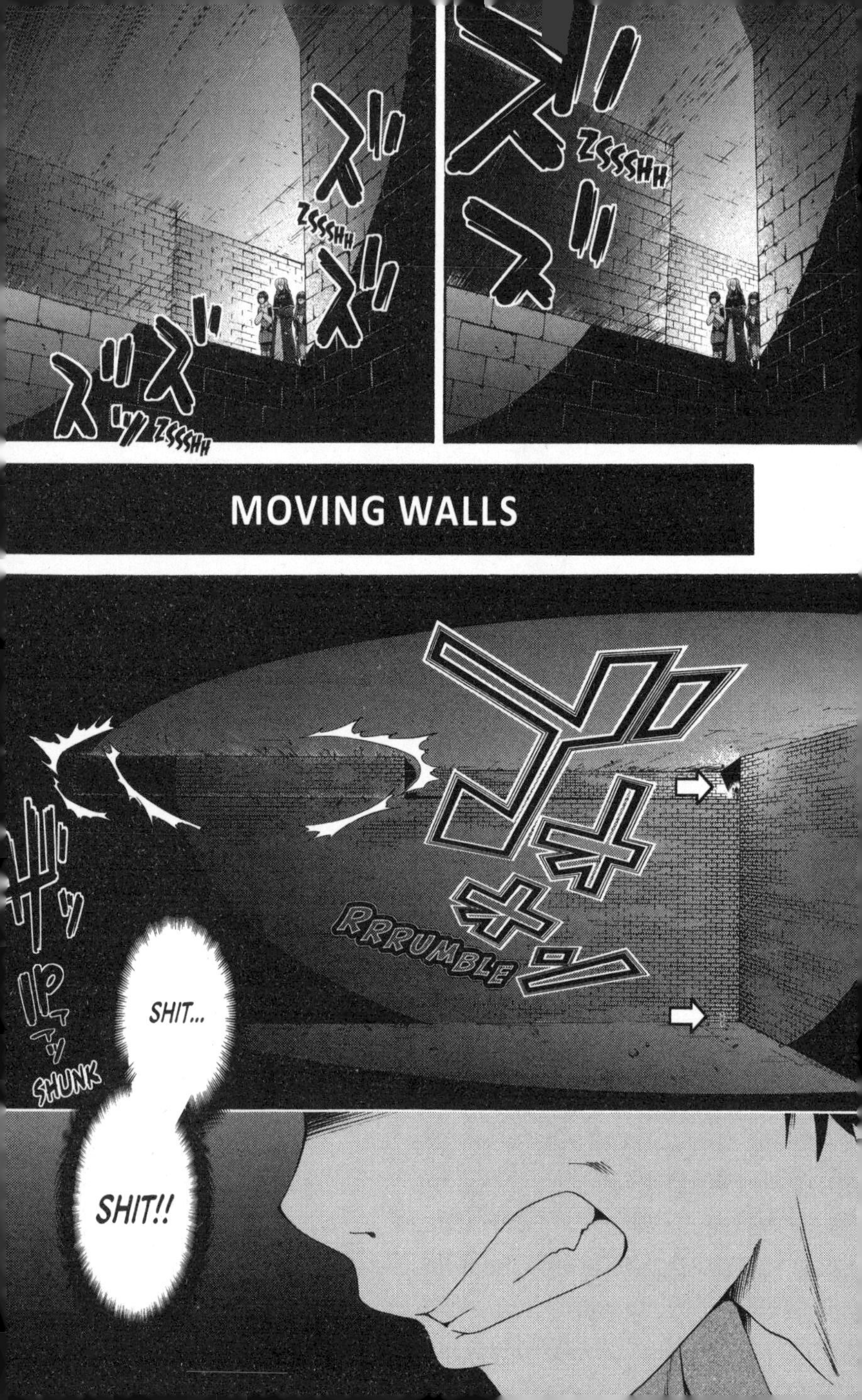
ZSSSHH
ZSSSHH
ZSSSHH
MOVING WALLS
RRRUMBLE
SHUNK
SHIT...
SHIT!!

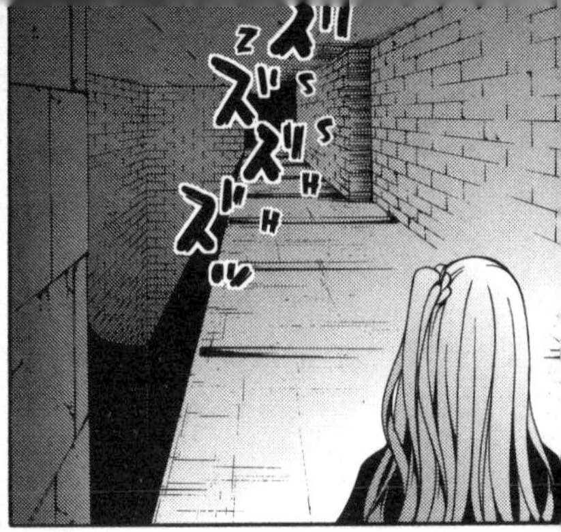
ZSSHH

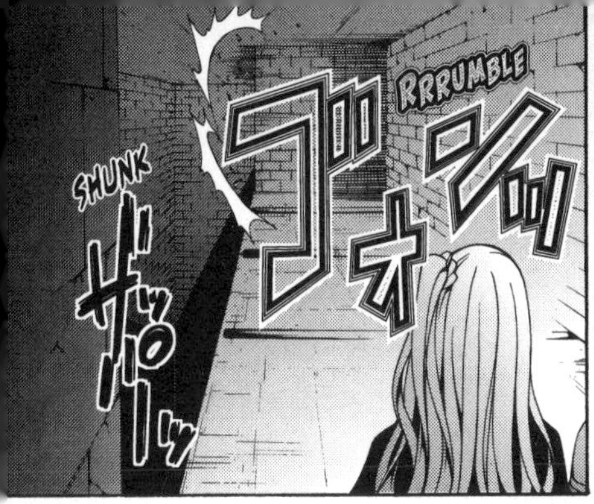
RRRUMBLE
SHUNK

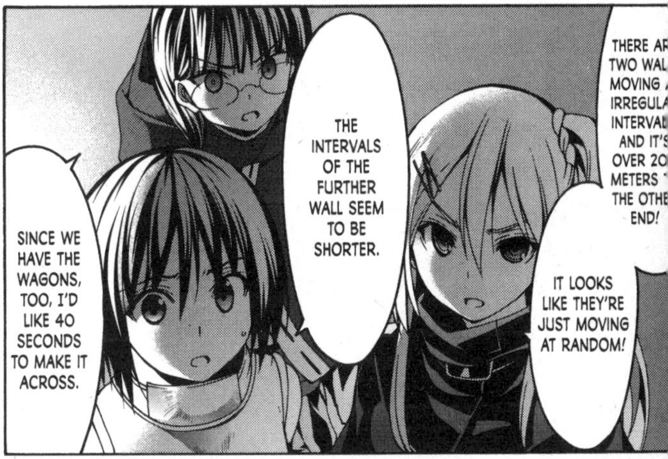
THERE AR TWO WAL MOVING IRREGUL INTERVAL AND IT'S OVER 20 METERS THE OTHE END!
IT LOOKS LIKE THEY'RE JUST MOVING AT RANDOM!
THE INTERVALS OF THE FURTHER WALL SEEM TO BE SHORTER.
SINCE WE HAVE THE WAGONS, TOO, I'D LIKE 40 SECONDS TO MAKE IT ACROSS.

THE WALLS...

...JUDGING BY TH SOUND, APPEAR BE POWERED BY MECHANISM LIKE DEER SCARER, I THAT WHEN THE WA ACCUMULATES T A CERTAIN LEVEL IT'S TRIGGERED TURN BACK.*

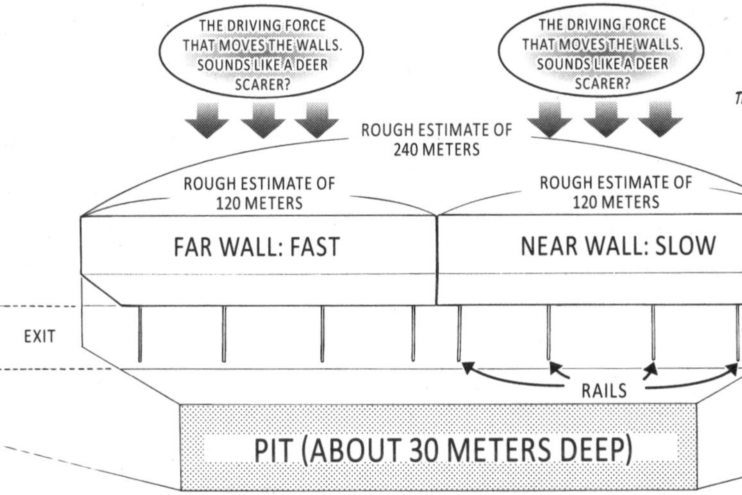
THE DRIVING FORCE THAT MOVES THE WALLS. SOUNDS LIKE A DEER SCARER?
THE DRIVING FORCE THAT MOVES THE WALLS. SOUNDS LIKE A DEER SCARER?
ROUGH ESTIMATE OF 240 METERS
ROUGH ESTIMATE OF 120 METERS
ROUGH ESTIMATE OF 120 METERS
FAR WALL: FAST
NEAR WALL: SLOW
EXIT
ENTRA (CURRE LOCATI
RAILS
PIT (ABOUT 30 METERS DEEP)

*A deer scarer is a small bamboo water fountain device that make clunking sound near hot springs for the purpose of keeping deer a

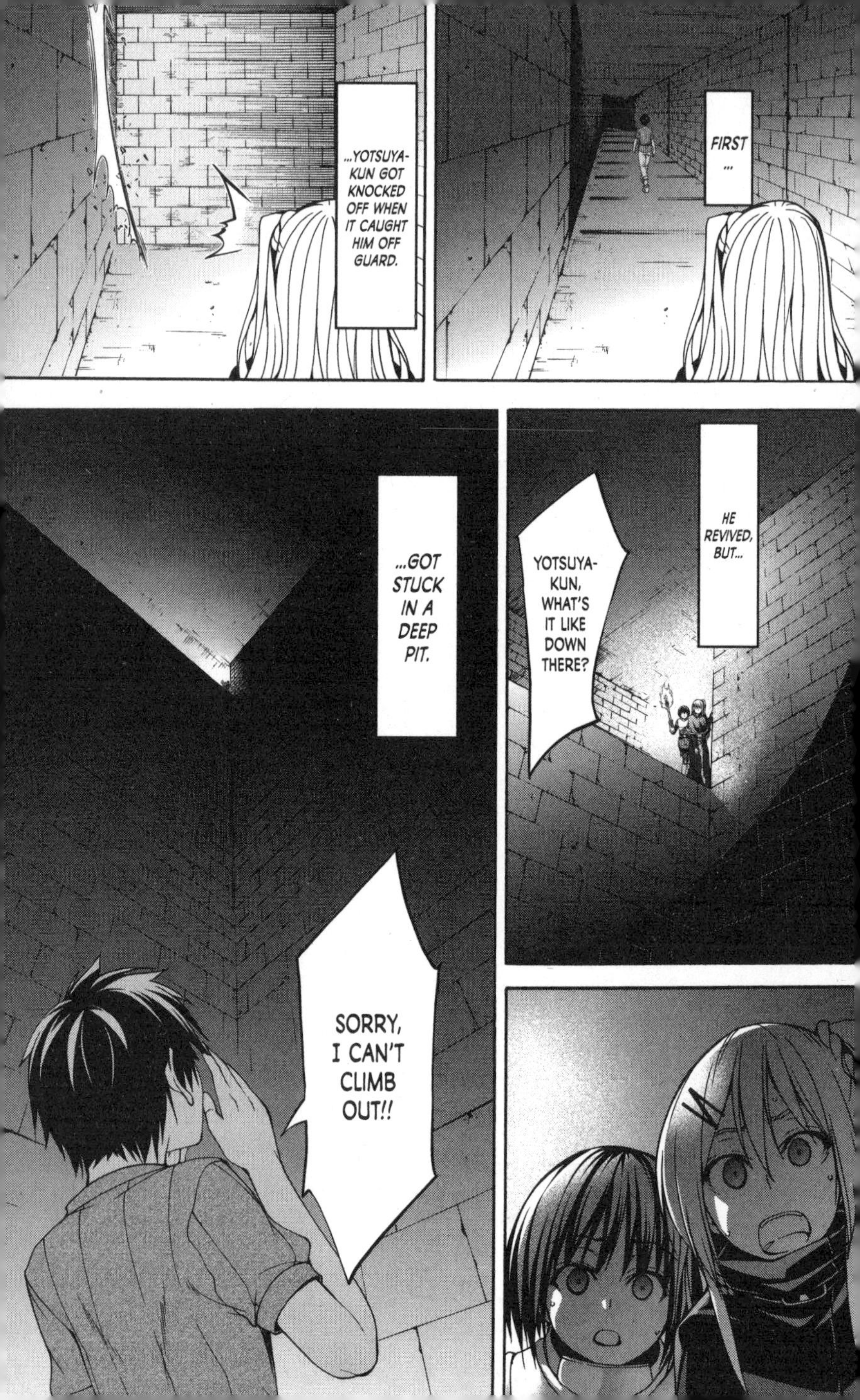
FIRST ...
...YOTSUYA-KUN GOT KNOCKED OFF WHEN IT CAUGHT HIM OFF GUARD.
HE REVIVED, BUT...
YOTSUYA-KUN, WHAT'S IT LIKE DOWN THERE?
...GOT STUCK IN A DEEP PIT.
SORRY, I CAN'T CLIMB OUT!!

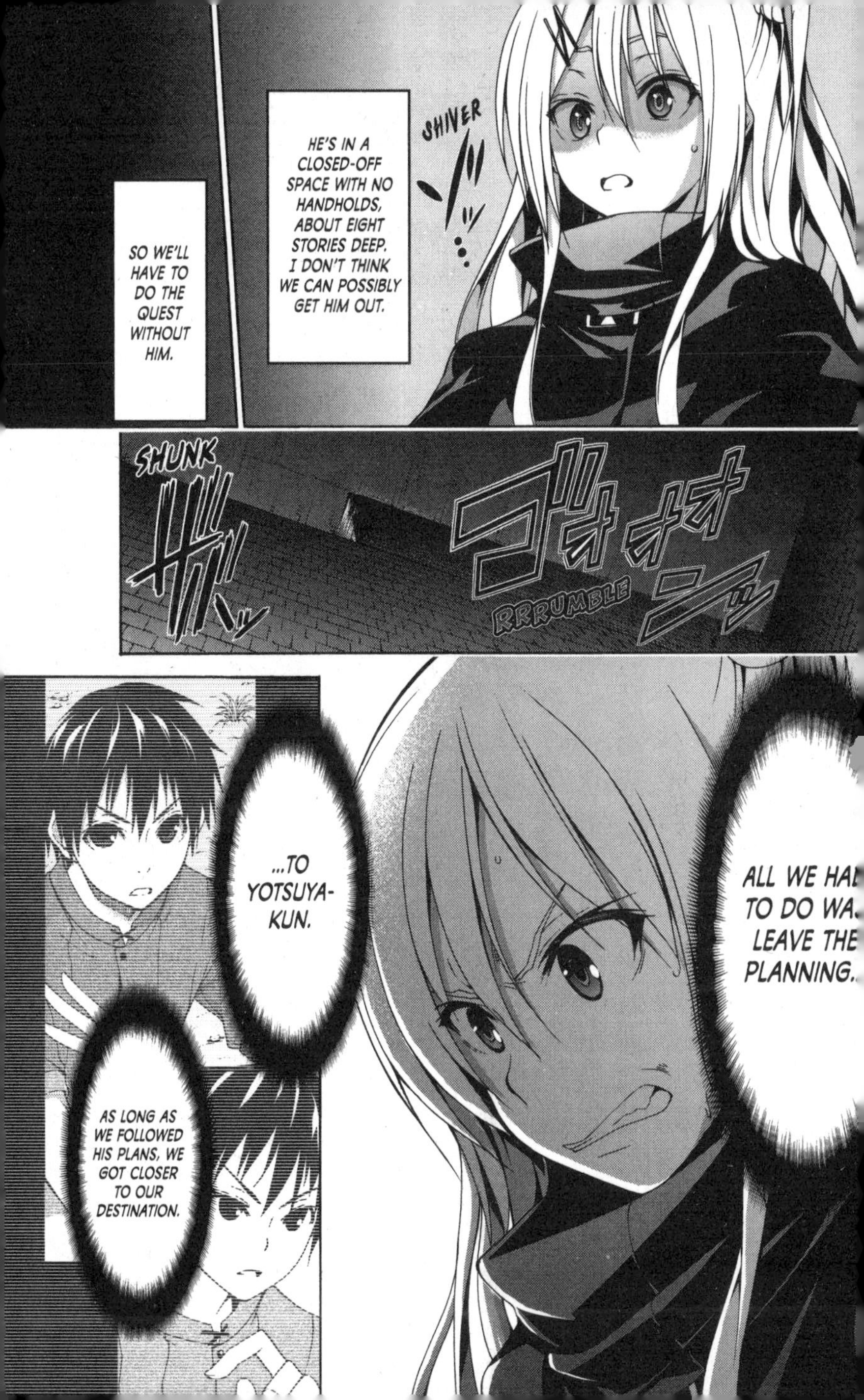
SHIVER
HE'S IN A CLOSED-OFF SPACE WITH NO HANDHOLDS, ABOUT EIGHT STORIES DEEP. I DON'T THINK WE CAN POSSIBLY GET HIM OUT.
SO WE'LL HAVE TO DO THE QUEST WITHOUT HIM.
RRRUMBLE
SHUNK
ALL WE HA TO DO WA LEAVE THE PLANNING.
...TO YOTSUYA-KUN.
AS LONG AS WE FOLLOWED HIS PLANS, WE GOT CLOSER TO OUR DESTINATION.

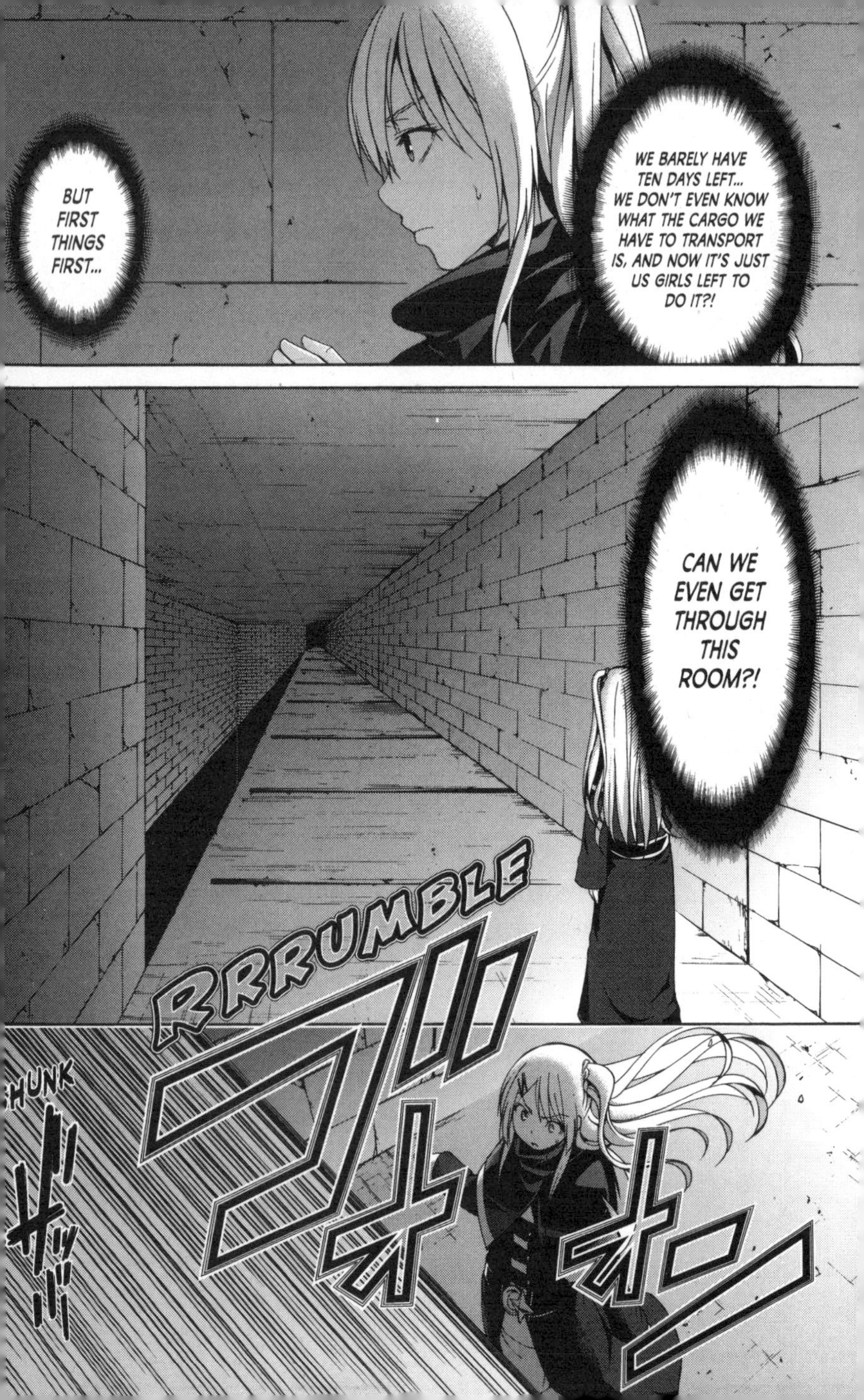
WE BARELY HAVE TEN DAYS LEFT... WE DON'T EVEN KNOW WHAT THE CARGO WE HAVE TO TRANSPORT IS, AND NOW IT'S JUST US GIRLS LEFT TO DO IT?!
BUT FIRST THINGS FIRST...
CAN WE EVEN GET THROUGH THIS ROOM?!
RRRUMBLE
HUNK

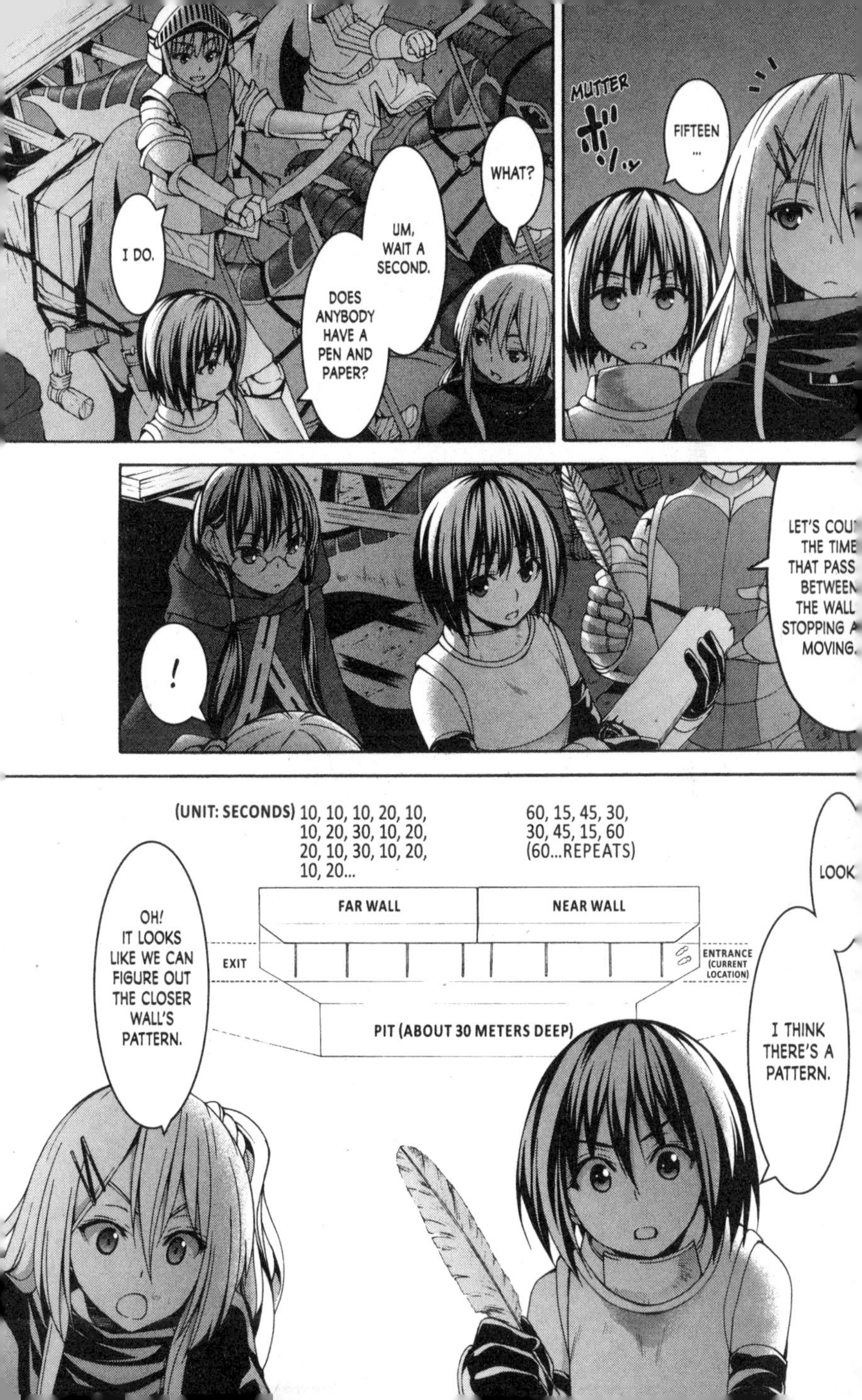
MUTTER
FIFTEEN ...
WHAT?
UM, WAIT A SECOND.
DOES ANYBODY HAVE A PEN AND PAPER?
I DO.
LET'S COU THE TIME THAT PASS BETWEEN THE WALL STOPPING A MOVING.
!
LOOK
I THINK THERE'S A PATTERN.
(UNIT: SECONDS) 10, 10, 10, 20, 10, 10, 20, 30, 10, 20, 20, 10, 30, 10, 20, 10, 20...
60, 15, 45, 30, 30, 45, 15, 60 (60...REPEATS)
FAR WALL
NEAR WALL
EXIT
ENTRANCE (CURRENT LOCATION)
PIT (ABOUT 30 METERS DEEP)
OH! IT LOOKS LIKE WE CAN FIGURE OUT THE CLOSER WALL'S PATTERN.

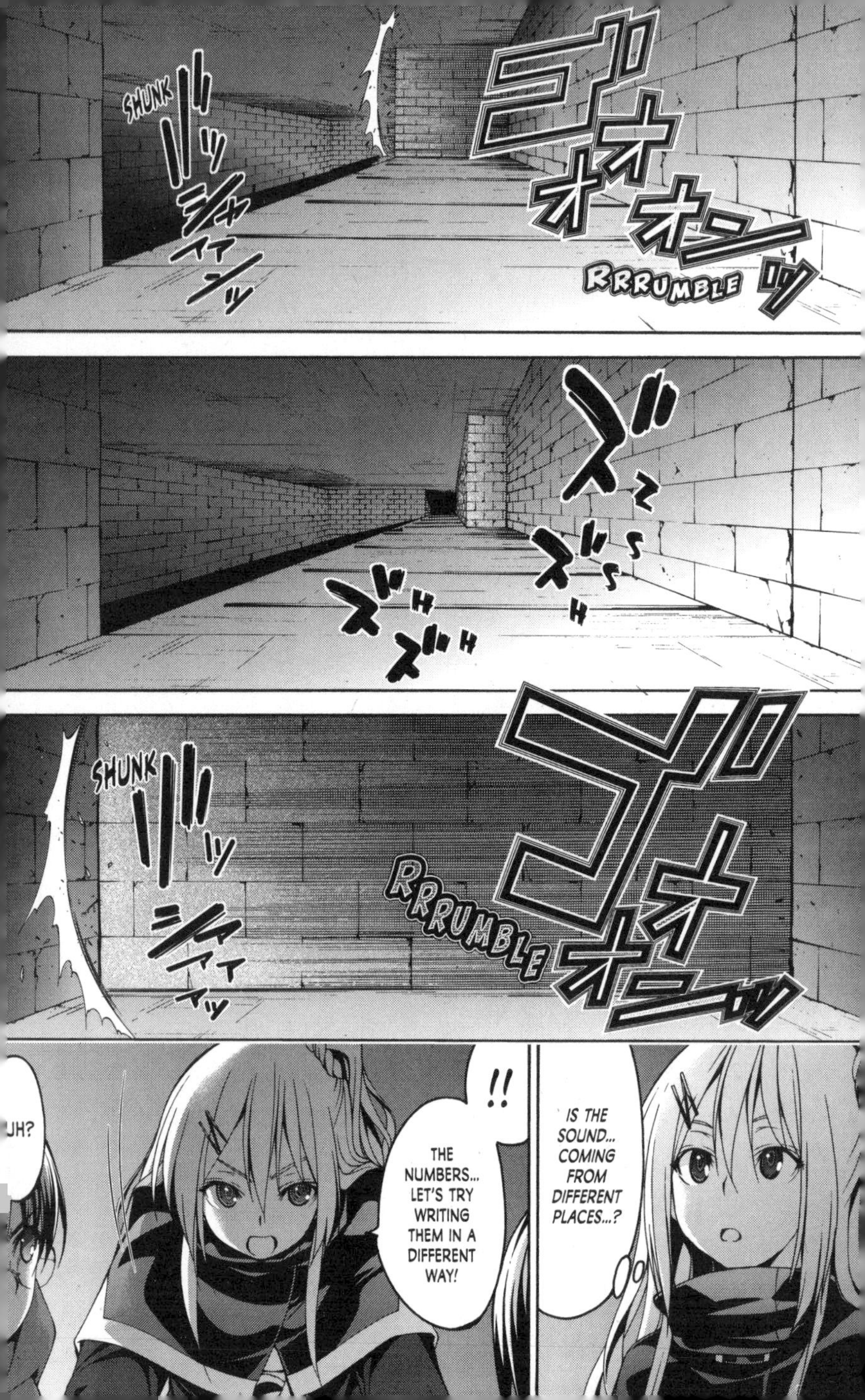
RRRUMBLE
SHUNK
RRRUMBLE
SHUNK
IS THE SOUND... COMING FROM DIFFERENT PLACES...?
!!
THE NUMBERS... LET'S TRY WRITING THEM IN A DIFFERENT WAY!
JH?

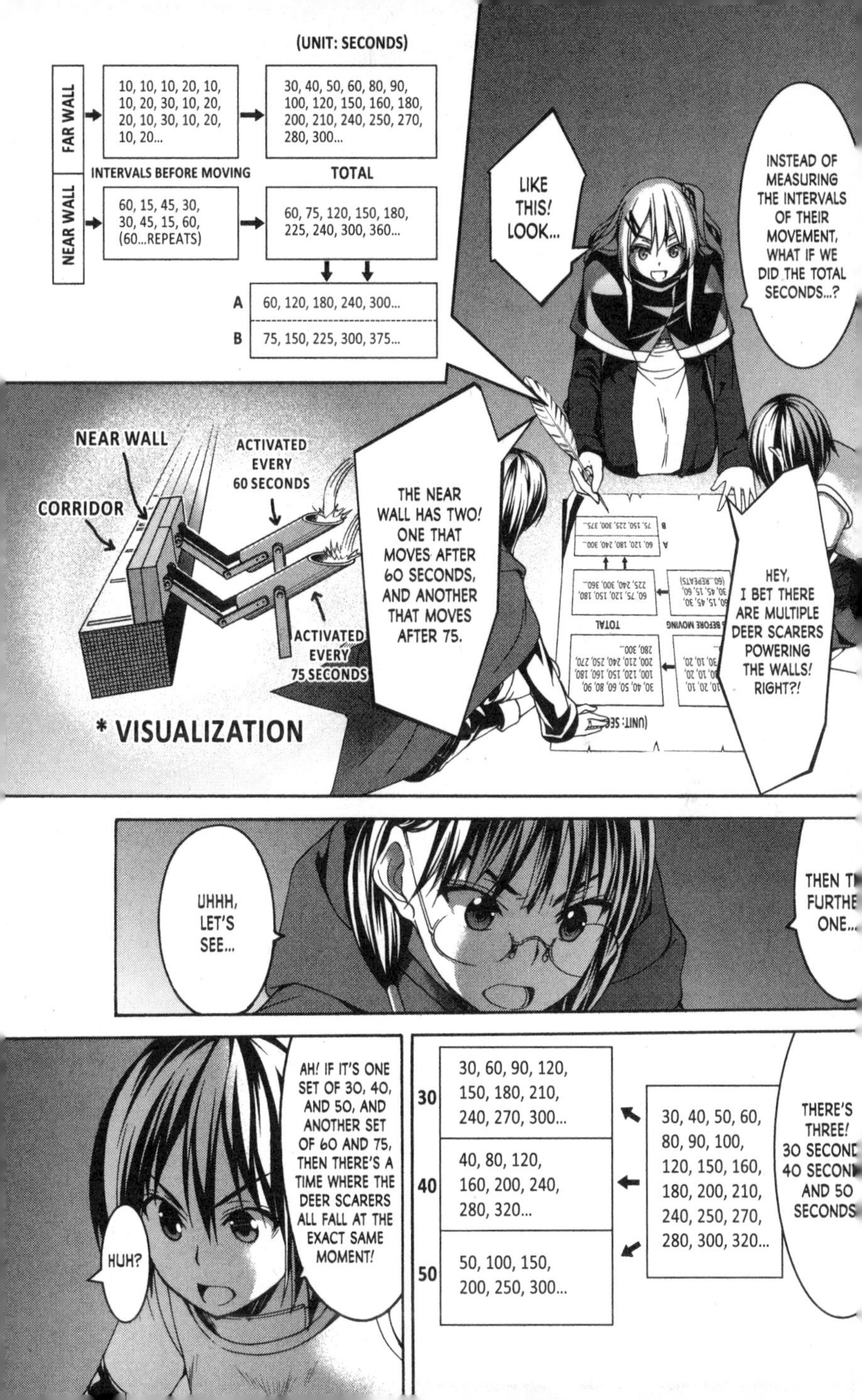
INSTEAD OF MEASURING THE INTERVALS OF THEIR MOVEMENT, WHAT IF WE DID THE TOTAL SECONDS...?
LIKE THIS! LOOK...
(UNIT: SECONDS)
FAR WALL
10, 10, 10, 20, 10, 10, 20, 30, 10, 20, 20, 10, 30, 10, 20, 10, 20...
30, 40, 50, 60, 80, 90, 100, 120, 150, 160, 180, 200, 210, 240, 250, 270, 280, 300...
INTERVALS BEFORE MOVING
TOTAL
NEAR WALL
60, 15, 45, 30, 30, 45, 15, 60, (60...REPEATS)
60, 75, 120, 150, 180, 225, 240, 300, 360...
A
60, 120, 180, 240, 300...
B
75, 150, 225, 300, 375...
HEY, I BET THERE ARE MULTIPLE DEER SCARERS POWERING THE WALLS! RIGHT?!
THE NEAR WALL HAS TWO! ONE THAT MOVES AFTER 60 SECONDS, AND ANOTHER THAT MOVES AFTER 75.
NEAR WALL
ACTIVATED EVERY 60 SECONDS
CORRIDOR
ACTIVATED EVERY 75 SECONDS
* VISUALIZATION
THEN T
FURTHE
ONE...
UHHH, LET'S SEE...
THERE'S THREE! 30 SECONE 40 SECON AND 50 SECONDS
30, 40, 50, 60, 80, 90, 100, 120, 150, 160, 180, 200, 210, 240, 250, 270, 280, 300, 320...
30
30, 60, 90, 120, 150, 180, 210, 240, 270, 300...
40
40, 80, 120, 160, 200, 240, 280, 320...
50
50, 100, 150, 200, 250, 300...
AH! IF IT'S ONE SET OF 30, 40, AND 50, AND ANOTHER SET OF 60 AND 75, THEN THERE'S A TIME WHERE THE DEER SCARERS ALL FALL AT THE EXACT SAME MOMENT!
HUH?

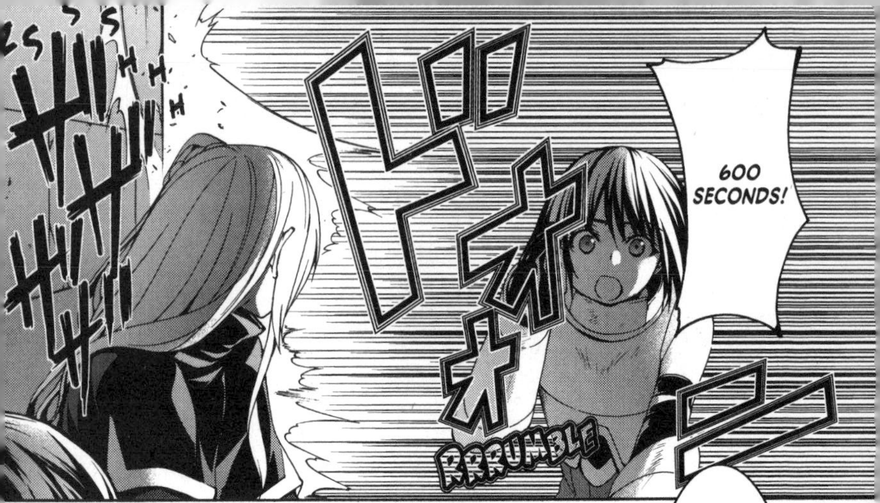
600 SECONDS!
RRRUMBLE
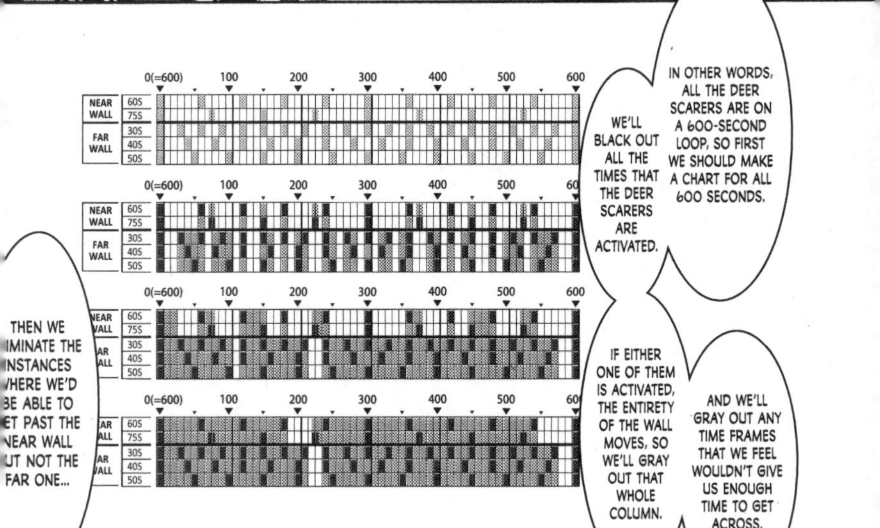
IN OTHER WORDS, ALL THE DEER SCARERS ARE ON A 600-SECOND LOOP, SO FIRST WE SHOULD MAKE A CHART FOR ALL 600 SECONDS.
WE'LL BLACK OUT ALL THE TIMES THAT THE DEER SCARERS ARE ACTIVATED.
0(=600) 100 200 300 400 500 600
NEAR WALL 60S 75S
FAR WALL 30S 40S 50S
IF EITHER ONE OF THEM IS ACTIVATED, THE ENTIRETY OF THE WALL MOVES, SO WE'LL GRAY OUT THAT WHOLE COLUMN.
AND WE'LL GRAY OUT ANY TIME FRAMES THAT WE FEEL WOULDN'T GIVE US ENOUGH TIME TO GET ACROSS.
THEN WE IMINATE THE INSTANCES HERE WE'D BE ABLE TO ET PAST THE NEAR WALL UT NOT THE FAR ONE...
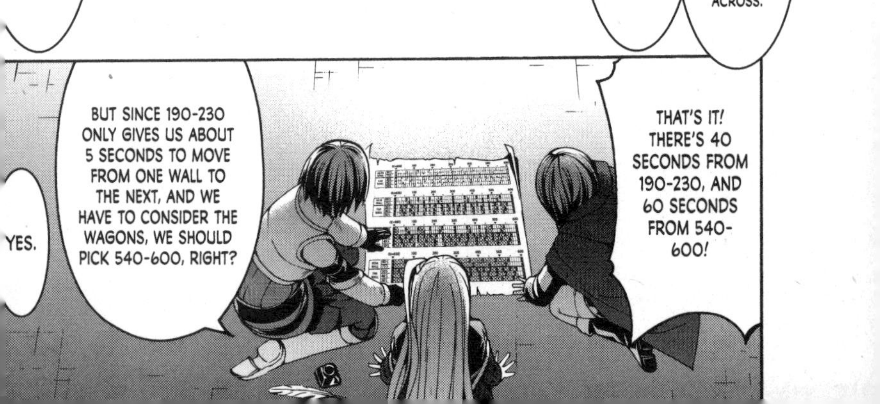
THAT'S IT! THERE'S 40 SECONDS FROM 190-230, AND 60 SECONDS FROM 540-600!
BUT SINCE 190-230 ONLY GIVES US ABOUT 5 SECONDS TO MOVE FROM ONE WALL TO THE NEXT, AND WE HAVE TO CONSIDER THE WAGONS, WE SHOULD PICK 540-600, RIGHT?
YES.

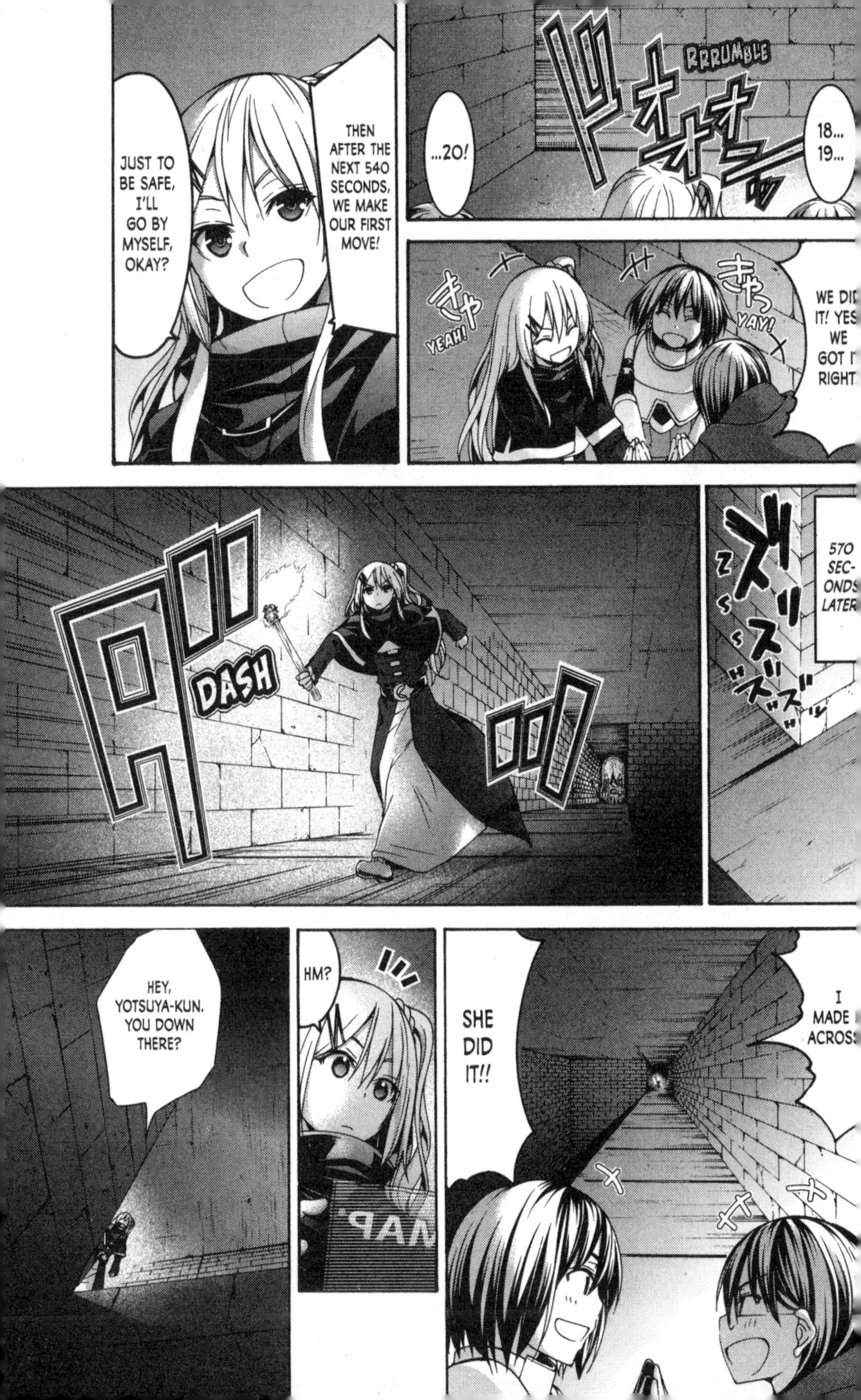
18... 19...
RRRUMBLE
...20!
YAY!
YEAH!
WE DID IT! YES WE GOT I RIGHT.
THEN AFTER THE NEXT 540 SECONDS, WE MAKE OUR FIRST MOVE!
JUST TO BE SAFE, I'LL GO BY MYSELF, OKAY?
570 SEC-ONDS LATER
DASH
I MADE ACROSS
SHE DID IT!!
HM?
MAP
HEY, YOTSUYA-KUN. YOU DOWN THERE?

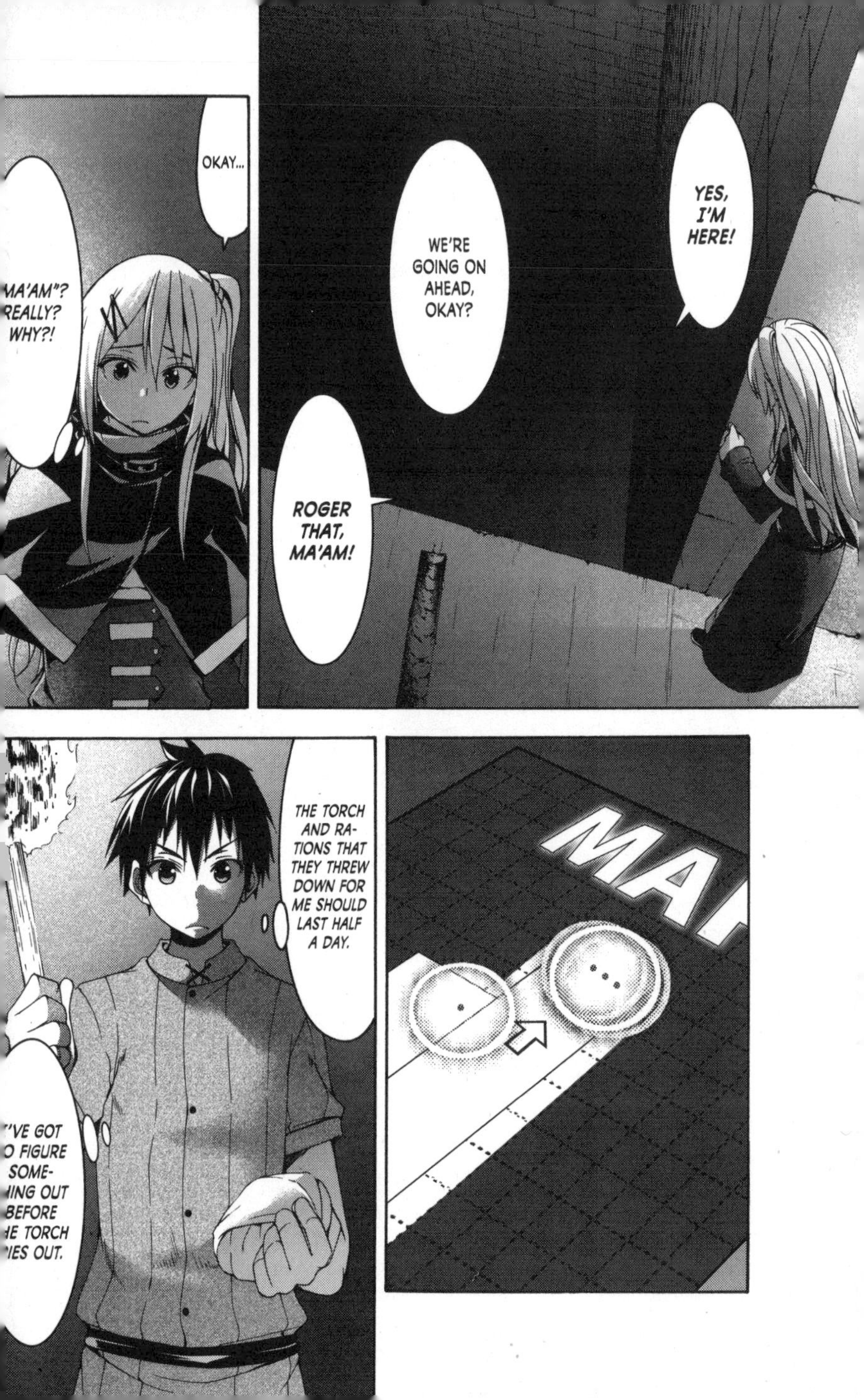
YES, I'M HERE!
WE'RE GOING ON AHEAD, OKAY?
ROGER THAT, MA'AM!
OKAY...
MA'AM"? REALLY? WHY?!
MA
THE TORCH AND RA-TIONS THAT THEY THREW DOWN FOR ME SHOULD LAST HALF A DAY.
'VE GOT O FIGURE SOME-ING OUT BEFORE HE TORCH IES OUT.

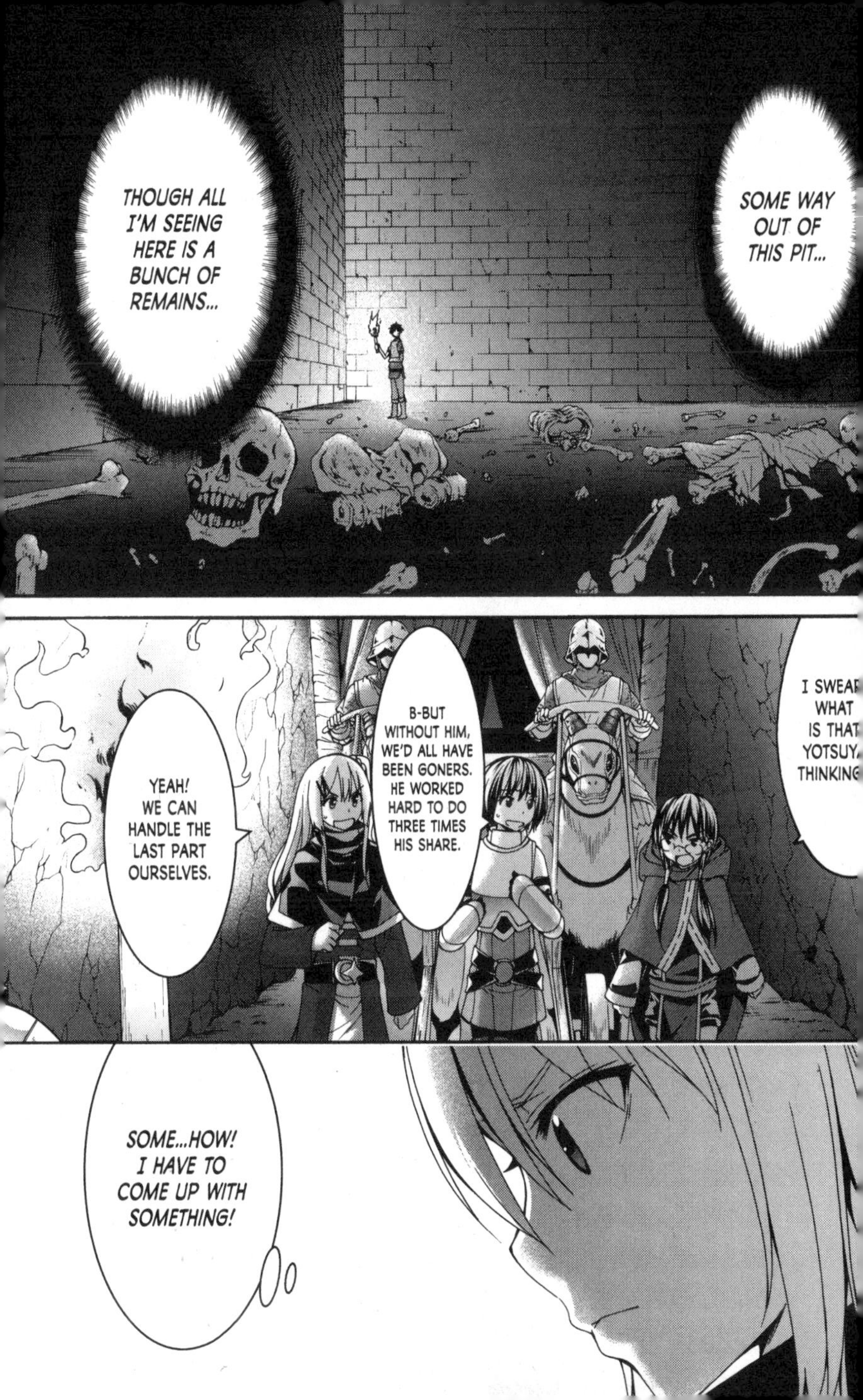
SOME WAY OUT OF THIS PIT...
THOUGH ALL I'M SEEING HERE IS A BUNCH OF REMAINS...
I SWEA WHAT IS THAT YOTSUY THINKING
B-BUT WITHOUT HIM, WE'D ALL HAVE BEEN GONERS. HE WORKED HARD TO DO THREE TIMES HIS SHARE.
YEAH! WE CAN HANDLE THE LAST PART OURSELVES.
SOME...HOW! I HAVE TO COME UP WITH SOMETHING!

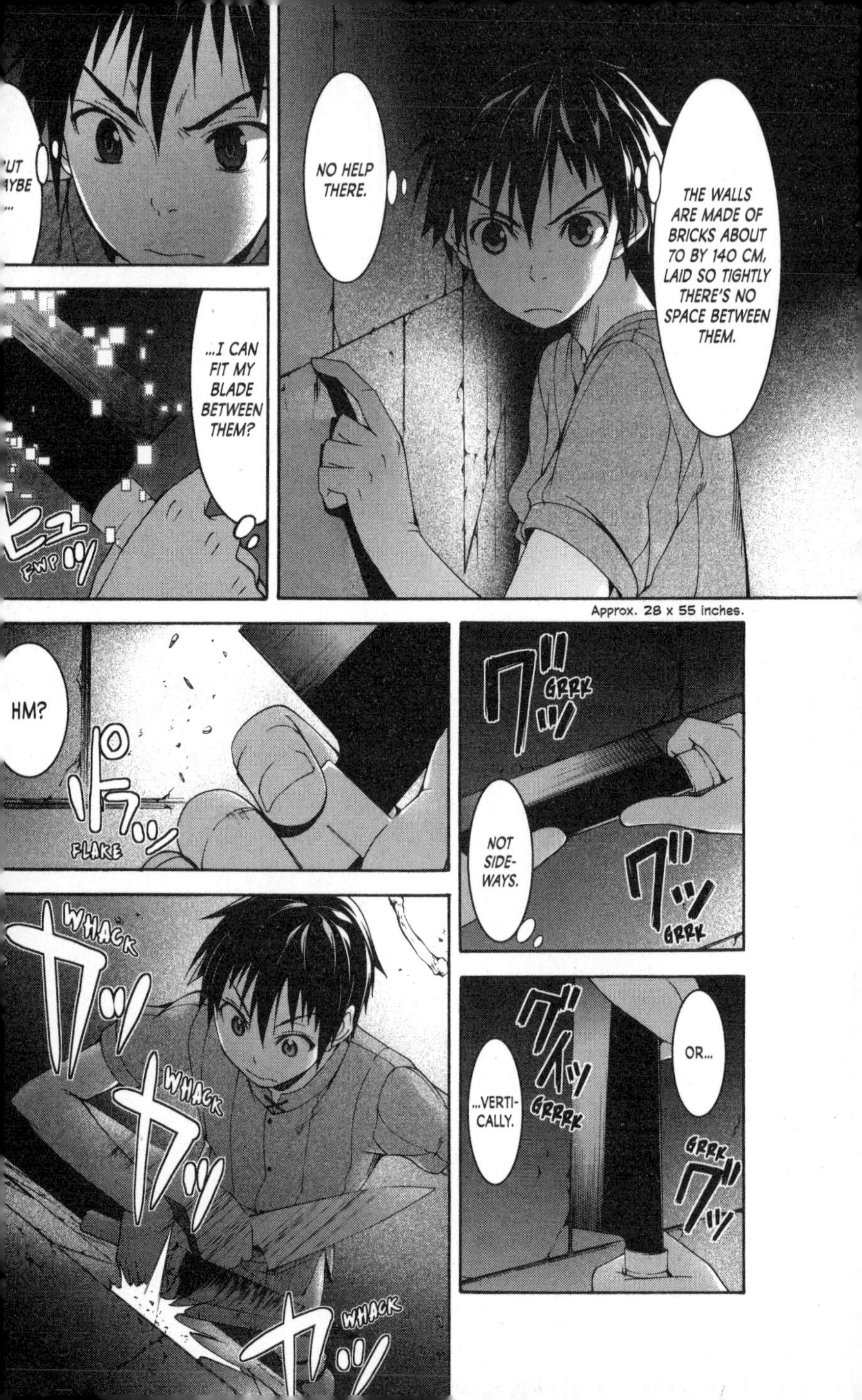
THE WALLS ARE MADE OF BRICKS ABOUT 70 BY 140 CM, LAID SO TIGHTLY THERE'S NO SPACE BETWEEN THEM.
NO HELP THERE.
...I CAN FIT MY BLADE BETWEEN THEM?
FWP
GRRK
NOT SIDEWAYS.
GRRK
HM?
FLAKE
OR...
GRRRK
...VERTI-CALLY.
GRRK
WHACK
WHACK
WHACK
Approx. 28 x 55 inches.

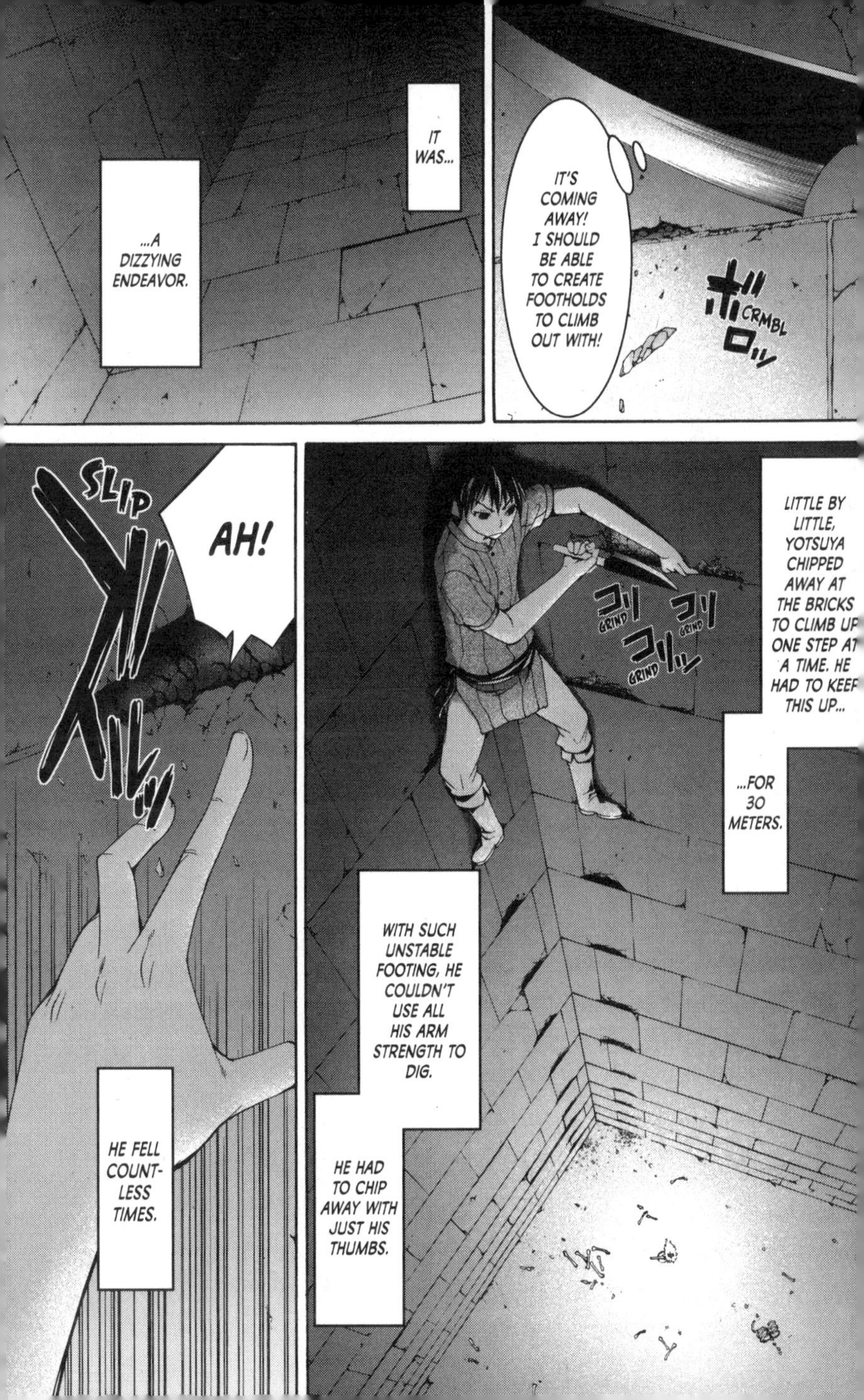
IT'S COMING AWAY! I SHOULD BE ABLE TO CREATE FOOTHOLDS TO CLIMB OUT WITH!
CRMBL
IT WAS...
...A DIZZYING ENDEAVOR.
LITTLE BY LITTLE, YOTSUYA CHIPPED AWAY AT THE BRICKS TO CLIMB UP ONE STEP AT A TIME. HE HAD TO KEEP THIS UP...
GRIND GRIND GRIND
...FOR 30 METERS.
WITH SUCH UNSTABLE FOOTING, HE COULDN'T USE ALL HIS ARM STRENGTH TO DIG.
HE HAD TO CHIP AWAY WITH JUST HIS THUMBS.
SLIP
AH!
HE FELL COUNT-LESS TIMES.

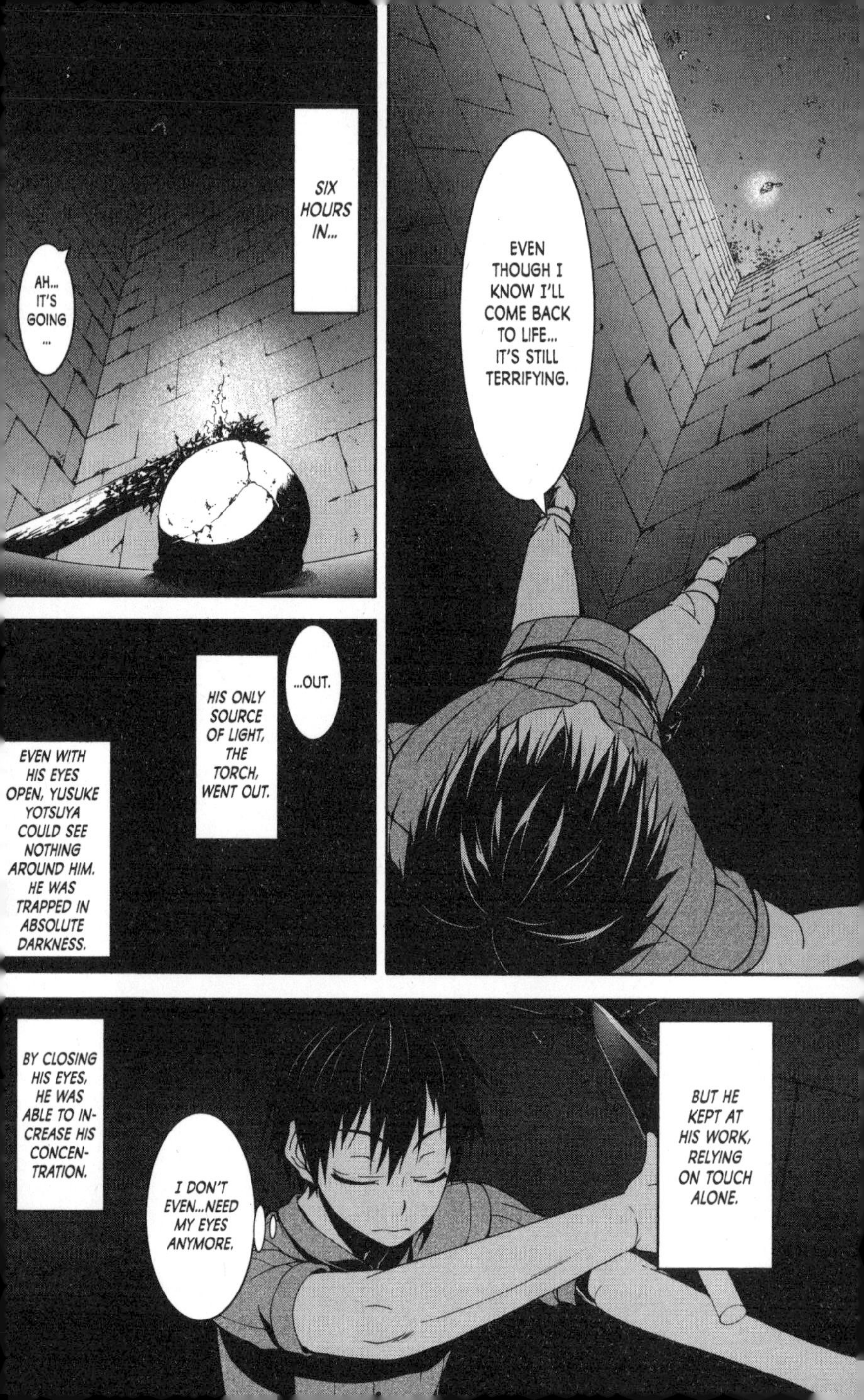
EVEN THOUGH I KNOW I'LL COME BACK TO LIFE... IT'S STILL TERRIFYING.
SIX HOURS IN...
AH... IT'S GOING ...
...OUT.
HIS ONLY SOURCE OF LIGHT, THE TORCH, WENT OUT.
EVEN WITH HIS EYES OPEN, YUSUKE YOTSUYA COULD SEE NOTHING AROUND HIM. HE WAS TRAPPED IN ABSOLUTE DARKNESS.
BUT HE KEPT AT HIS WORK, RELYING ON TOUCH ALONE.
I DON'T EVEN...NEED MY EYES ANYMORE.
BY CLOSING HIS EYES, HE WAS ABLE TO IN-CREASE HIS CONCEN-TRATION.

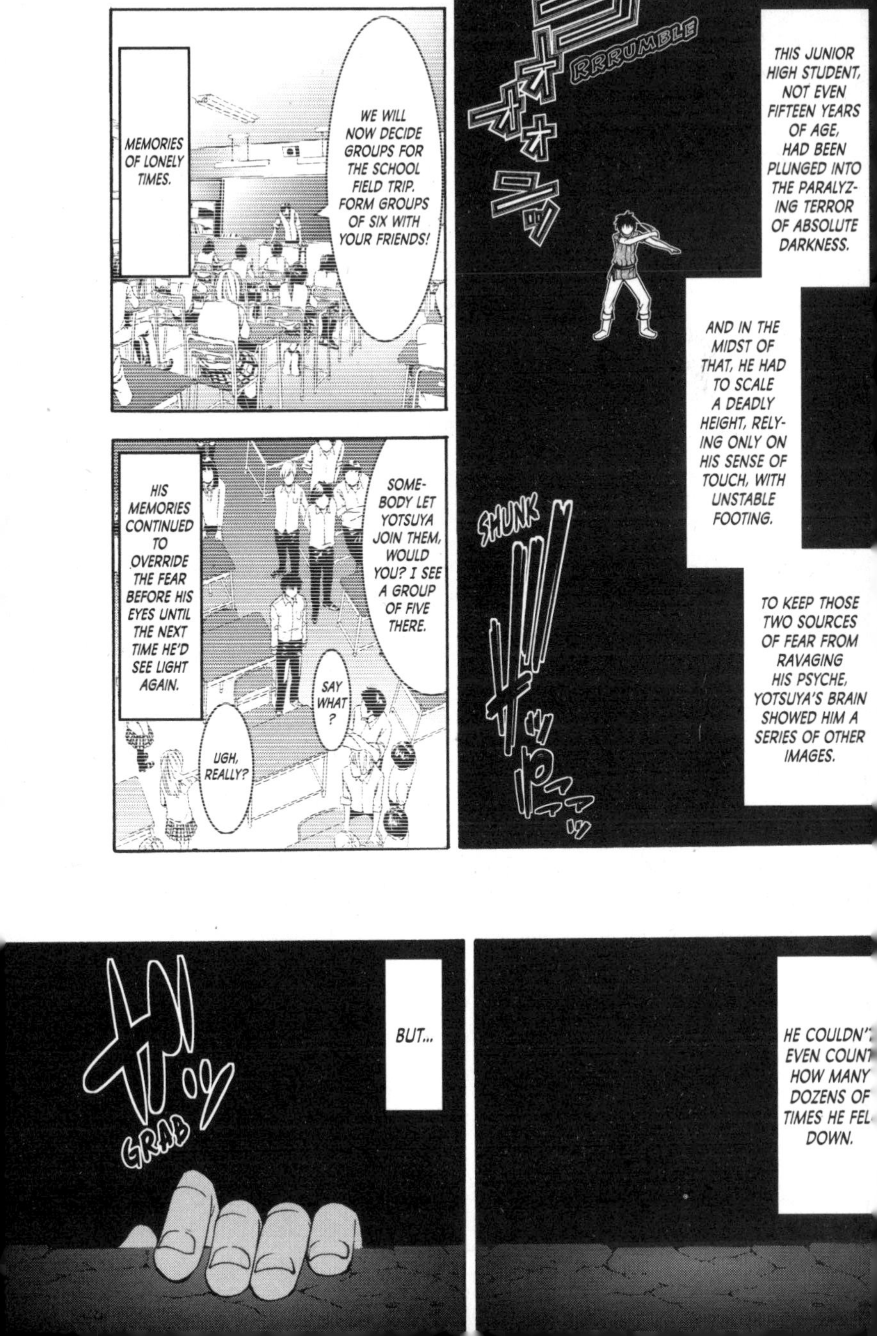
RRRUMBLE
THIS JUNIOR HIGH STUDENT, NOT EVEN FIFTEEN YEARS OF AGE, HAD BEEN PLUNGED INTO THE PARALYZ-ING TERROR OF ABSOLUTE DARKNESS.
AND IN THE MIDST OF THAT, HE HAD TO SCALE A DEADLY HEIGHT, RELY-ING ONLY ON HIS SENSE OF TOUCH, WITH UNSTABLE FOOTING.
SHUNK
TO KEEP THOSE TWO SOURCES OF FEAR FROM RAVAGING HIS PSYCHE, YOTSUYA'S BRAIN SHOWED HIM A SERIES OF OTHER IMAGES.
WE WILL NOW DECIDE GROUPS FOR THE SCHOOL FIELD TRIP. FORM GROUPS OF SIX WITH YOUR FRIENDS!
MEMORIES OF LONELY TIMES.
SOME-BODY LET YOTSUYA JOIN THEM, WOULD YOU? I SEE A GROUP OF FIVE THERE.
HIS MEMORIES CONTINUED TO OVERRIDE THE FEAR BEFORE HIS EYES UNTIL THE NEXT TIME HE'D SEE LIGHT AGAIN.
SAY WHAT?
UGH, REALLY?
HE COULDN' EVEN COUN HOW MANY DOZENS OF TIMES HE FEL DOWN.
BUT...
GRAB

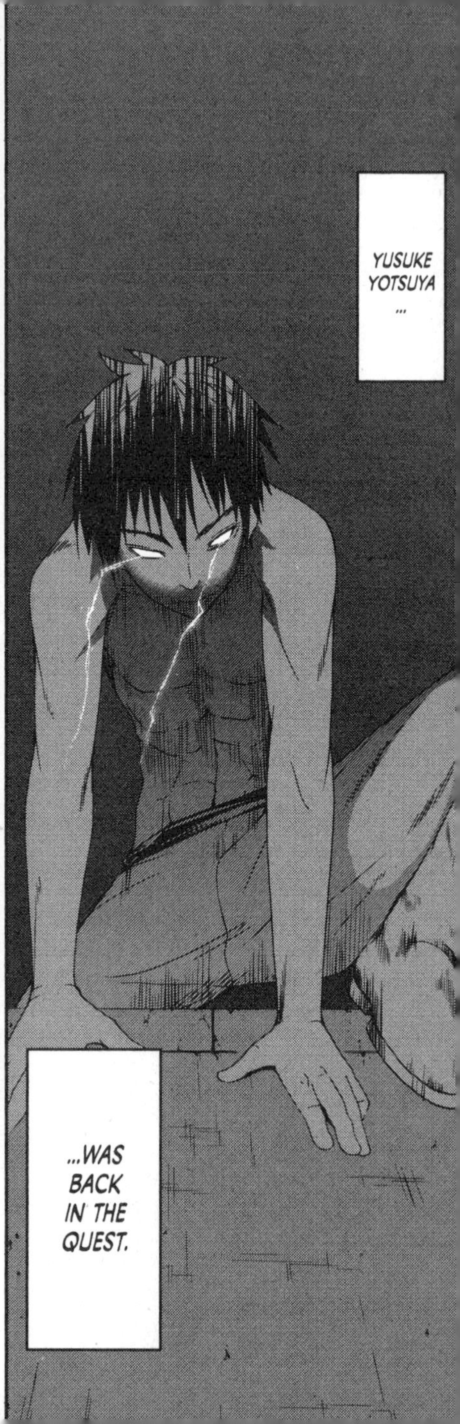
YUSUKE YOTSUYA ...
...WAS BACK IN THE QUEST.

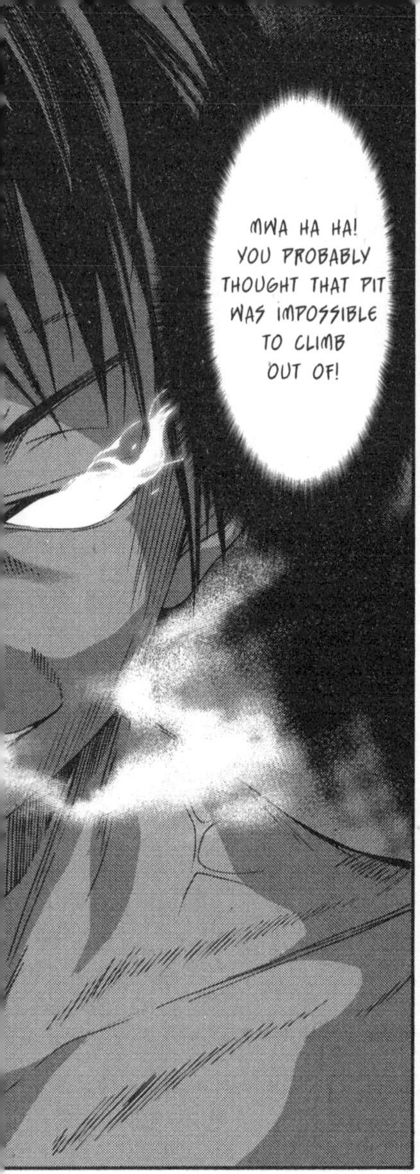
MWA HA HA! YOU PROBABLY THOUGHT THAT PIT WAS IMPOSSIBLE TO CLIMB OUT OF!

10 DAYS AND
5 HOURS

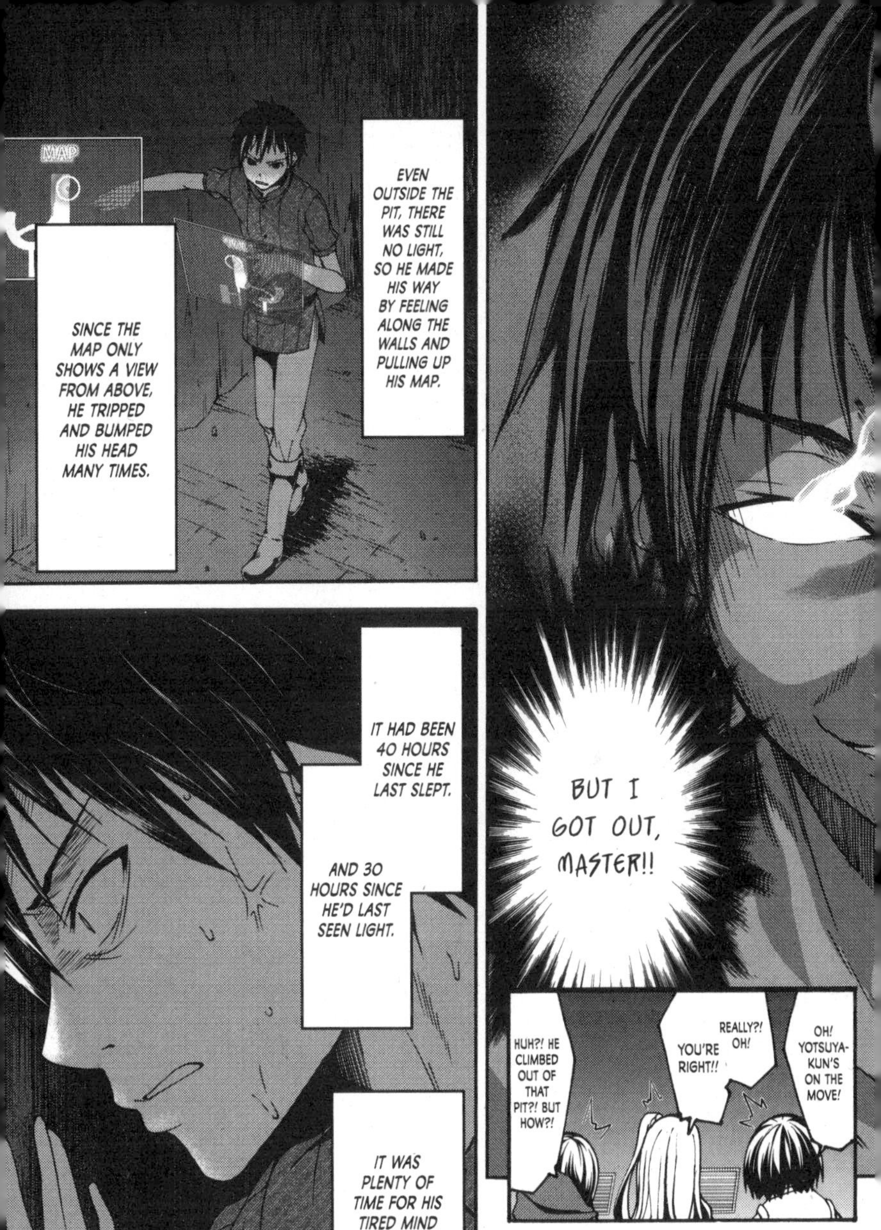
MAP
EVEN OUTSIDE THE PIT, THERE WAS STILL NO LIGHT, SO HE MADE HIS WAY BY FEELING ALONG THE WALLS AND PULLING UP HIS MAP.
SINCE THE MAP ONLY SHOWS A VIEW FROM ABOVE, HE TRIPPED AND BUMPED HIS HEAD MANY TIMES.
IT HAD BEEN 40 HOURS SINCE HE LAST SLEPT.
AND 30 HOURS SINCE HE'D LAST SEEN LIGHT.
IT WAS PLENTY OF TIME FOR HIS TIRED MIND TO START BELIEVING THAT HE WAS ALL ALONE IN THE WORLD.
BUT I GOT OUT, MASTER!!
OH! YOTSUYA-KUN'S ON THE MOVE!
REALLY?! OH!
YOU'RE RIGHT!!
HUH?! HE CLIMBED OUT OF THAT PIT?! BUT HOW?!

QUEST REMAINING TIME:

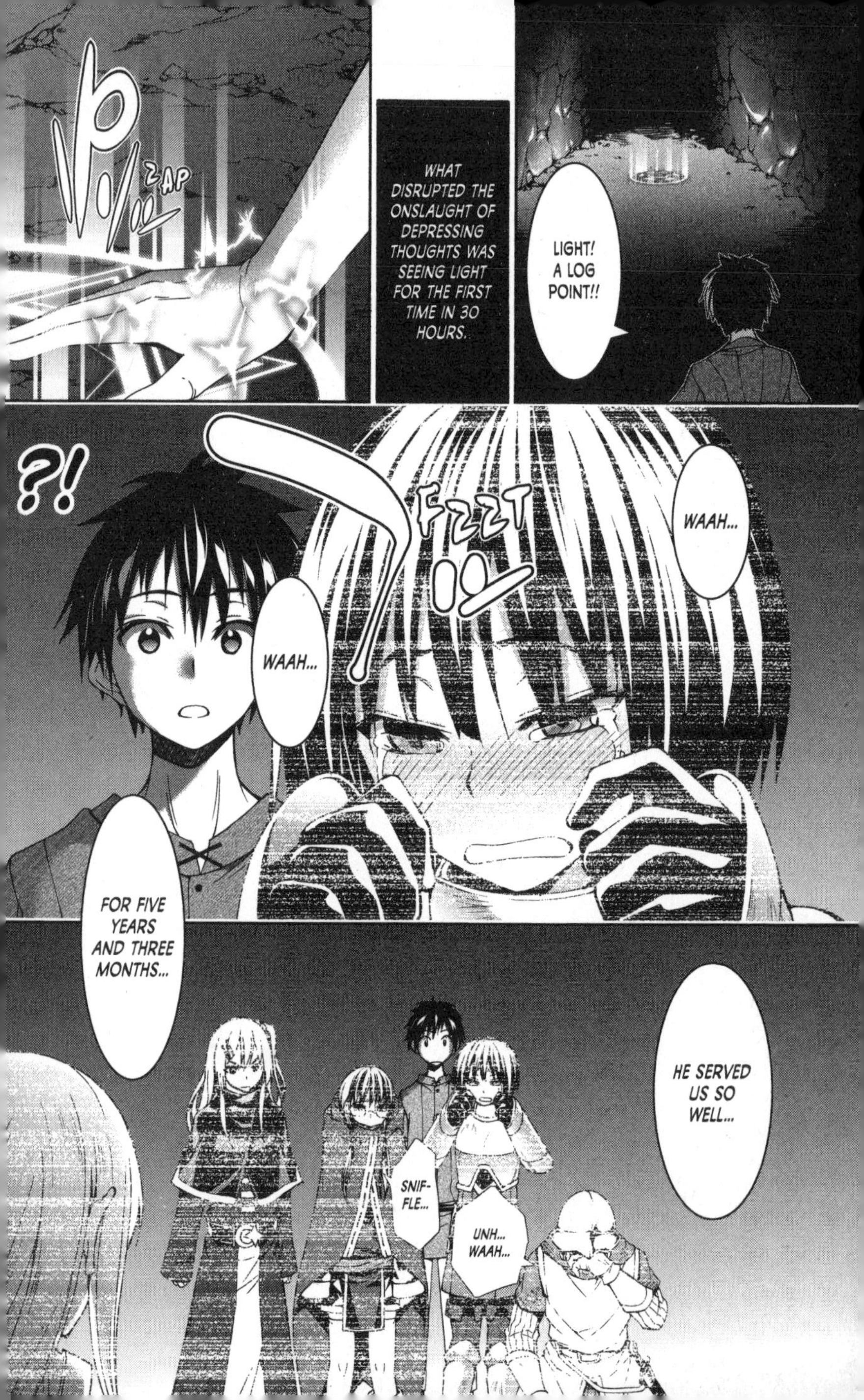
LIGHT! A LOG POINT!!
WHAT DISRUPTED THE ONSLAUGHT OF DEPRESSING THOUGHTS WAS SEEING LIGHT FOR THE FIRST TIME IN 30 HOURS.
ZAP
WAAH...
FZZT
WAAH...
?!
HE SERVED US SO WELL...
UNH... WAAH...
SNIF-FLE...
FOR FIVE YEARS AND THREE MONTHS...

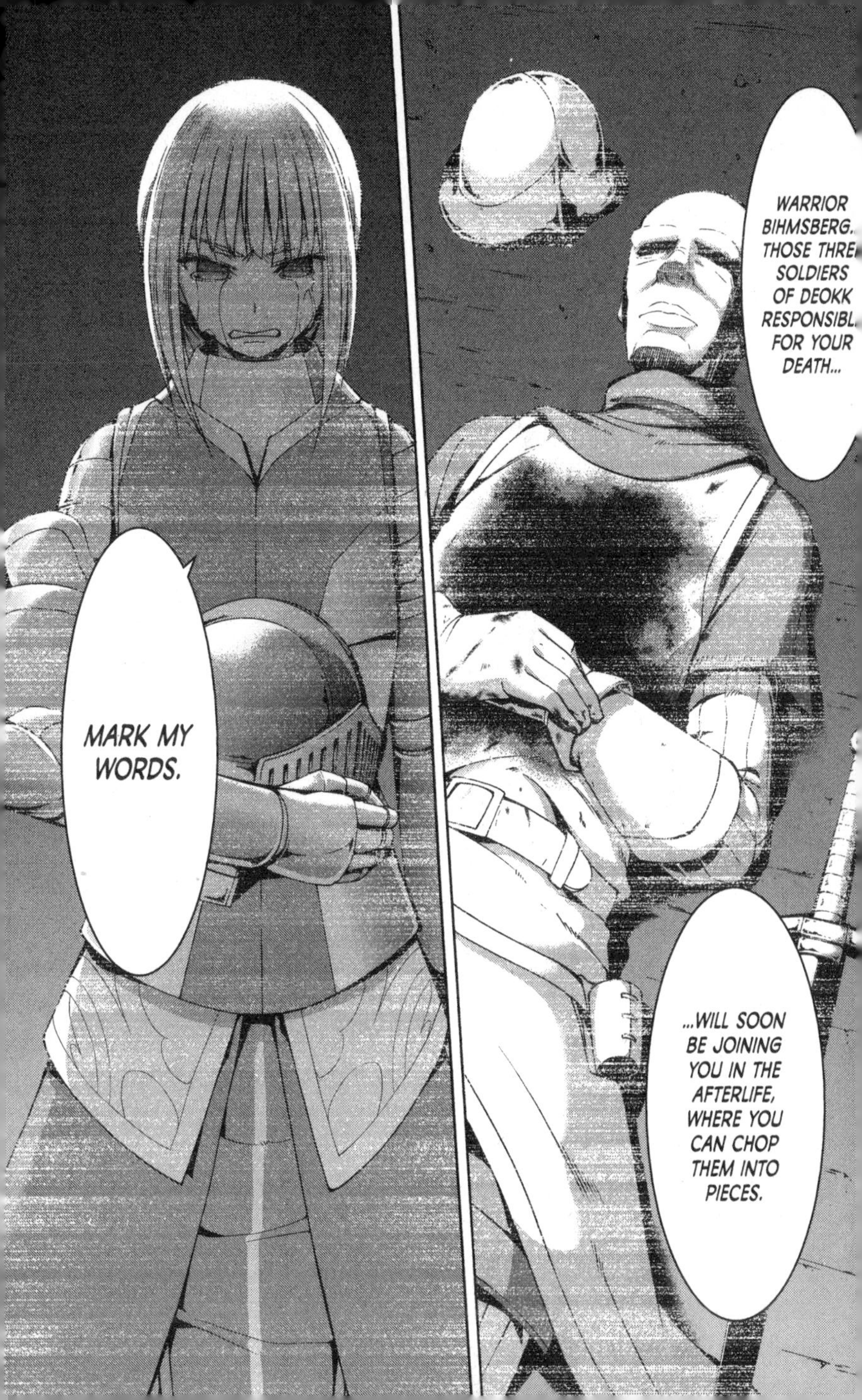
WARRIOR BIHMSBERG. THOSE THRE SOLDIERS OF DEOKK RESPONSIBL FOR YOUR DEATH...
...WILL SOON BE JOINING YOU IN THE AFTERLIFE, WHERE YOU CAN CHOP THEM INTO PIECES.
MARK MY WORDS.

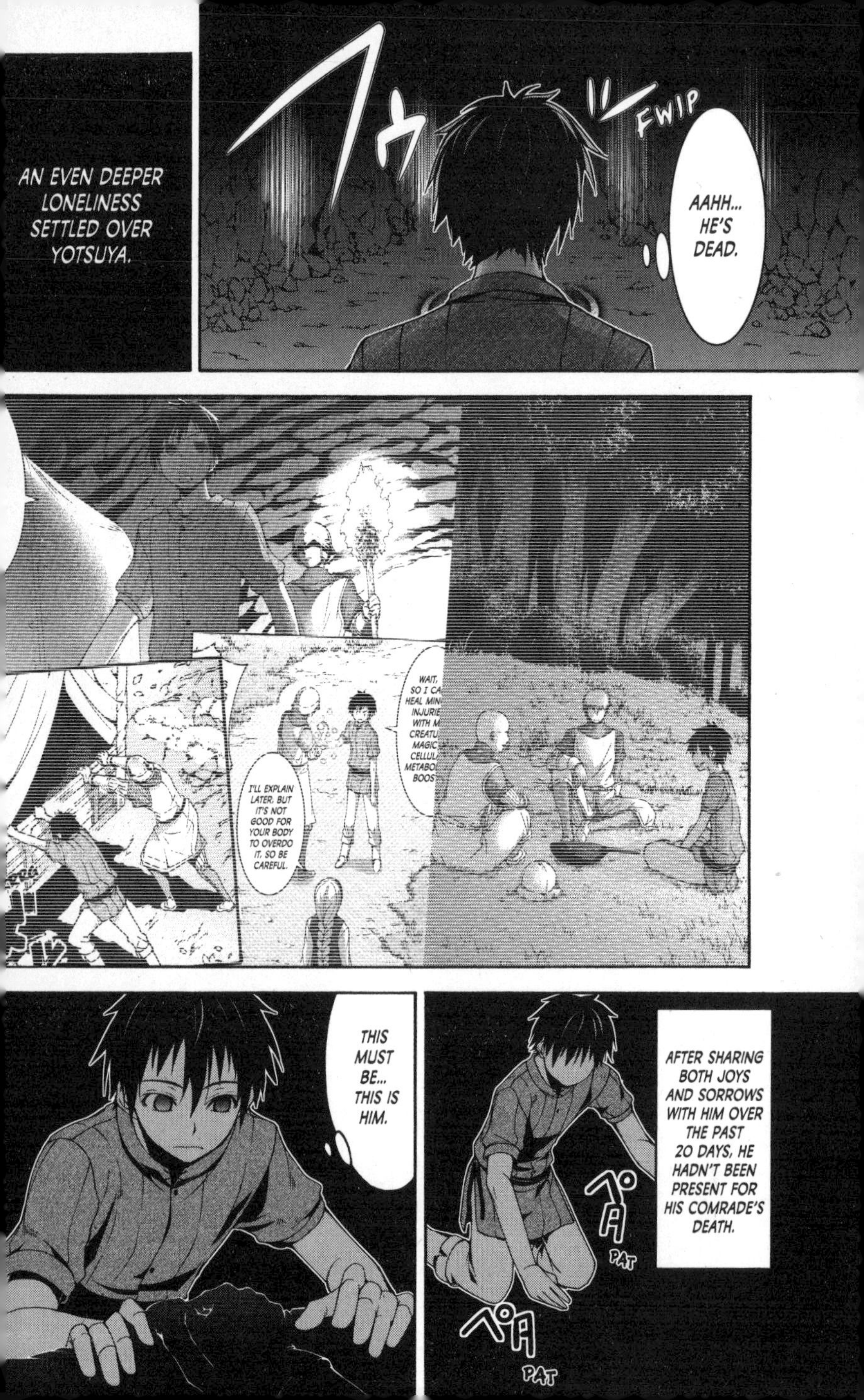
FWIP
AAHH... HE'S DEAD.
AN EVEN DEEPER LONELINESS SETTLED OVER YOTSUYA.
I'LL EXPLAIN LATER. BUT IT'S NOT GOOD FOR YOUR BODY TO OVERDO IT, SO BE CAREFUL.
AFTER SHARING BOTH JOYS AND SORROWS WITH HIM OVER THE PAST 20 DAYS, HE HADN'T BEEN PRESENT FOR HIS COMRADE'S DEATH.
PAT
PAT
THIS MUST BE... THIS IS HIM.

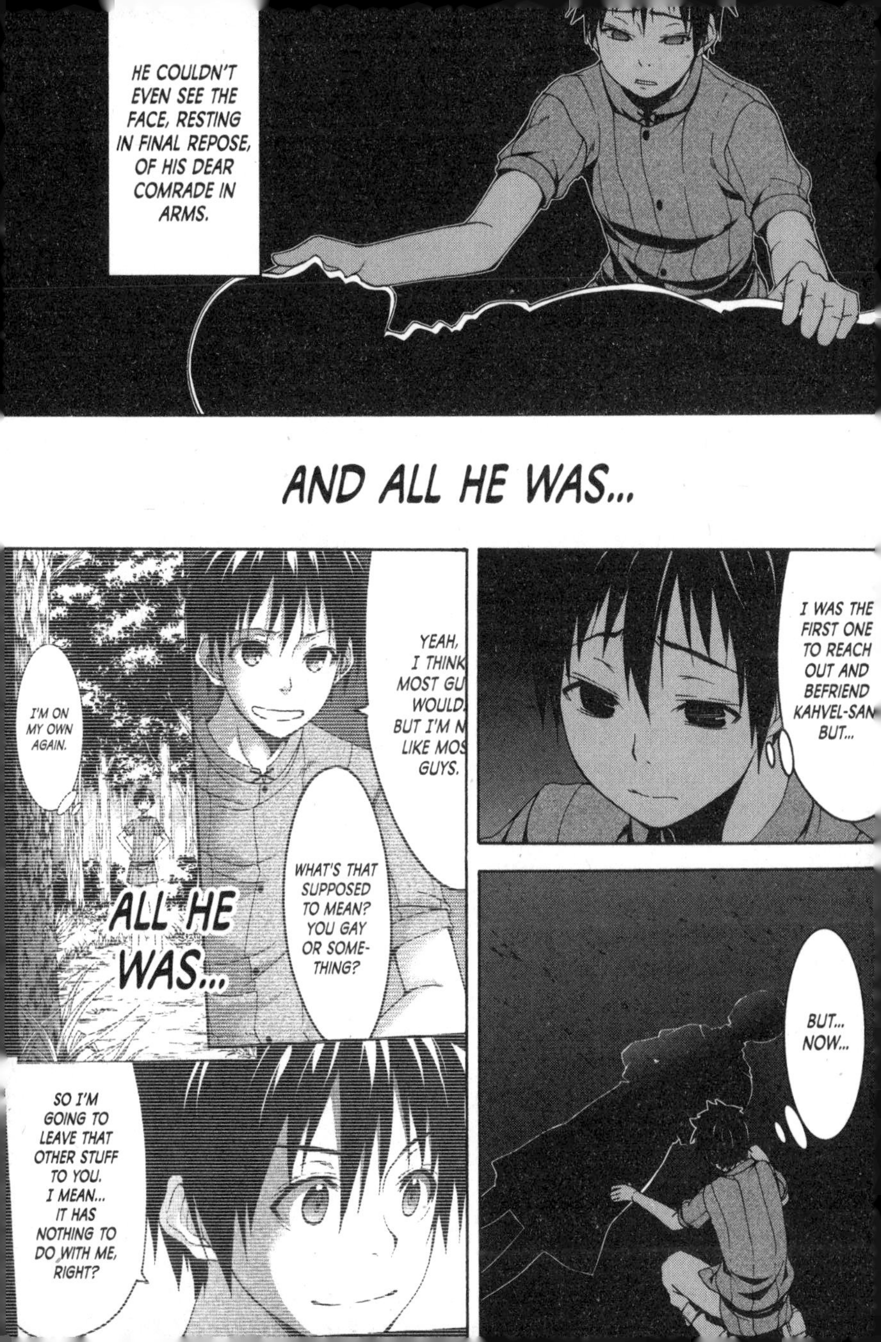
HE COULDN'T EVEN SEE THE FACE, RESTING IN FINAL REPOSE, OF HIS DEAR COMRADE IN ARMS.
AND ALL HE WAS...
I WAS THE FIRST ONE TO REACH OUT AND BEFRIEND KAHVEL-SAN BUT...
YEAH, I THINK MOST GU WOULD. BUT I'M N LIKE MOS GUYS.
WHAT'S THAT SUPPOSED TO MEAN? YOU GAY OR SOME-THING?
I'M ON MY OWN AGAIN.
ALL HE WAS...
SO I'M GOING TO LEAVE THAT OTHER STUFF TO YOU. I MEAN... IT HAS NOTHING TO DO WITH ME, RIGHT?
BUT... NOW...

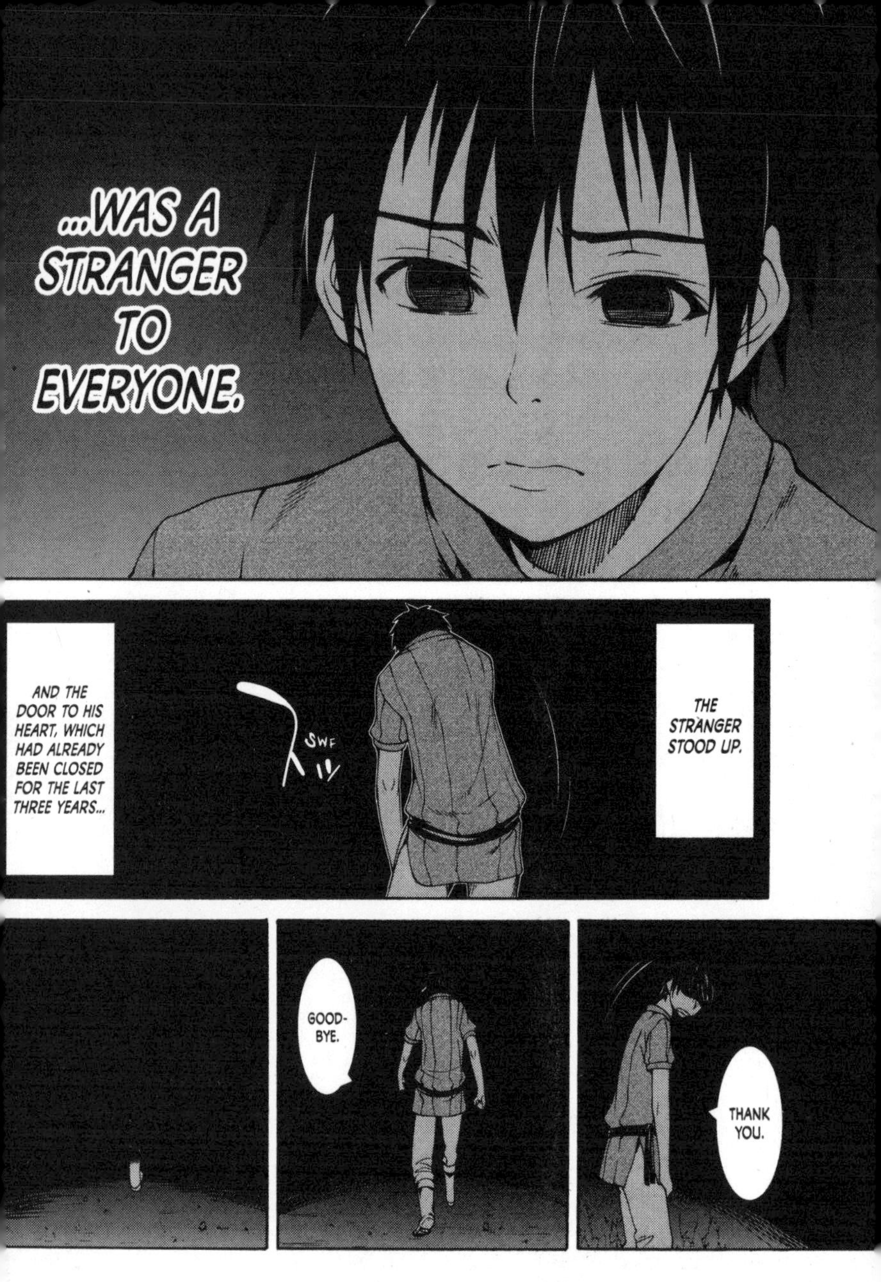
...WAS A STRANGER TO EVERYONE.
THE STRANGER STOOD UP.
SWF
AND THE DOOR TO HIS HEART, WHICH HAD ALREADY BEEN CLOSED FOR THE LAST THREE YEARS...
THANK YOU.
GOOD-BYE.
...LOCKED TIGHT.

QUEST REMAINING TIME: 8 DAYS AND 21 HOURS

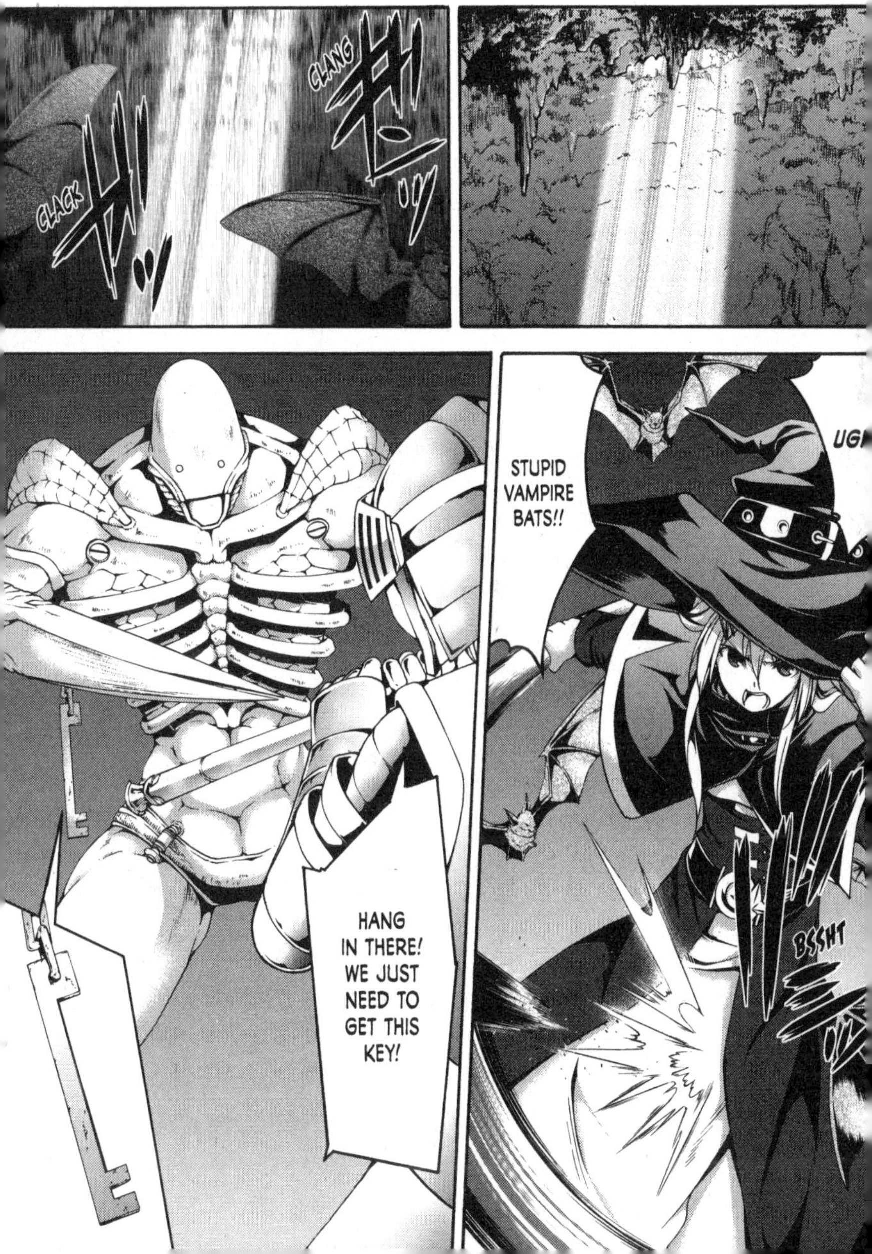
CLANG
CLACK
UG
STUPID VAMPIRE BATS!!
BSSHT
HANG IN THERE! WE JUST NEED TO GET THIS KEY!

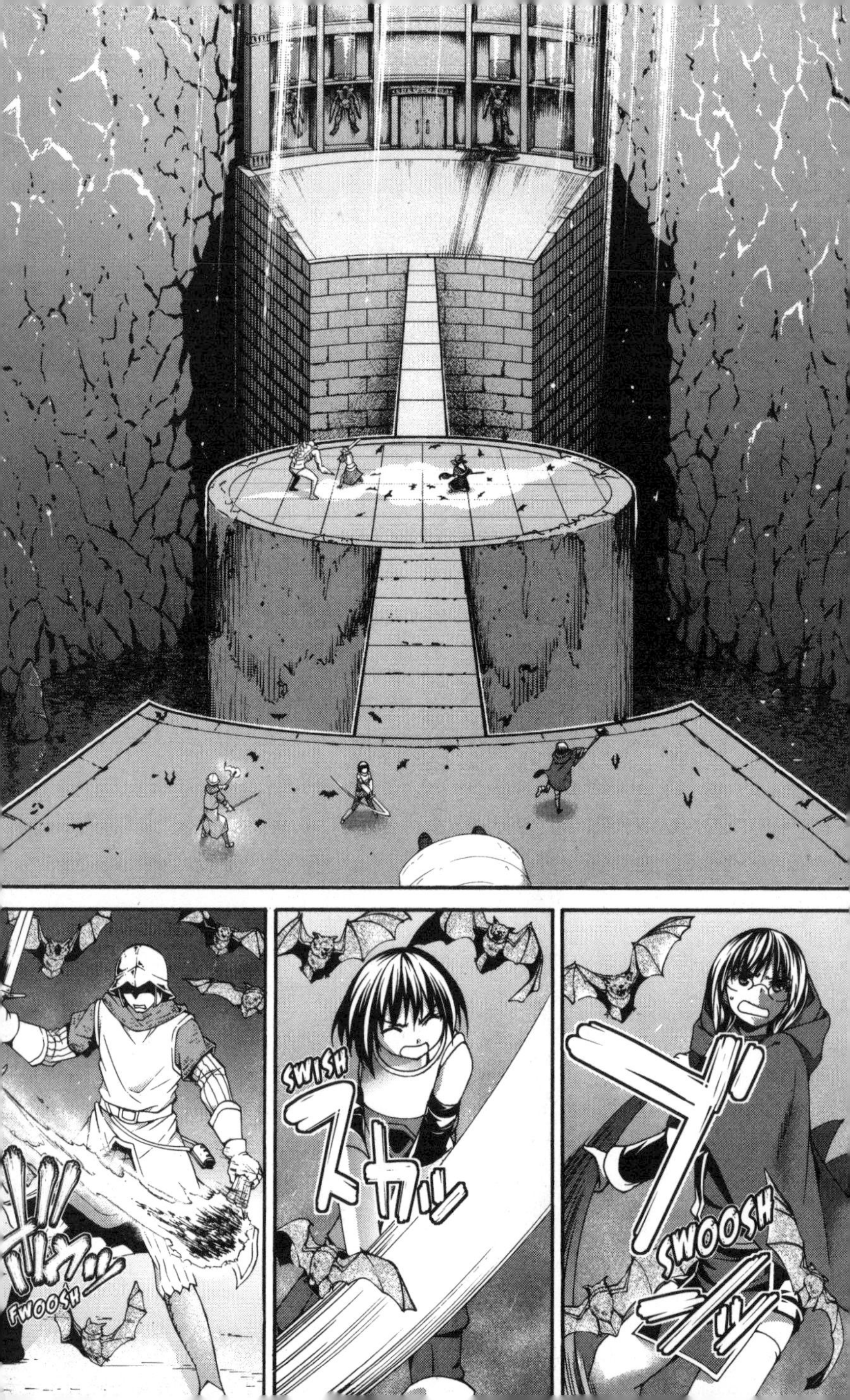
SWOOSH
SWISH
FWOOSH

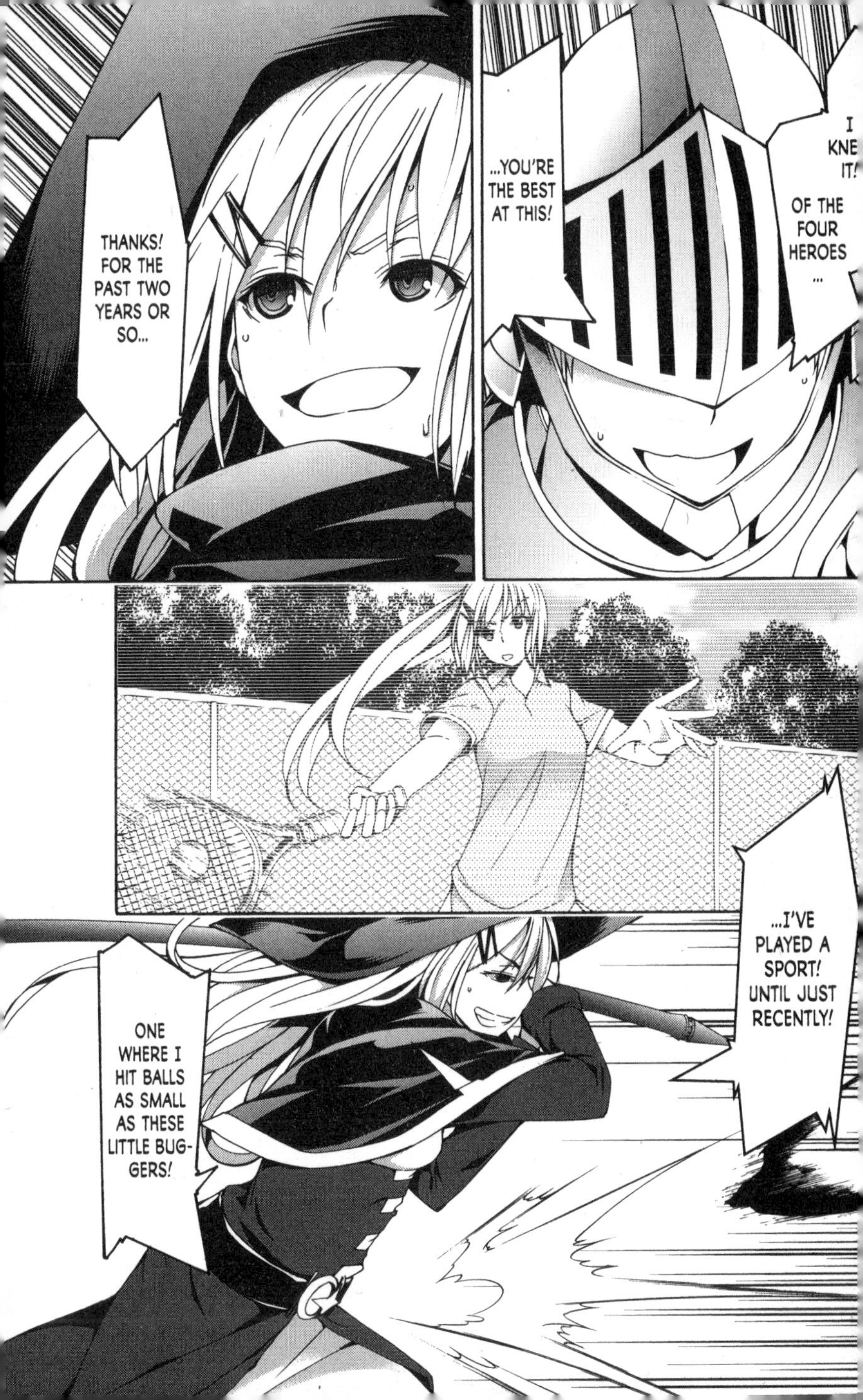
I KNE IT!
OF THE FOUR HEROES ...
...YOU'RE THE BEST AT THIS!
THANKS! FOR THE PAST TWO YEARS OR SO...
...I'VE PLAYED A SPORT! UNTIL JUST RECENTLY!
ONE WHERE I HIT BALLS AS SMALL AS THESE LITTLE BUG-GERS!

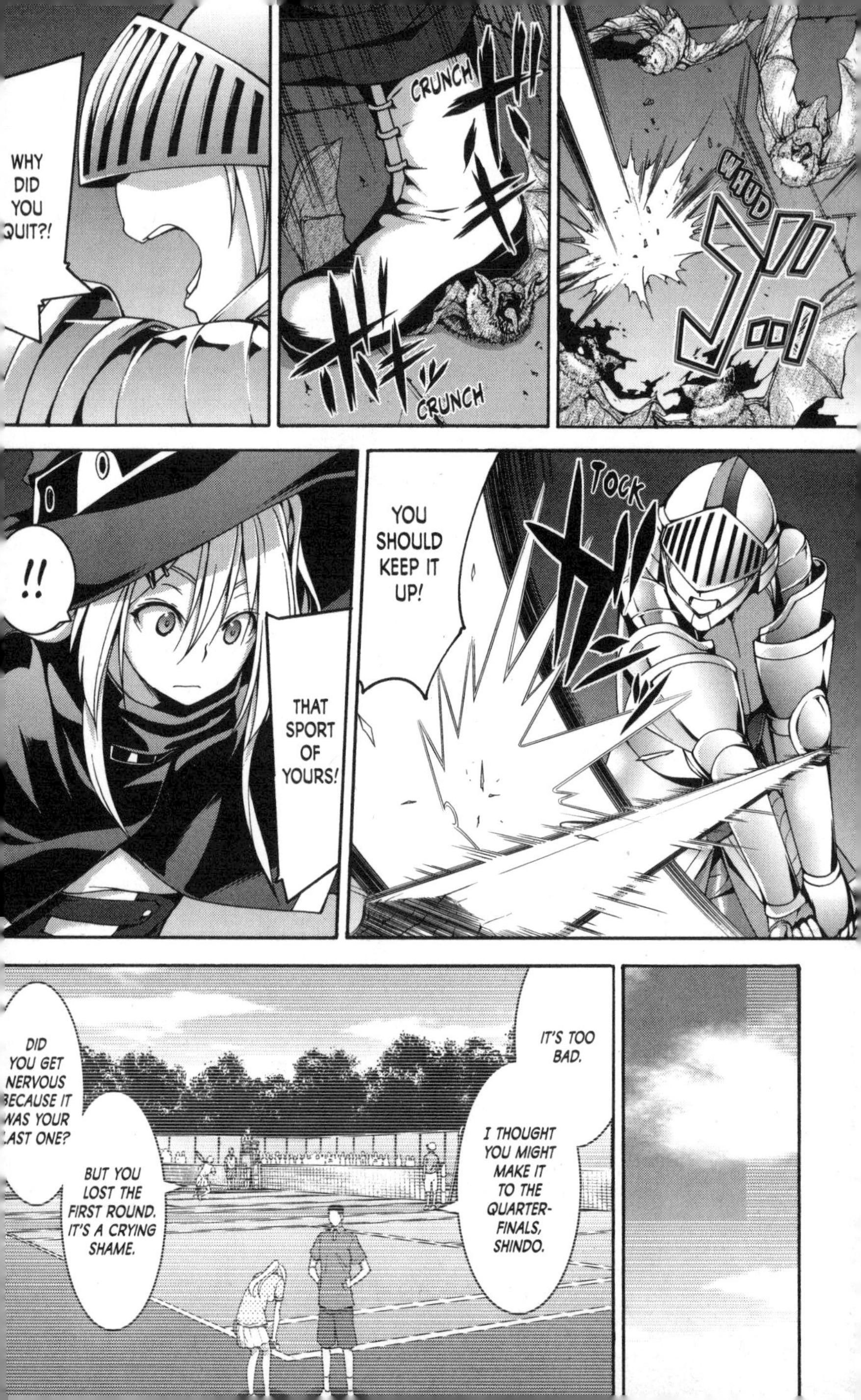
WHUD
CRUNCH
CRUNCH
WHY DID YOU QUIT?!
TOCK
YOU SHOULD KEEP IT UP!
THAT SPORT OF YOURS!
!!
IT'S TOO BAD.
I THOUGHT YOU MIGHT MAKE IT TO THE QUARTER-FINALS, SHINDO.
DID YOU GET NERVOUS BECAUSE IT WAS YOUR LAST ONE?
BUT YOU LOST THE FIRST ROUND. IT'S A CRYING SHAME.

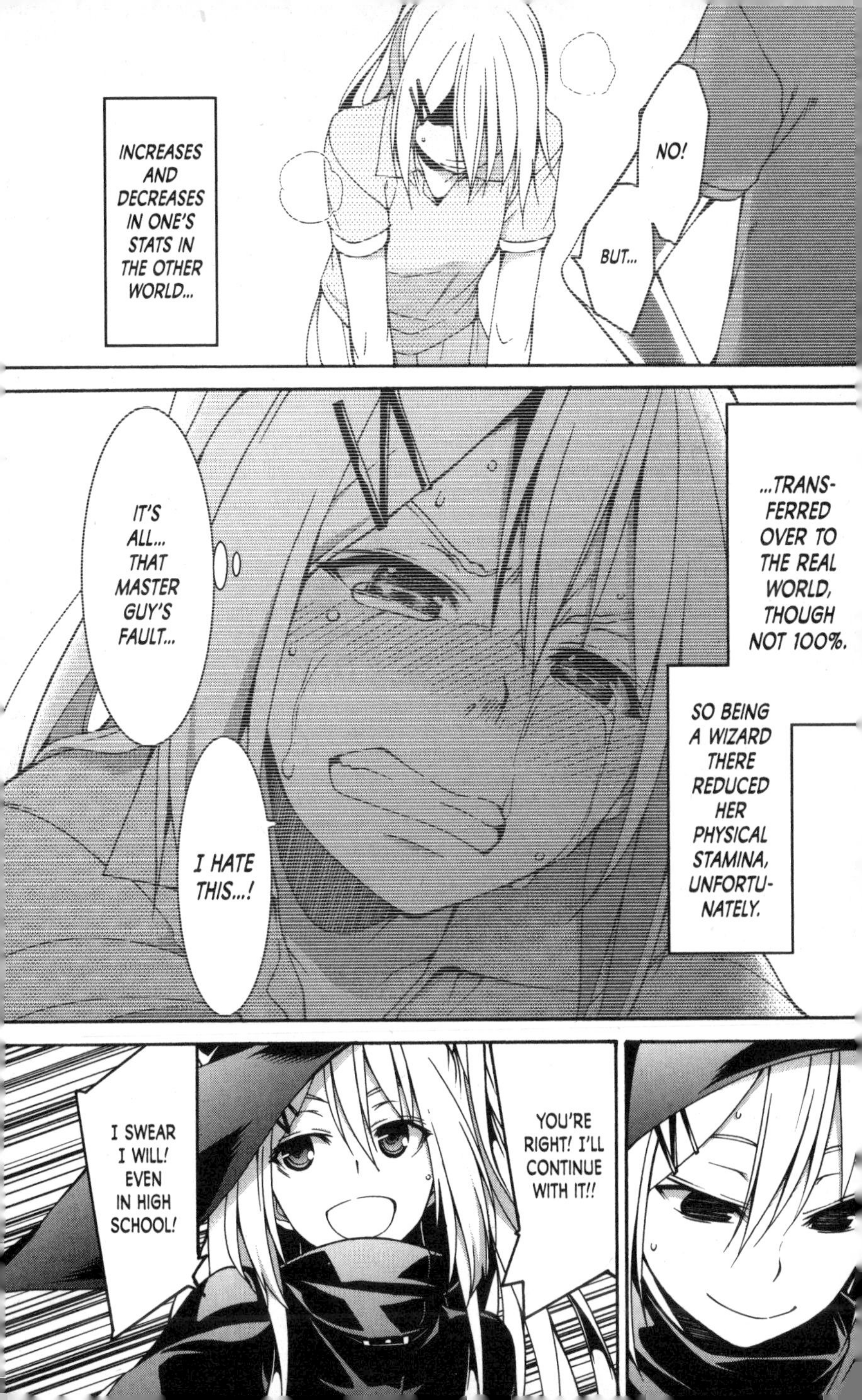
NO!
BUT...
INCREASES AND DECREASES IN ONE'S STATS IN THE OTHER WORLD...
...TRANS-FERRED OVER TO THE REAL WORLD, THOUGH NOT 100%.
SO BEING A WIZARD THERE REDUCED HER PHYSICAL STAMINA, UNFORTU-NATELY.
IT'S ALL... THAT MASTER GUY'S FAULT...
I HATE THIS...!
YOU'RE RIGHT! I'LL CONTINUE WITH IT!!
I SWEAR I WILL! EVEN IN HIGH SCHOOL!

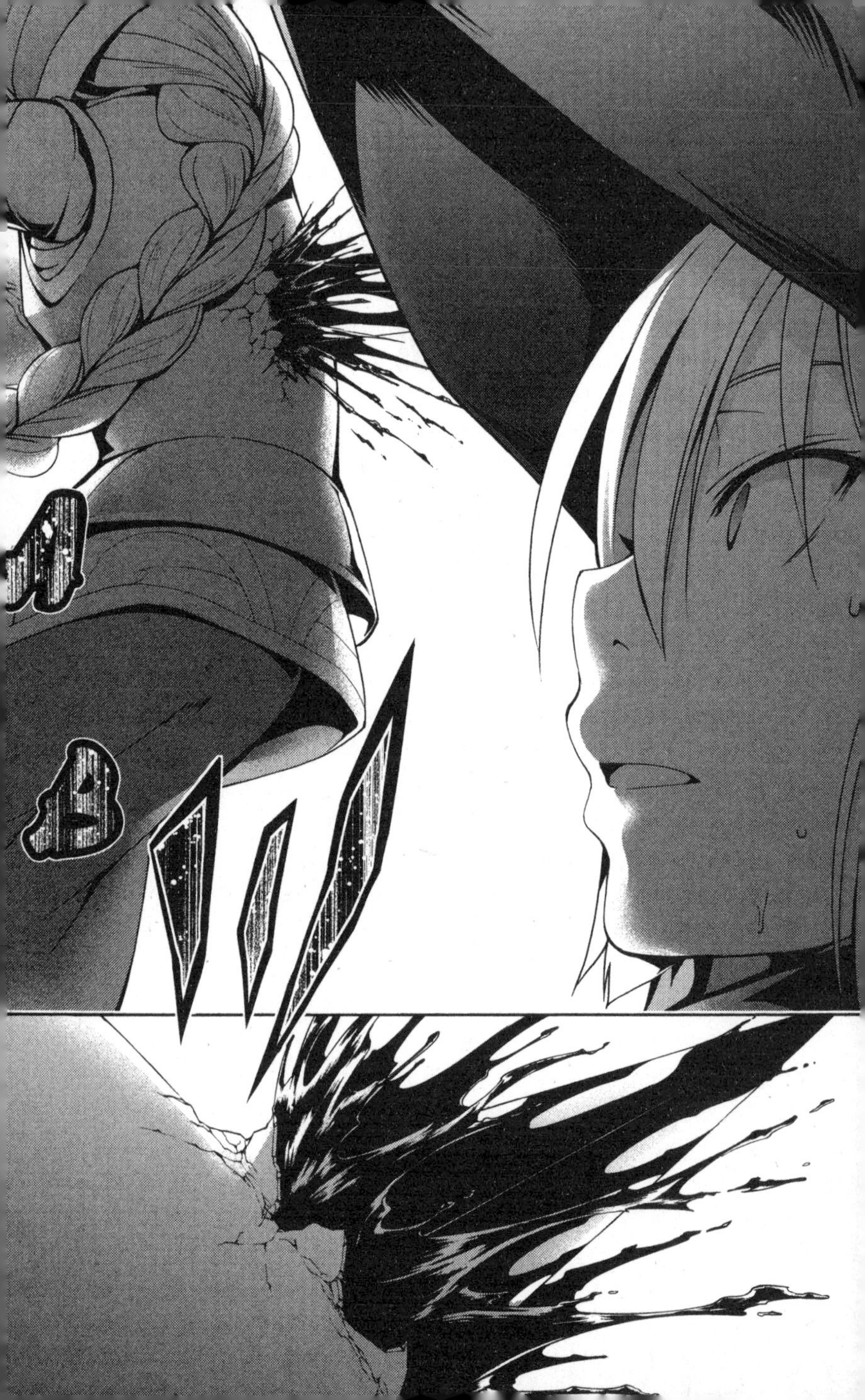

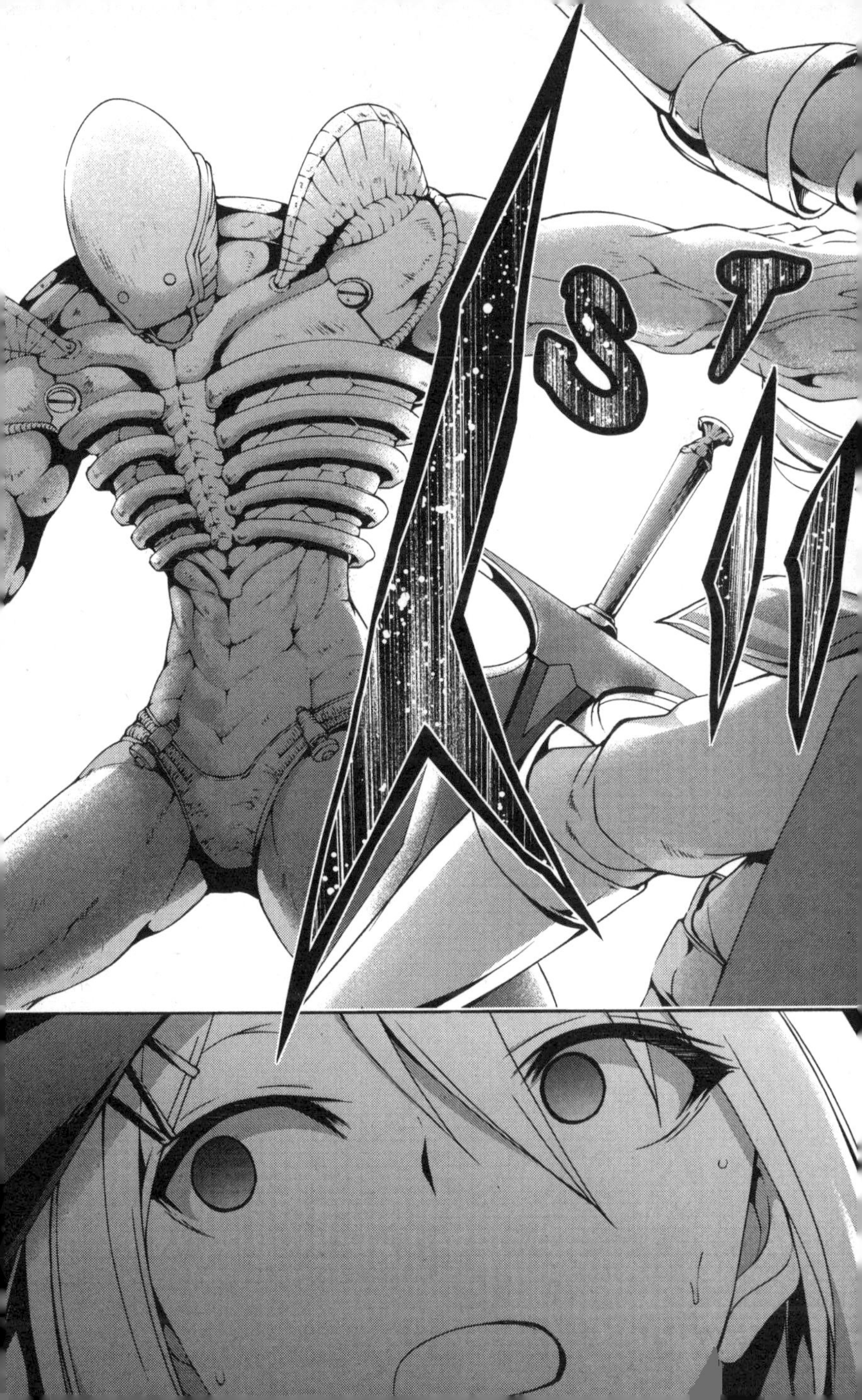

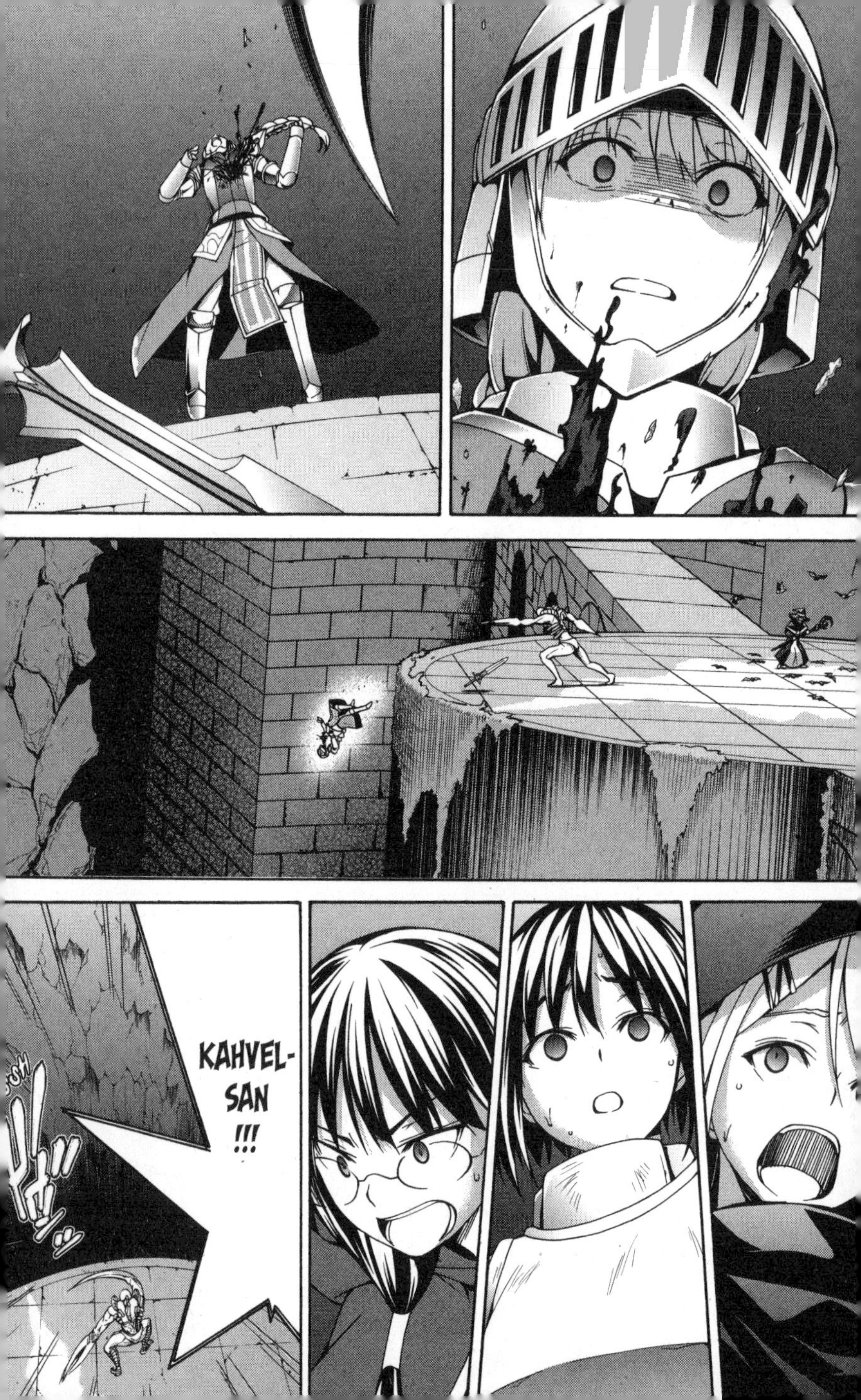
KAHVEL-SAN !!!

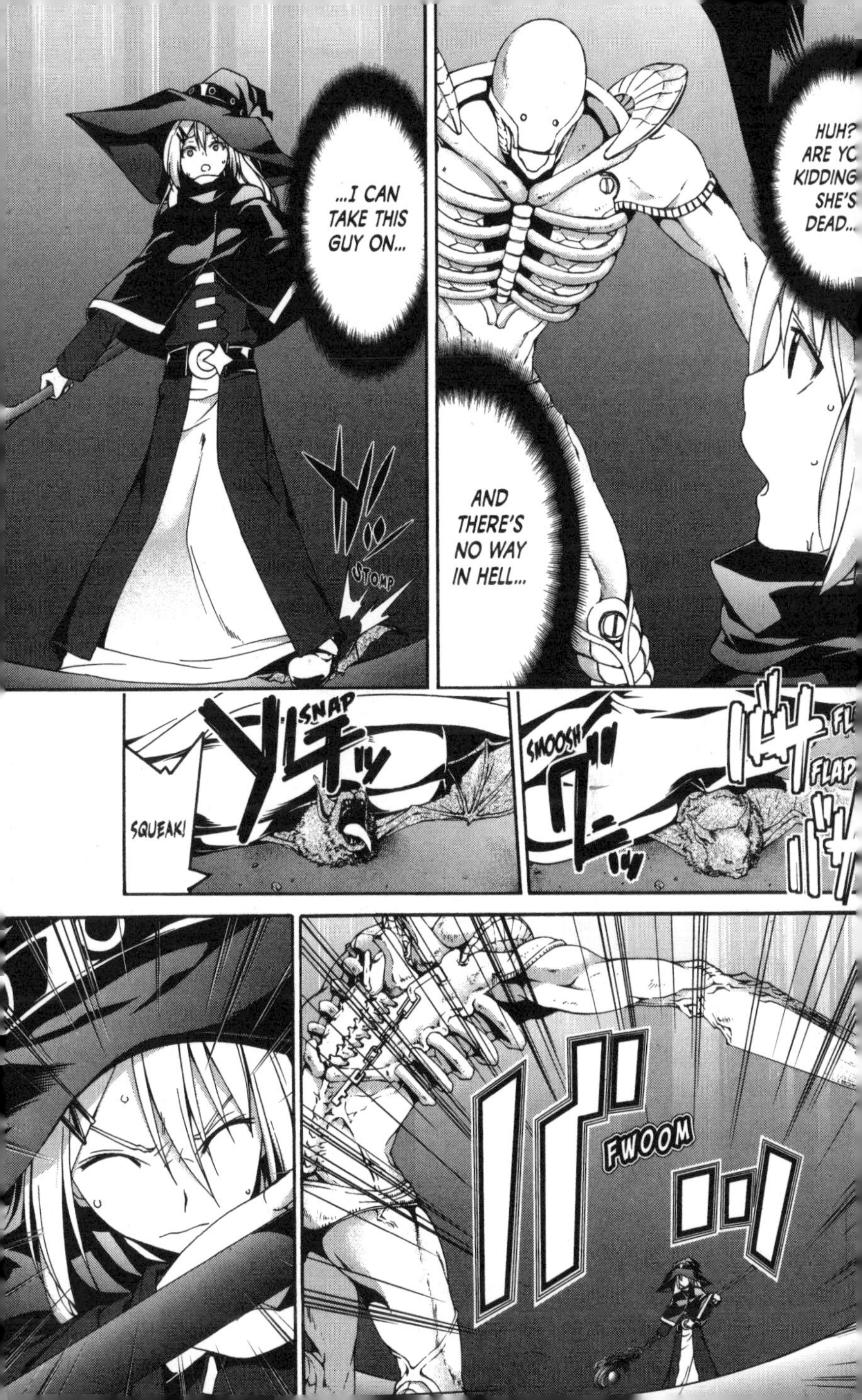
HUH? ARE YO KIDDING SHE'S DEAD...
AND THERE'S NO WAY IN HELL...
...I CAN TAKE THIS GUY ON...
STOMP
FLAP
SMOOSH
SNAP
SQUEAK!
FWOOM

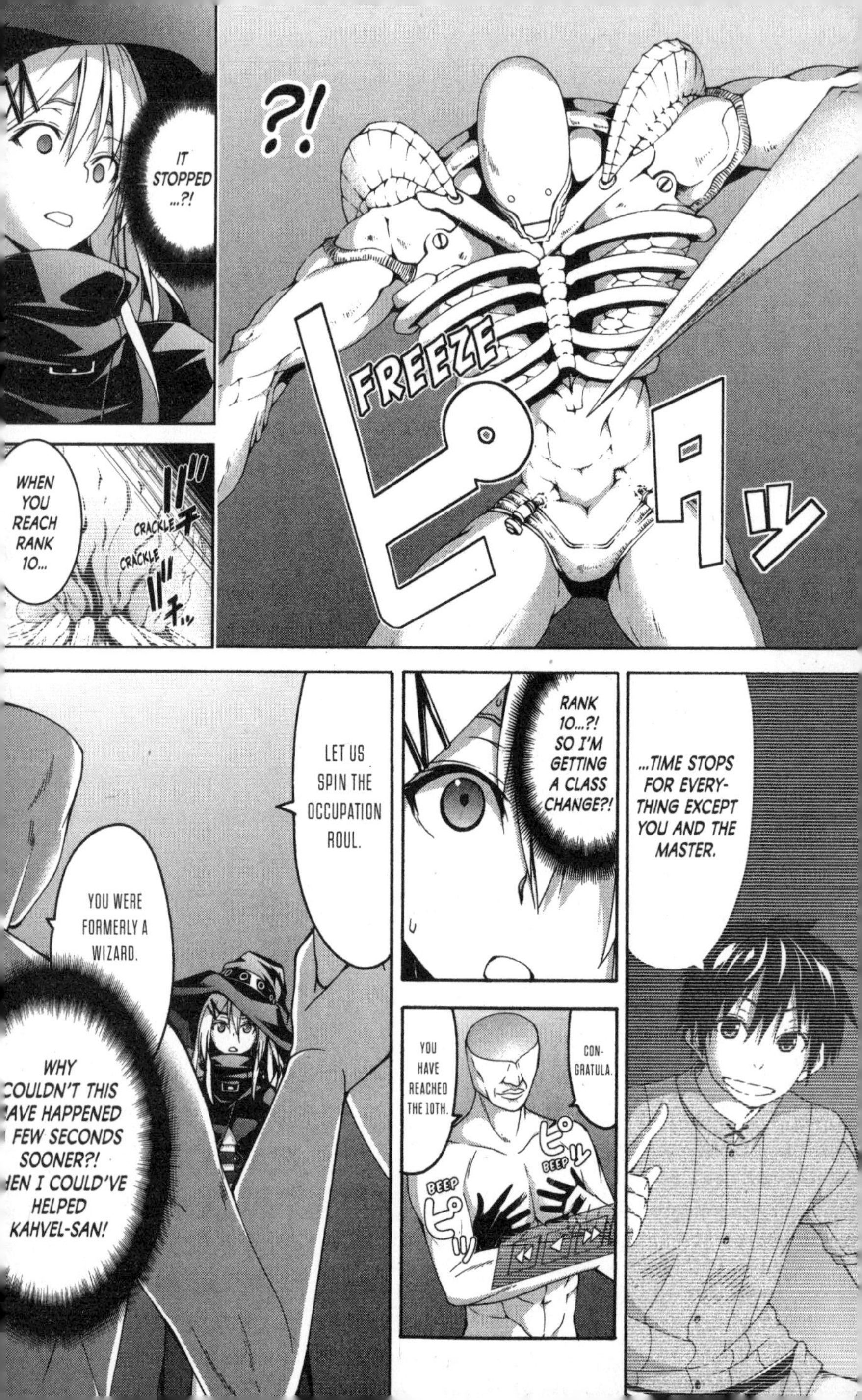
?!
FREEZE
IT STOPPED ...?!
WHEN YOU REACH RANK 10...
CRACKLE
CRACKLE
...TIME STOPS FOR EVERY-THING EXCEPT YOU AND THE MASTER.
RANK 10...?! SO I'M GETTING A CLASS CHANGE?!
CON-GRATULA.
YOU HAVE REACHED THE 10TH.
BEEP
BEEP
LET US SPIN THE OCCUPATION ROUL.
YOU WERE FORMERLY A WIZARD.
WHY COULDN'T THIS AVE HAPPENED FEW SECONDS SOONER?! HEN I COULD'VE HELPED KAHVEL-SAN!

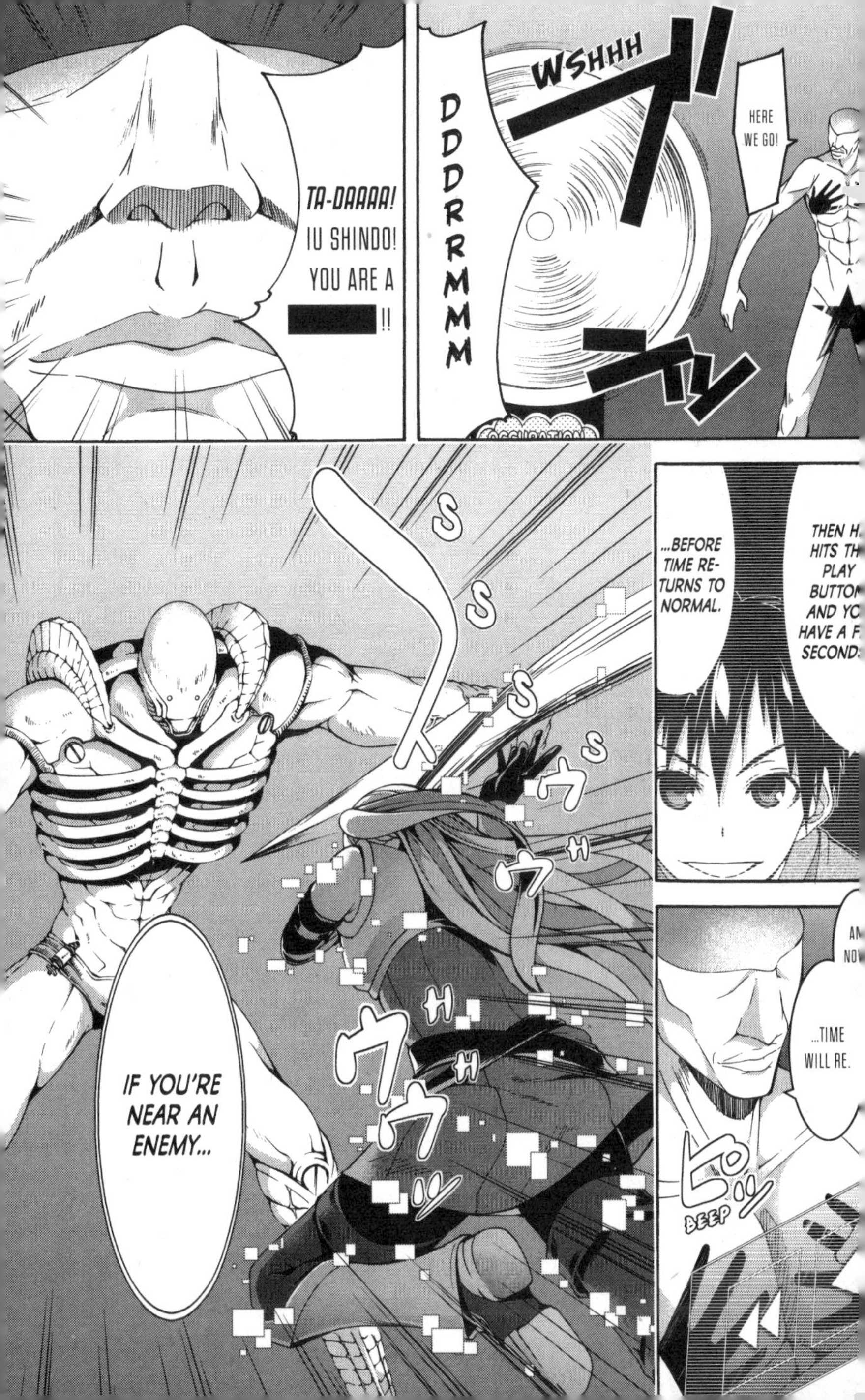
HERE WE GO!
WSHHH
DDDRRMMM
TA-DAAAA! IU SHINDO! YOU ARE A [redacted]!!
THEN H HITS TH PLAY BUTTO AND YO HAVE A F SECONDS
...BEFORE TIME RE-TURNS TO NORMAL.
AN NO
...TIME WILL RE.
BEEP
S
S
S
S
H
H
H
IF YOU'RE NEAR AN ENEMY...

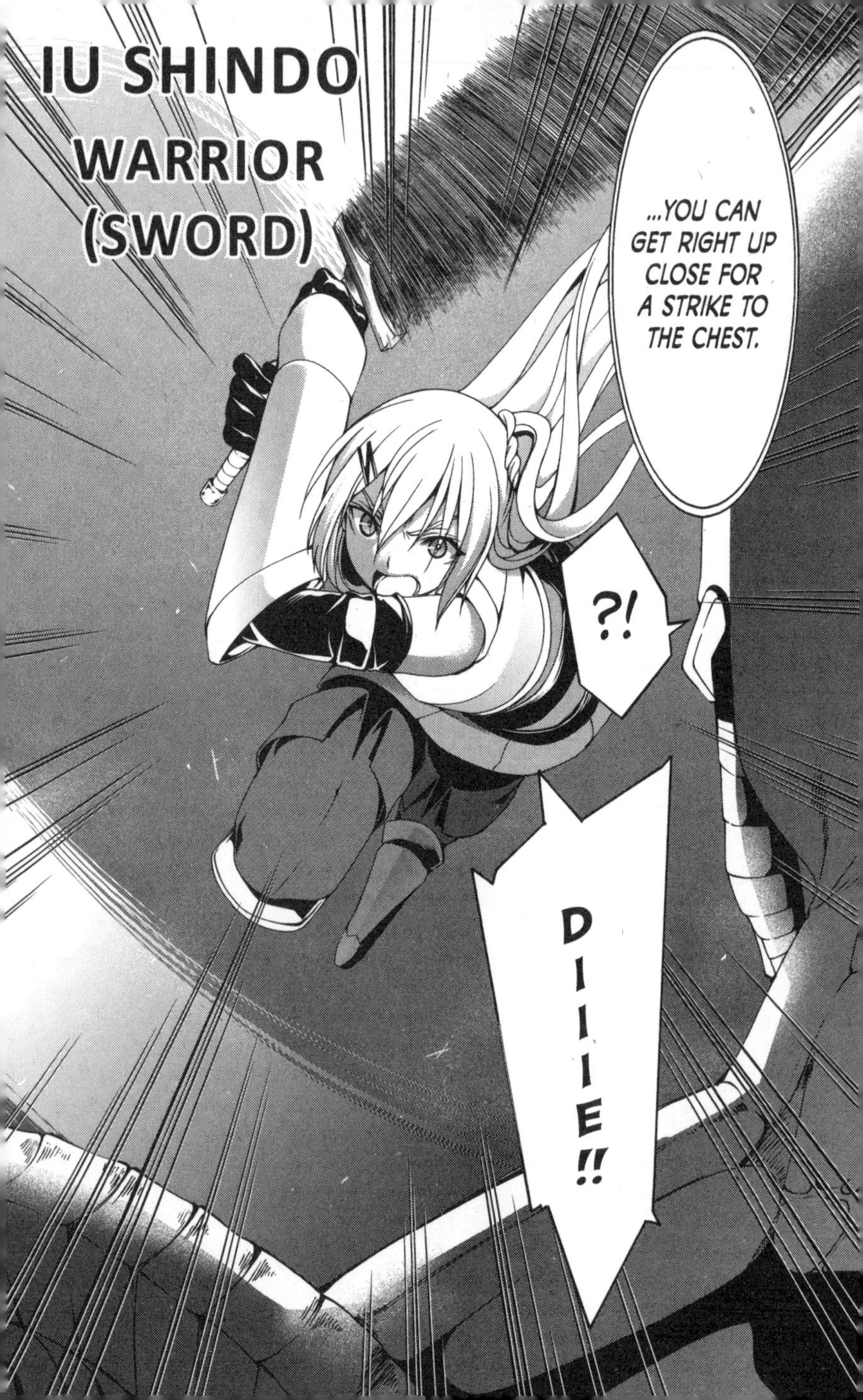
IU SHINDO
WARRIOR
(SWORD)
...YOU CAN GET RIGHT UP CLOSE FOR A STRIKE TO THE CHEST.
?!
DIIIE!!

*In many cases, there's information that the characters know about in the story that hasn't been mentioned yet, so I'll take this opportunity to share it here.

CLASS CHANGE

When one's rank reaches Rank 10, the Master shows up and spins the occupation roulette wheel again. As that is happening, time is stopped for everyone except the Master and the player undergoing the class change.

INHERITANCE OF SKILLS AND ITEMS

When one undergoes a class change, one's clothing will change to that of the new occupation, but the former occupation's weapons and outfit are stored in the Item Box and can be retrieved from it. Skills are also inherited and can continue to be employed. (An example of a hybrid outfit can be seen here. →)

RANK UP BONUS

In addition to the inheritance of weaponry, clothing, and skills, an item called the **"Rank Up Bonus" (RUB)** is added to the skill listing, enabling stats transfer. The value transferred is that of half of the stats (health, upper body, lower body, involuntary muscle, and strength) at Rank 10.

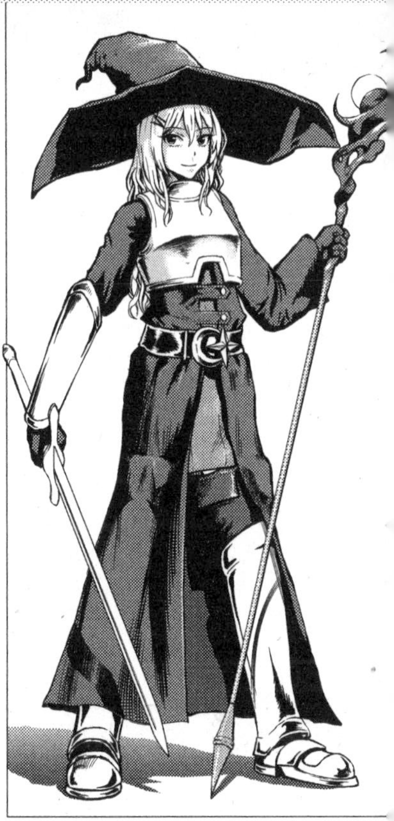

For every increase in rank, each stat increases by 1%. (Except when going from Rank 1 to 2, where they increase by 2%.) By the time a character levels up from Rank 1 to Rank 10, every one of their stats increases by 10%.

So far, the only Warrior class that has appeared in the story is Warrior (Sword), but all three types of Wizards (Heat, Wind, Creature) have appeared.

The Wizards' stats at Rank 1 are all 80%.

WIZARD (HEAT, WIND, CREATURE)			
RANK	1	2	10
HEALTH	80%	82%	90%
UPPER BODY	80%	82%	90%
LOWER BODY	80%	82%	90%
INVOLUNTARY MUSCLE	80%	82%	90%
STRENGTH	80%	82%	90%

So, the **RUB** of someone with the experience of being a Wizard is:

90%=-10%
-10%÷2=-5%

So, all stats are reduced by 5%. At the end of Chapter 7, Iu Shindo became a Warrior (Sword) who is 5% weaker than usual, but can use wind magic.

IU SHINDO	WARRIOR (SWD)	RANK 1	
	BASE VALUE	RUB	TOTAL VALUE
HEALTH	220%	-5%	215%
UPPER BODY	190%	-5%	185%
LOWER BODY	180%	-5%	175%
INVOLUNTARY MUSCLE	170%	-5%	165%
STRENGTH	190%	-5%	185%

Illustration and Text: Naoki Yamaka

RANK

The difficulty of increasing in rank varies depending on the class. From the easiest to the most difficult, the order goes:

OTHER (5 MISC. TYPES) → WARRIOR → WIZARD

Thieves and Hunters have yet to appear, so they're still unknown.

OCCUPATION ROULETTE DETAILS (EARLY VERSION)		
WARRIOR (SWORD)	20%	8/40
WARRIOR (SPEAR)	12.5%	5/40
WARRIOR (AX)	12.5%	5/40
WIZARD (HEAT)	12.5%	5/40
WIZARD (WIND)	12.5%	5/40
WIZARD (CREATURE)	12.5%	5/40
THIEF	7.5%	3/40
HUNTER	7.5%	3/40
OTHER (5 MISC. TYPES)	0.5% EACH	1/200
	2.5% TOTAL	1/40

STATS

Health = One's stamina. Think of it as pertaining to one's lung capacity, blood circulation efficiency, and metabolic rate.

Upper Body = One's voluntary muscle strength from the waist up. Changes in it aren't always visually evident.

Lower Body = One's voluntary muscle strength from the waist down.

Involuntary Muscle = This pertains to muscles that function without a person's conscious volition. This includes the heart, other internal organs, etc.

Strength = The power to counter all outside forces that could damage one's health. Besides defensive strength against physical attacks, it's the strength to cope with temperature changes, oxygen deprivation, electricity, poison, sickness, and more. The first four stats have base values determined by the player's class, but strength is determined by calculating the average of the other four stats. It can be rounded off when it appears in the display.

WIZARDS' STATS

MP = A value recorded separately from the above five stats. One gains it for the first time upon becoming a Wizard. It's like the fuel needed for casting a spell. There's the current value and the maximum value, which are like the remaining amount and the maximum fuel tank capacity, respectively.

Magic (Heat, Wind, Creature) = The amount of fuel needed to cast each kind of spell. MP is shared between all spells, but magic has individual values by type. When a spell is cast, the MP consumed is determined by multiplying the force, duration, range, and proximity (the further away from the target the wielder is, the more MP is consumed).

MP CONSUMED = FORCE × DURATION × RANGE × DISTANCE FROM TARGET ÷ MAGIC (OF EACH TYPE)

MP × MAGIC ≥ FORCE × DURATION × RANGE × DISTANCE

There were a few scenes where just using magic for a second completely drained a character's MP. That's because they used it all up by applying the highest possible force for the longest possible duration. At their current magic and MP levels, they don't have the power to do any real damage, though.

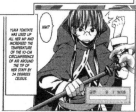

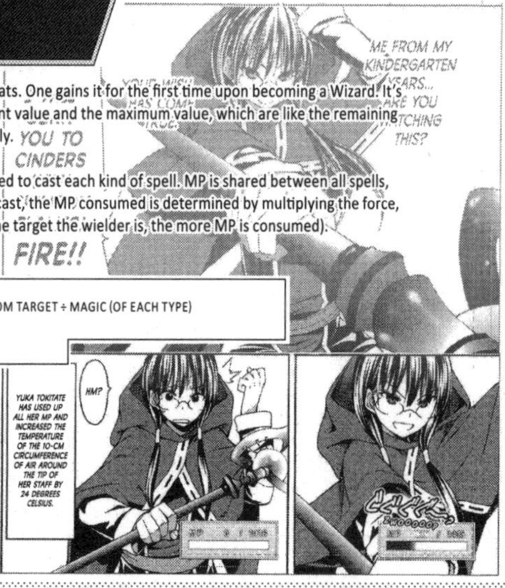

YOU TO CINDERS
FIRE!!
HM?
YUKA TOKITATE HAS USED UP ALL HER MP AND INCREASED THE TEMPERATURE OF THE 10-CM CIRCUMFERENCE OF AIR AROUND THE TIP OF HER STAFF BY 24 DEGREES CELSIUS.

Text: Naoki Yamakawa

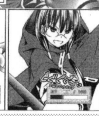

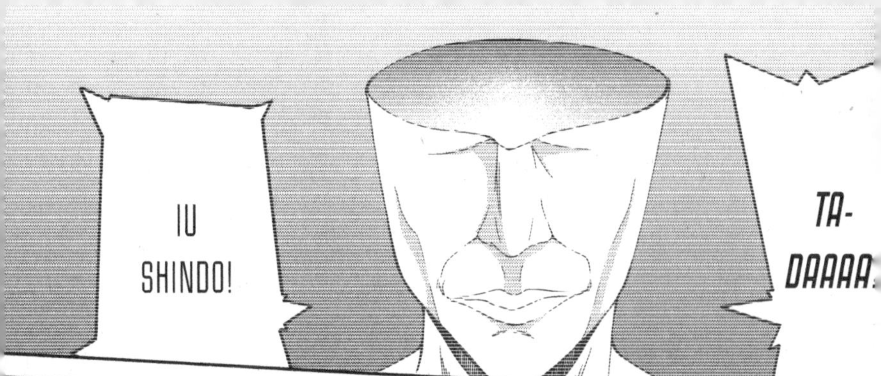
TA-
DAAAA.
IU
SHINDO!

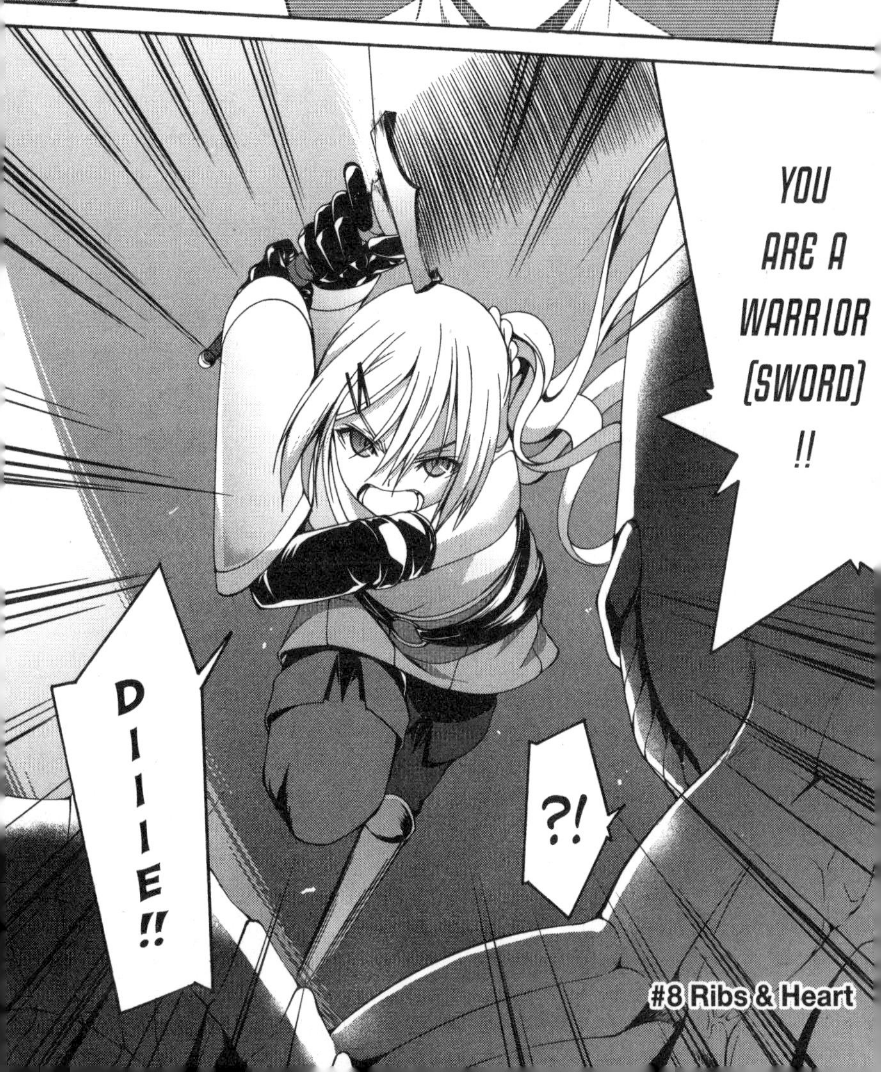
YOU
ARE A
WARRIOR
(SWORD)
!!
?!
DIIIE!!
#8 Ribs & Heart

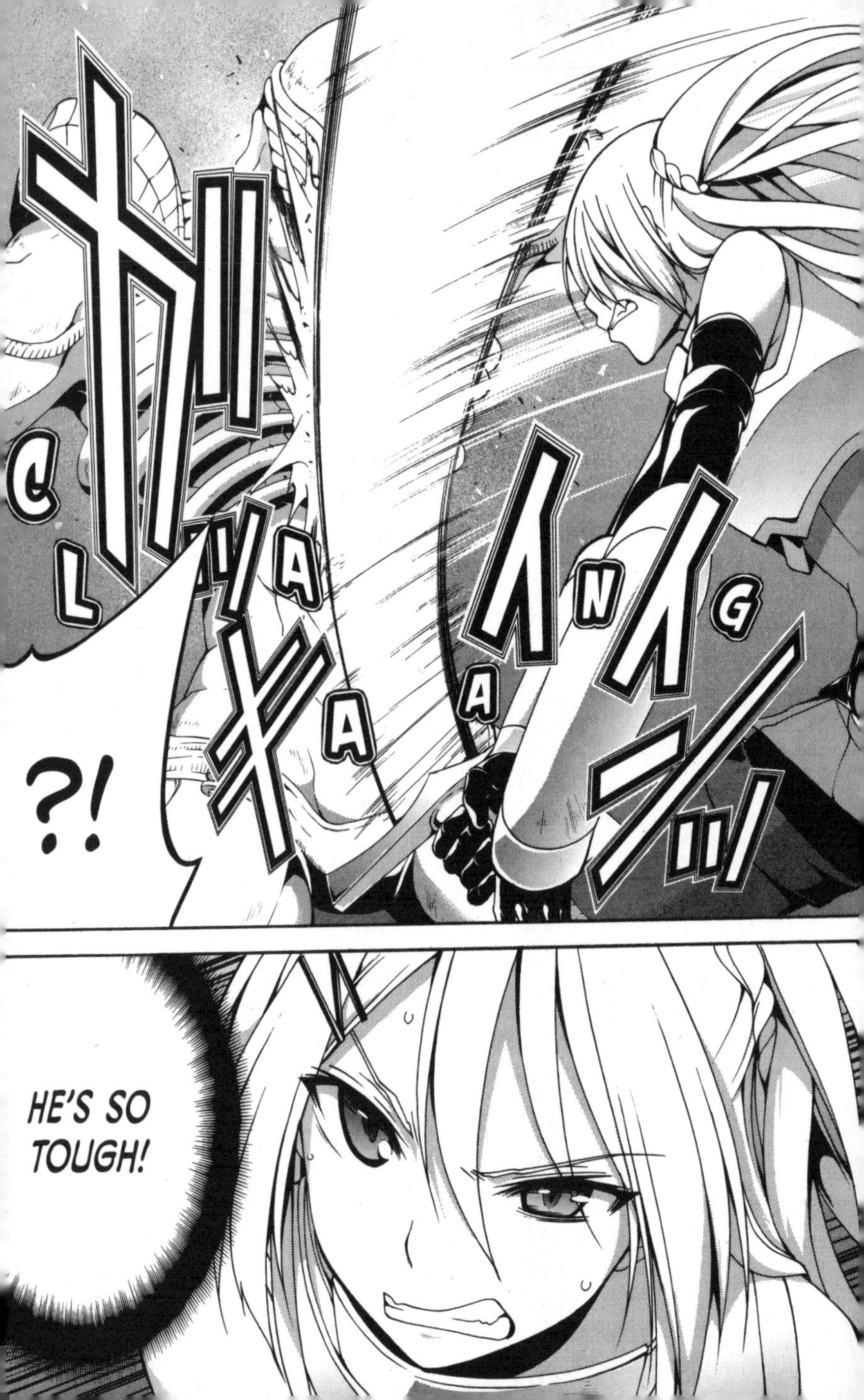
ガキィン
CLAAAANG
?!
HE'S SO TOUGH!

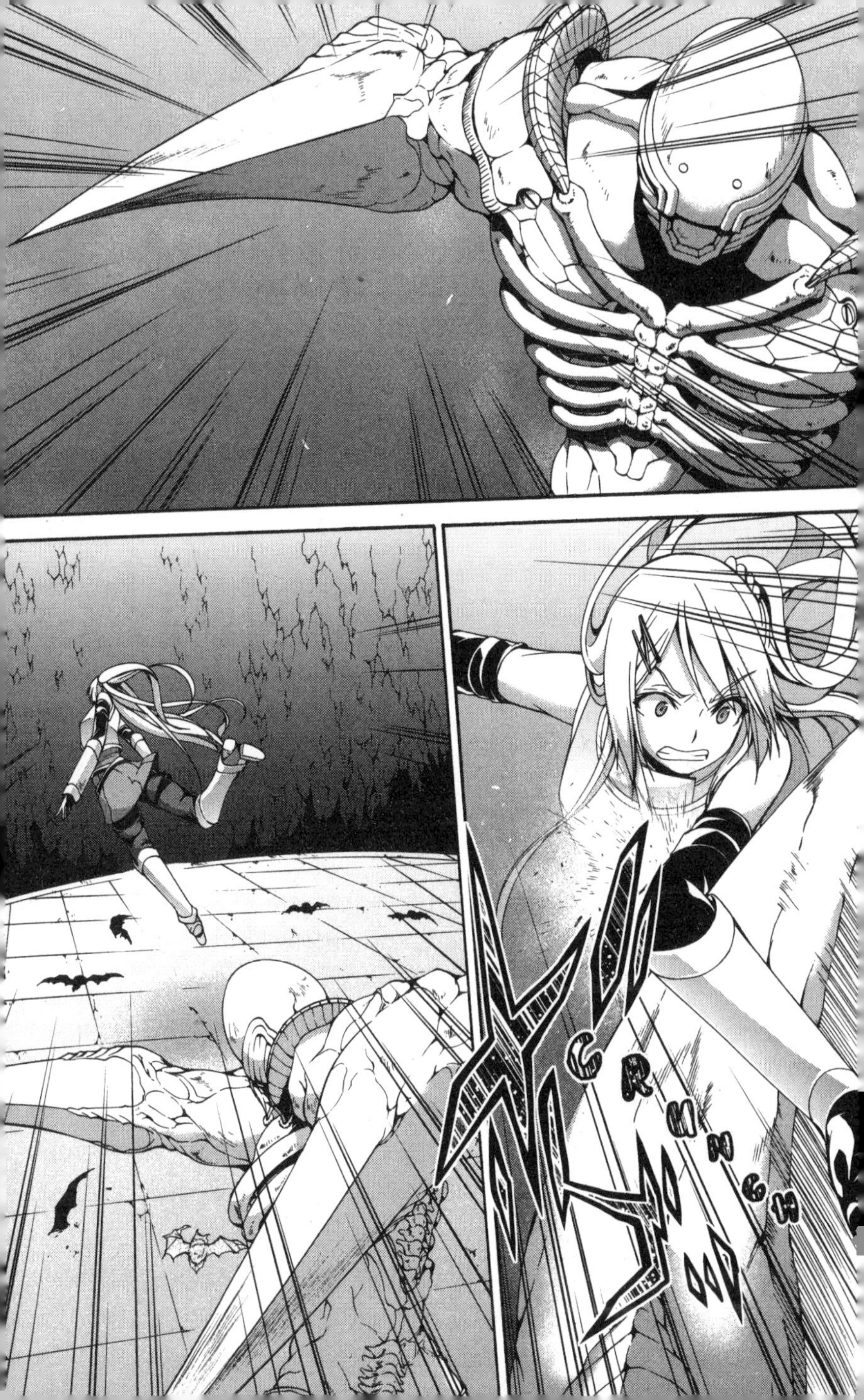
CRUNCH

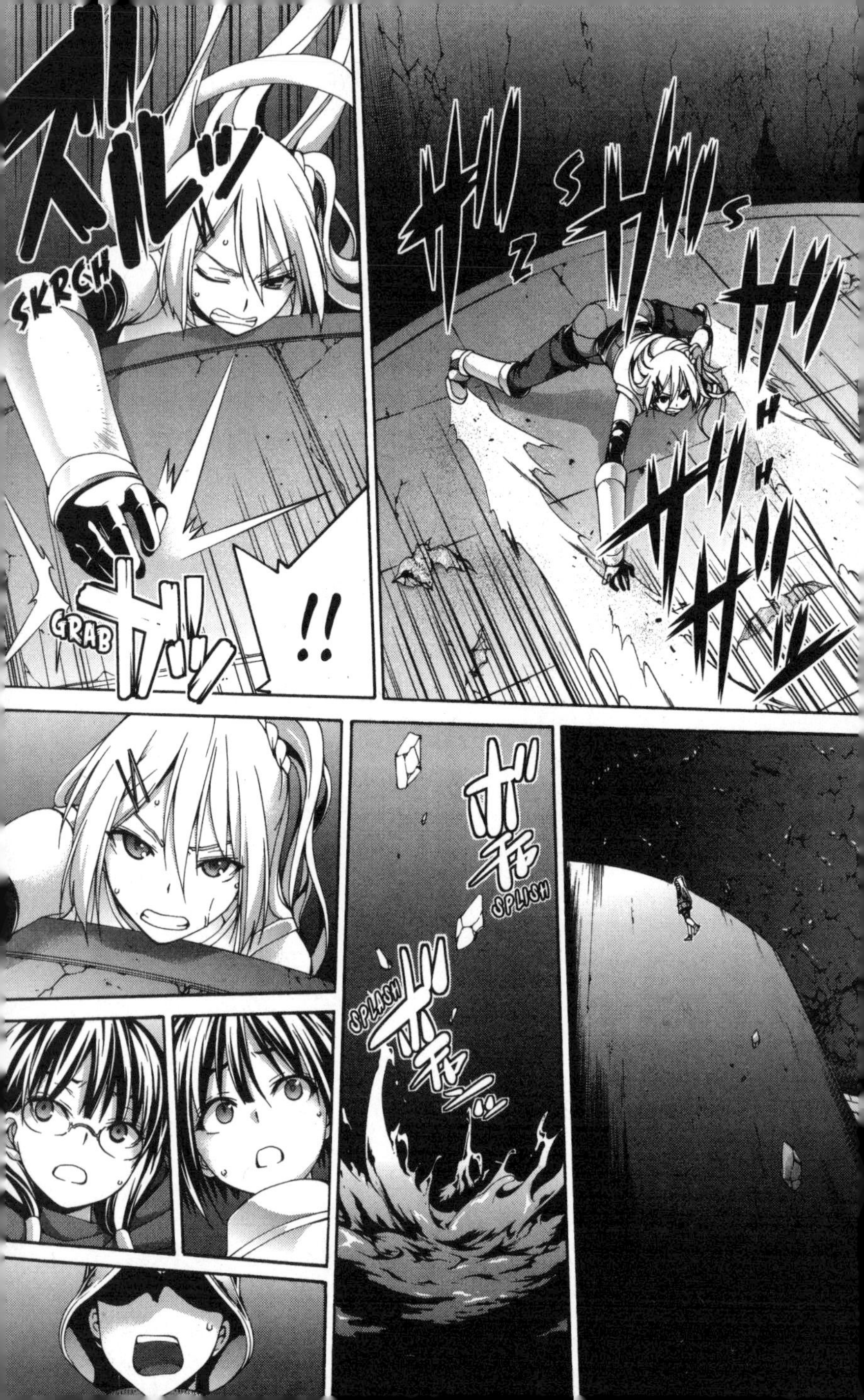
ザ S Z ザ S ザ H ザ H ザ ザ
ズルッ
SKRCH
ガッ
GRAB
!!
ザバ
SPLISH
ザバーッ
SPLASH

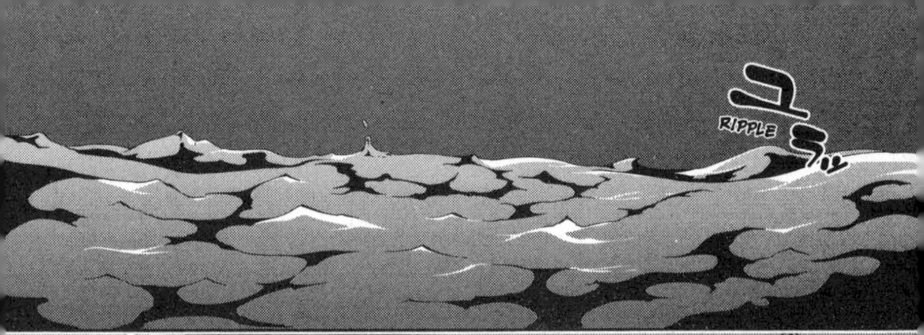
ユラッ
RIPPLE

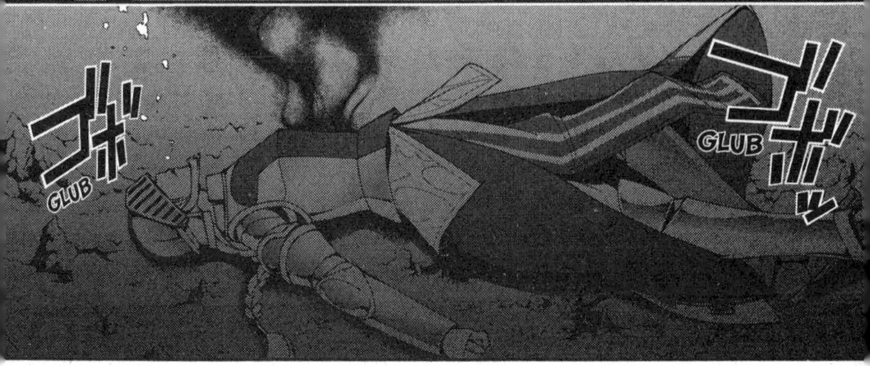
ゴボッ
GLUB
GLUB

FIVE MINUTES EARLIER...

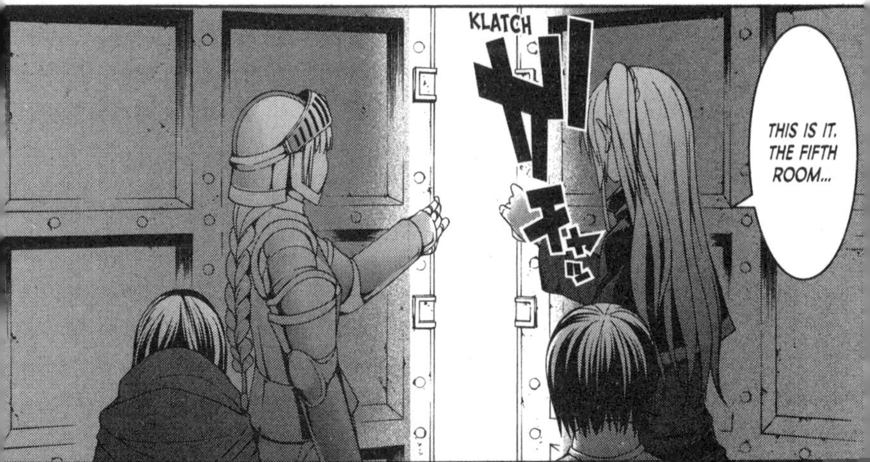
THIS IS IT. THE FIFTH ROOM...
ガチャッ
KLATCH

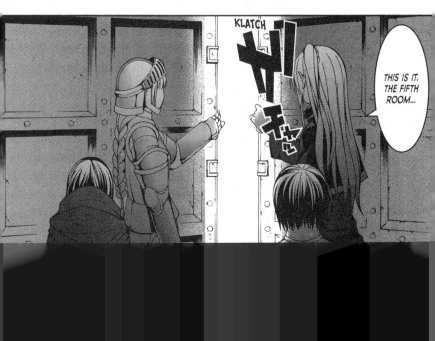

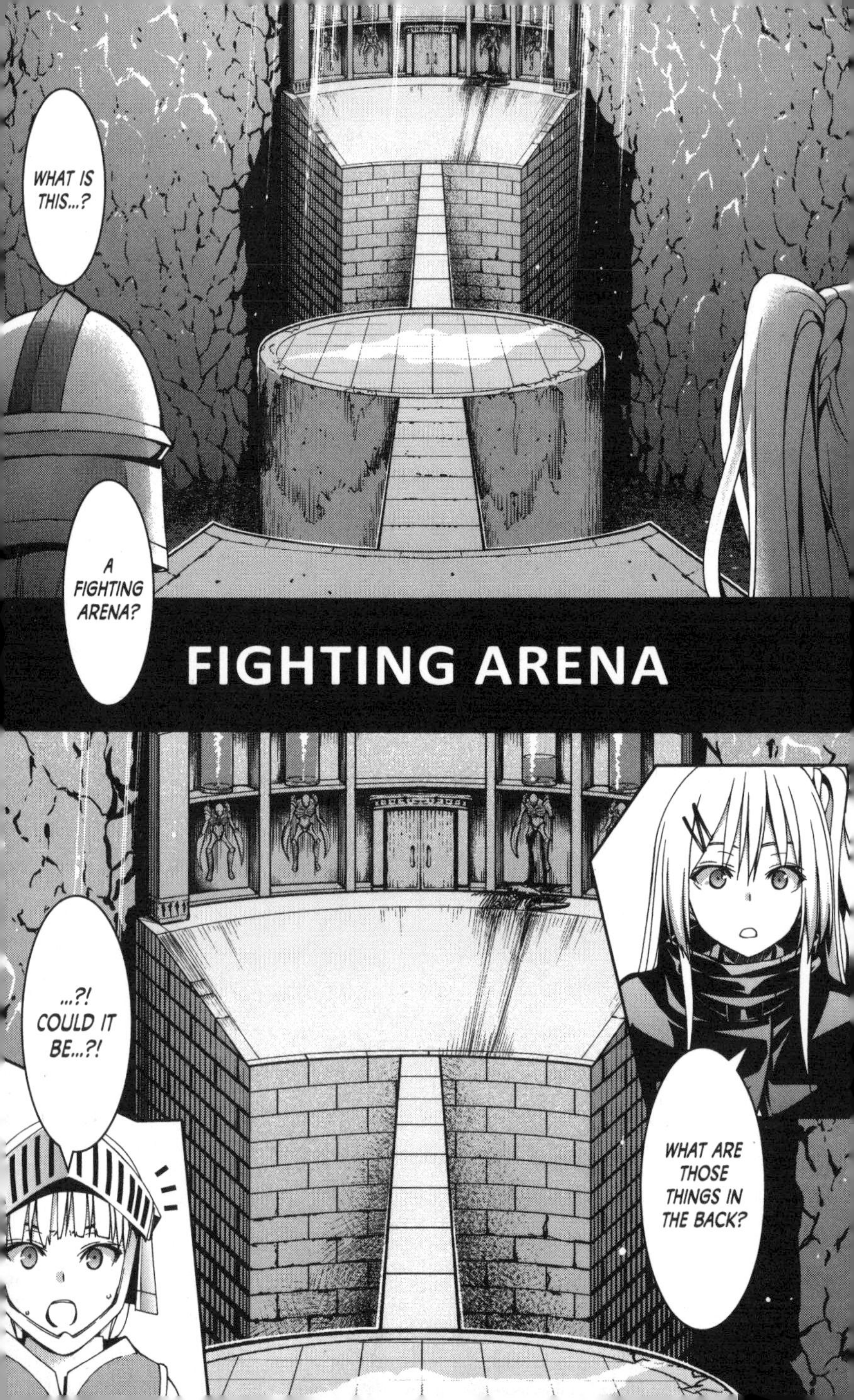
WHAT IS THIS...?
A FIGHTING ARENA?
FIGHTING ARENA
WHAT ARE THOSE THINGS IN THE BACK?
...?! COULD IT BE...?!

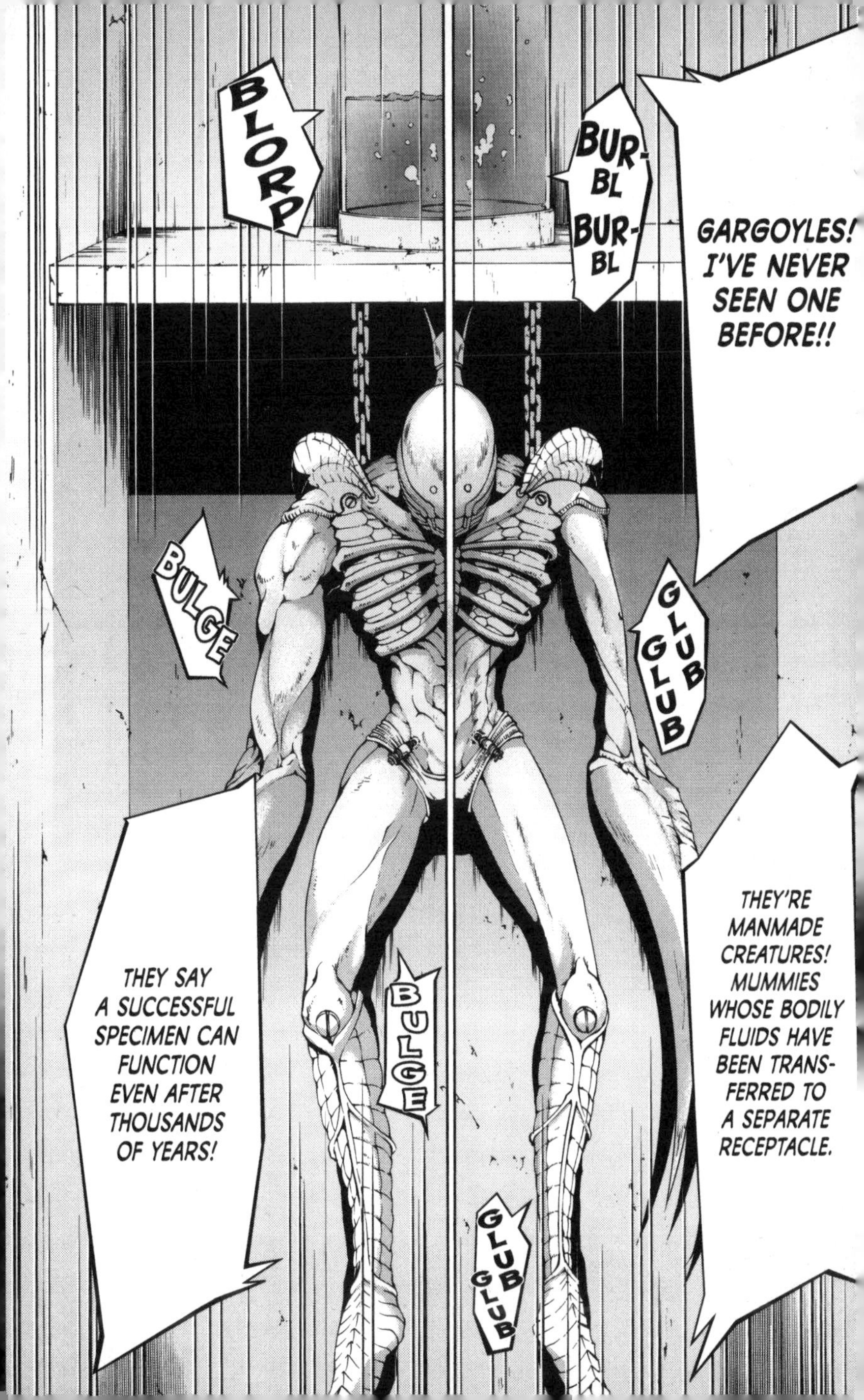
GARGOYLES! I'VE NEVER SEEN ONE BEFORE!!
BUR-BL BUR-BL
BLORP
GLUB GLUB
BULGE
THEY'RE MANMADE CREATURES! MUMMIES WHOSE BODILY FLUIDS HAVE BEEN TRANS-FERRED TO A SEPARATE RECEPTACLE.
THEY SAY A SUCCESSFUL SPECIMEN CAN FUNCTION EVEN AFTER THOUSANDS OF YEARS!
BULGE
GLUB GLUB

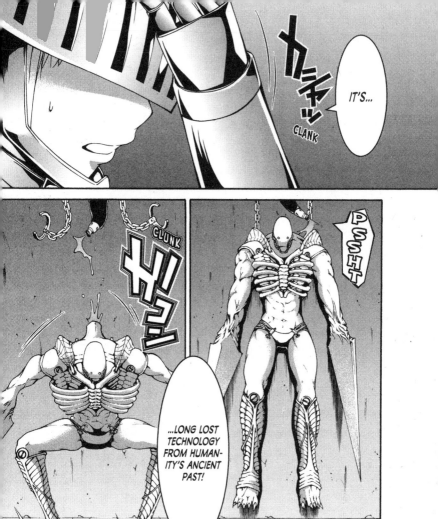

IT'S...

CLANK

CLUNK

PSSHT

...LONG LOST TECHNOLOGY FROM HUMAN-ITY'S ANCIENT PAST!

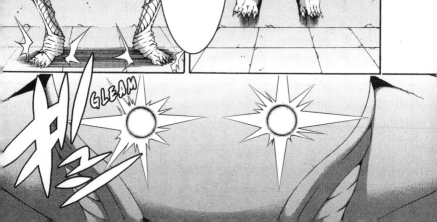

GLEAM

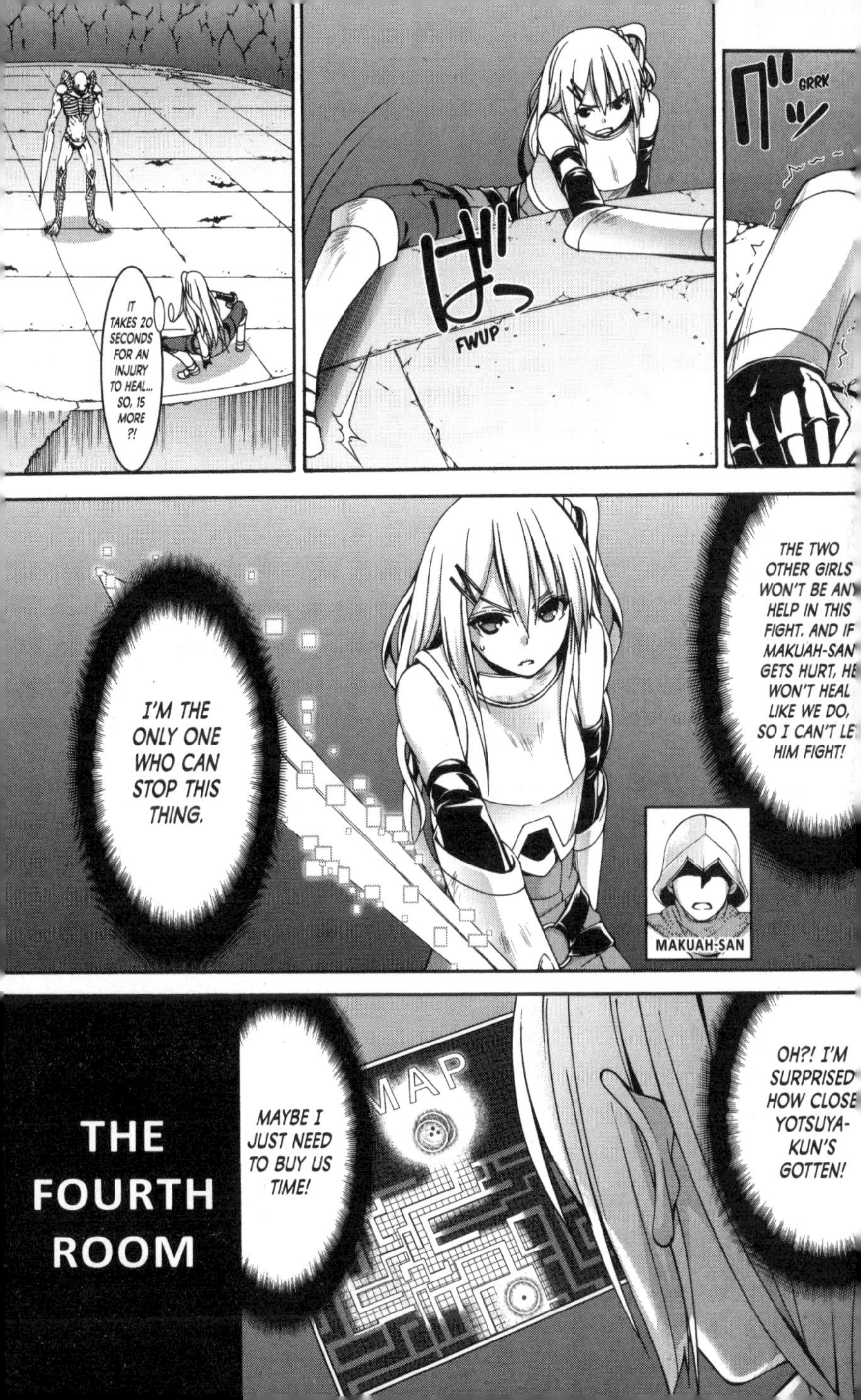
GRRK
FWUP
IT TAKES 20 SECONDS FOR AN INJURY TO HEAL... SO, 15 MORE ?!
THE TWO OTHER GIRLS WON'T BE ANY HELP IN THIS FIGHT. AND IF MAKUAH-SAN GETS HURT, HE WON'T HEAL LIKE WE DO, SO I CAN'T LET HIM FIGHT!
MAKUAH-SAN
I'M THE ONLY ONE WHO CAN STOP THIS THING.
OH?! I'M SURPRISED HOW CLOSE YOTSUYA-KUN'S GOTTEN!
MAP
MAYBE I JUST NEED TO BUY US TIME!
THE FOURTH ROOM

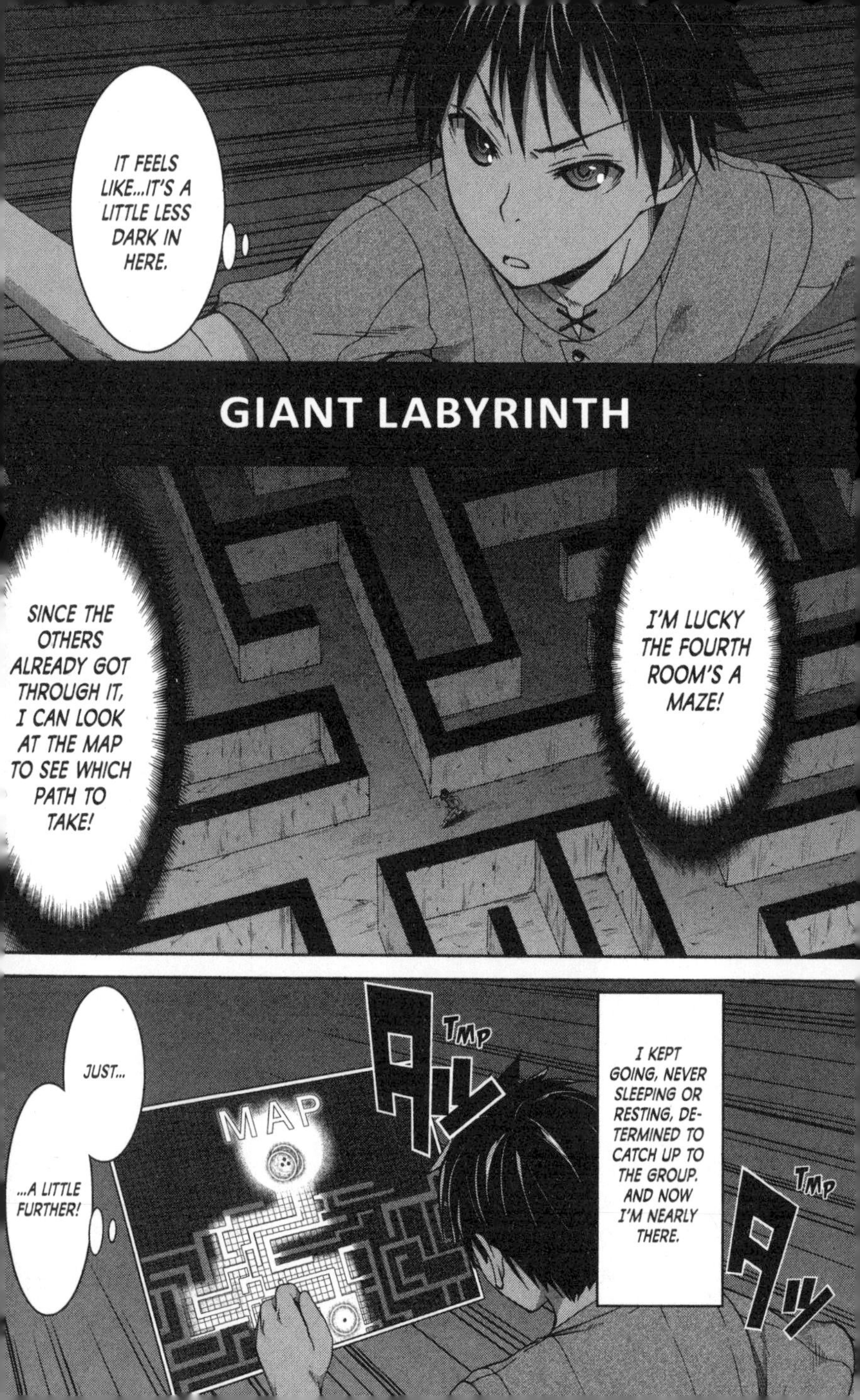
IT FEELS LIKE...IT'S A LITTLE LESS DARK IN HERE.
GIANT LABYRINTH
I'M LUCKY THE FOURTH ROOM'S A MAZE!
SINCE THE OTHERS ALREADY GOT THROUGH IT, I CAN LOOK AT THE MAP TO SEE WHICH PATH TO TAKE!
I KEPT GOING, NEVER SLEEPING OR RESTING, DE-TERMINED TO CATCH UP TO THE GROUP. AND NOW I'M NEARLY THERE.
TMP
TMP
MAP
JUST...
...A LITTLE FURTHER!

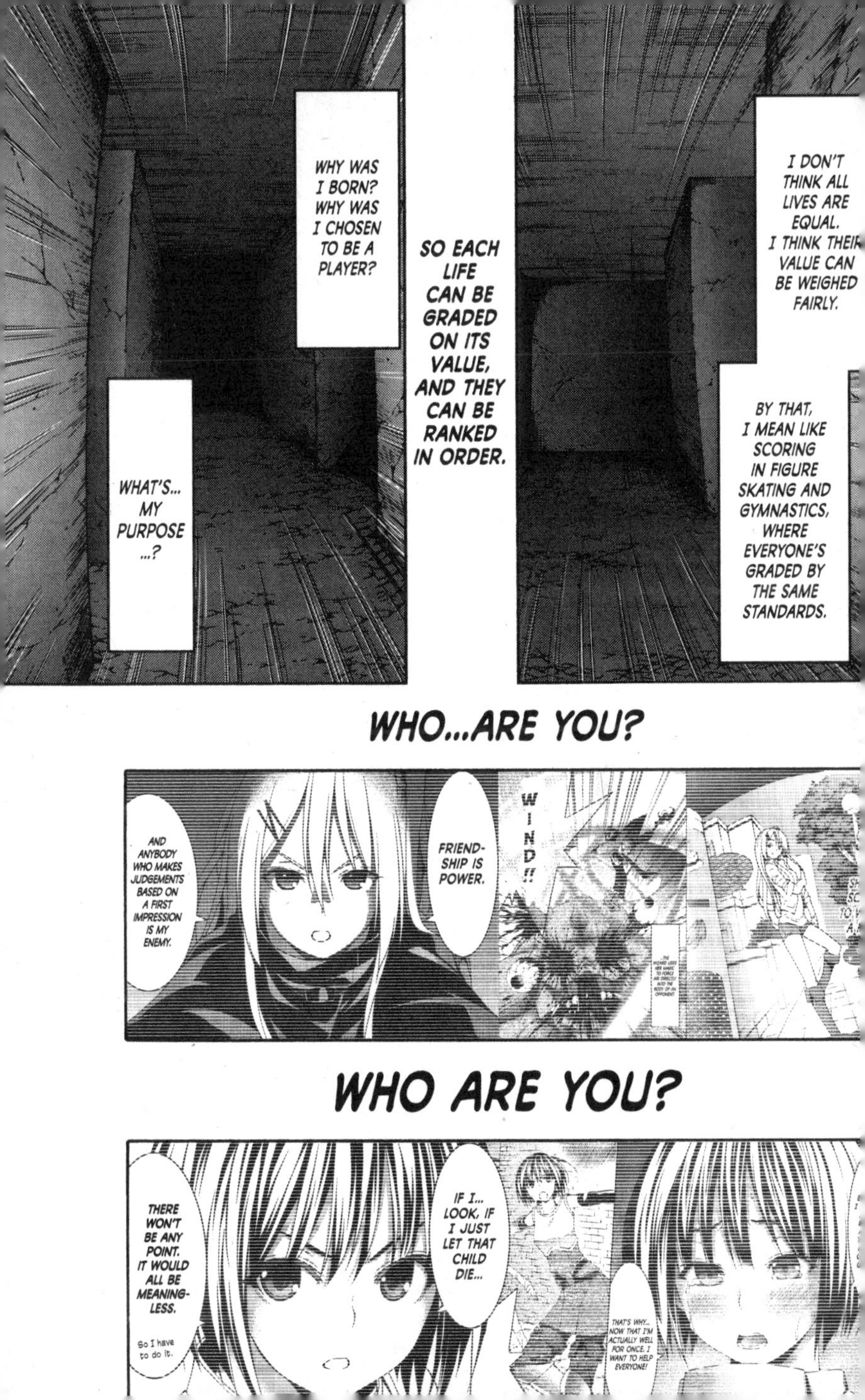
I DON'T THINK ALL LIVES ARE EQUAL. I THINK THEIR VALUE CAN BE WEIGHED FAIRLY.
BY THAT, I MEAN LIKE SCORING IN FIGURE SKATING AND GYMNASTICS, WHERE EVERYONE'S GRADED BY THE SAME STANDARDS.
SO EACH LIFE CAN BE GRADED ON ITS VALUE, AND THEY CAN BE RANKED IN ORDER.
WHY WAS I BORN? WHY WAS I CHOSEN TO BE A PLAYER?
WHAT'S... MY PURPOSE ...?
WHO...ARE YOU?
...THE WIZARD USES HER MAGIC TO FORCE AIR DIRECTLY INTO THE BODY OF AN OPPONENT.
WIND!!
FRIEND-SHIP IS POWER.
AND ANYBODY WHO MAKES JUDGEMENTS BASED ON A FIRST IMPRESSION IS MY ENEMY.
WHO ARE YOU?
THAT'S WHY... NOW THAT I'M ACTUALLY WELL FOR ONCE, I WANT TO HELP EVERYONE!
IF I... LOOK, IF I JUST LET THAT CHILD DIE...
THERE WON'T BE ANY POINT. IT WOULD ALL BE MEANING-LESS.
So I have to do it.

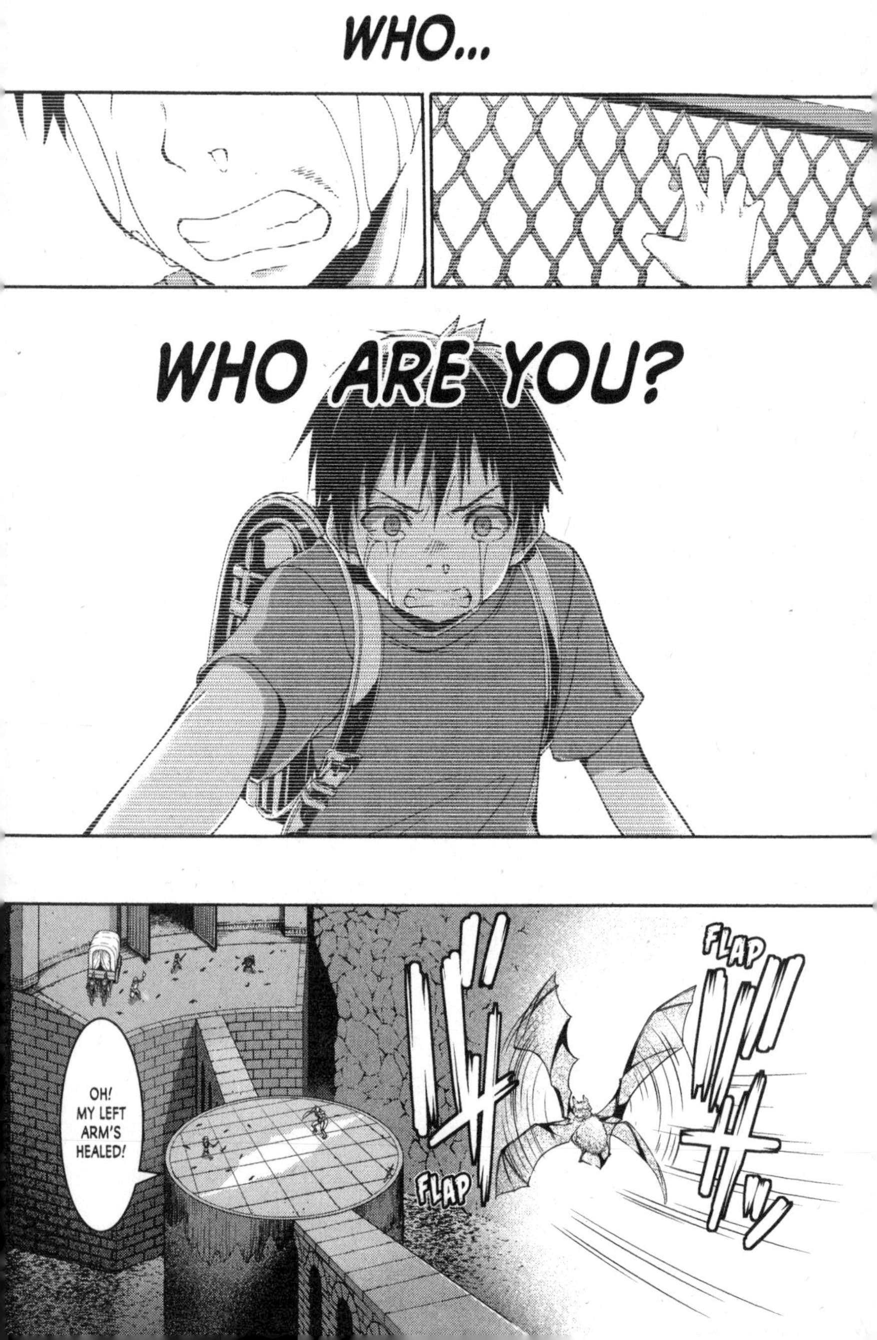
WHO...
WHO ARE YOU?
FLAP
OH! MY LEFT ARM'S HEALED!
FLAP

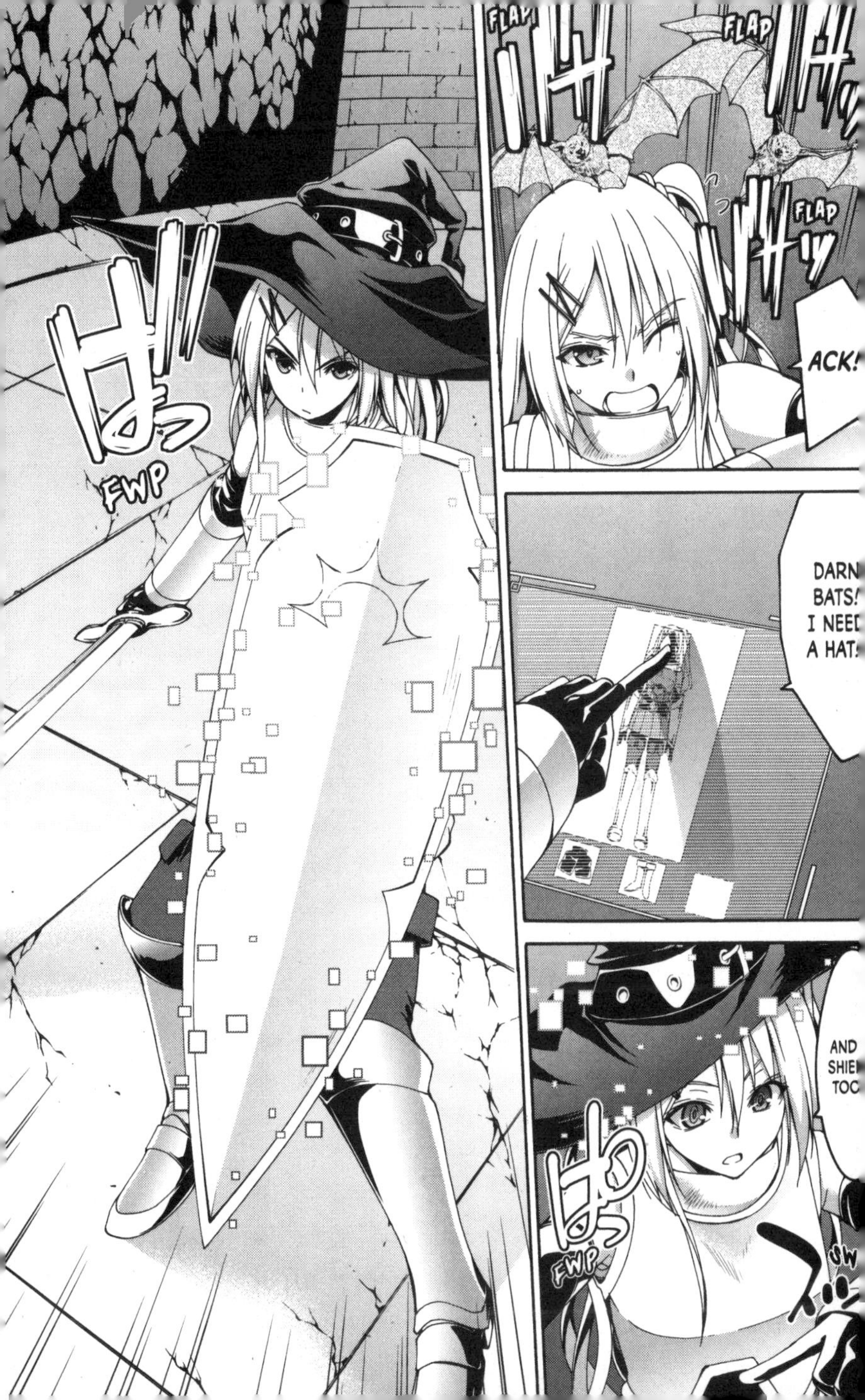
FLAP
FLAP
FLAP
ACK!
DARN BATS! I NEED A HAT!
AND SHIEL TOO
FWP
FWP

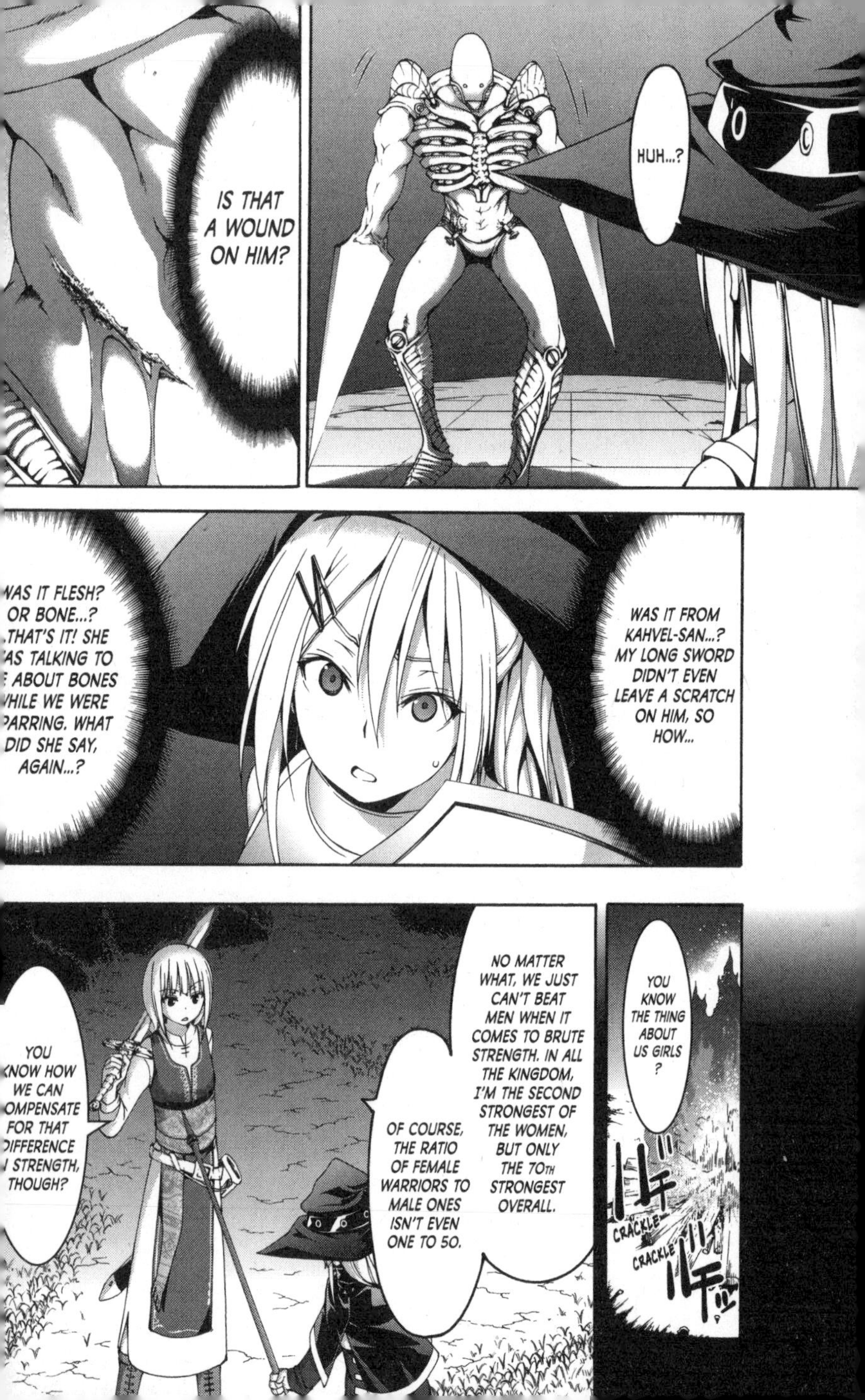
HUH...?
IS THAT A WOUND ON HIM?
WAS IT FROM KAHVEL-SAN...? MY LONG SWORD DIDN'T EVEN LEAVE A SCRATCH ON HIM, SO HOW...
VAS IT FLESH? OR BONE...? .THAT'S IT! SHE 'AS TALKING TO E ABOUT BONES VHILE WE WERE PARRING. WHAT DID SHE SAY, AGAIN...?
YOU KNOW THE THING ABOUT US GIRLS ?
CRACKLE
CRACKLE
NO MATTER WHAT, WE JUST CAN'T BEAT MEN WHEN IT COMES TO BRUTE STRENGTH. IN ALL THE KINGDOM, I'M THE SECOND STRONGEST OF THE WOMEN, BUT ONLY THE 70TH STRONGEST OVERALL.
OF COURSE, THE RATIO OF FEMALE WARRIORS TO MALE ONES ISN'T EVEN ONE TO 50.
YOU KNOW HOW WE CAN OMPENSATE FOR THAT DIFFERENCE STRENGTH, THOUGH?

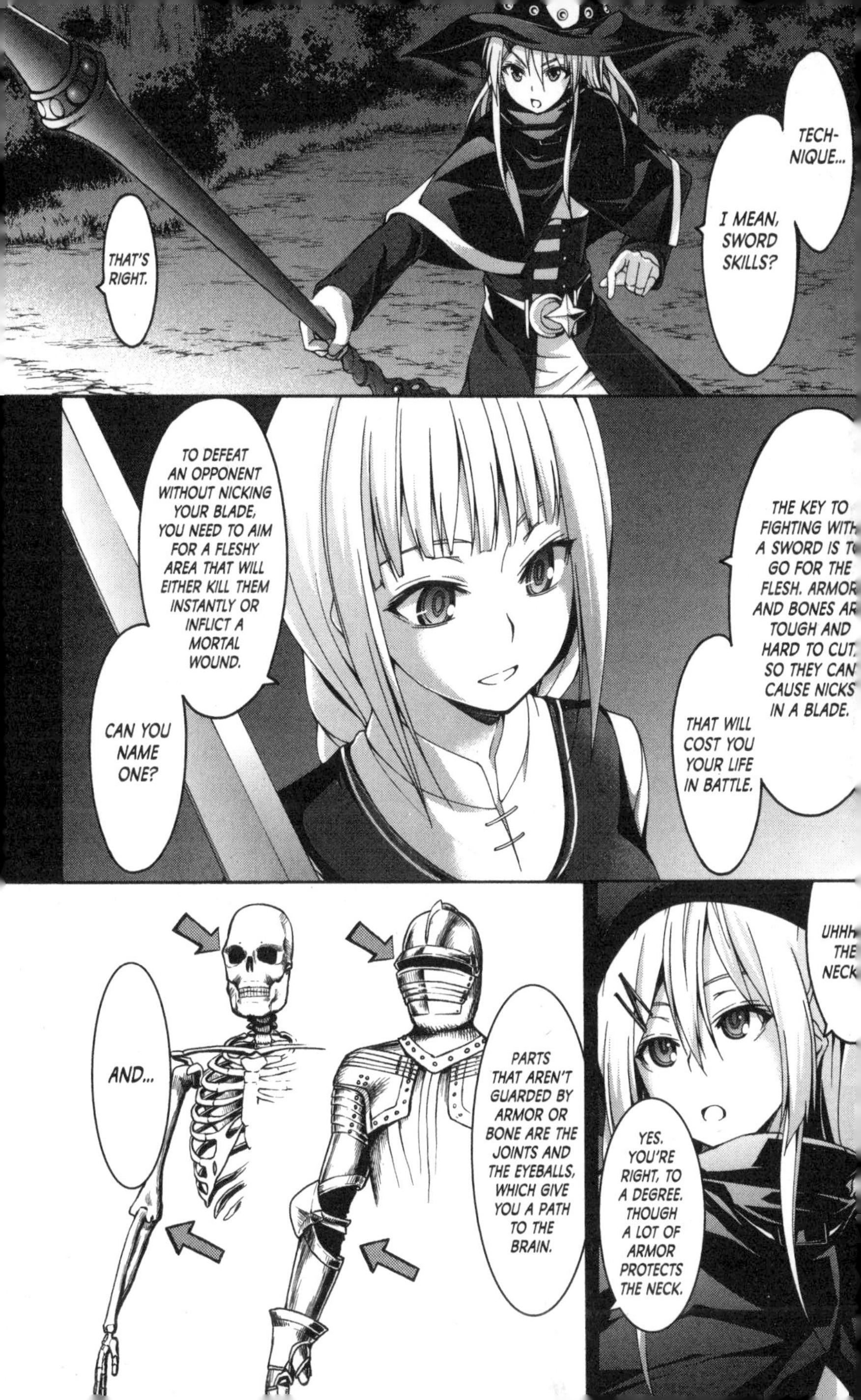
TECH-NIQUE...
I MEAN, SWORD SKILLS?
THAT'S RIGHT.
THE KEY TO FIGHTING WITH A SWORD IS T GO FOR THE FLESH. ARMOR AND BONES AR TOUGH AND HARD TO CUT, SO THEY CAN CAUSE NICKS IN A BLADE.
THAT WILL COST YOU YOUR LIFE IN BATTLE.
TO DEFEAT AN OPPONENT WITHOUT NICKING YOUR BLADE, YOU NEED TO AIM FOR A FLESHY AREA THAT WILL EITHER KILL THEM INSTANTLY OR INFLICT A MORTAL WOUND.
CAN YOU NAME ONE?
UHHH THE NECK
YES. YOU'RE RIGHT, TO A DEGREE. THOUGH A LOT OF ARMOR PROTECTS THE NECK.
PARTS THAT AREN'T GUARDED BY ARMOR OR BONE ARE THE JOINTS AND THE EYEBALLS, WHICH GIVE YOU A PATH TO THE BRAIN.
AND...

THE HEART.
HUH? BUT THE HEART...
THAT'S RIGHT. AT FIRST GLANCE, IT APPEARS TO BE PROTECTED BY BOTH ARMOR AND BONE.
SO YOU HAVE TO BYPASS THOSE AND STAB FROM ABOVE OR BELOW.
FROM ABOVE, YOU GO FROM HERE DOWN.
FROM BELOW, YOU GO FROM HERE UP.
AS LONG AS YOUR OPPONENT ISN'T WEARING A FULL SUIT OF ARMOR, THERE'S USUALLY A SEAM YOU CAN SLIP THROUGH.

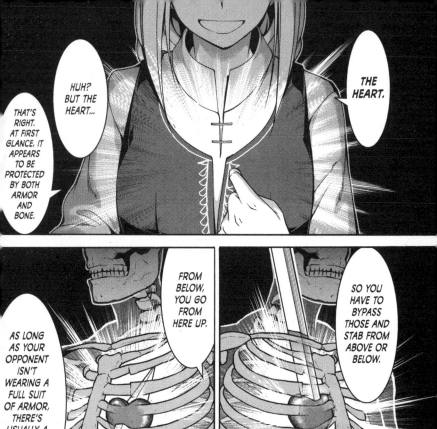

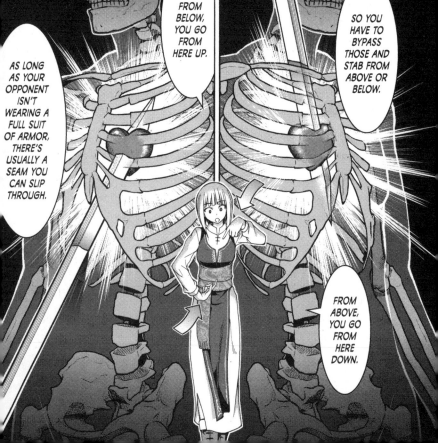

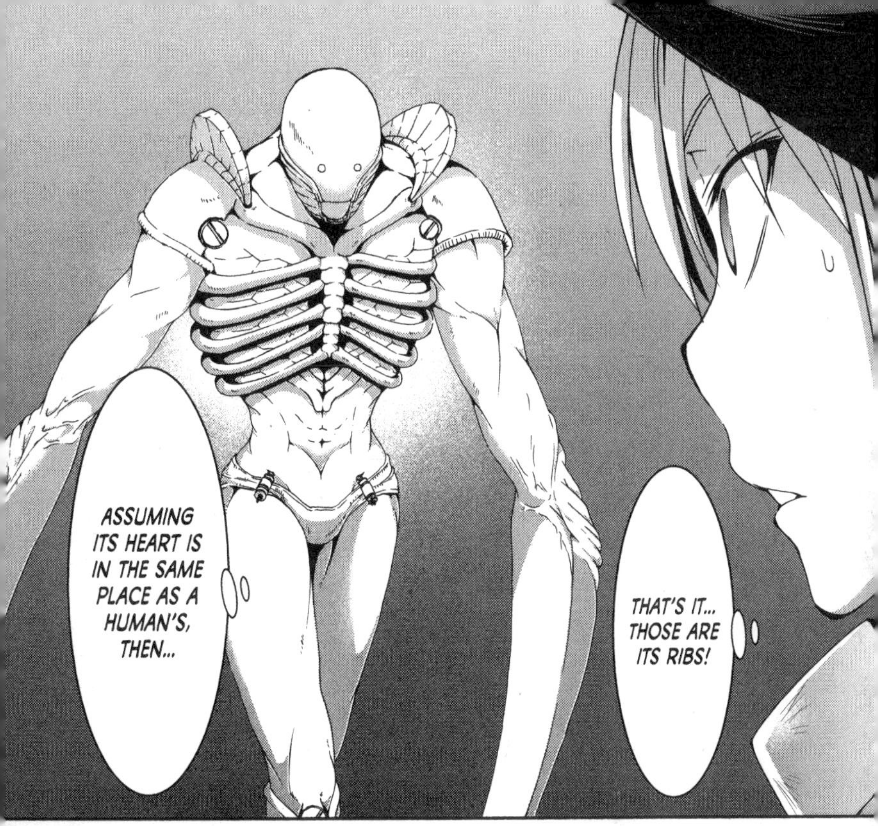
THAT'S IT... THOSE ARE ITS RIBS!
ASSUMING ITS HEART IS IN THE SAME PLACE AS A HUMAN'S, THEN...
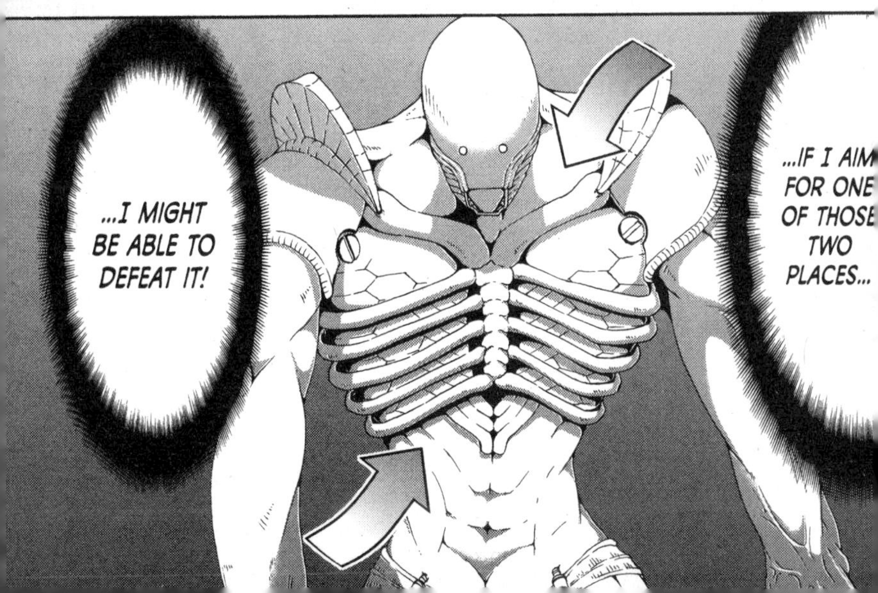
...IF I AIM FOR ONE OF THOSE TWO PLACES...
...I MIGHT BE ABLE TO DEFEAT IT!

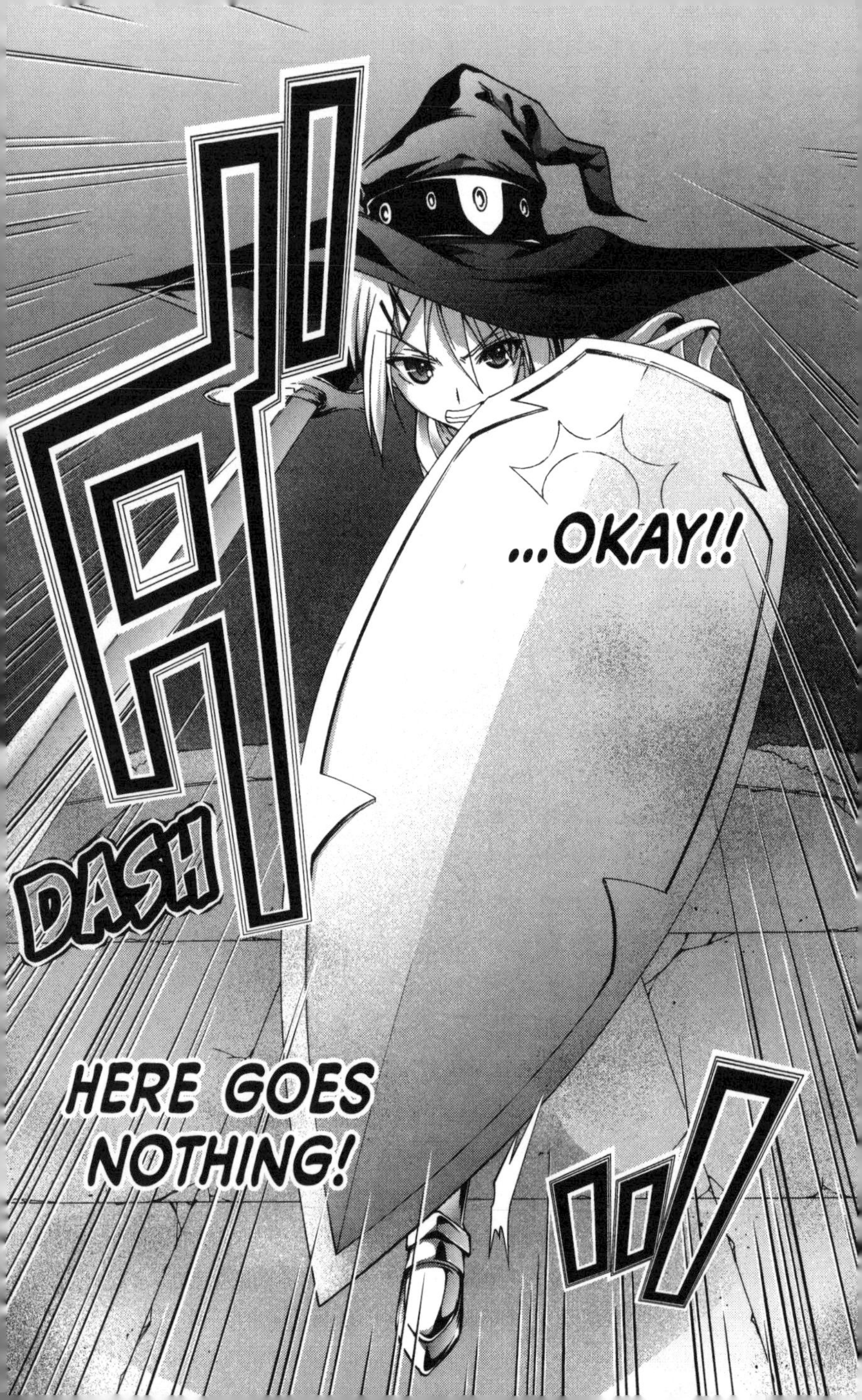
...OKAY!!
DASH
HERE GOES NOTHING!

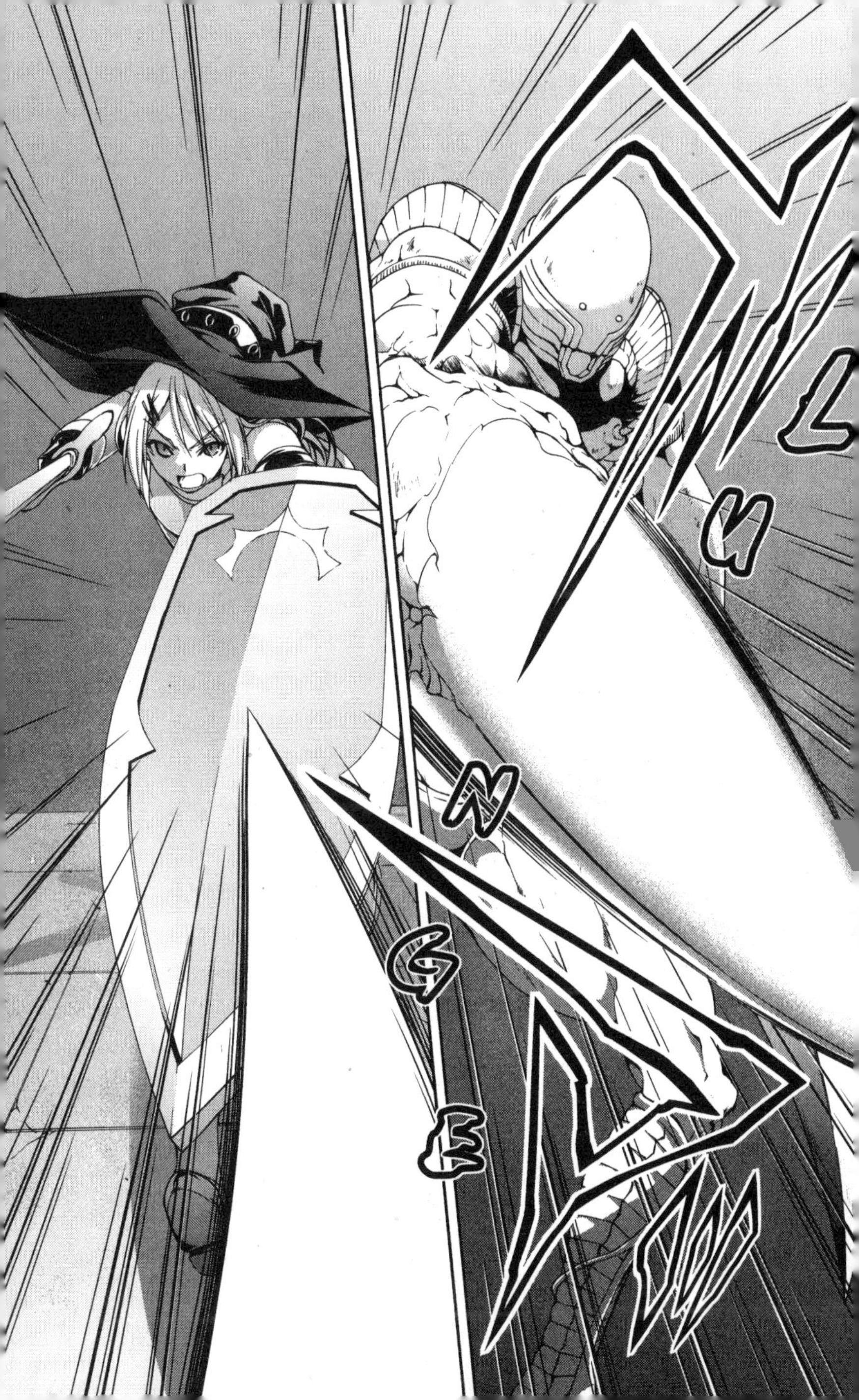
LUNGE

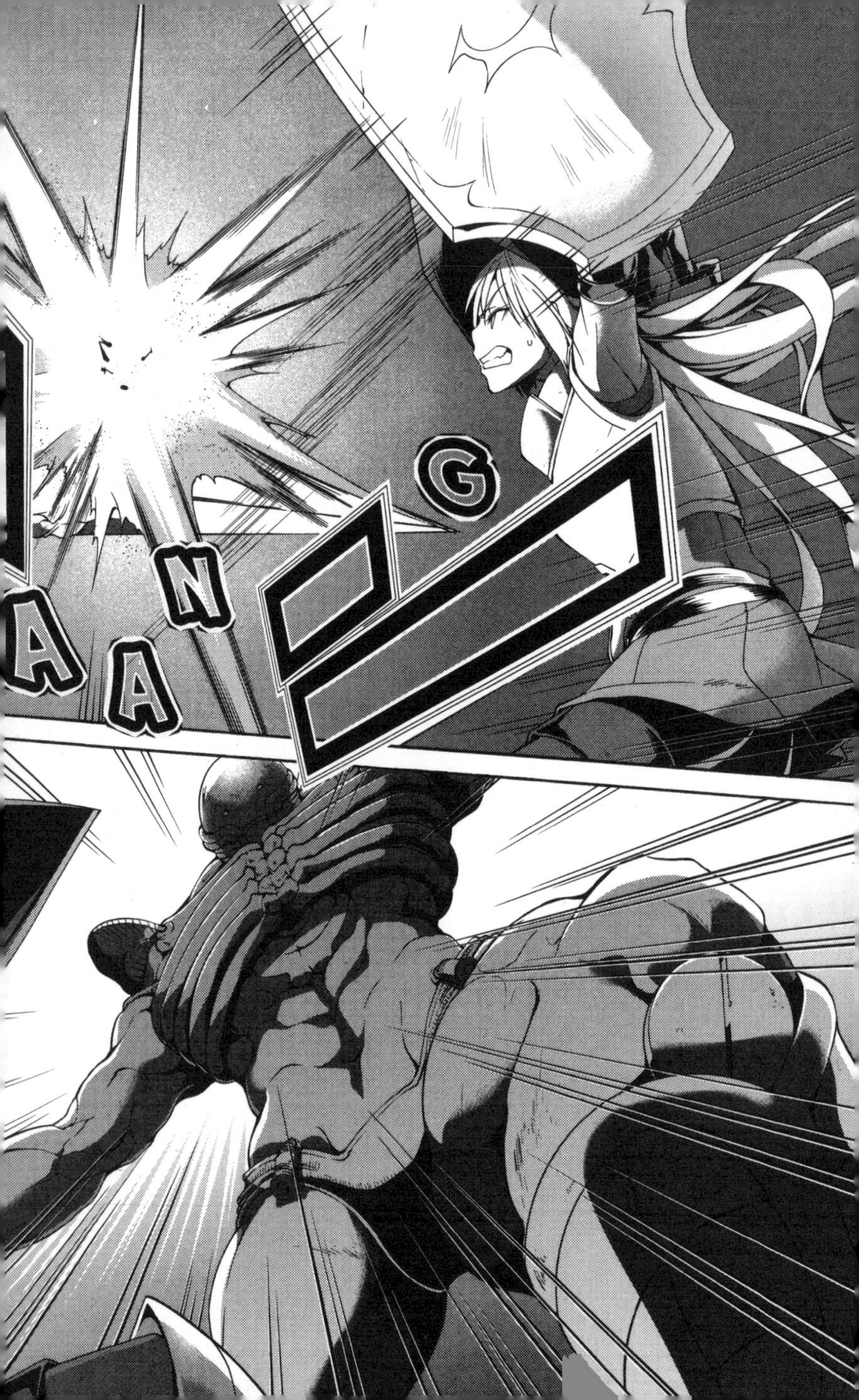
AANG

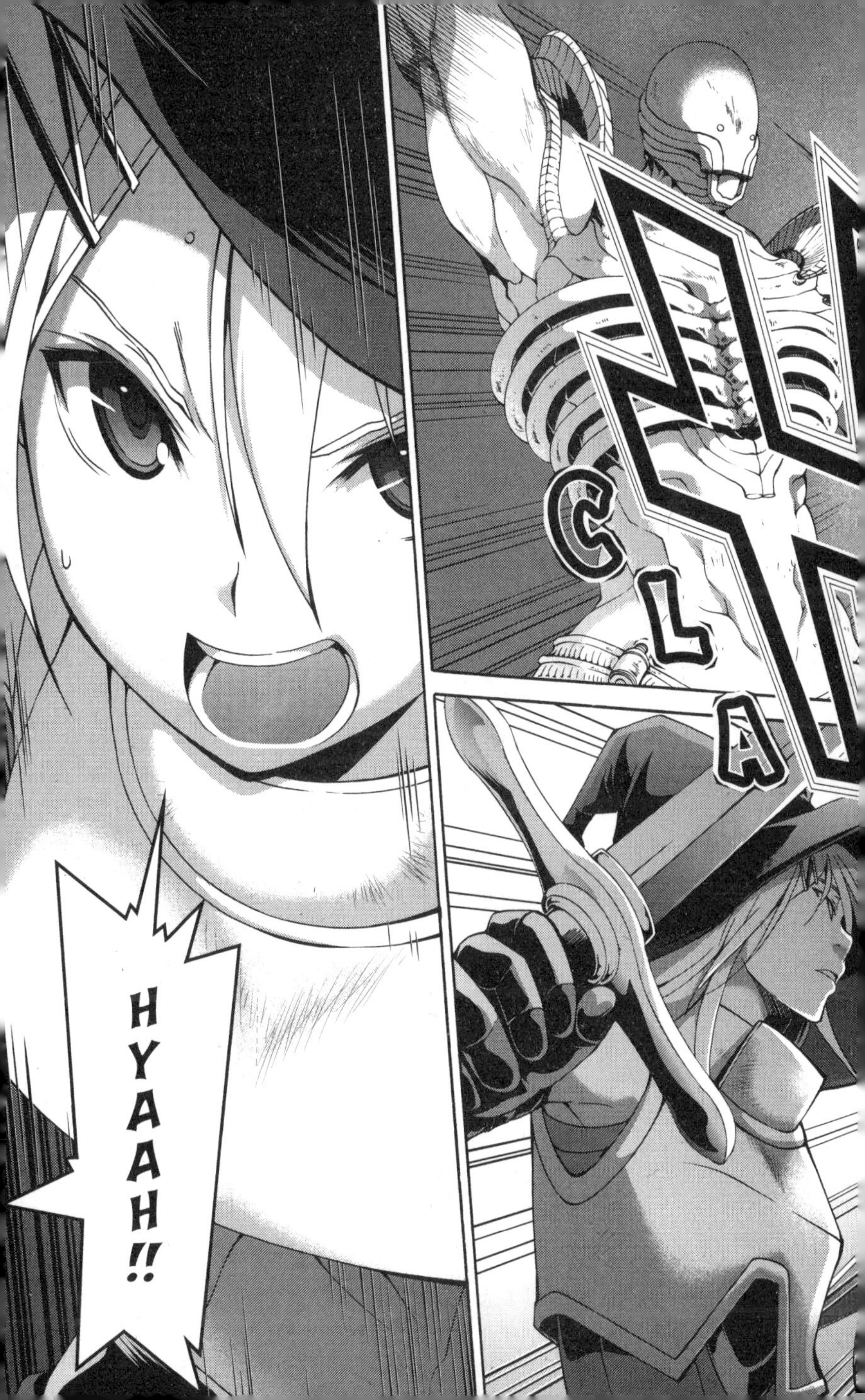
CLA
HYAAH!!

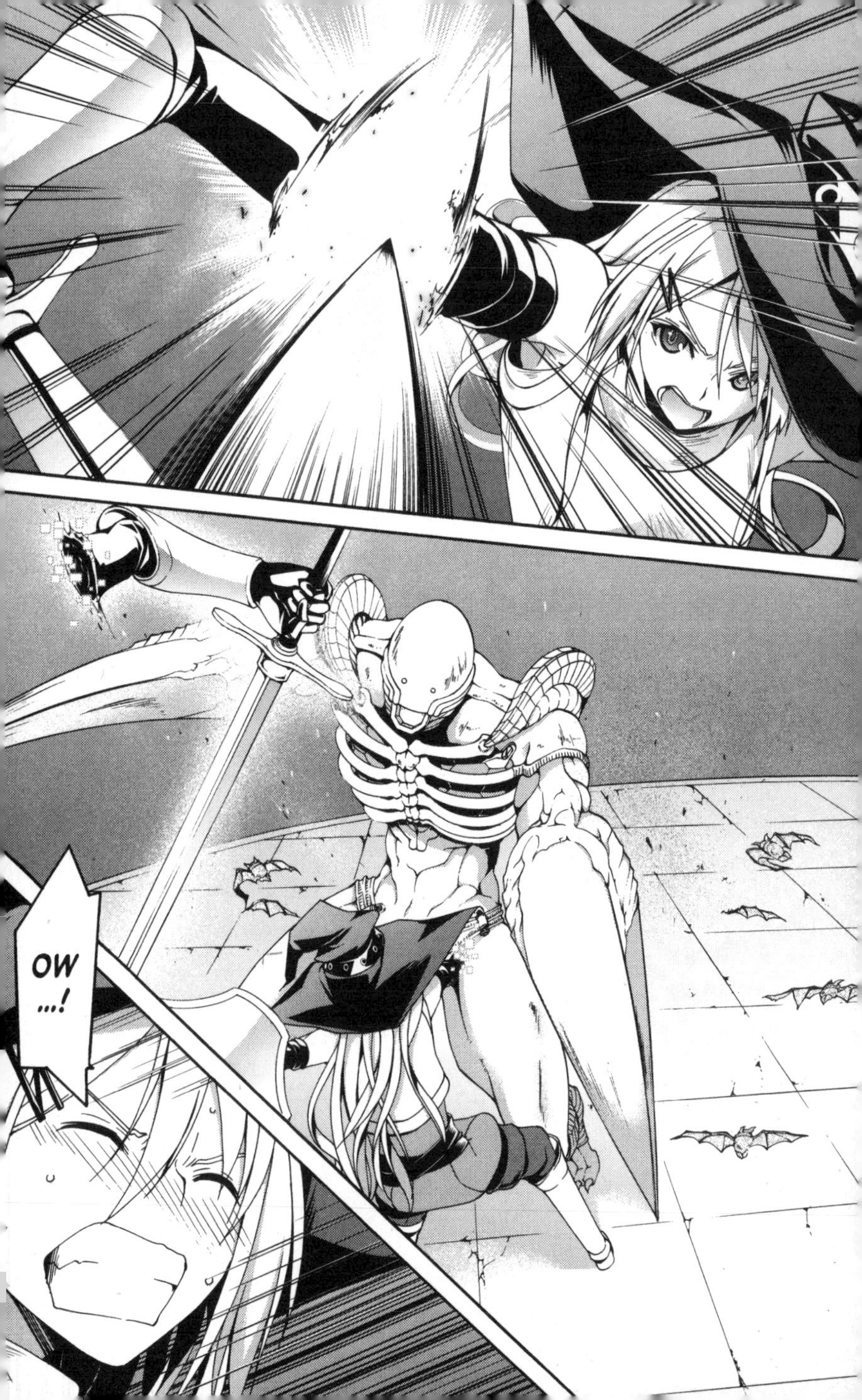
OW ...!

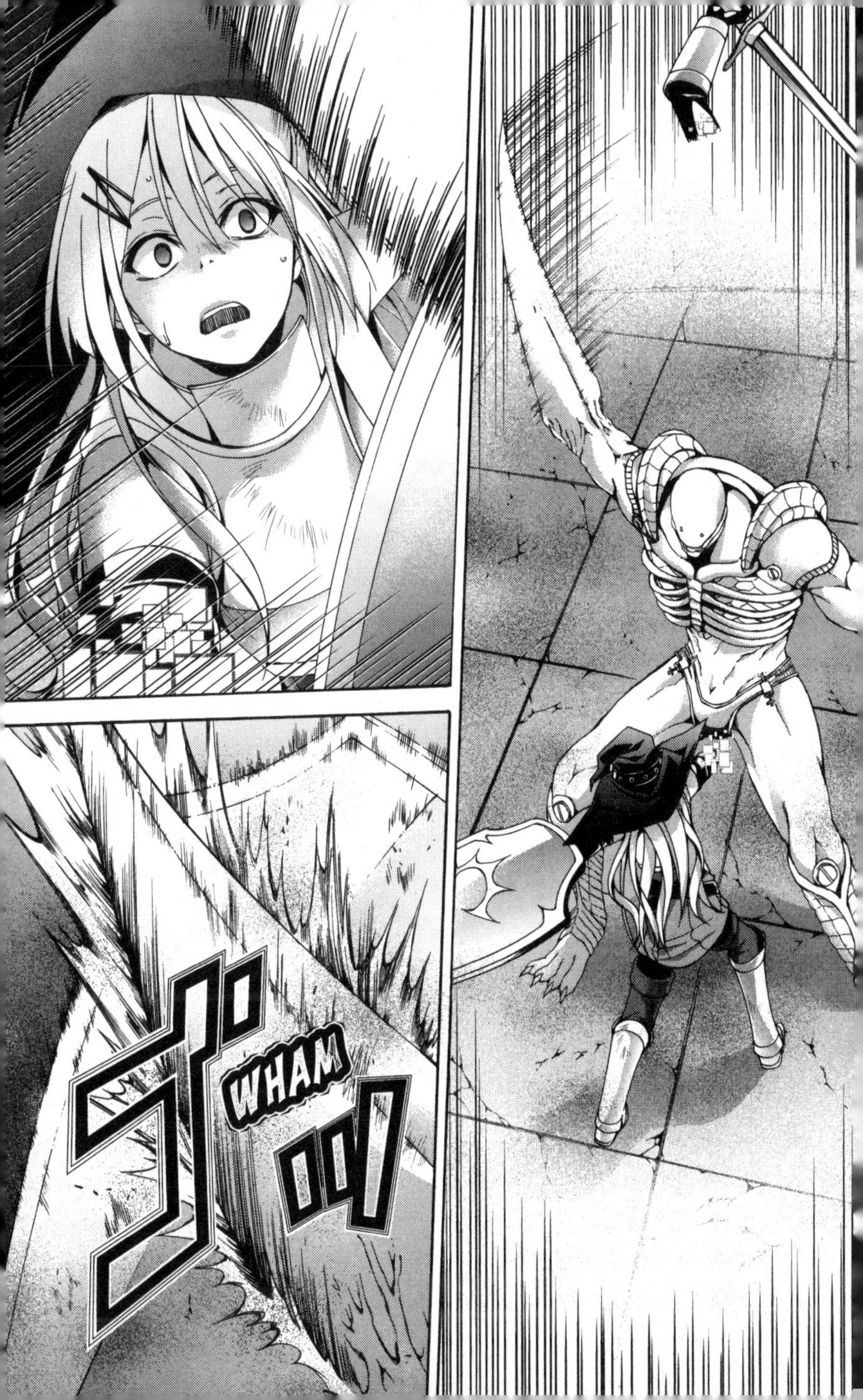
WHAM

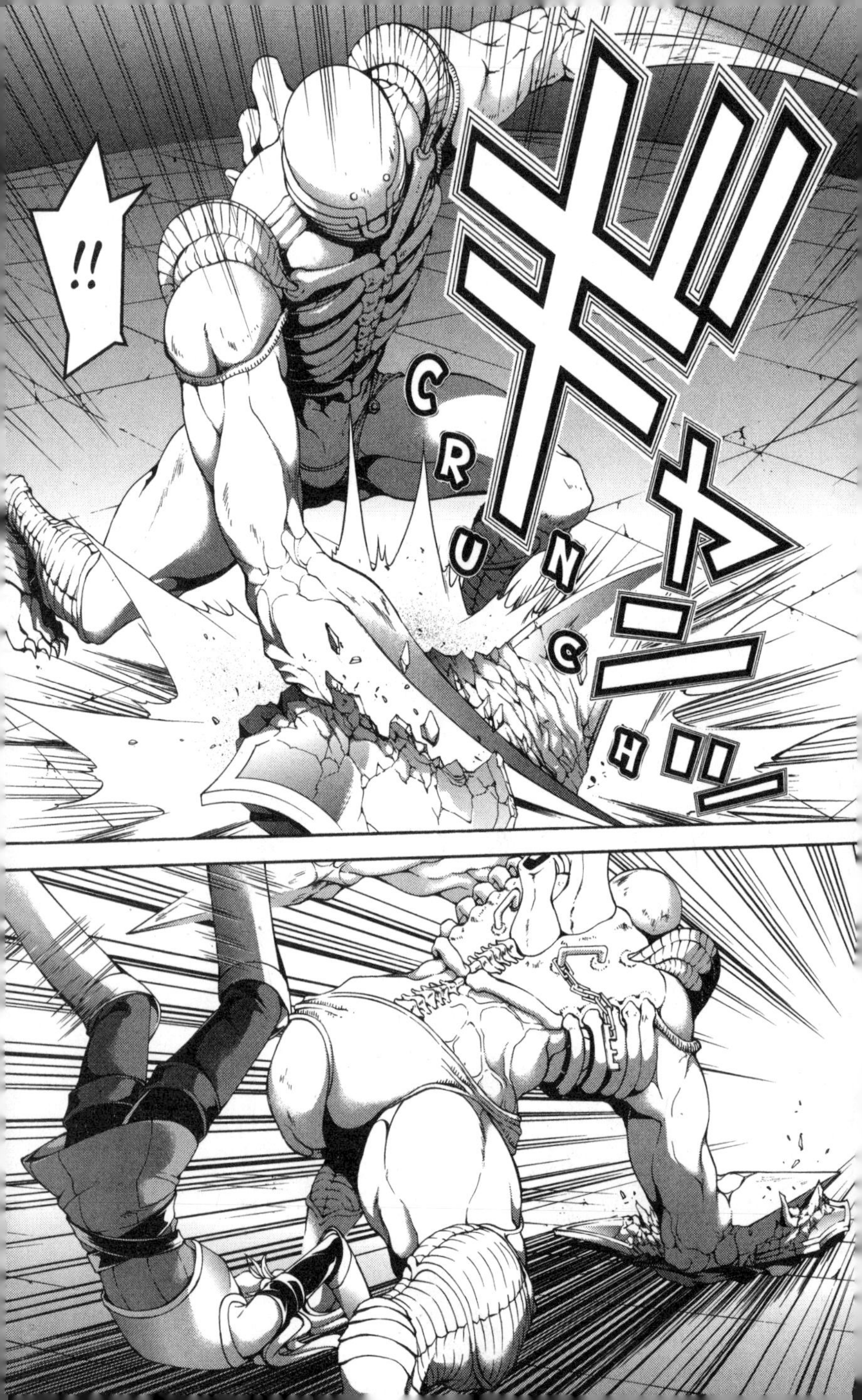
CRUNCH
!!

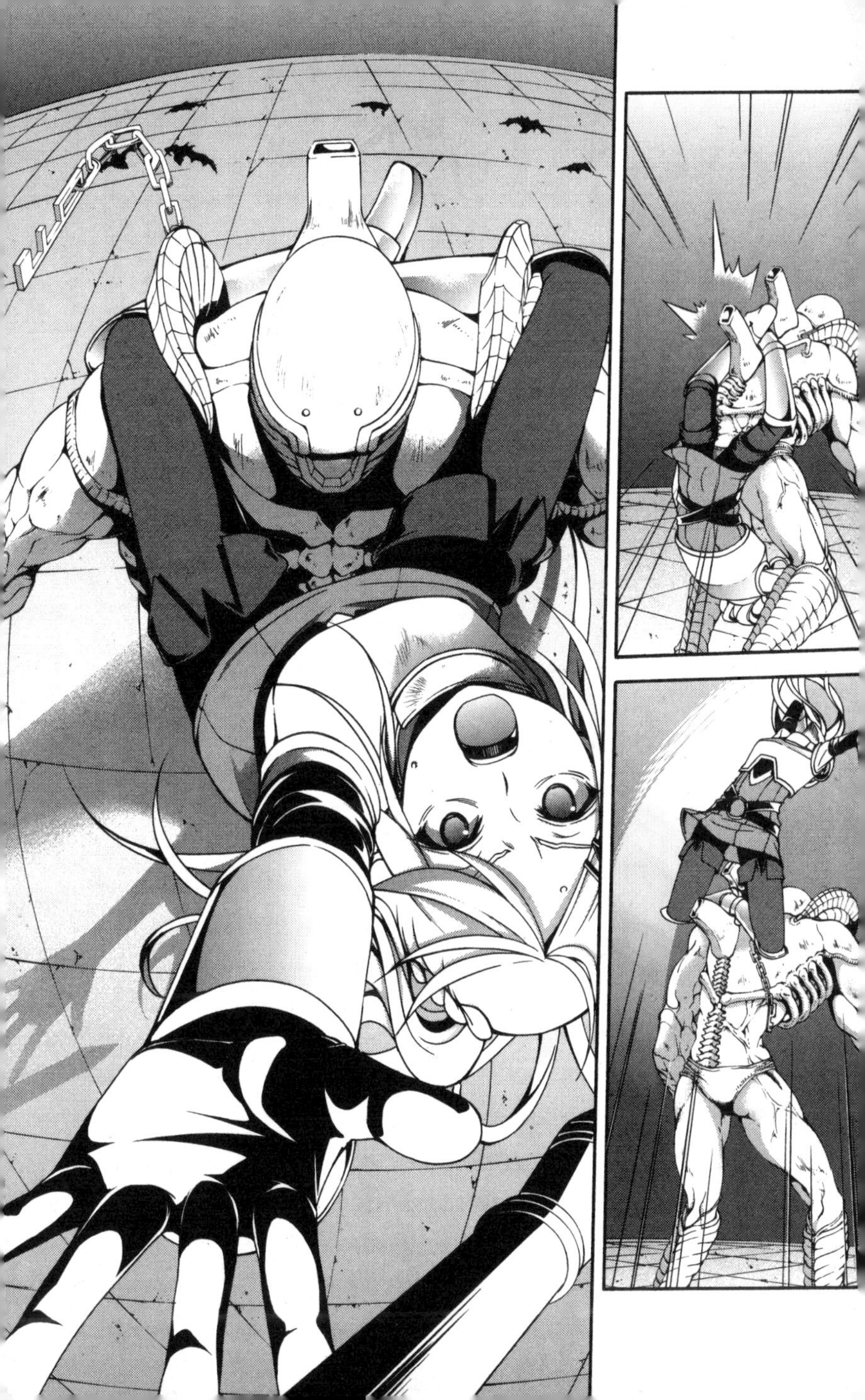

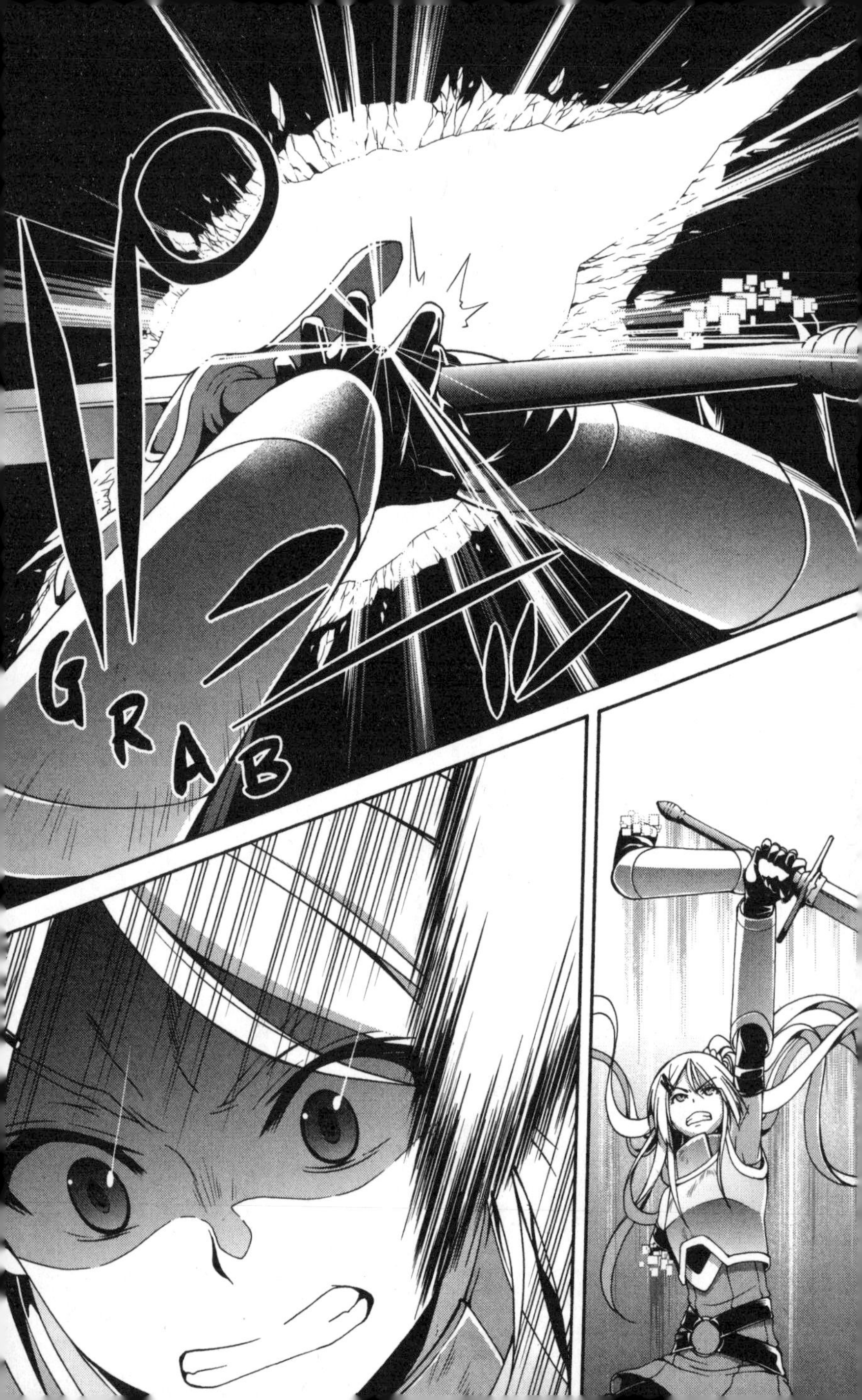
GRAB

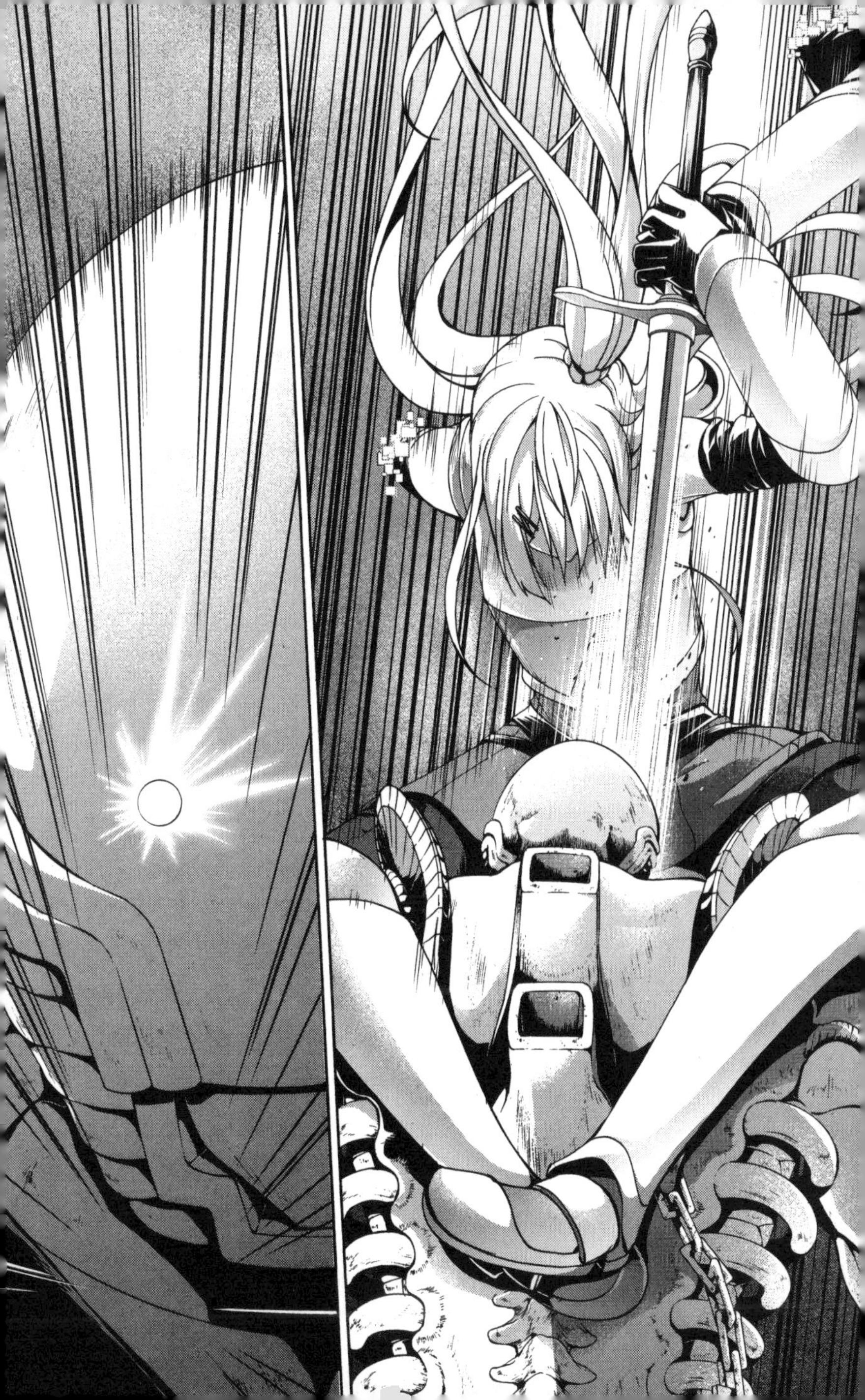

THE MEANING OF LIFE

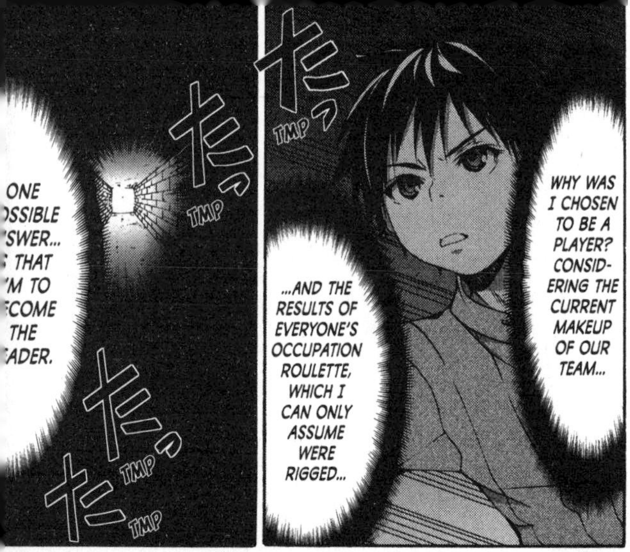
TMP
WHY WAS I CHOSEN TO BE A PLAYER? CONSID-ERING THE CURRENT MAKEUP OF OUR TEAM...
...AND THE RESULTS OF EVERYONE'S OCCUPATION ROULETTE, WHICH I CAN ONLY ASSUME WERE RIGGED...
TMP
ONE
SSIBLE
SWER...
THAT
M TO
COME
THE
ADER.
TMP
TMP

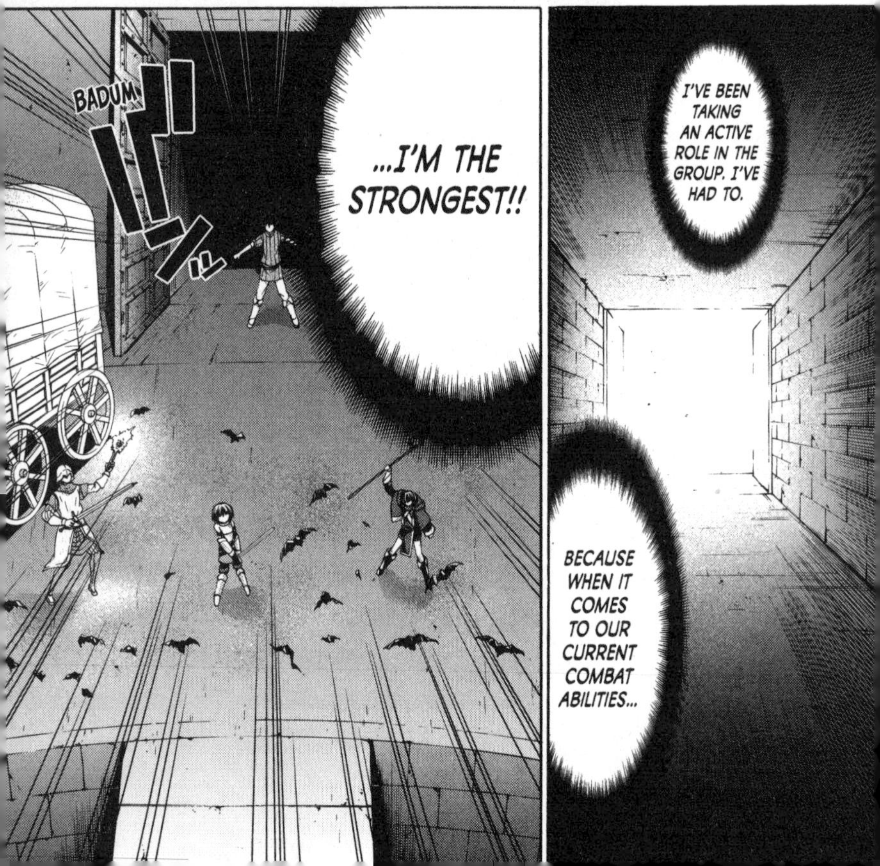
I'VE BEEN TAKING AN ACTIVE ROLE IN THE GROUP. I'VE HAD TO.
BECAUSE WHEN IT COMES TO OUR CURRENT COMBAT ABILITIES...
...I'M THE STRONGEST!!
BADUM

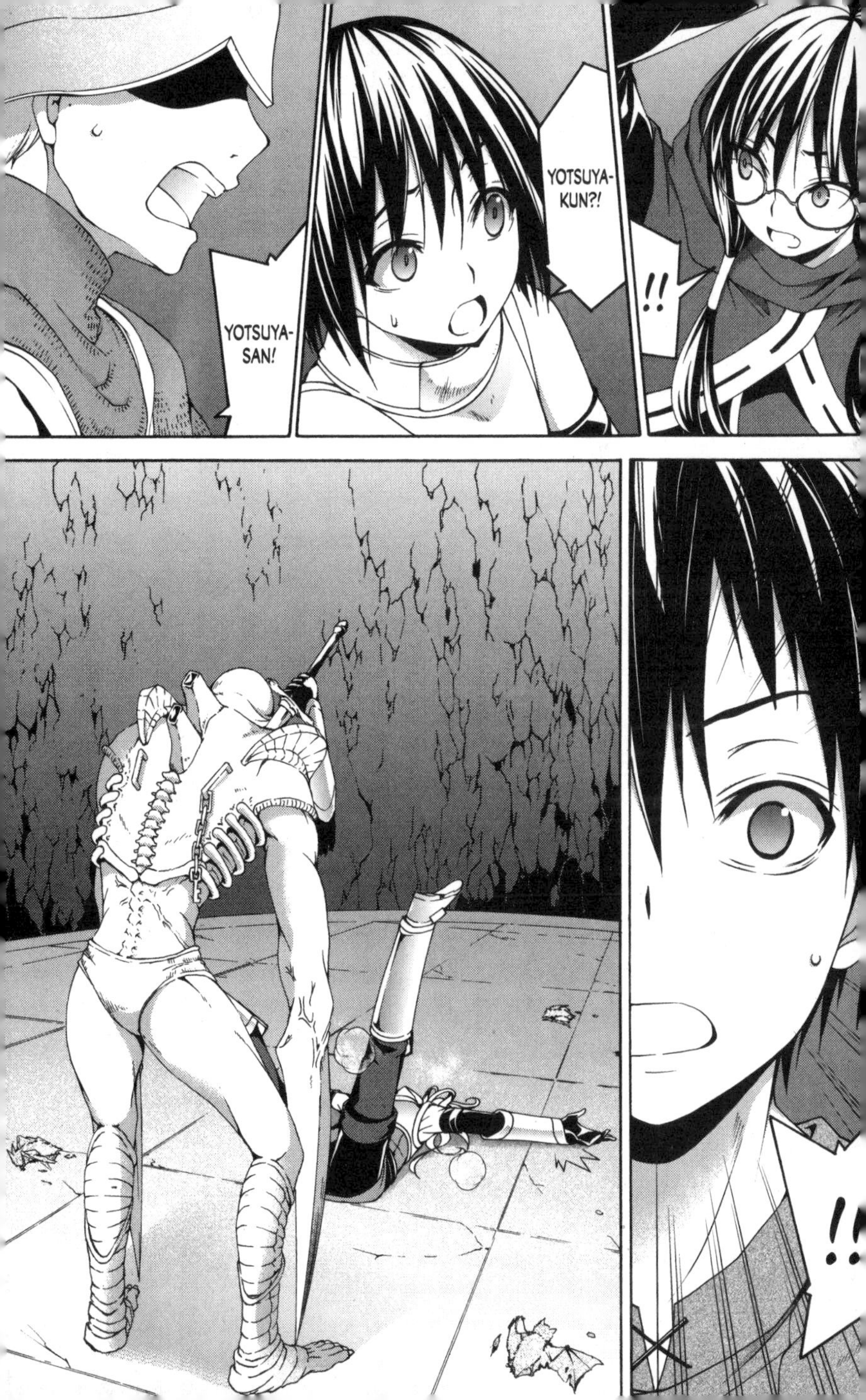
!!
YOTSUYA-KUN?!
YOTSUYA-SAN!
!!

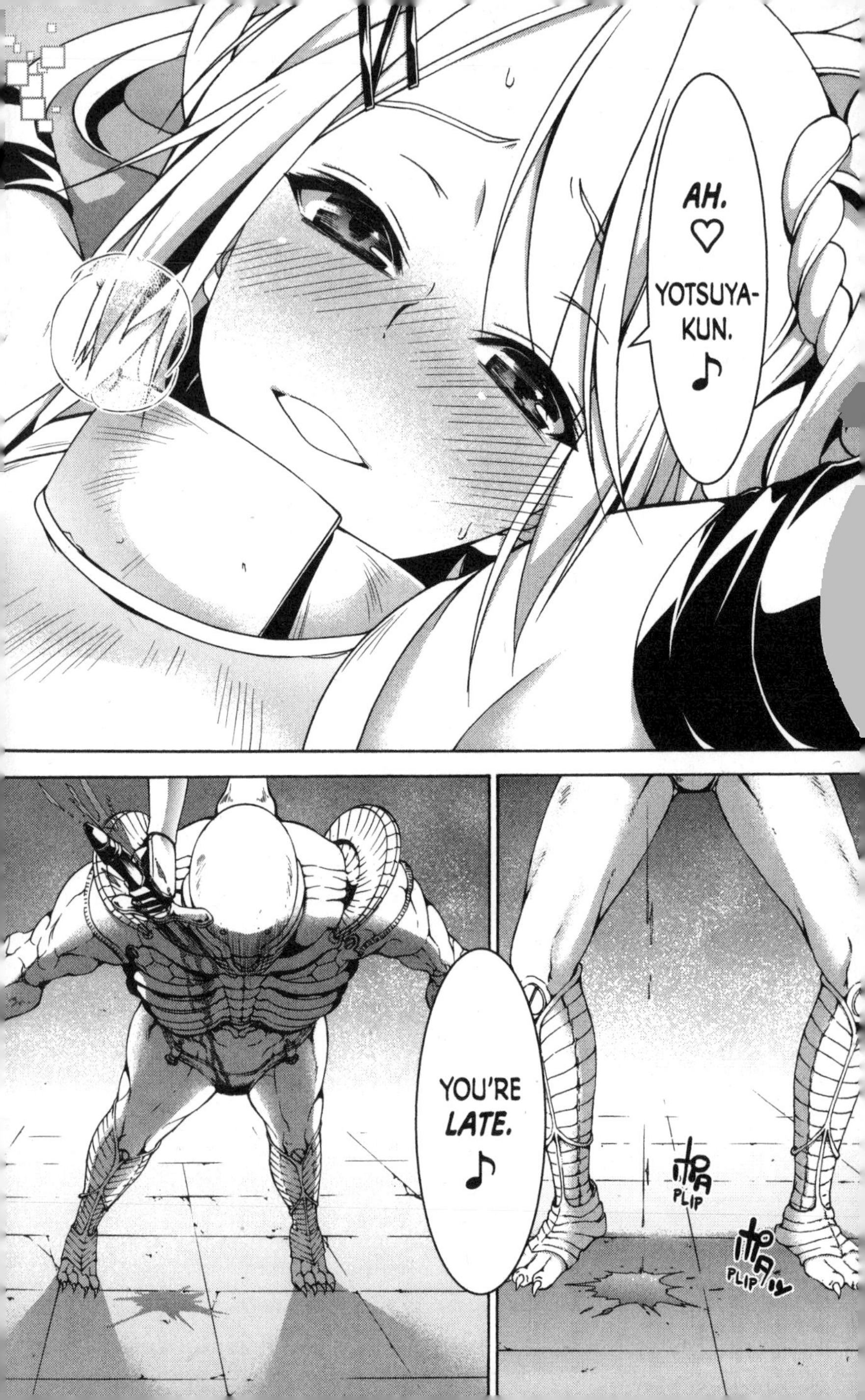
AH. ♡ YOTSUYA-KUN. ♪
PLIP
PLIP
YOU'RE *LATE.* ♪

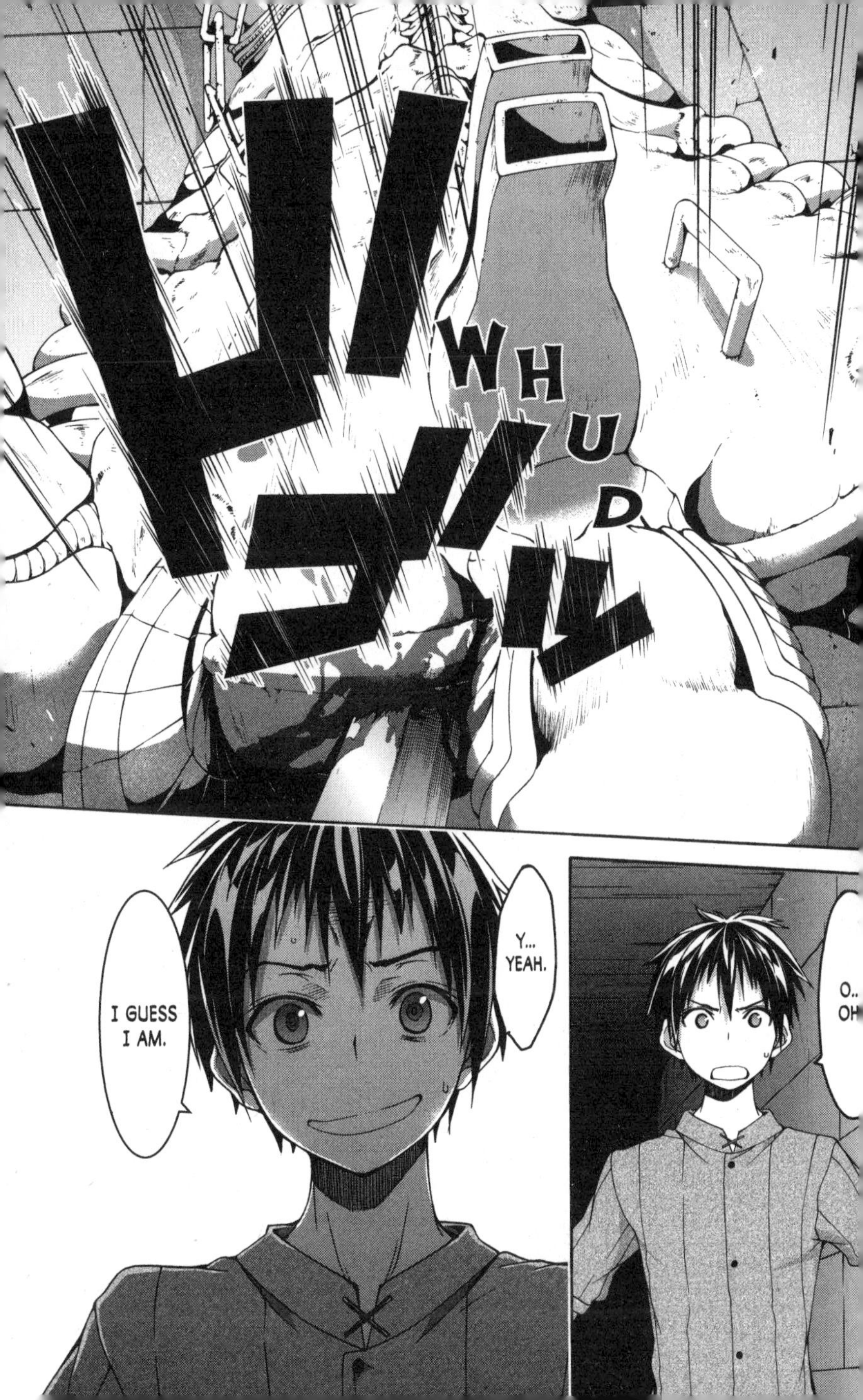
WHUD
O.. OH
Y... YEAH.
I GUESS I AM.

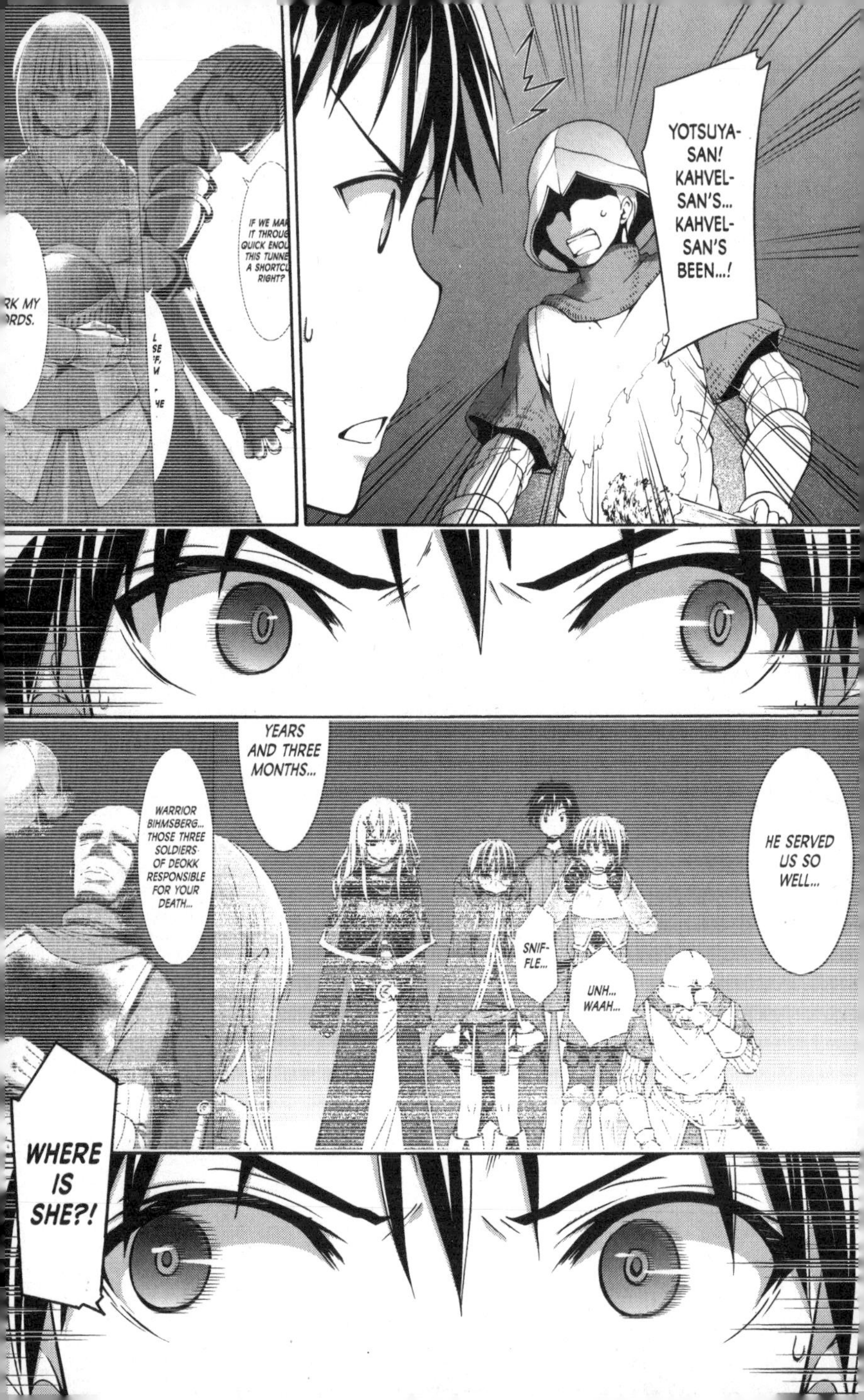
YOTSUYA-SAN! KAHVEL-SAN'S... KAHVEL-SAN'S BEEN...!
HE SERVED US SO WELL...
UNH... WAAH...
SNIFF-LE...
YEARS AND THREE MONTHS...
WARRIOR BIHMSBERG... THOSE THREE SOLDIERS OF DEOKK RESPONSIBLE FOR YOUR DEATH...
WHERE IS SHE?!

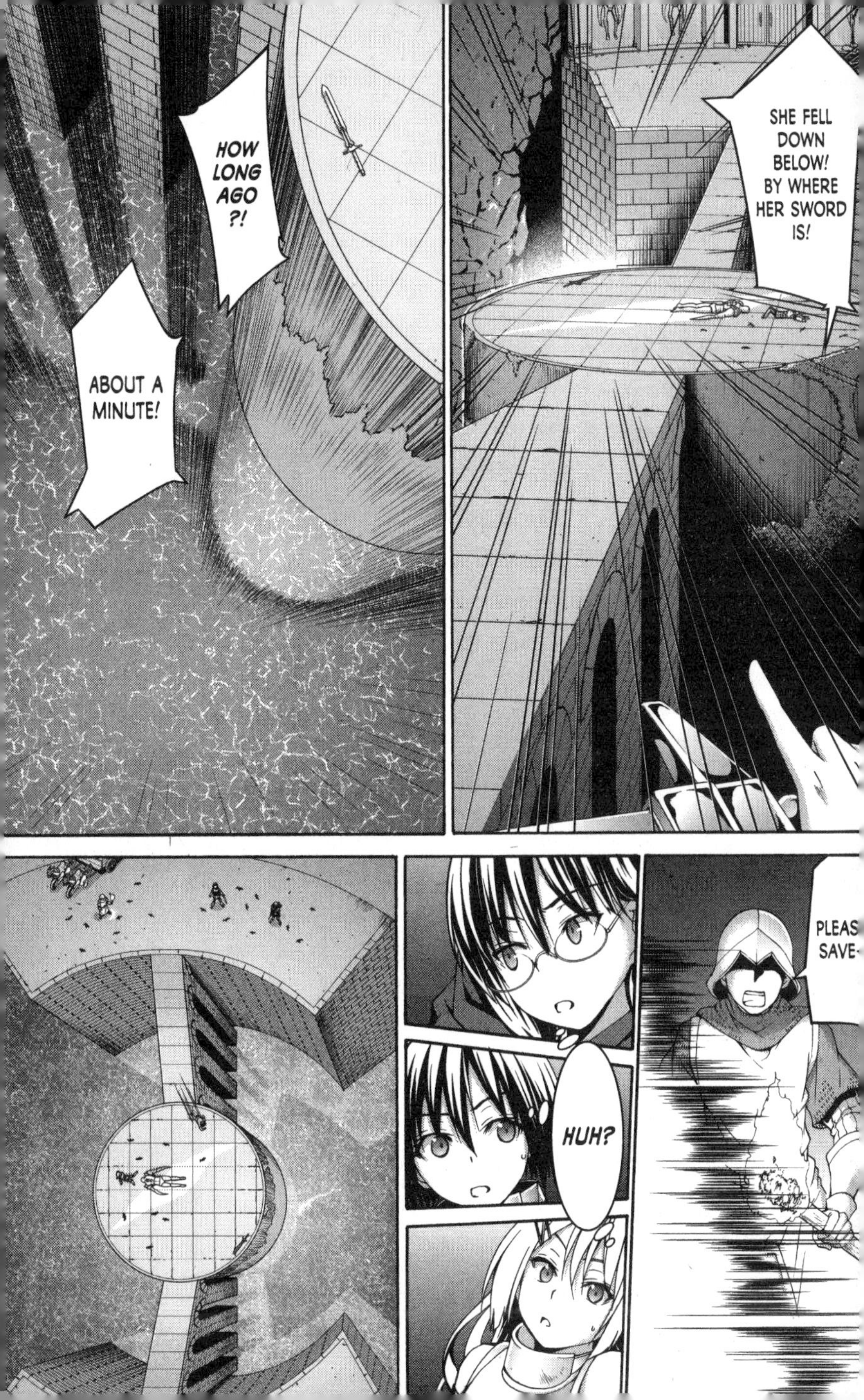
SHE FELL DOWN BELOW! BY WHERE HER SWORD IS!
HOW LONG AGO ?!
ABOUT A MINUTE!
PLEAS SAVE-
HUH?

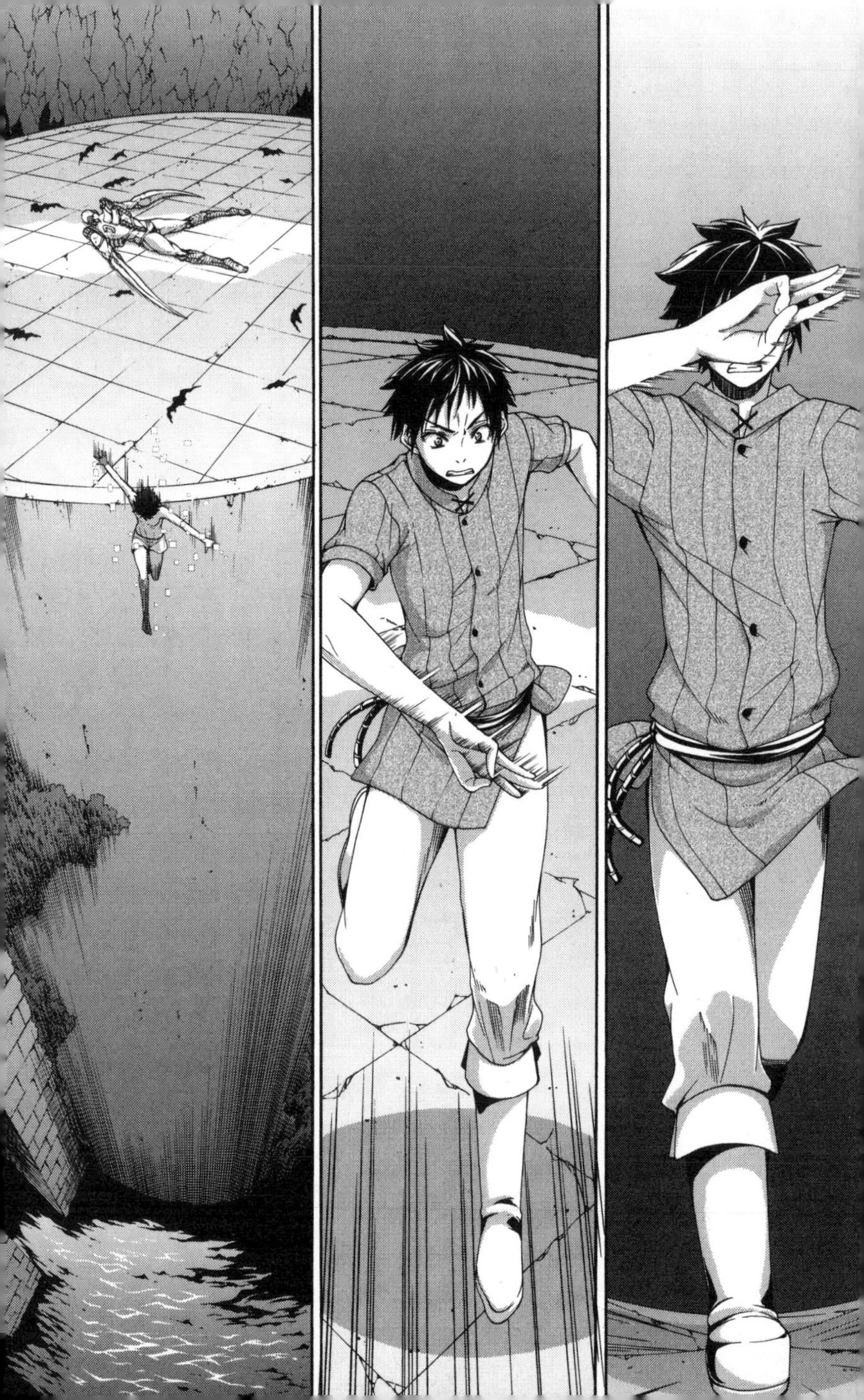

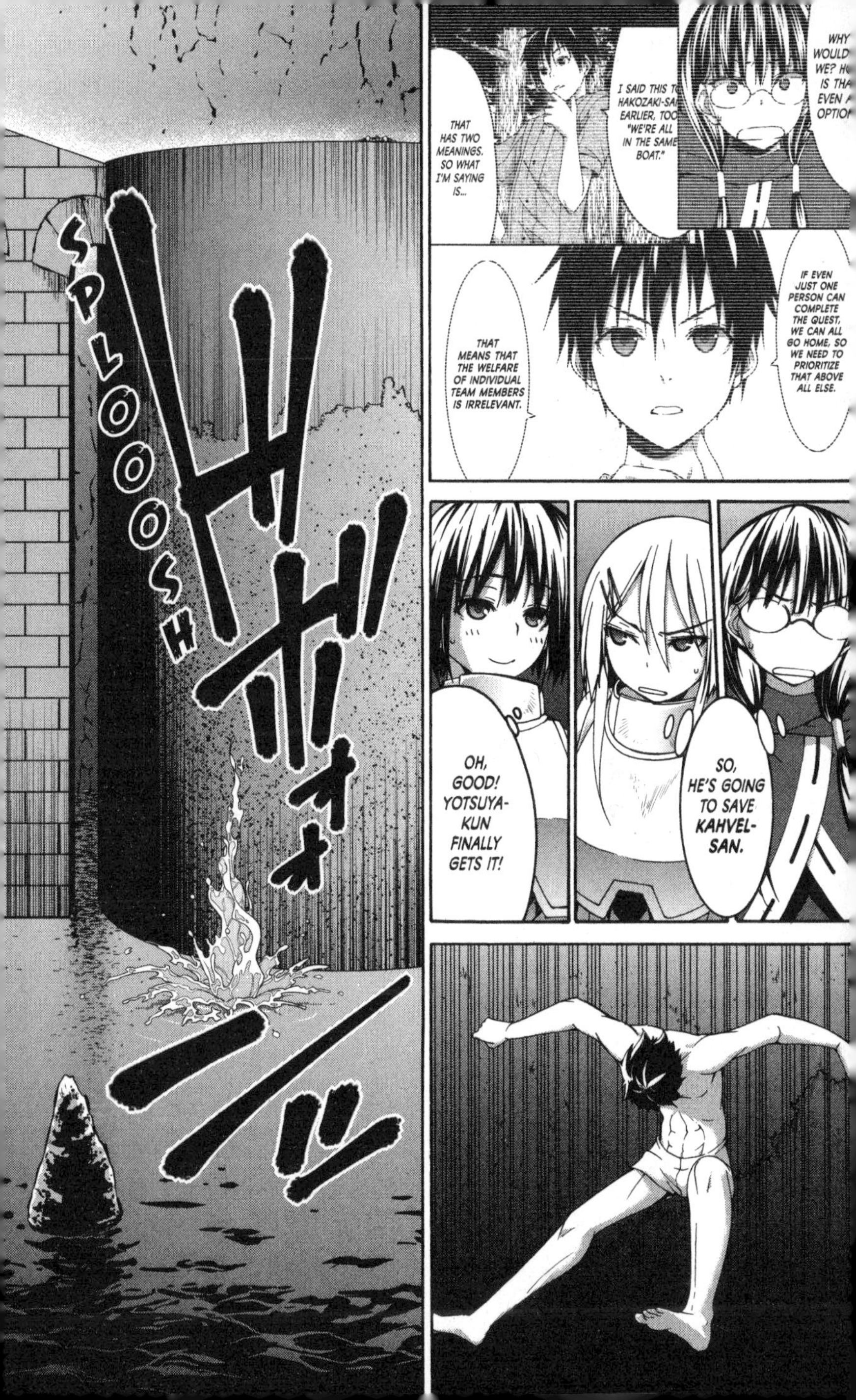
WHY WOULD WE? HO IS THA EVEN A OPTIO
I SAID THIS TO HAKOZAKI-SA EARLIER, TOO "WE'RE ALL IN THE SAME BOAT."
THAT HAS TWO MEANINGS. SO WHAT I'M SAYING IS...
IF EVEN JUST ONE PERSON CAN COMPLETE THE QUEST, WE CAN ALL GO HOME, SO WE NEED TO PRIORITIZE THAT ABOVE ALL ELSE.
THAT MEANS THAT THE WELFARE OF INDIVIDUAL TEAM MEMBERS IS IRRELEVANT.
SO, HE'S GOING TO SAVE KAHVEL-SAN.
OH, GOOD! YOTSUYA-KUN FINALLY GETS IT!
SPLOOOSH

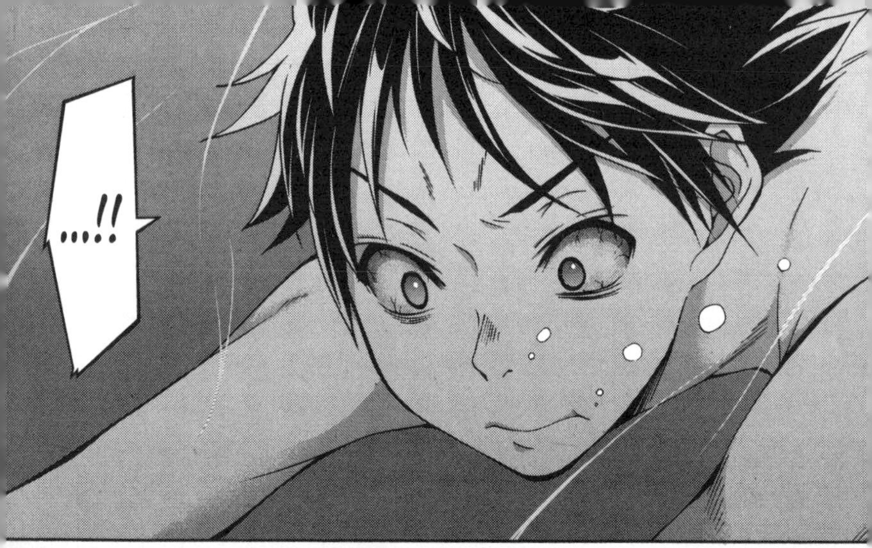
...!!
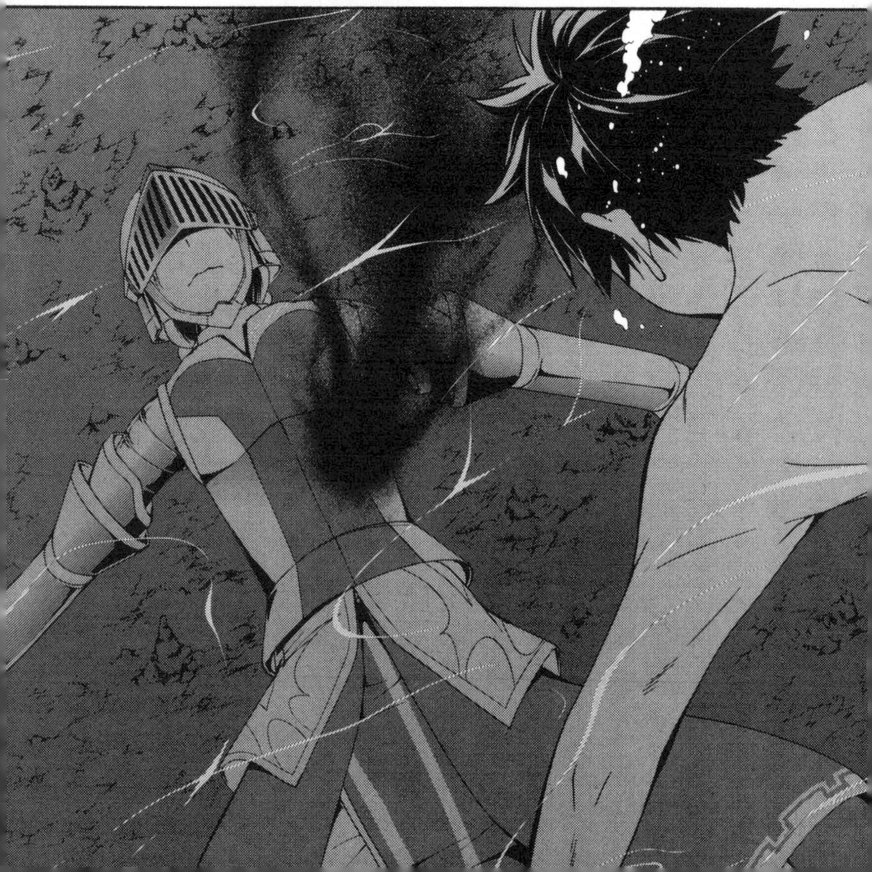

COVER ILLUSTRATION: ROUGH SKETCH

ROUGH SKETCH OF
ANOTHER ILLUSTRATION

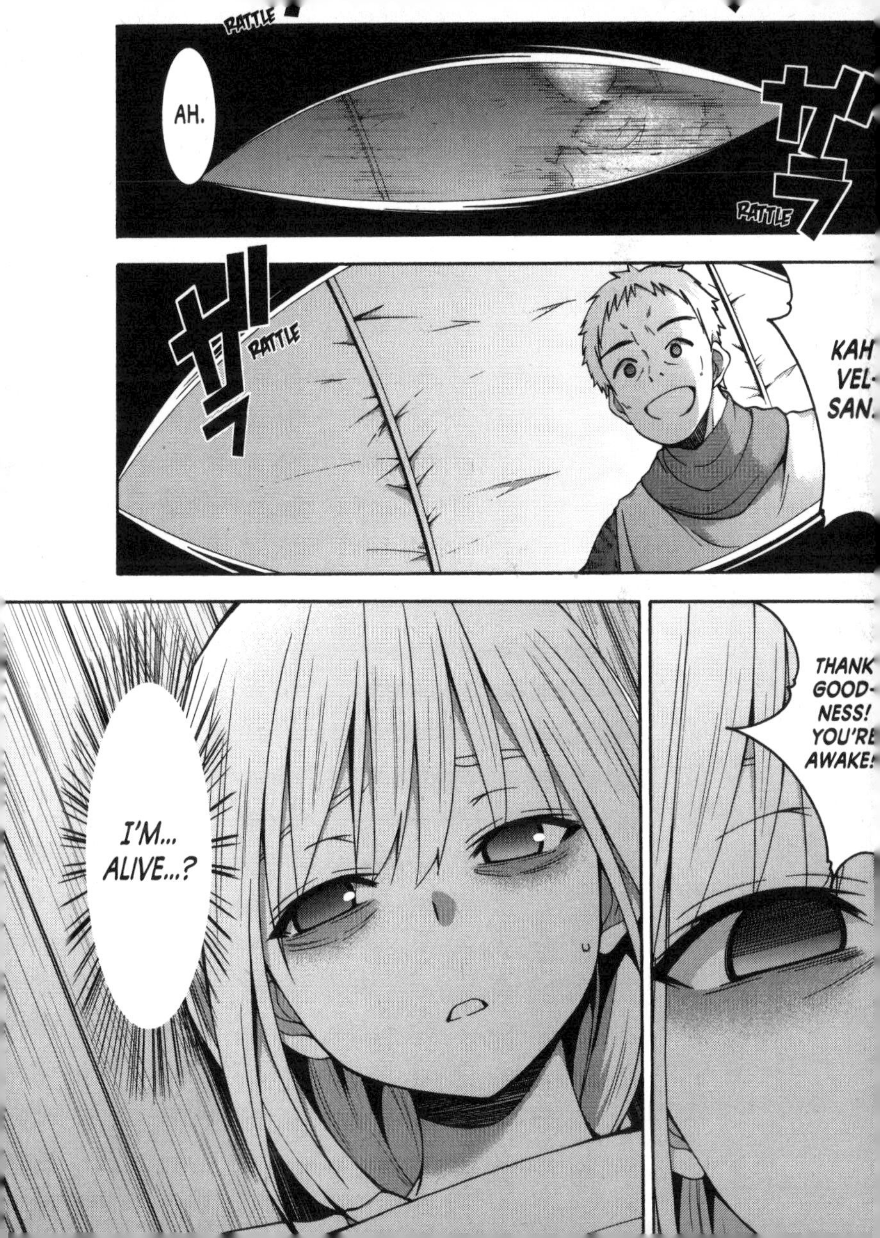
RATTLE
AH.
ザラ
RATTLE
ザラ
RATTLE
KAH VEL- SAN.
THANK GOODNESS! YOU'RE AWAKE!
I'M... ALIVE...?

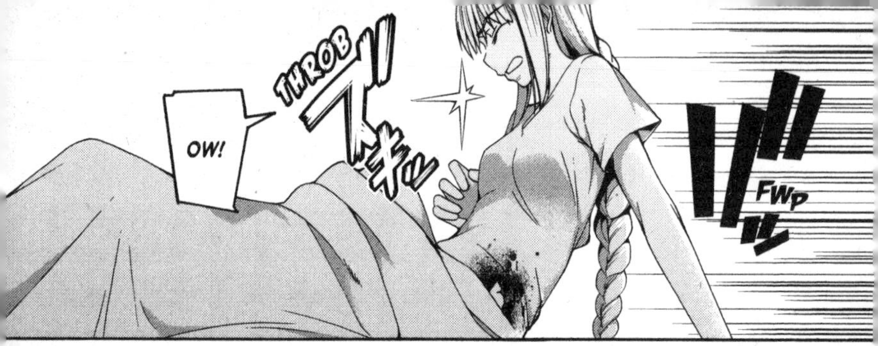
FWP
THROB
OW!
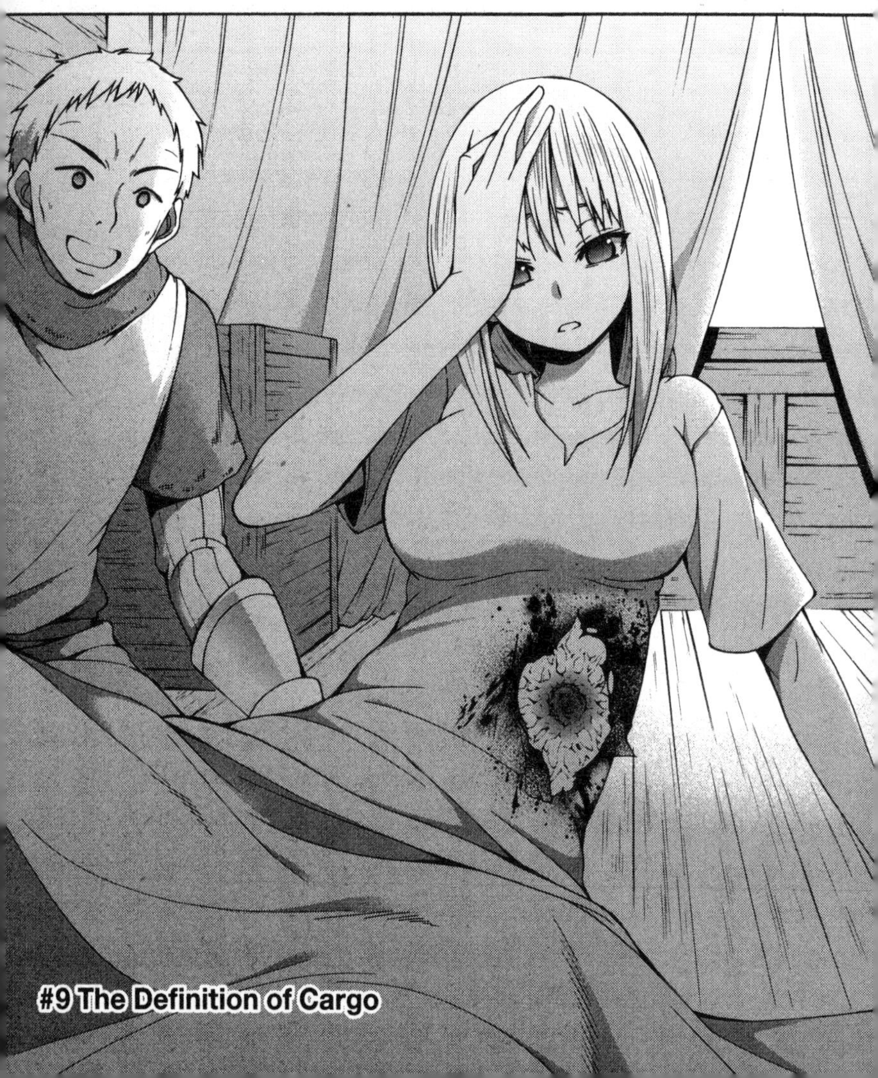
#9 The Definition of Cargo

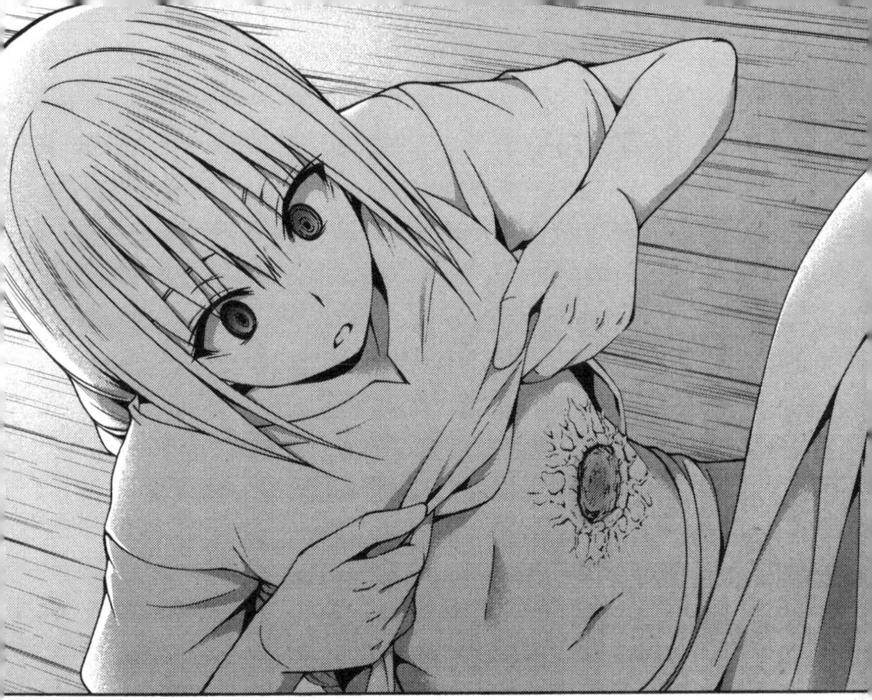

CREATURE MAGIC CAN SPEED UP THE METABOLISM OF CELLS. IN OTHER WORDS, IT CAN MAKE WOUNDS HEAL FASTER.

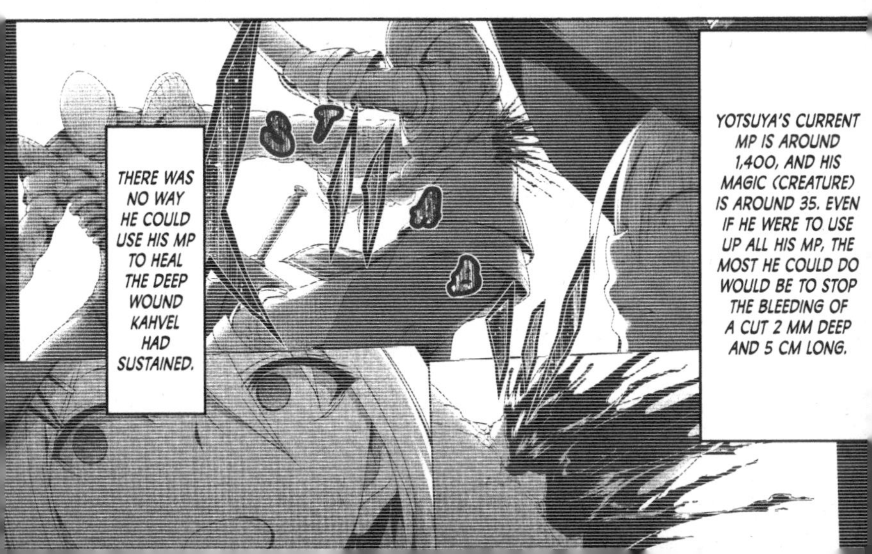
YOTSUYA'S CURRENT MP IS AROUND 1,400, AND HIS MAGIC (CREATURE) IS AROUND 35. EVEN IF HE WERE TO USE UP ALL HIS MP, THE MOST HE COULD DO WOULD BE TO STOP THE BLEEDING OF A CUT 2 MM DEEP AND 5 CM LONG.
THERE WAS NO WAY HE COULD USE HIS MP TO HEAL THE DEEP WOUND KAHVEL HAD SUSTAINED.

BUT MP CAN ALSO BE DRAWN FROM THE BLOOD OF LIVING CREATURES.

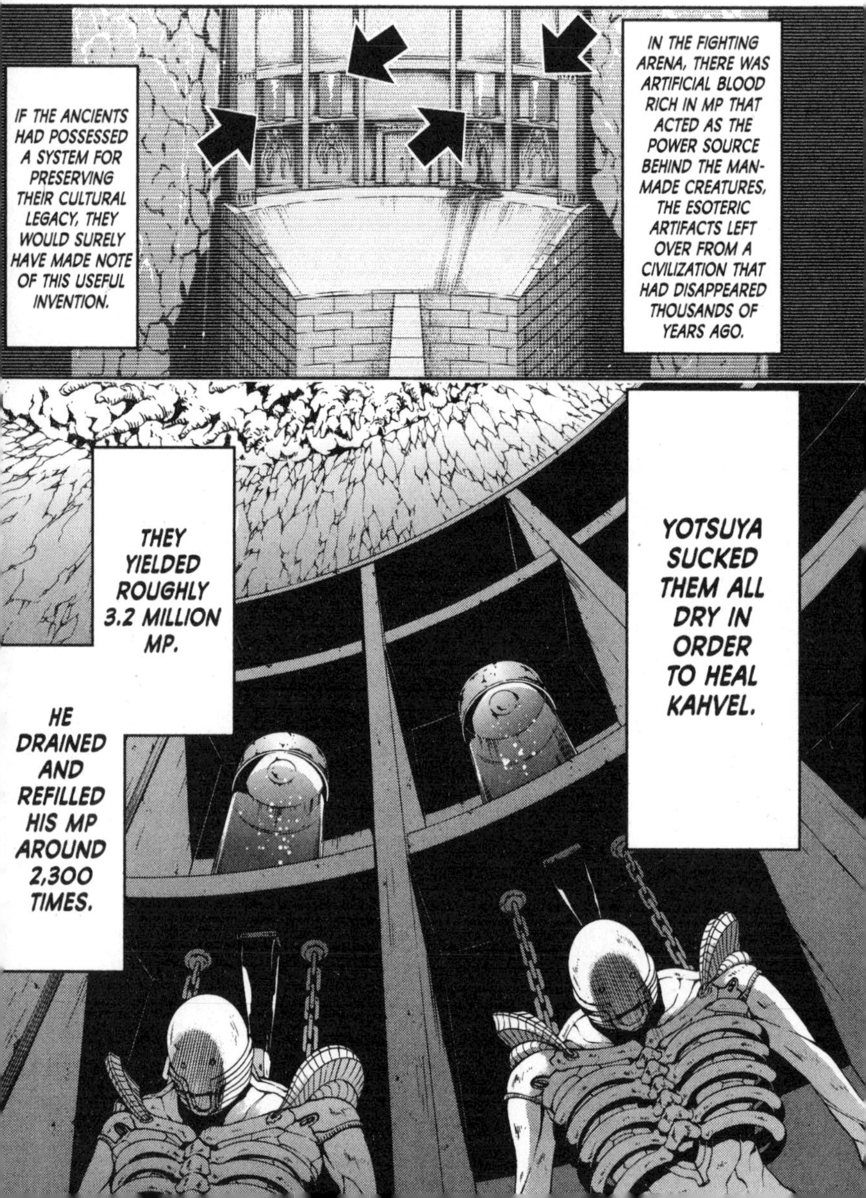
IN THE FIGHTING ARENA, THERE WAS ARTIFICIAL BLOOD RICH IN MP THAT ACTED AS THE POWER SOURCE BEHIND THE MAN-MADE CREATURES, THE ESOTERIC ARTIFACTS LEFT OVER FROM A CIVILIZATION THAT HAD DISAPPEARED THOUSANDS OF YEARS AGO.
IF THE ANCIENTS HAD POSSESSED A SYSTEM FOR PRESERVING THEIR CULTURAL LEGACY, THEY WOULD SURELY HAVE MADE NOTE OF THIS USEFUL INVENTION.
YOTSUYA SUCKED THEM ALL DRY IN ORDER TO HEAL KAHVEL.
THEY YIELDED ROUGHLY 3.2 MILLION MP.
HE DRAINED AND REFILLED HIS MP AROUND 2,300 TIMES.

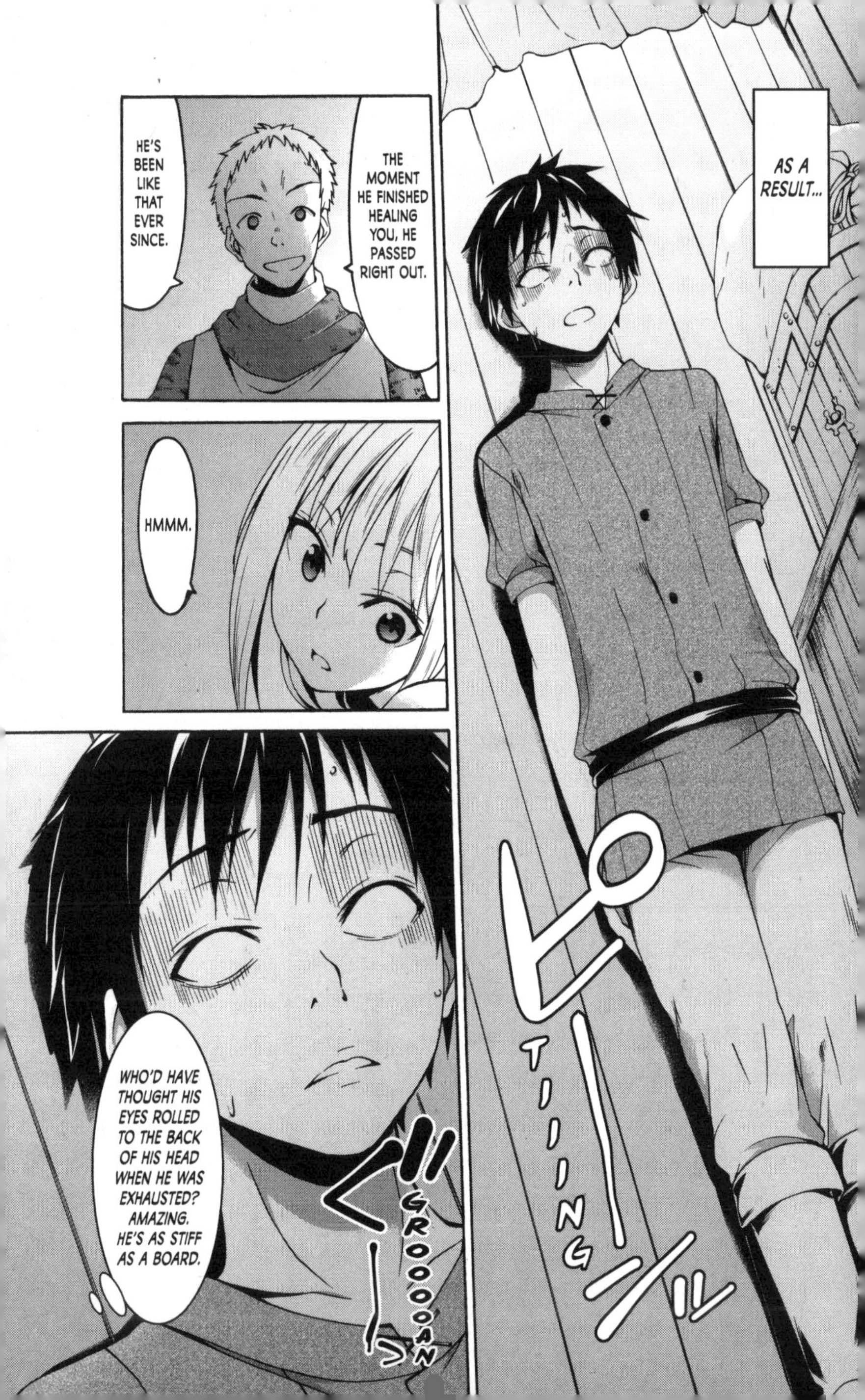
AS A RESULT...
TIIIING
THE MOMENT HE FINISHED HEALING YOU, HE PASSED RIGHT OUT.
HE'S BEEN LIKE THAT EVER SINCE.
HMMM.
WHO'D HAVE THOUGHT HIS EYES ROLLED TO THE BACK OF HIS HEAD WHEN HE WAS EXHAUSTED? AMAZING. HE'S AS STIFF AS A BOARD.
GROOOOAN

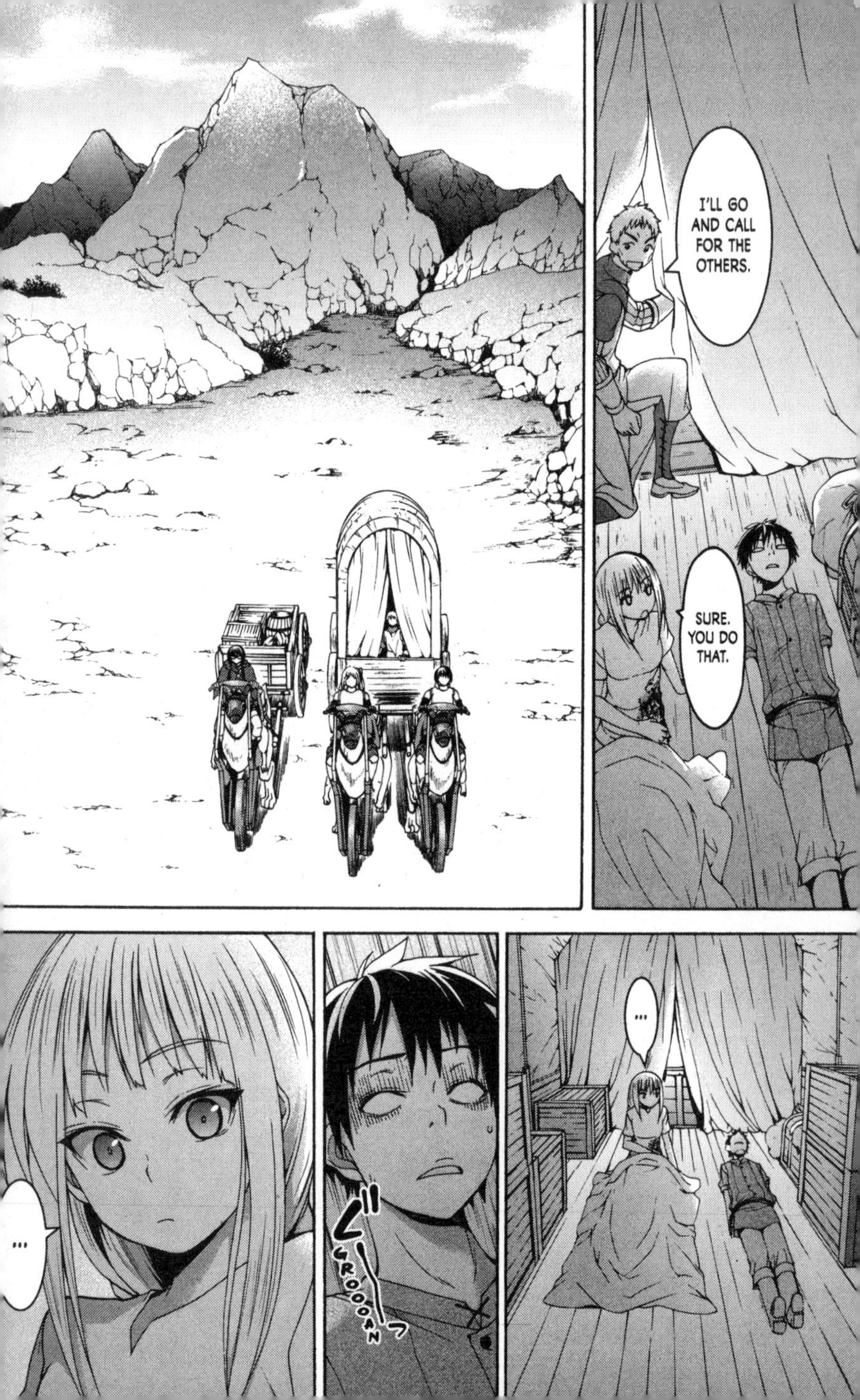
I'LL GO AND CALL FOR THE OTHERS.
SURE. YOU DO THAT.
...
GROOOAN
...

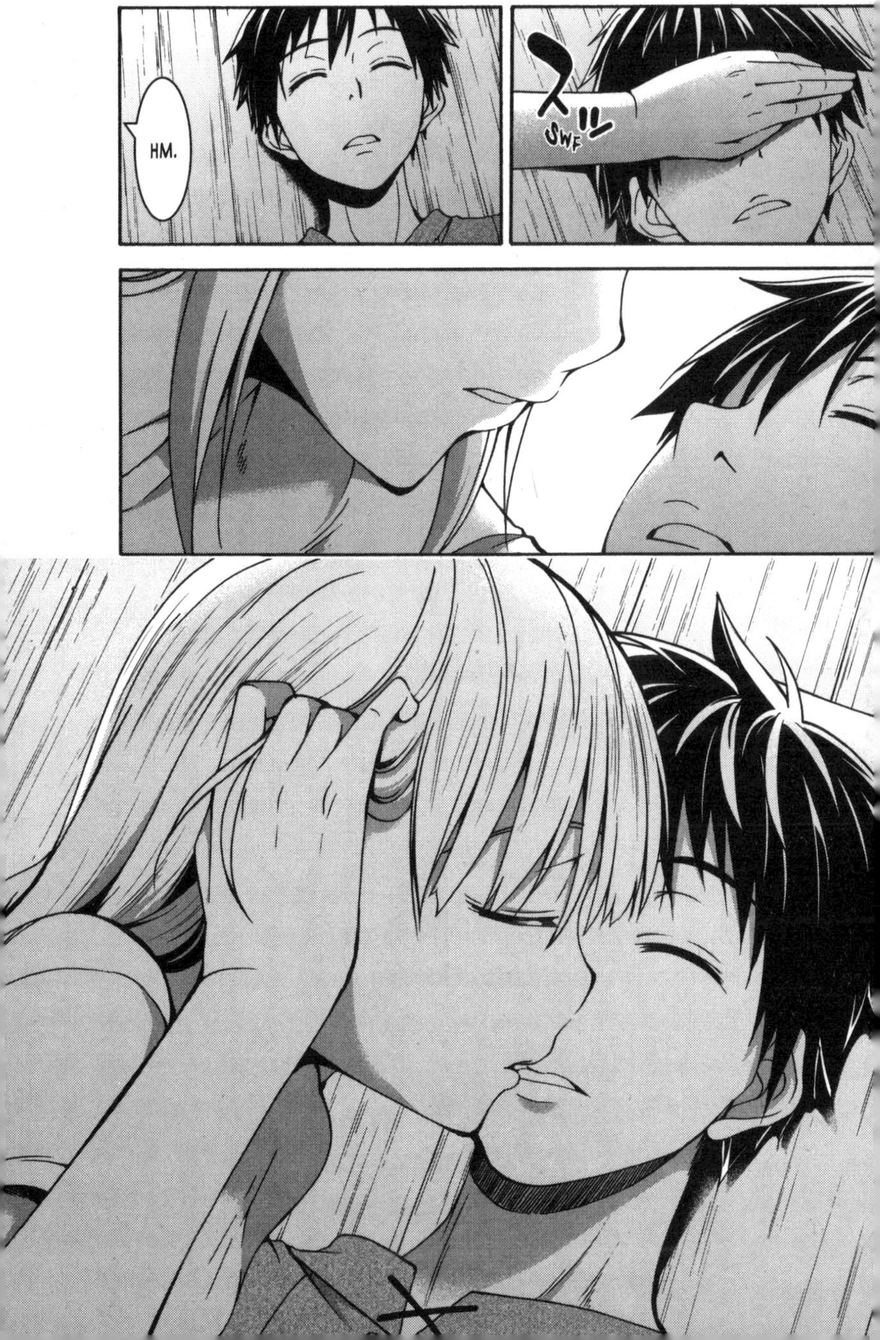
スッ
SWF
HM.

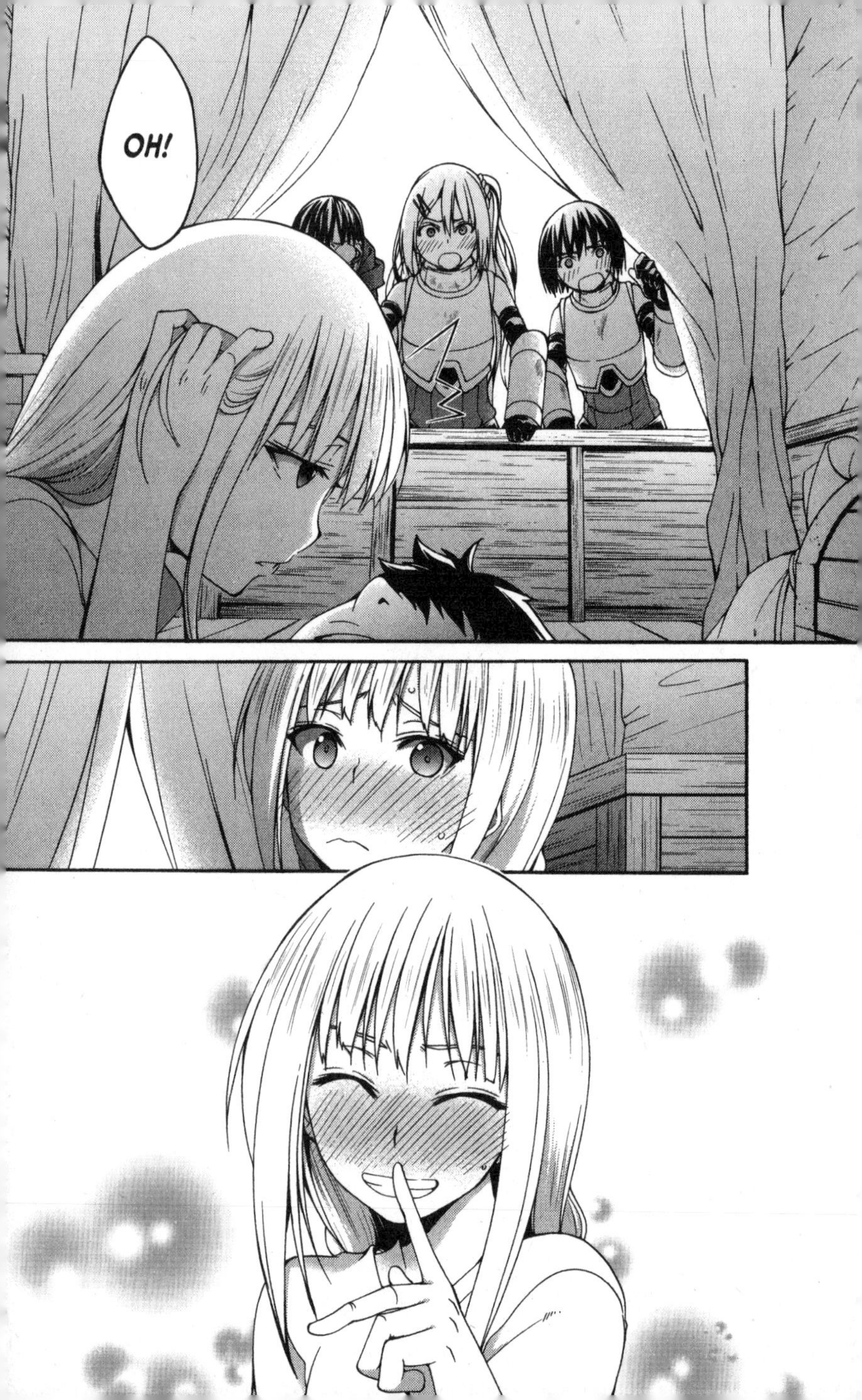
OH!

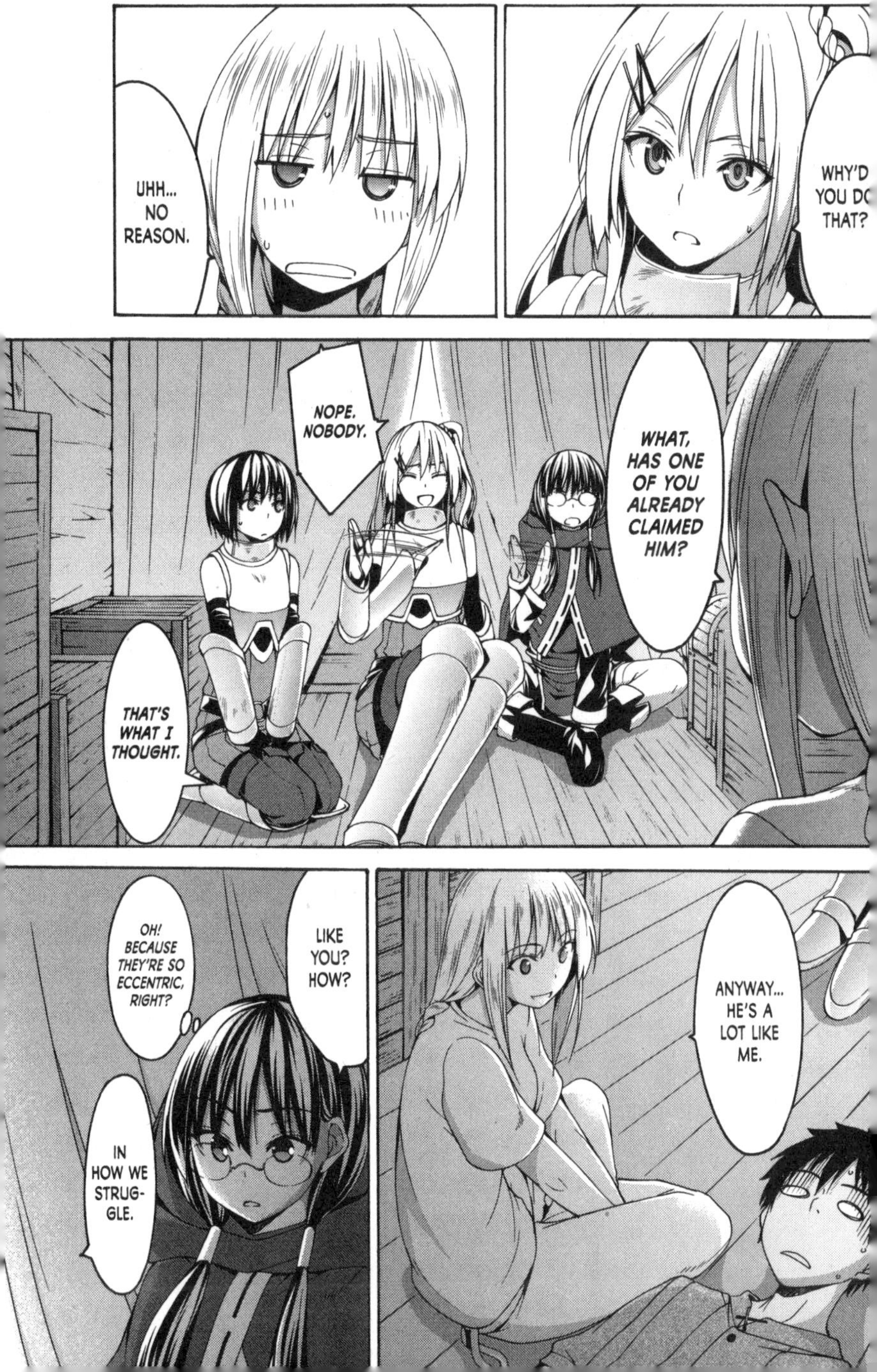
WHY'D YOU DO THAT?
UHH... NO REASON.
WHAT, HAS ONE OF YOU ALREADY CLAIMED HIM?
NOPE. NOBODY.
THAT'S WHAT I THOUGHT.
ANYWAY... HE'S A LOT LIKE ME.
LIKE YOU? HOW?
OH! BECAUSE THEY'RE SO ECCENTRIC, RIGHT?
IN HOW WE STRUG-GLE.

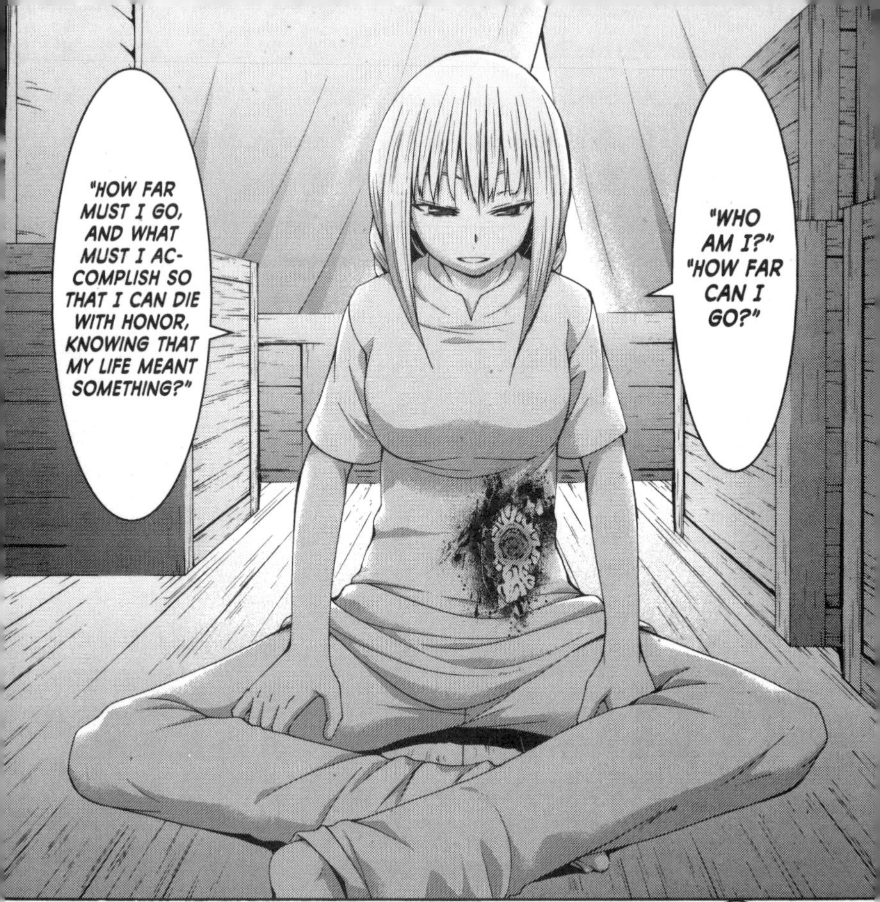
"WHO AM I?" "HOW FAR CAN I GO?"
"HOW FAR MUST I GO, AND WHAT MUST I ACCOMPLISH SO THAT I CAN DIE WITH HONOR, KNOWING THAT MY LIFE MEANT SOMETHING?"

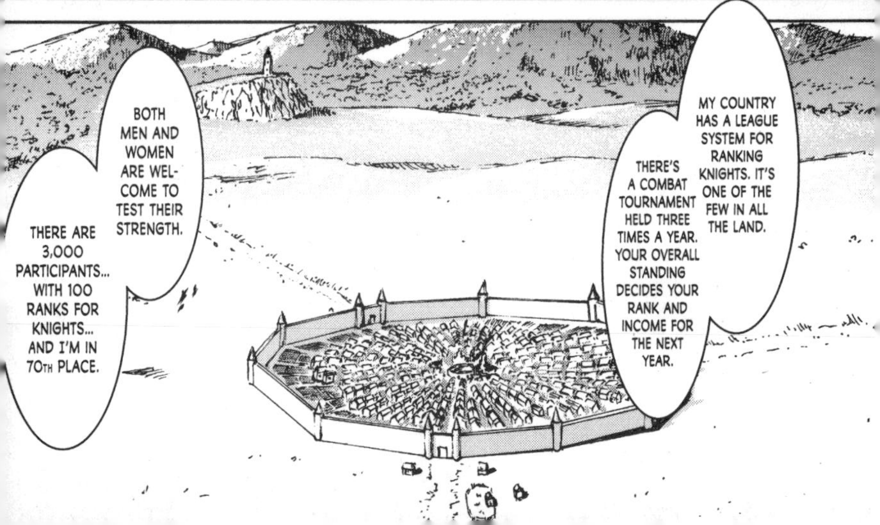
MY COUNTRY HAS A LEAGUE SYSTEM FOR RANKING KNIGHTS. IT'S ONE OF THE FEW IN ALL THE LAND.
THERE'S A COMBAT TOURNAMENT HELD THREE TIMES A YEAR. YOUR OVERALL STANDING DECIDES YOUR RANK AND INCOME FOR THE NEXT YEAR.
BOTH MEN AND WOMEN ARE WELCOME TO TEST THEIR STRENGTH.
THERE ARE 3,000 PARTICIPANTS... WITH 100 RANKS FOR KNIGHTS... AND I'M IN 70TH PLACE.

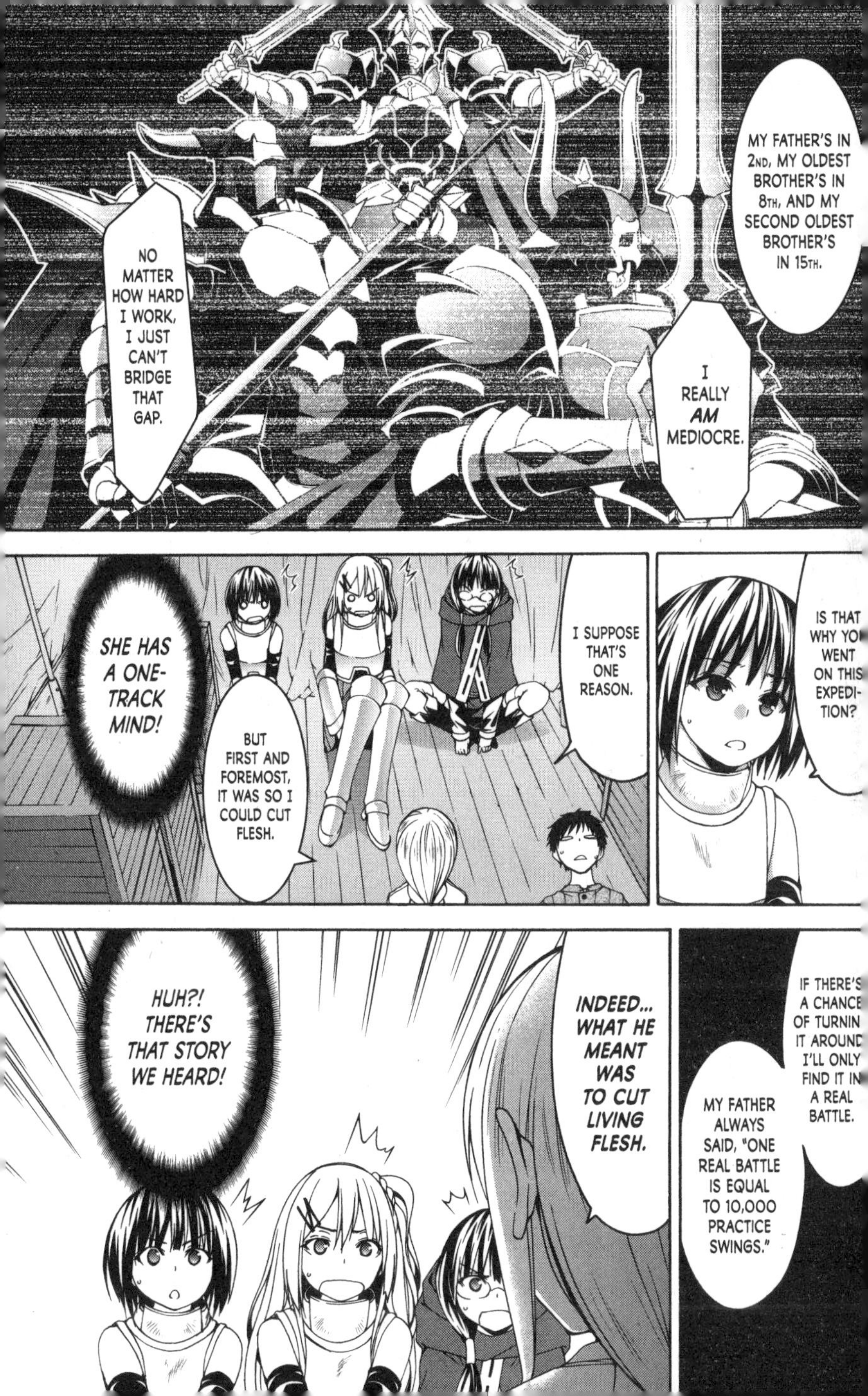
MY FATHER'S IN 2ND, MY OLDEST BROTHER'S IN 8TH, AND MY SECOND OLDEST BROTHER'S IN 15TH.
NO MATTER HOW HARD I WORK, I JUST CAN'T BRIDGE THAT GAP.
I REALLY *AM* MEDIOCRE.
IS THAT WHY YO WENT ON THIS EXPEDITION?
I SUPPOSE THAT'S ONE REASON.
BUT FIRST AND FOREMOST, IT WAS SO I COULD CUT FLESH.
SHE HAS A ONE-TRACK MIND!
MY FATHER ALWAYS SAID, "ONE REAL BATTLE IS EQUAL TO 10,000 PRACTICE SWINGS."
IF THERE'S A CHANCE OF TURNIN IT AROUND I'LL ONLY FIND IT IN A REAL BATTLE.
INDEED... WHAT HE MEANT WAS TO CUT LIVING FLESH.
HUH?! THERE'S THAT STORY WE HEARD!

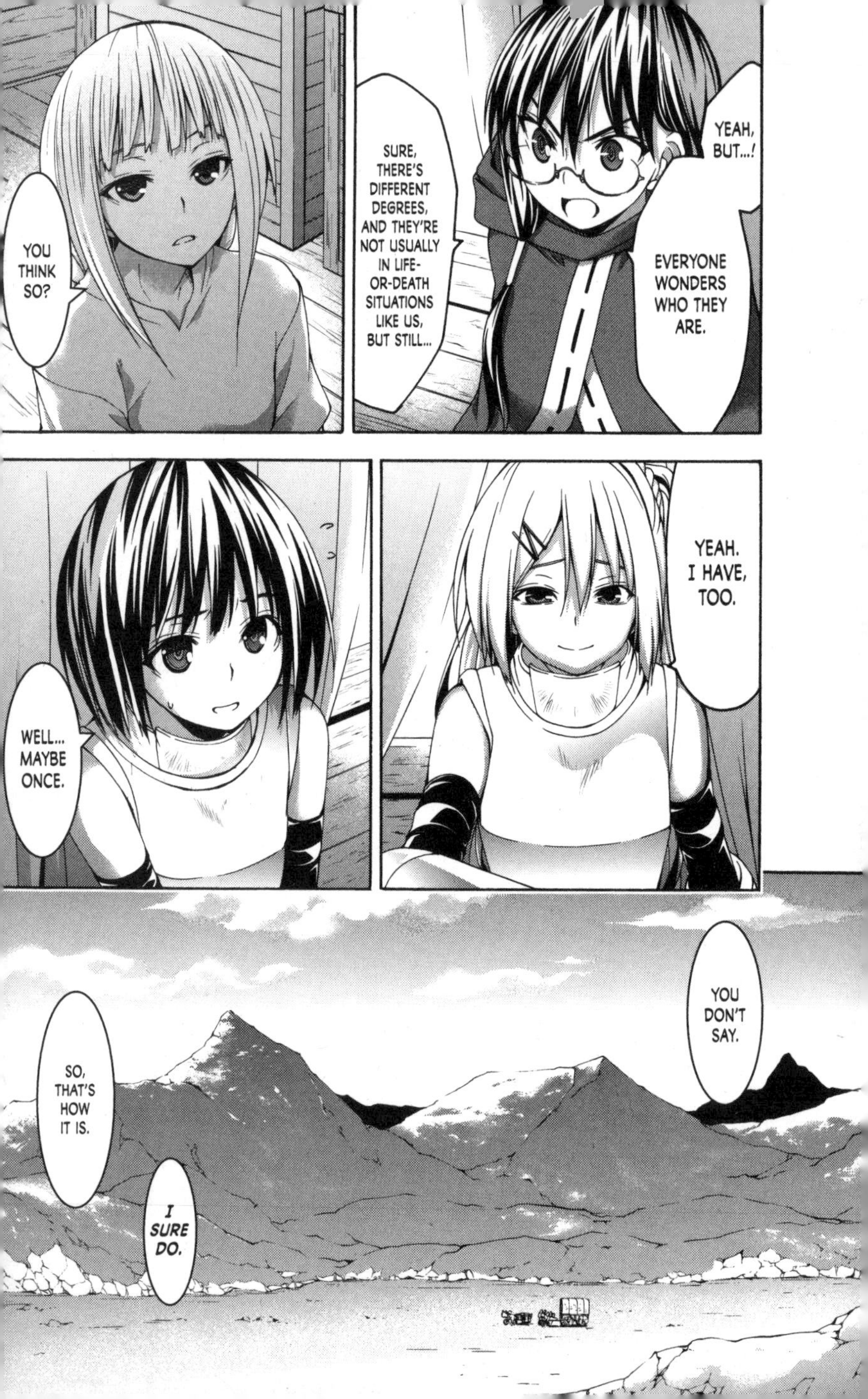
YEAH, BUT...!
EVERYONE WONDERS WHO THEY ARE.
SURE, THERE'S DIFFERENT DEGREES, AND THEY'RE NOT USUALLY IN LIFE-OR-DEATH SITUATIONS LIKE US, BUT STILL...
YOU THINK SO?
YEAH. I HAVE, TOO.
WELL... MAYBE ONCE.
YOU DON'T SAY.
SO, THAT'S HOW IT IS.
I SURE DO.

REMAINING TIME:
8 DAYS AND 17 HOURS → 7 DAYS AND 10 HOURS

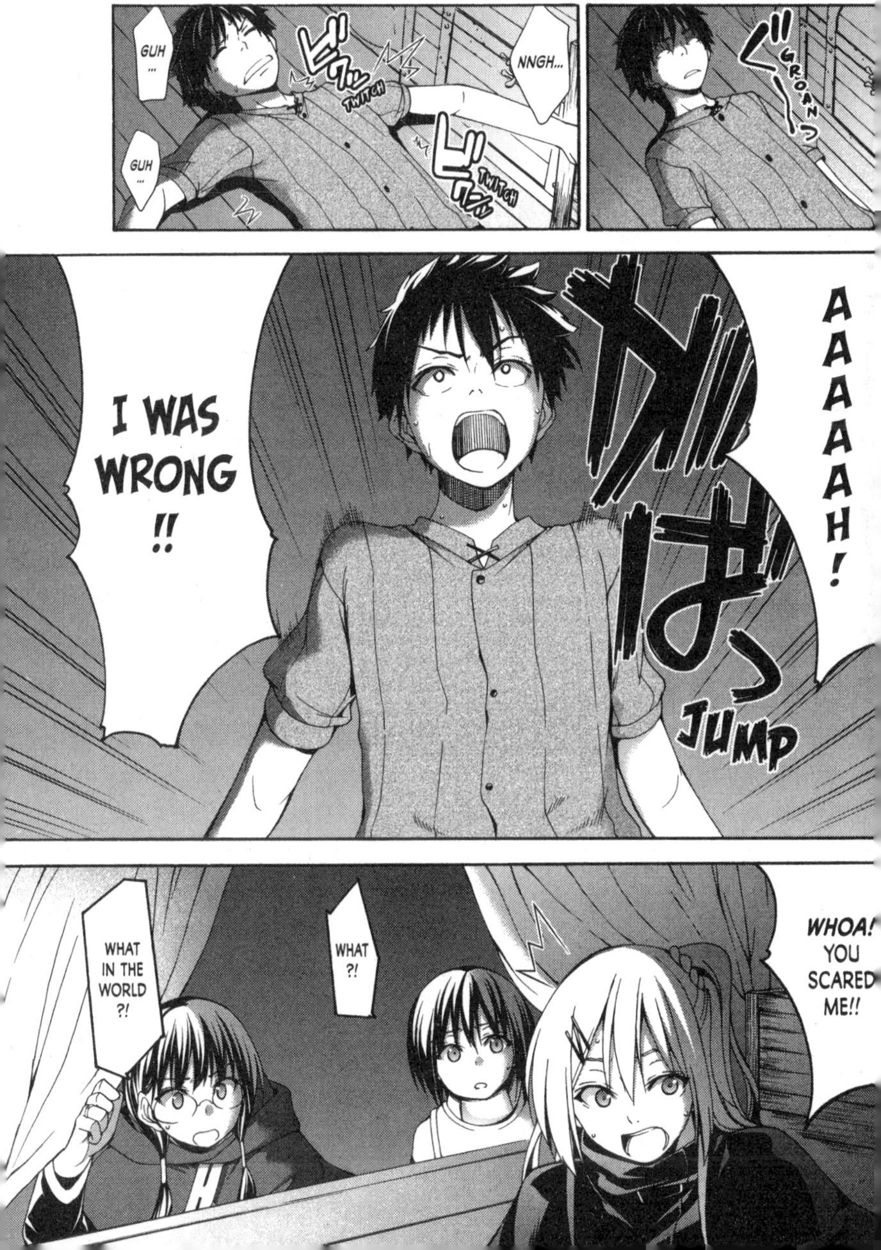
GROAN
NNGH...
TWITCH
GUH ...
GUH ...
TWITCH
AAAAAAH!
JUMP
I WAS WRONG !!
WHOA! YOU SCARED ME!!
WHAT ?!
WHAT IN THE WORLD ?!

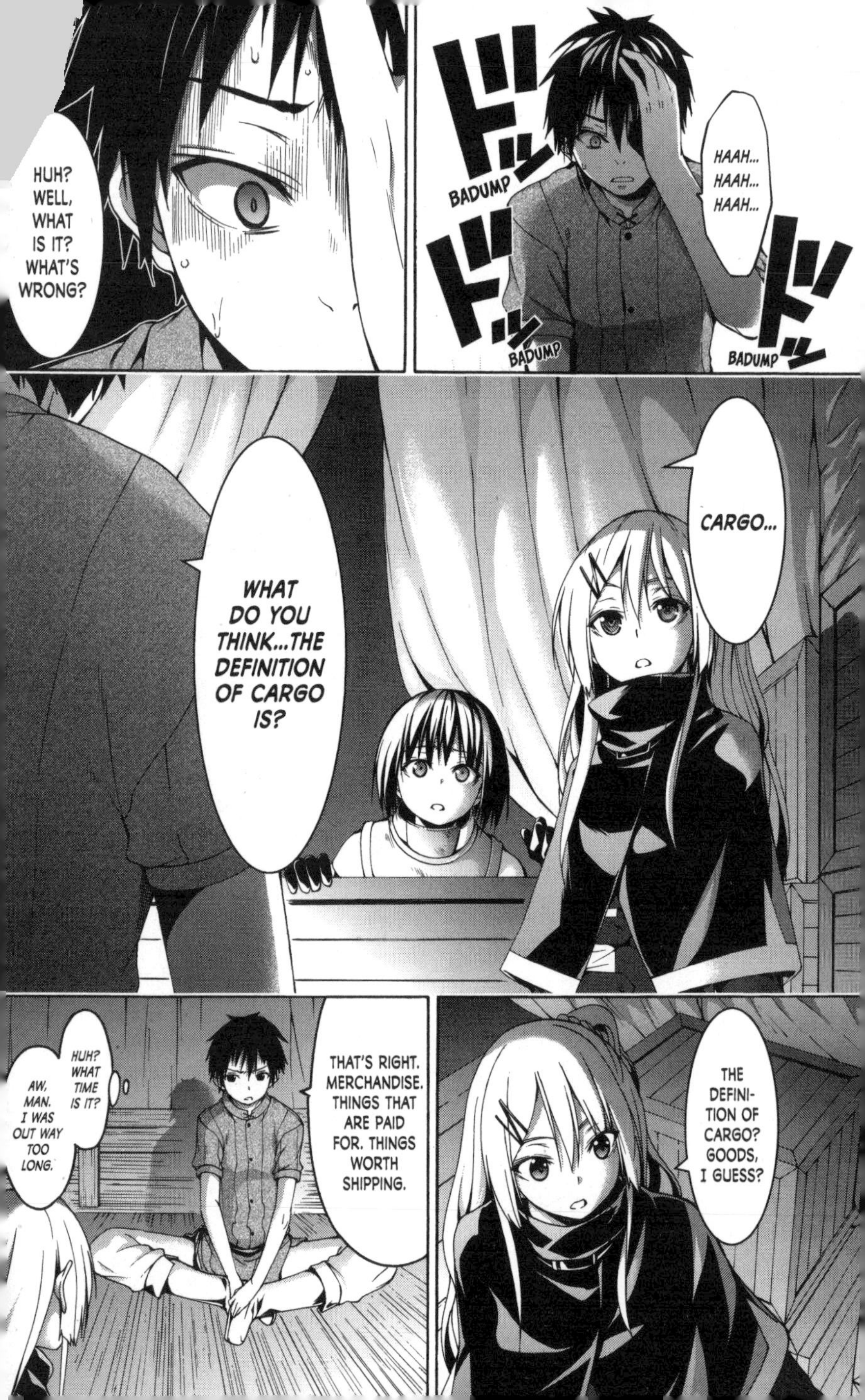
ドッ BADUMP
ドッ BADUMP
ドッ BADUMP
HAAH... HAAH... HAAH...
HUH? WELL, WHAT IS IT? WHAT'S WRONG?
CARGO...
WHAT DO YOU THINK...THE DEFINITION OF CARGO IS?
THE DEFINITION OF CARGO? GOODS, I GUESS?
THAT'S RIGHT. MERCHANDISE. THINGS THAT ARE PAID FOR. THINGS WORTH SHIPPING.
HUH? WHAT TIME IS IT?
AW, MAN. I WAS OUT WAY TOO LONG.

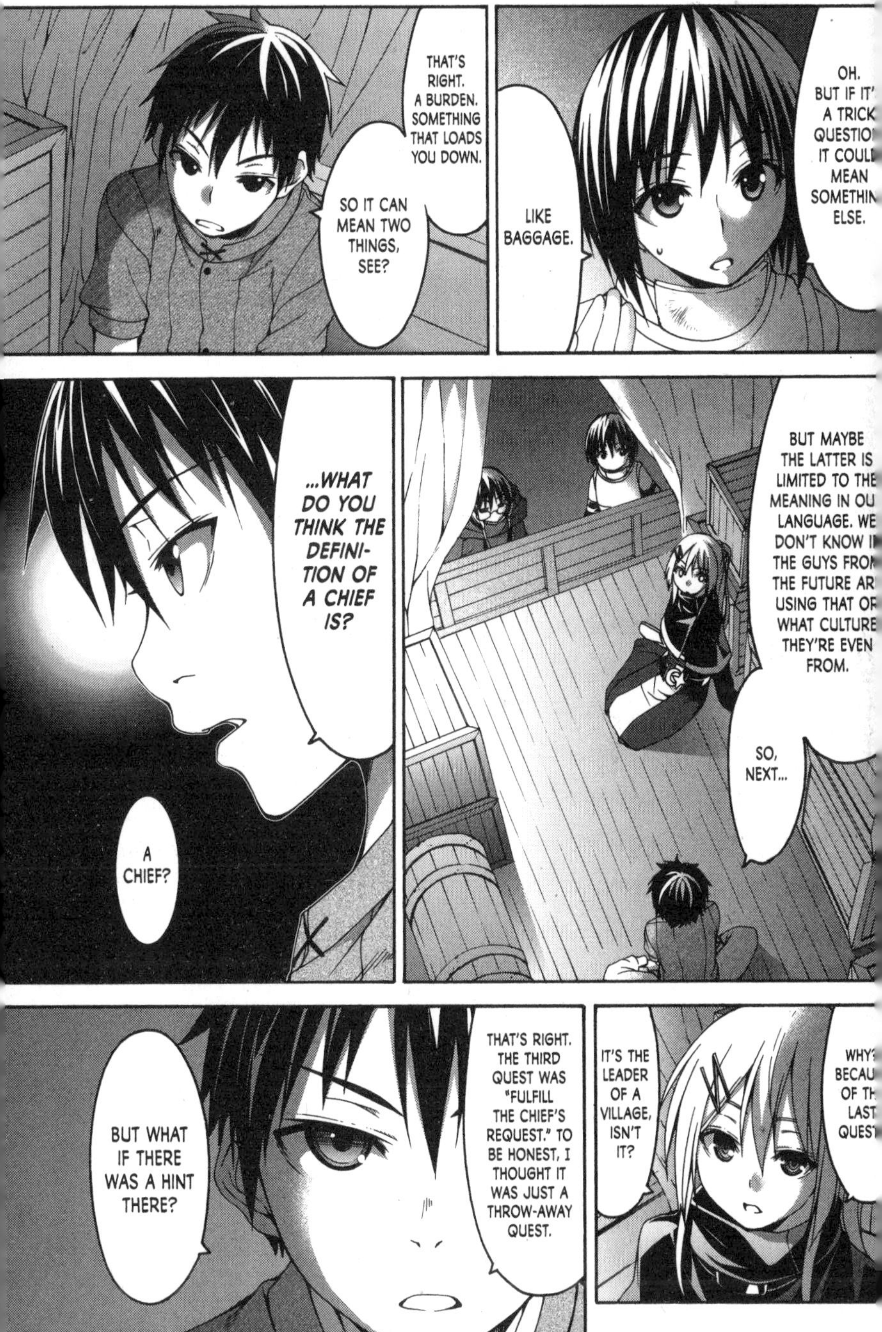
OH. BUT IF IT' A TRICK QUESTIO IT COUL MEAN SOMETHIN ELSE.
LIKE BAGGAGE.
THAT'S RIGHT. A BURDEN. SOMETHING THAT LOADS YOU DOWN.
SO IT CAN MEAN TWO THINGS, SEE?
BUT MAYBE THE LATTER IS LIMITED TO THE MEANING IN OU LANGUAGE. WE DON'T KNOW I THE GUYS FROM THE FUTURE AR USING THAT OR WHAT CULTURE THEY'RE EVEN FROM.
SO, NEXT...
...WHAT DO YOU THINK THE DEFINITION OF A CHIEF IS?
A CHIEF?
WHY? BECAU OF TH LAST QUEST
IT'S THE LEADER OF A VILLAGE, ISN'T IT?
THAT'S RIGHT. THE THIRD QUEST WAS "FULFILL THE CHIEF'S REQUEST." TO BE HONEST, I THOUGHT IT WAS JUST A THROW-AWAY QUEST.
BUT WHAT IF THERE WAS A HINT THERE?

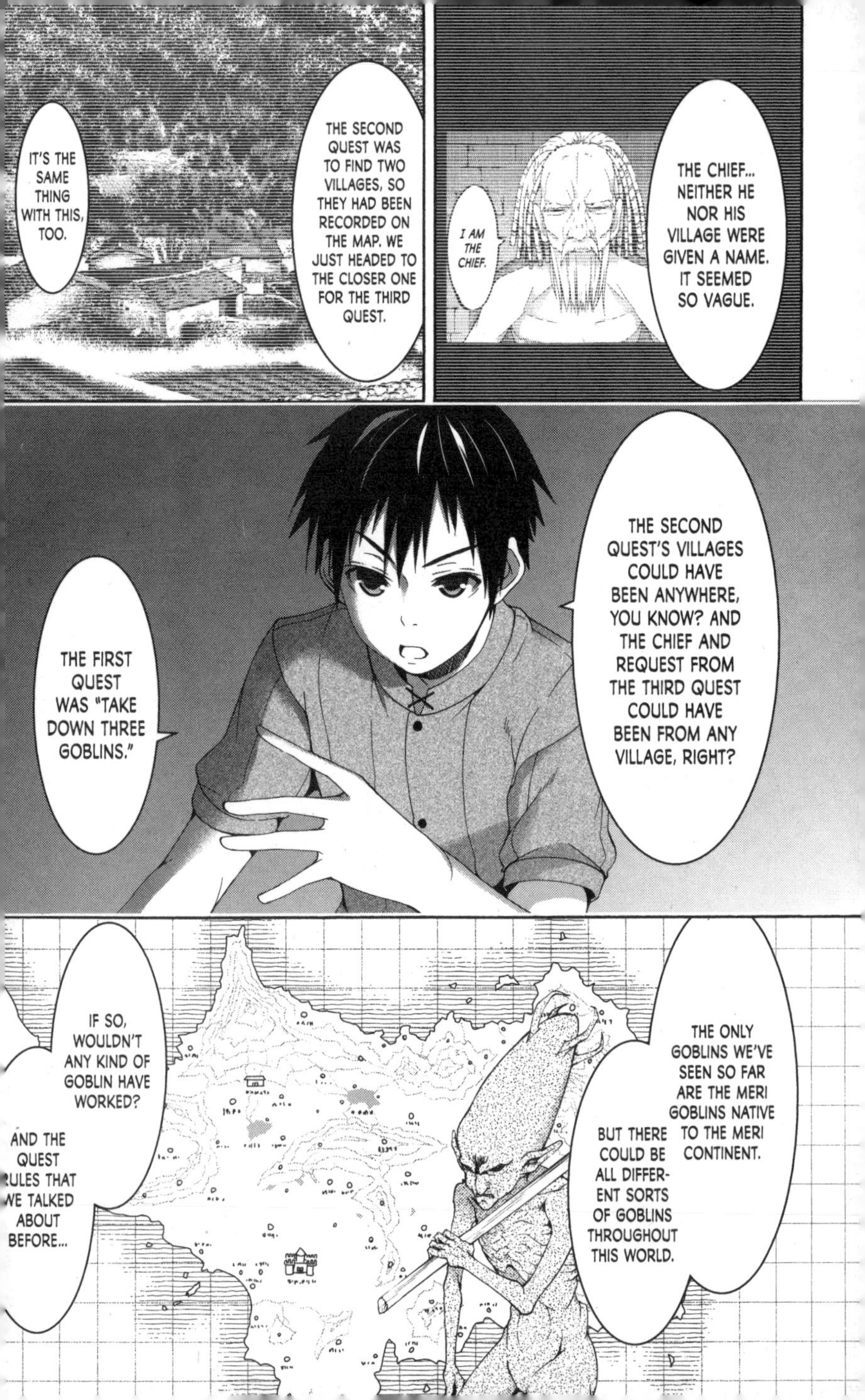
THE CHIEF... NEITHER HE NOR HIS VILLAGE WERE GIVEN A NAME. IT SEEMED SO VAGUE.
I AM THE CHIEF.
THE SECOND QUEST WAS TO FIND TWO VILLAGES, SO THEY HAD BEEN RECORDED ON THE MAP. WE JUST HEADED TO THE CLOSER ONE FOR THE THIRD QUEST.
IT'S THE SAME THING WITH THIS, TOO.
THE SECOND QUEST'S VILLAGES COULD HAVE BEEN ANYWHERE, YOU KNOW? AND THE CHIEF AND REQUEST FROM THE THIRD QUEST COULD HAVE BEEN FROM ANY VILLAGE, RIGHT?
THE FIRST QUEST WAS "TAKE DOWN THREE GOBLINS."
THE ONLY GOBLINS WE'VE SEEN SO FAR ARE THE MERI GOBLINS NATIVE TO THE MERI CONTINENT.
BUT THERE COULD BE ALL DIFFER-ENT SORTS OF GOBLINS THROUGHOUT THIS WORLD.
IF SO, WOULDN'T ANY KIND OF GOBLIN HAVE WORKED?
AND THE QUEST RULES THAT WE TALKED ABOUT BEFORE...

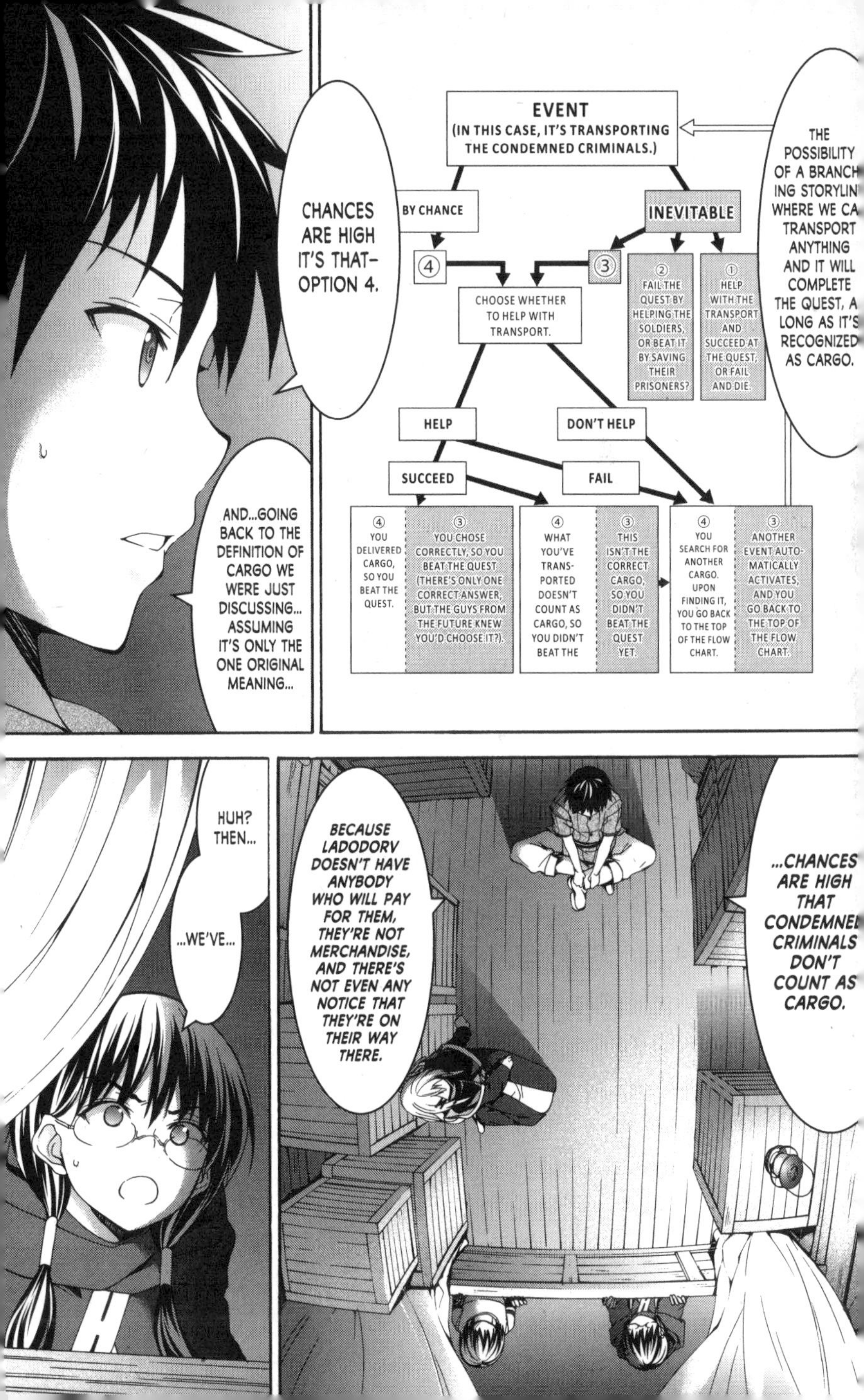
THE POSSIBILITY OF A BRANCH ING STORYLIN WHERE WE CA TRANSPORT ANYTHING AND IT WILL COMPLETE THE QUEST, A LONG AS IT'S RECOGNIZED AS CARGO.
EVENT (IN THIS CASE, IT'S TRANSPORTING THE CONDEMNED CRIMINALS.)
BY CHANCE
INEVITABLE
④
③
② FAIL THE QUEST BY HELPING THE SOLDIERS, OR BEAT IT BY SAVING THEIR PRISONERS?
① HELP WITH THE TRANSPORT AND SUCCEED AT THE QUEST, OR FAIL AND DIE.
CHOOSE WHETHER TO HELP WITH TRANSPORT.
HELP
DON'T HELP
SUCCEED
FAIL
④ YOU DELIVERED CARGO, SO YOU BEAT THE QUEST.
③ YOU CHOSE CORRECTLY, SO YOU BEAT THE QUEST (THERE'S ONLY ONE CORRECT ANSWER, BUT THE GUYS FROM THE FUTURE KNEW YOU'D CHOOSE IT?).
④ WHAT YOU'VE TRANS-PORTED DOESN'T COUNT AS CARGO, SO YOU DIDN'T BEAT THE
③ THIS ISN'T THE CORRECT CARGO, SO YOU DIDN'T BEAT THE QUEST YET.
④ YOU SEARCH FOR ANOTHER CARGO. UPON FINDING IT, YOU GO BACK TO THE TOP OF THE FLOW CHART.
③ ANOTHER EVENT AUTO-MATICALLY ACTIVATES, AND YOU GO BACK TO THE TOP OF THE FLOW CHART.
CHANCES ARE HIGH IT'S THAT— OPTION 4.
AND...GOING BACK TO THE DEFINITION OF CARGO WE WERE JUST DISCUSSING... ASSUMING IT'S ONLY THE ONE ORIGINAL MEANING...
...CHANCES ARE HIGH THAT CONDEMNEI CRIMINALS DON'T COUNT AS CARGO.
BECAUSE LADODORV DOESN'T HAVE ANYBODY WHO WILL PAY FOR THEM, THEY'RE NOT MERCHANDISE, AND THERE'S NOT EVEN ANY NOTICE THAT THEY'RE ON THEIR WAY THERE.
HUH? THEN...
...WE'VE...

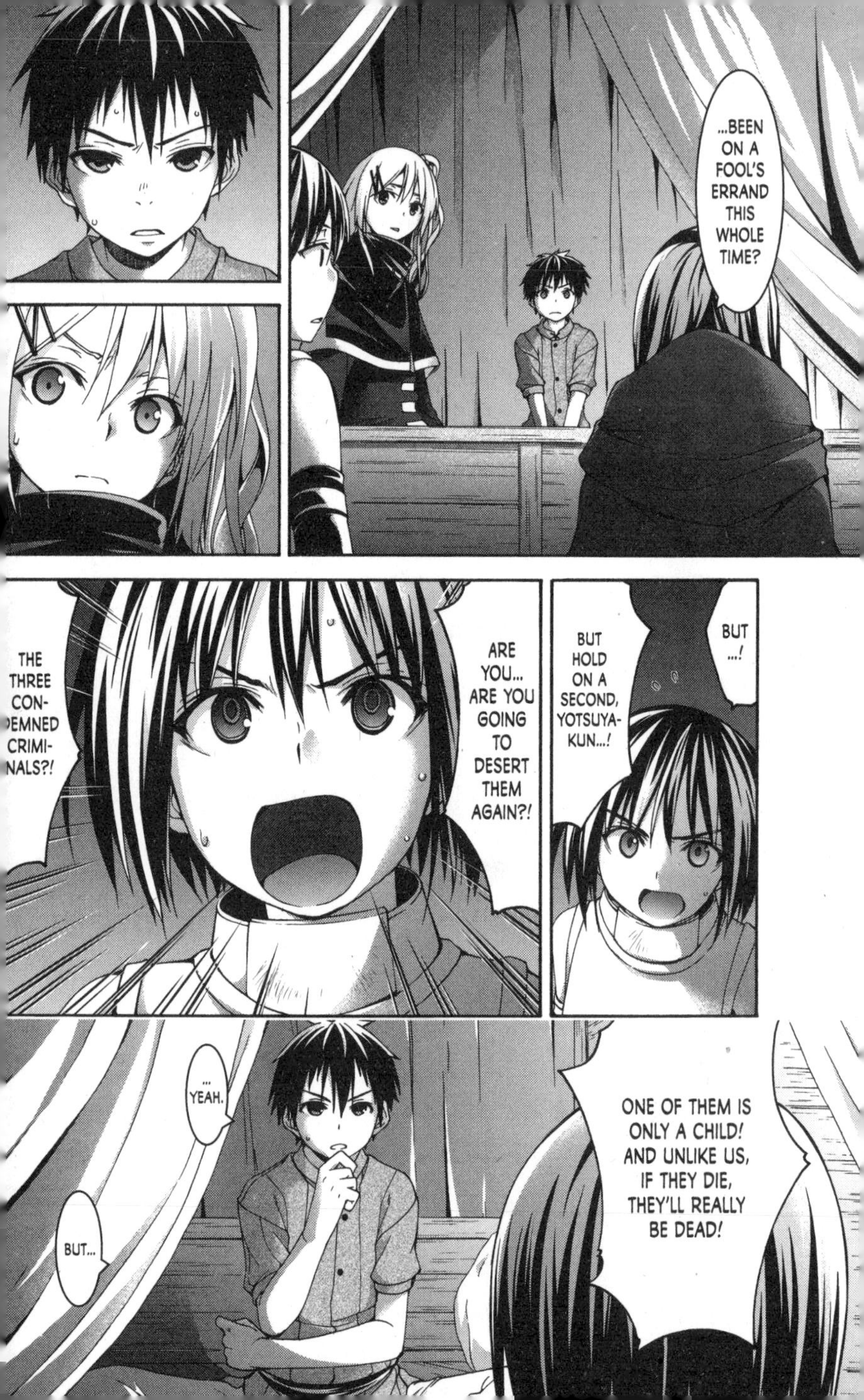
...BEEN ON A FOOL'S ERRAND THIS WHOLE TIME?
BUT ...!
BUT HOLD ON A SECOND, YOTSUYA-KUN...!
ARE YOU... ARE YOU GOING TO DESERT THEM AGAIN?!
THE THREE CON-EMNED CRIMI-NALS?!
ONE OF THEM IS ONLY A CHILD! AND UNLIKE US, IF THEY DIE, THEY'LL REALLY BE DEAD!
... YEAH.
BUT...

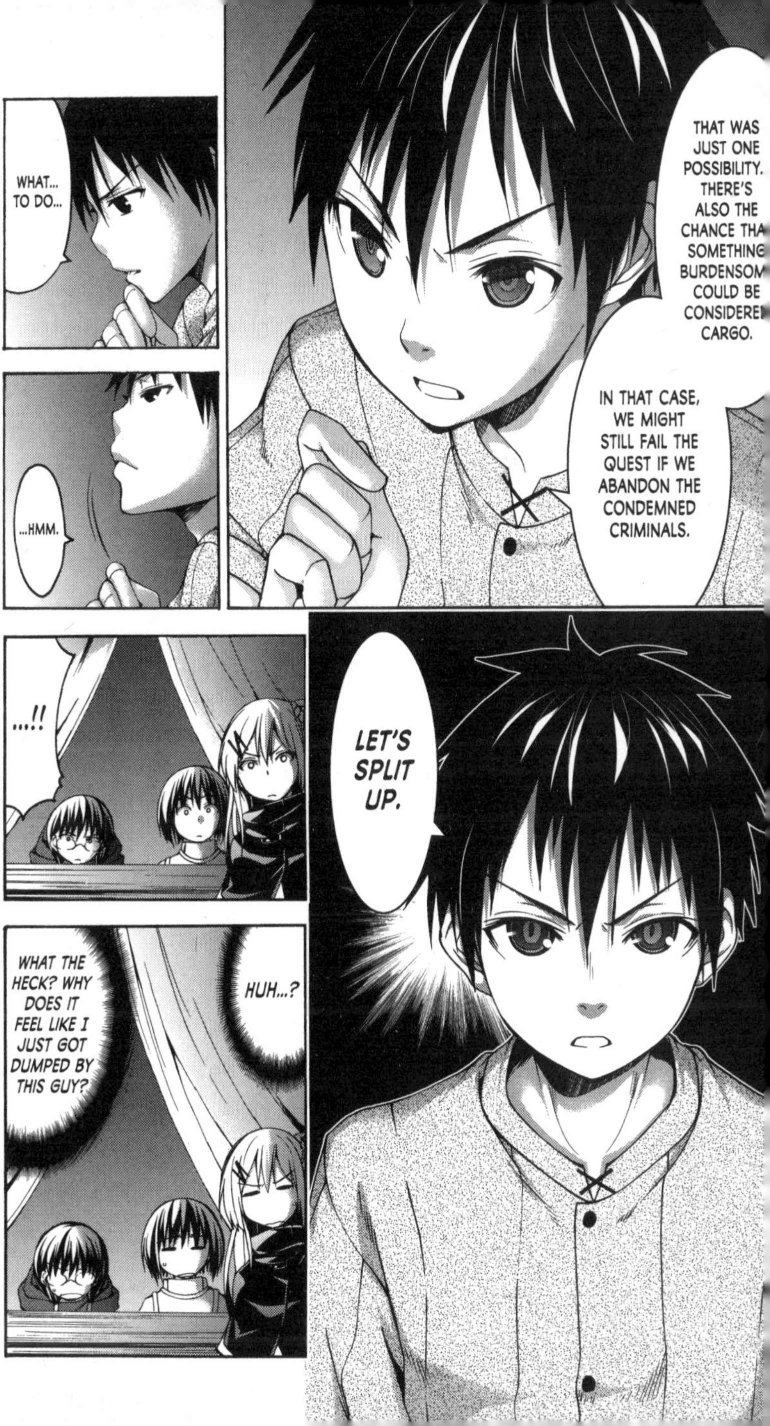
THAT WAS JUST ONE POSSIBILITY. THERE'S ALSO THE CHANCE THA SOMETHING BURDENSOM COULD BE CONSIDERE CARGO.
IN THAT CASE, WE MIGHT STILL FAIL THE QUEST IF WE ABANDON THE CONDEMNED CRIMINALS.
WHAT... TO DO...
...HMM.
LET'S SPLIT UP.
...!!
HUH...?
WHAT THE HECK? WHY DOES IT FEEL LIKE I JUST GOT DUMPED BY THIS GUY?

REMAINING TIME: 7 DAYS AND 1 HOUR

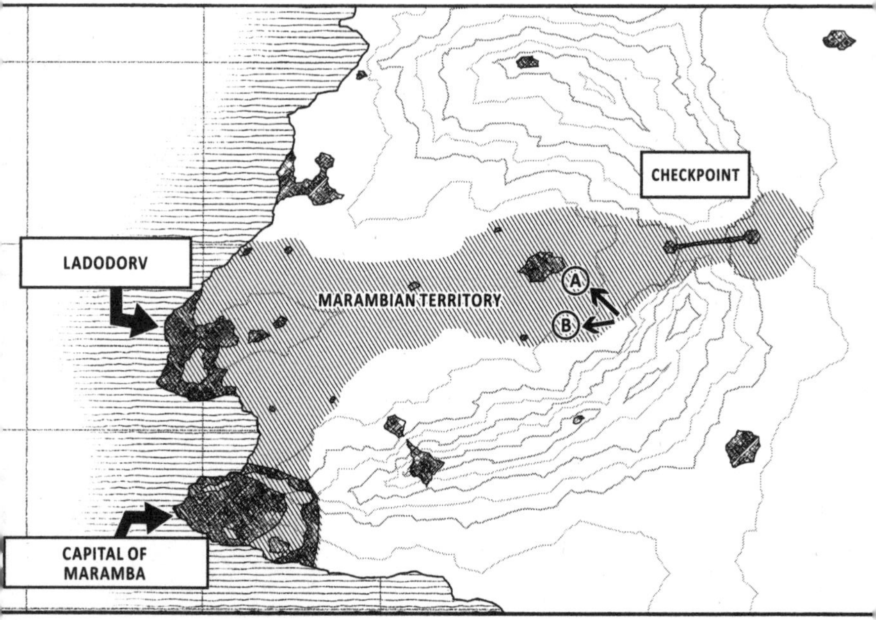
CHECKPOINT
LADODORV
MARAMBIAN TERRITORY
A
B
CAPITAL OF MARAMBA

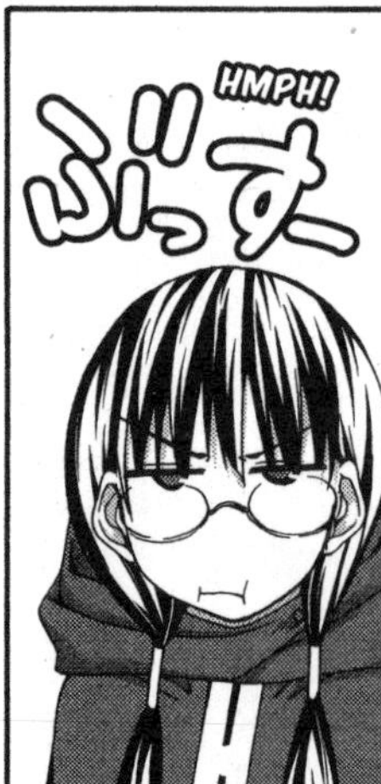
HMPH!
ぶーっすー

BEFORE SPLITTING UP...

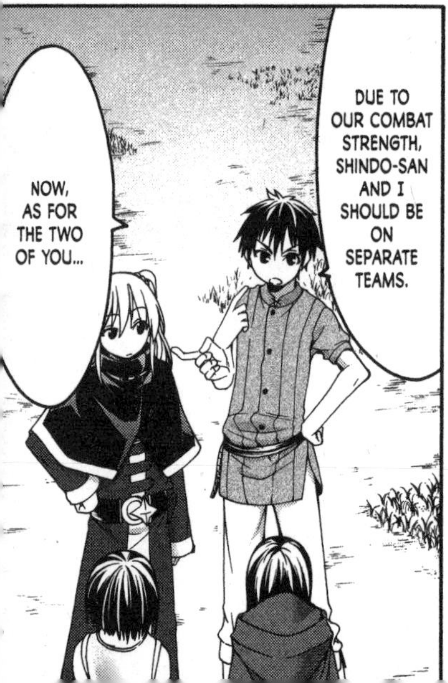
DUE TO OUR COMBAT STRENGTH, SHINDO-SAN AND I SHOULD BE ON SEPARATE TEAMS.
NOW, AS FOR THE TWO OF YOU...

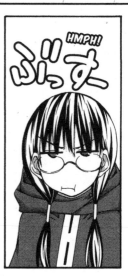

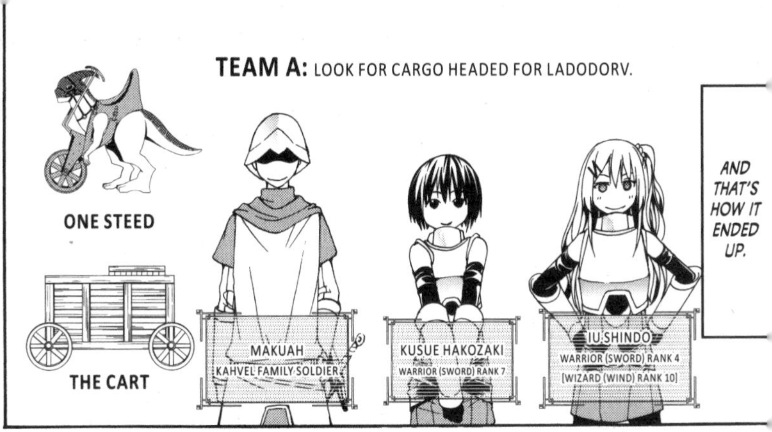
AND THAT'S HOW IT ENDED UP.
TEAM A: LOOK FOR CARGO HEADED FOR LADODORV.
ONE STEED
THE CART
MAKUAH
KAHVEL FAMILY SOLDIER
KUSUE HAKOZAKI
WARRIOR (SWORD) RANK 7
IU SHINDO
WARRIOR (SWORD) RANK 4
[WIZARD (WIND) RANK 10]

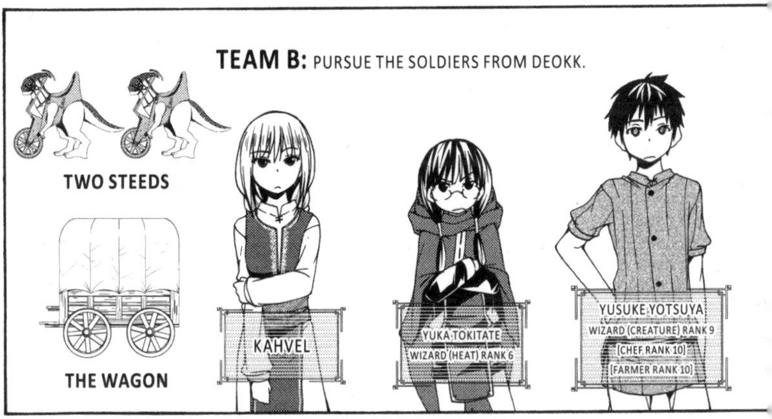
TEAM B: PURSUE THE SOLDIERS FROM DEOKK.
TWO STEEDS
THE WAGON
KAHVEL
YUKA TOKITATE
WIZARD (HEAT) RANK 6
YUSUKE YOTSUYA
WIZARD (CREATURE) RANK 9
[CHEF RANK 10]
[FARMER RANK 10]

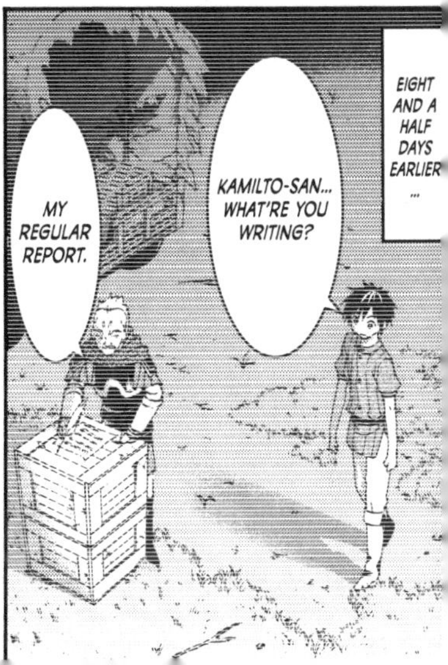
EIGHT AND A HALF DAYS EARLIER ...
KAMILTO-SAN... WHAT'RE YOU WRITING?
MY REGULAR REPORT.

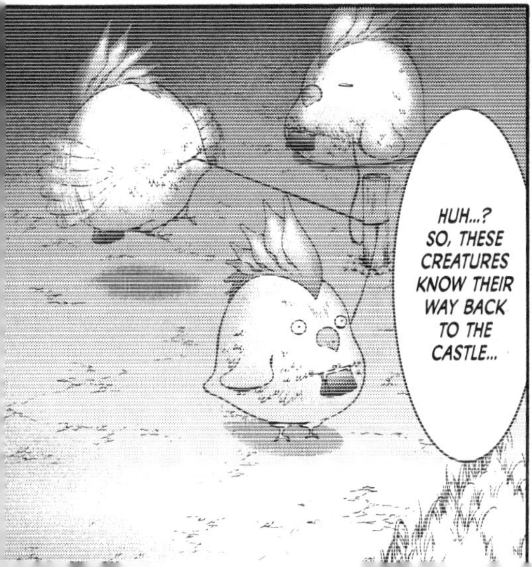
HUH...? SO, THESE CREATURES KNOW THEIR WAY BACK TO THE CASTLE...

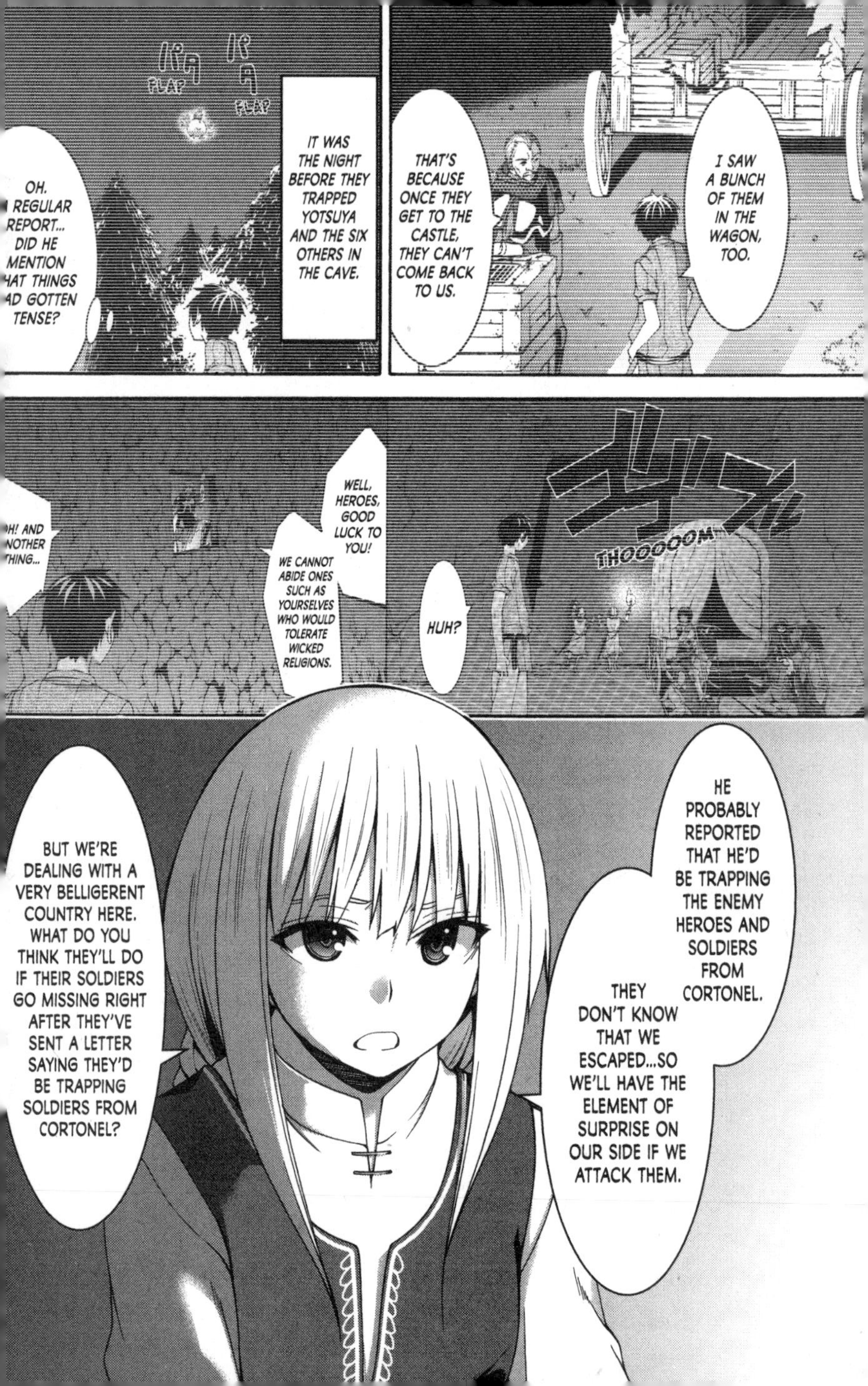
I SAW A BUNCH OF THEM IN THE WAGON, TOO.
THAT'S BECAUSE ONCE THEY GET TO THE CASTLE, THEY CAN'T COME BACK TO US.
IT WAS THE NIGHT BEFORE THEY TRAPPED YOTSUYA AND THE SIX OTHERS IN THE CAVE.
FLAP
FLAP
OH. REGULAR REPORT... DID HE MENTION HAT THINGS AD GOTTEN TENSE?
THOOOOOM
HUH?
WELL, HEROES, GOOD LUCK TO YOU!
WE CANNOT ABIDE ONES SUCH AS YOURSELVES WHO WOULD TOLERATE WICKED RELIGIONS.
H! AND NOTHER THING...
HE PROBABLY REPORTED THAT HE'D BE TRAPPING THE ENEMY HEROES AND SOLDIERS FROM CORTONEL.
THEY DON'T KNOW THAT WE ESCAPED...SO WE'LL HAVE THE ELEMENT OF SURPRISE ON OUR SIDE IF WE ATTACK THEM.
BUT WE'RE DEALING WITH A VERY BELLIGERENT COUNTRY HERE. WHAT DO YOU THINK THEY'LL DO IF THEIR SOLDIERS GO MISSING RIGHT AFTER THEY'VE SENT A LETTER SAYING THEY'D BE TRAPPING SOLDIERS FROM CORTONEL?

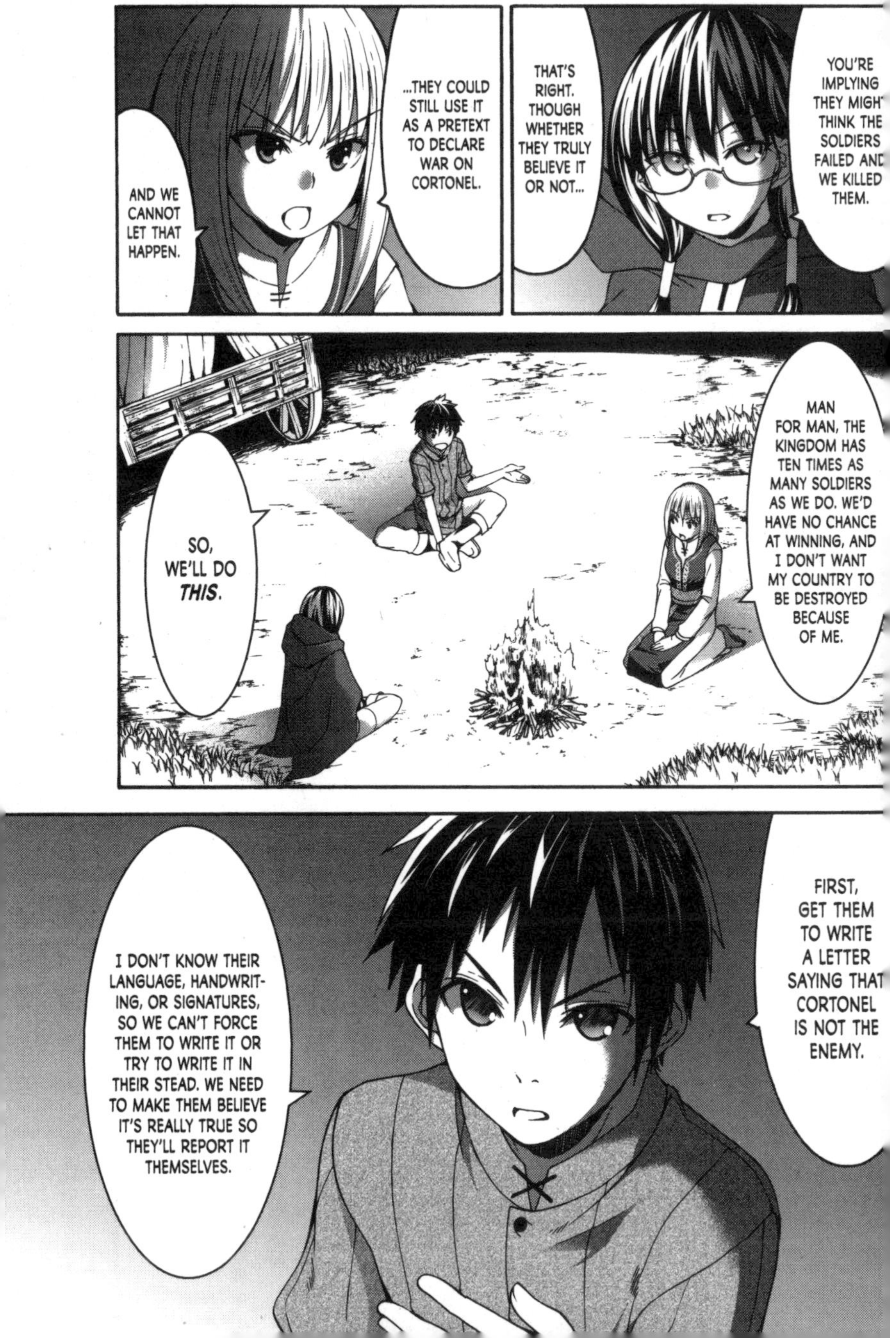
YOU'RE IMPLYING THEY MIGHT THINK THE SOLDIERS FAILED AND WE KILLED THEM.
THAT'S RIGHT. THOUGH WHETHER THEY TRULY BELIEVE IT OR NOT...
...THEY COULD STILL USE IT AS A PRETEXT TO DECLARE WAR ON CORTONEL.
AND WE CANNOT LET THAT HAPPEN.
MAN FOR MAN, THE KINGDOM HAS TEN TIMES AS MANY SOLDIERS AS WE DO. WE'D HAVE NO CHANCE AT WINNING, AND I DON'T WANT MY COUNTRY TO BE DESTROYED BECAUSE OF ME.
SO, WE'LL DO *THIS*.
FIRST, GET THEM TO WRITE A LETTER SAYING THAT CORTONEL IS NOT THE ENEMY.
I DON'T KNOW THEIR LANGUAGE, HANDWRIT-ING, OR SIGNATURES, SO WE CAN'T FORCE THEM TO WRITE IT OR TRY TO WRITE IT IN THEIR STEAD. WE NEED TO MAKE THEM BELIEVE IT'S REALLY TRUE SO THEY'LL REPORT IT THEMSELVES.

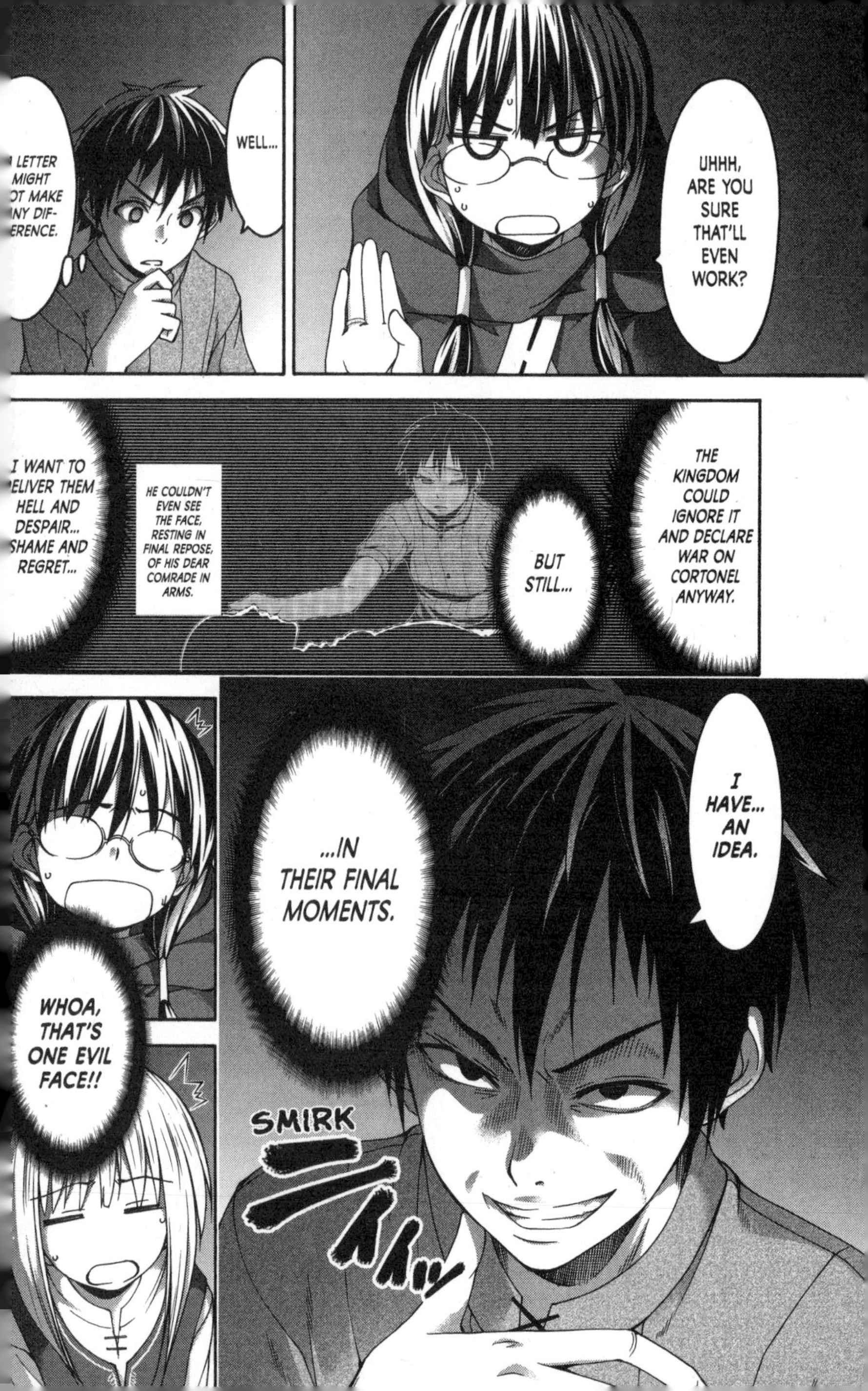
UHHH, ARE YOU SURE THAT'LL EVEN WORK?
WELL...
LETTER MIGHT OT MAKE NY DIF- ERENCE.
THE KINGDOM COULD IGNORE IT AND DECLARE WAR ON CORTONEL ANYWAY.
BUT STILL...
HE COULDN'T EVEN SEE THE FACE, RESTING IN FINAL REPOSE, OF HIS DEAR COMRADE IN ARMS.
I WANT TO ELIVER THEM HELL AND DESPAIR... HAME AND REGRET...
I HAVE... AN IDEA.
...IN THEIR FINAL MOMENTS.
WHOA, THAT'S ONE EVIL FACE!!
SMIRK

REMAINING TIME: 5 DAYS AND 17 HOURS

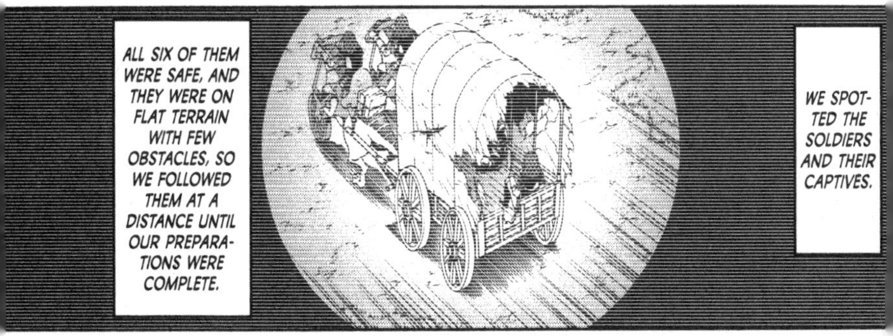
WE SPOTTED THE SOLDIERS AND THEIR CAPTIVES.
ALL SIX OF THEM WERE SAFE, AND THEY WERE ON FLAT TERRAIN WITH FEW OBSTACLES, SO WE FOLLOWED THEM AT A DISTANCE UNTIL OUR PREPARATIONS WERE COMPLETE.

REMAINING TIME: 5 DAYS AND 9 HOURS

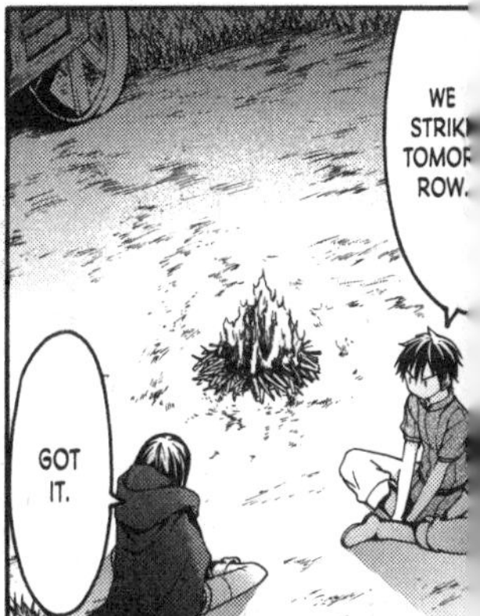
WE STRIK TOMOR ROW.
GOT IT.

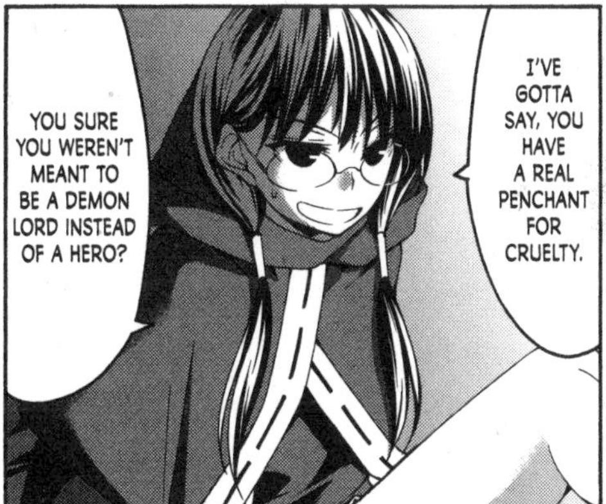
I'VE GOTTA SAY, YOU HAVE A REAL PENCHANT FOR CRUELTY.
YOU SURE YOU WEREN'T MEANT TO BE A DEMON LORD INSTEAD OF A HERO?

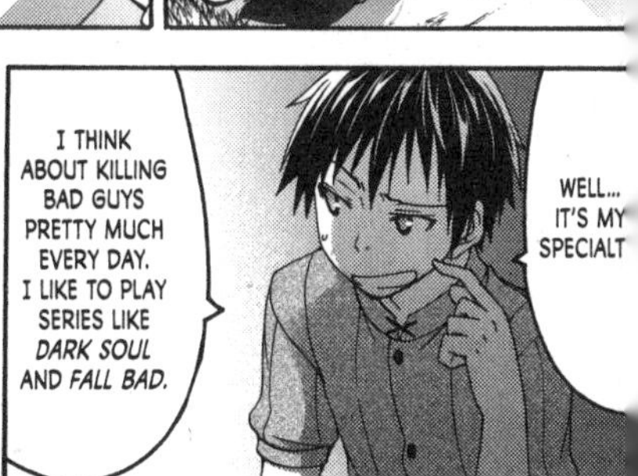
WELL... IT'S MY SPECIALT
I THINK ABOUT KILLING BAD GUYS PRETTY MUCH EVERY DAY. I LIKE TO PLAY SERIES LIKE *DARK SOUL* AND *FALL BAD*.

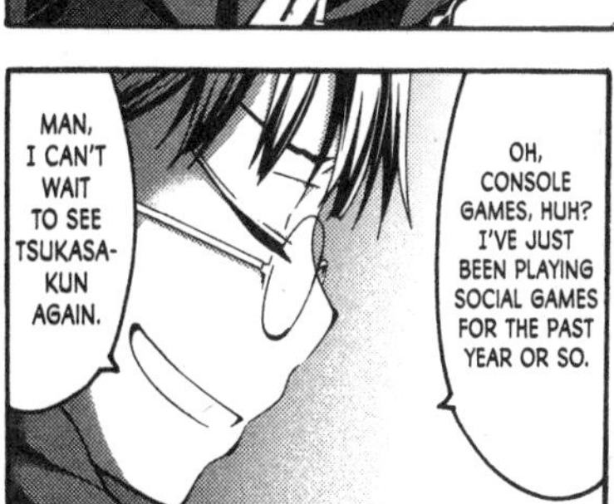
OH, CONSOLE GAMES, HUH? I'VE JUST BEEN PLAYING SOCIAL GAMES FOR THE PAST YEAR OR SO.
MAN, I CAN'T WAIT TO SEE TSUKASA-KUN AGAIN.

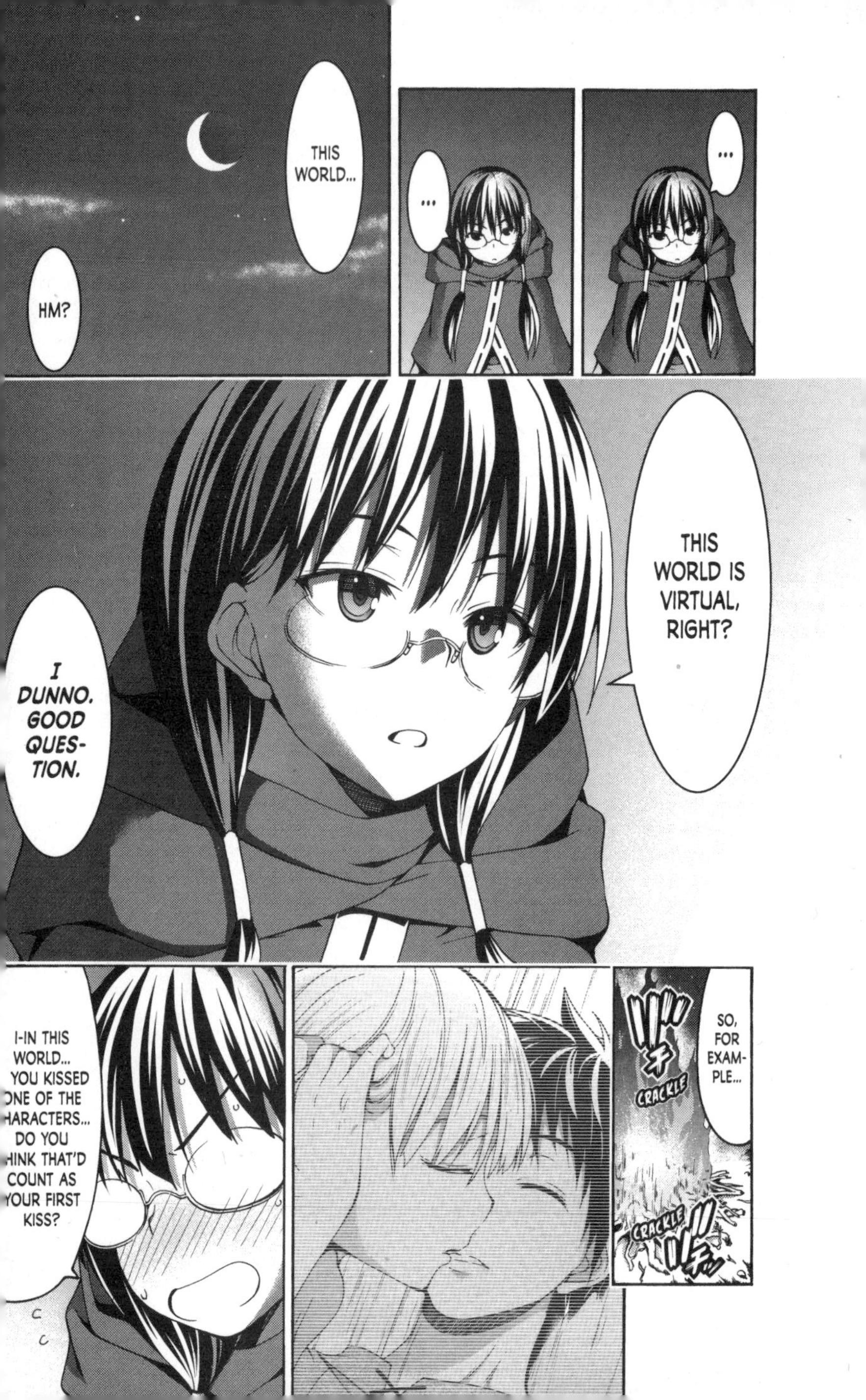
...
...
THIS WORLD...
HM?
THIS WORLD IS VIRTUAL, RIGHT?
I DUNNO. GOOD QUES-TION.
SO, FOR EXAMPLE...
CRACKLE
CRACKLE
I-IN THIS WORLD... YOU KISSED ONE OF THE CHARACTERS... DO YOU THINK THAT'D COUNT AS YOUR FIRST KISS?

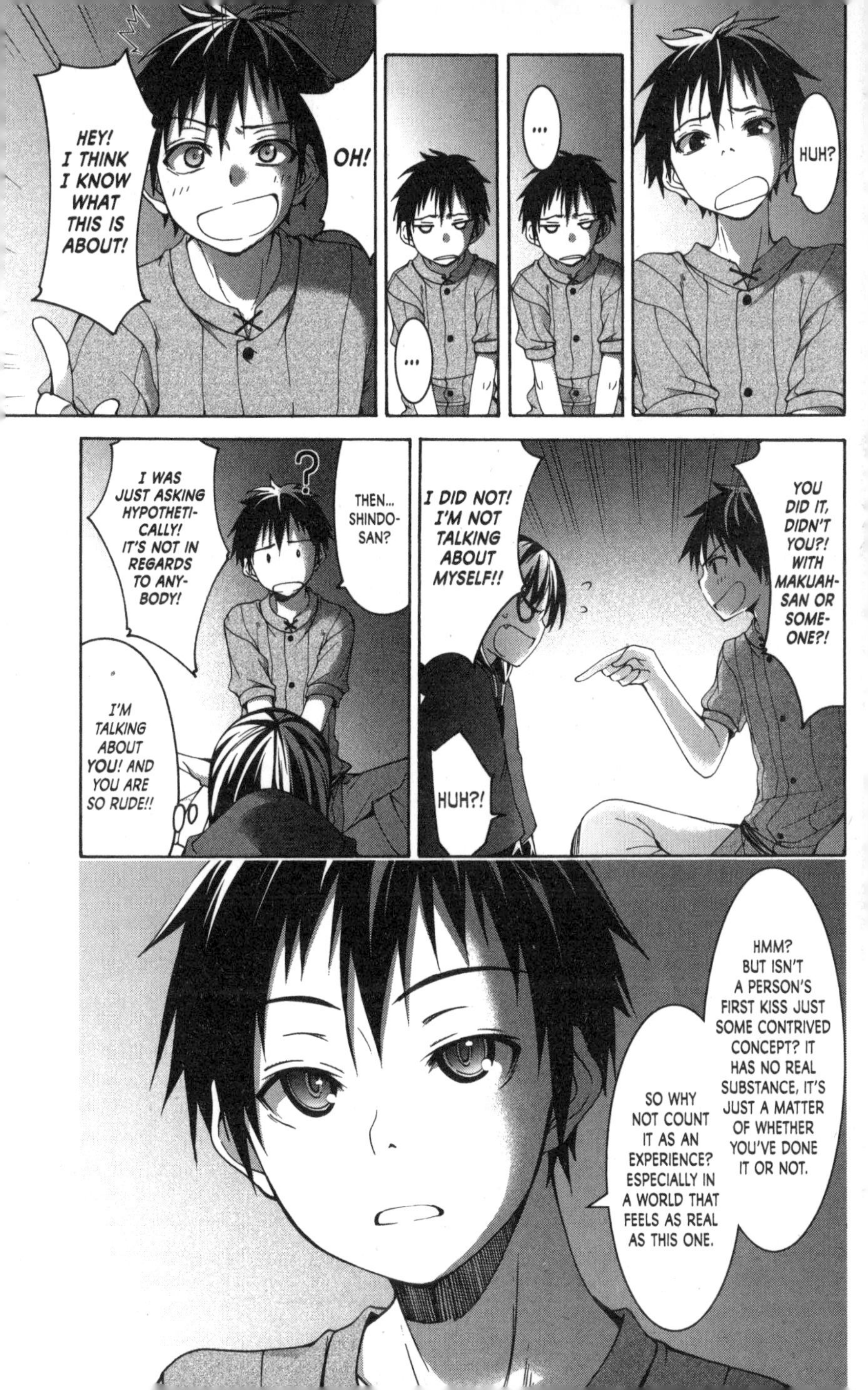
HUH?
...
...
OH!
HEY! I THINK I KNOW WHAT THIS IS ABOUT!
YOU DID IT, DIDN'T YOU?! WITH MAKUAH-SAN OR SOME-ONE?!
I DID NOT! I'M NOT TALKING ABOUT MYSELF!!
HUH?!
THEN... SHINDO-SAN?
I WAS JUST ASKING HYPOTHETI-CALLY! IT'S NOT IN REGARDS TO ANY-BODY!
I'M TALKING ABOUT YOU! AND YOU ARE SO RUDE!!
HMM? BUT ISN'T A PERSON'S FIRST KISS JUST SOME CONTRIVED CONCEPT? IT HAS NO REAL SUBSTANCE, IT'S JUST A MATTER OF WHETHER YOU'VE DONE IT OR NOT.
SO WHY NOT COUNT IT AS AN EXPERIENCE? ESPECIALLY IN A WORLD THAT FEELS AS REAL AS THIS ONE.

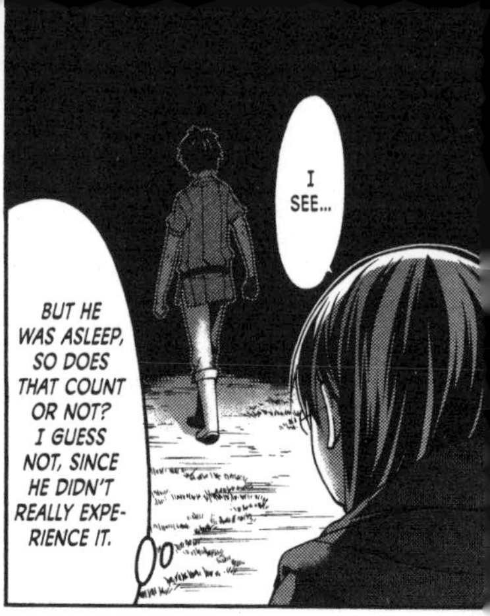
I SEE...
BUT HE WAS ASLEEP, SO DOES THAT COUNT OR NOT? I GUESS NOT, SINCE HE DIDN'T REALLY EXPE-RIENCE IT.
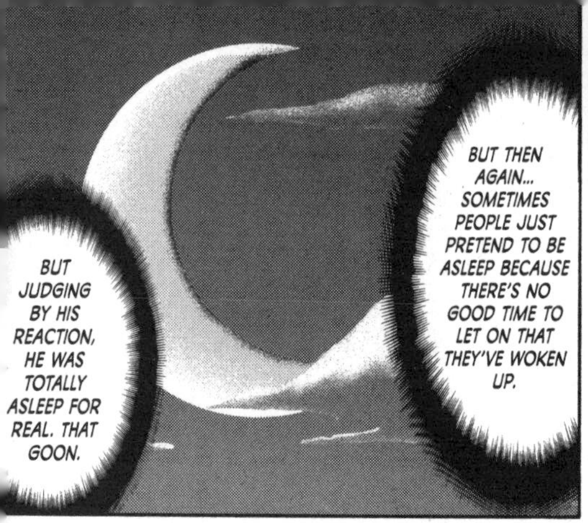
BUT THEN AGAIN... SOMETIMES PEOPLE JUST PRETEND TO BE ASLEEP BECAUSE THERE'S NO GOOD TIME TO LET ON THAT THEY'VE WOKEN UP.
BUT JUDGING BY HIS REACTION, HE WAS TOTALLY ASLEEP FOR REAL. THAT GOON.

REMAINING TIME: 4 DAYS AND 15 HOURS

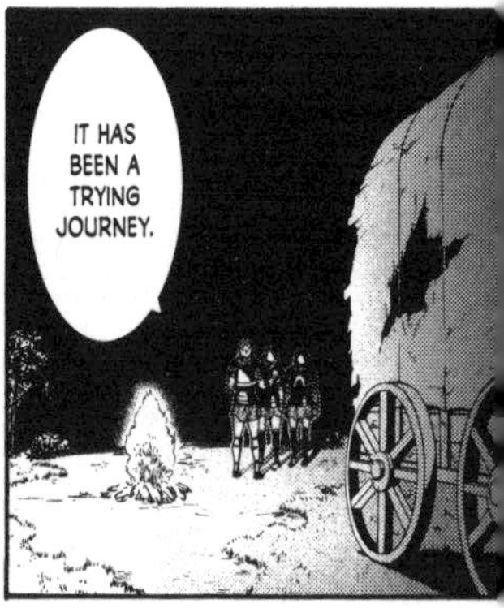
IT HAS BEEN A TRYING JOURNEY.
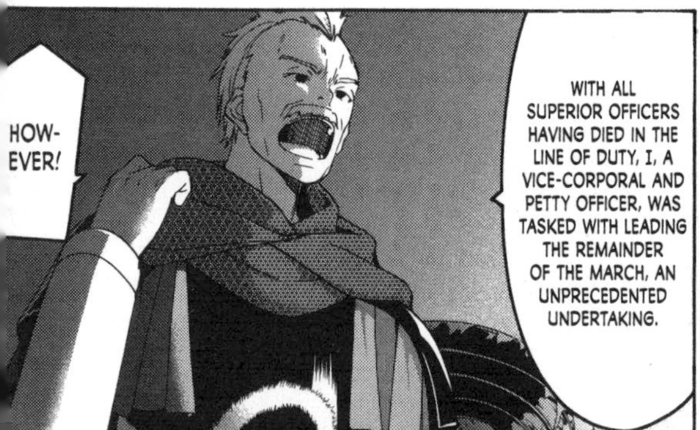
WITH ALL SUPERIOR OFFICERS HAVING DIED IN THE LINE OF DUTY, I, A VICE-CORPORAL AND PETTY OFFICER, WAS TASKED WITH LEADING THE REMAINDER OF THE MARCH, AN UNPRECEDENTED UNDERTAKING.
HOW-EVER!
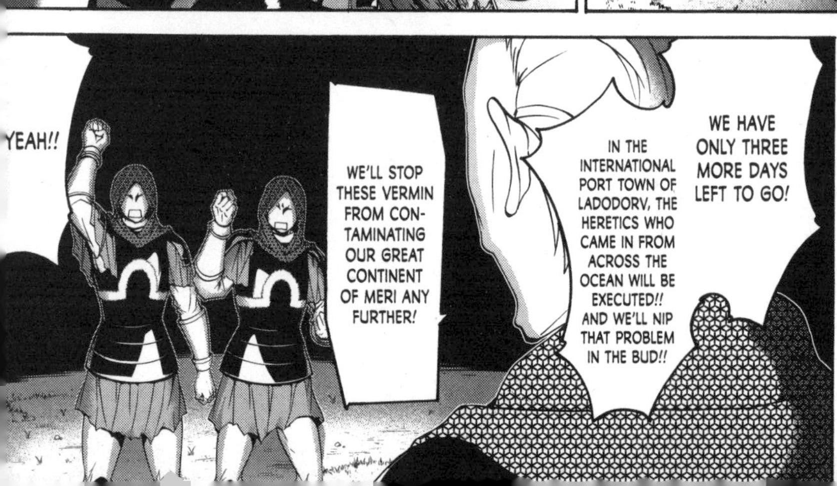
WE HAVE ONLY THREE MORE DAYS LEFT TO GO!
IN THE INTERNATIONAL PORT TOWN OF LADODORV, THE HERETICS WHO CAME IN FROM ACROSS THE OCEAN WILL BE EXECUTED!! AND WE'LL NIP THAT PROBLEM IN THE BUD!!
WE'LL STOP THESE VERMIN FROM CON-TAMINATING OUR GREAT CONTINENT OF MERI ANY FURTHER!
YEAH!!

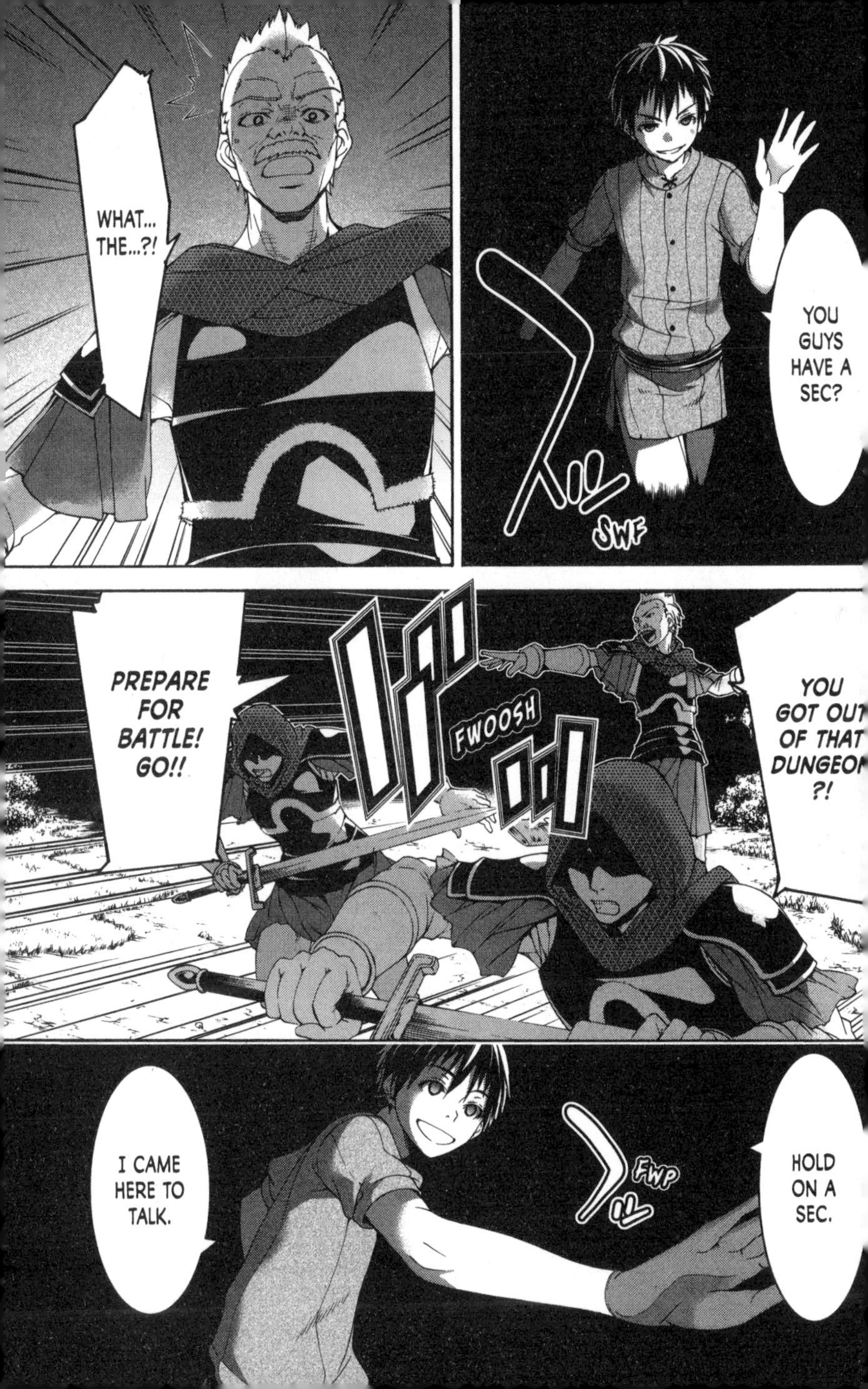

YOU GUYS HAVE A SEC?
SWF
WHAT... THE...?!
YOU GOT OUT OF THAT DUNGEON ?!
FWOOSH
PREPARE FOR BATTLE! GO!!
HOLD ON A SEC.
FWP
I CAME HERE TO TALK.

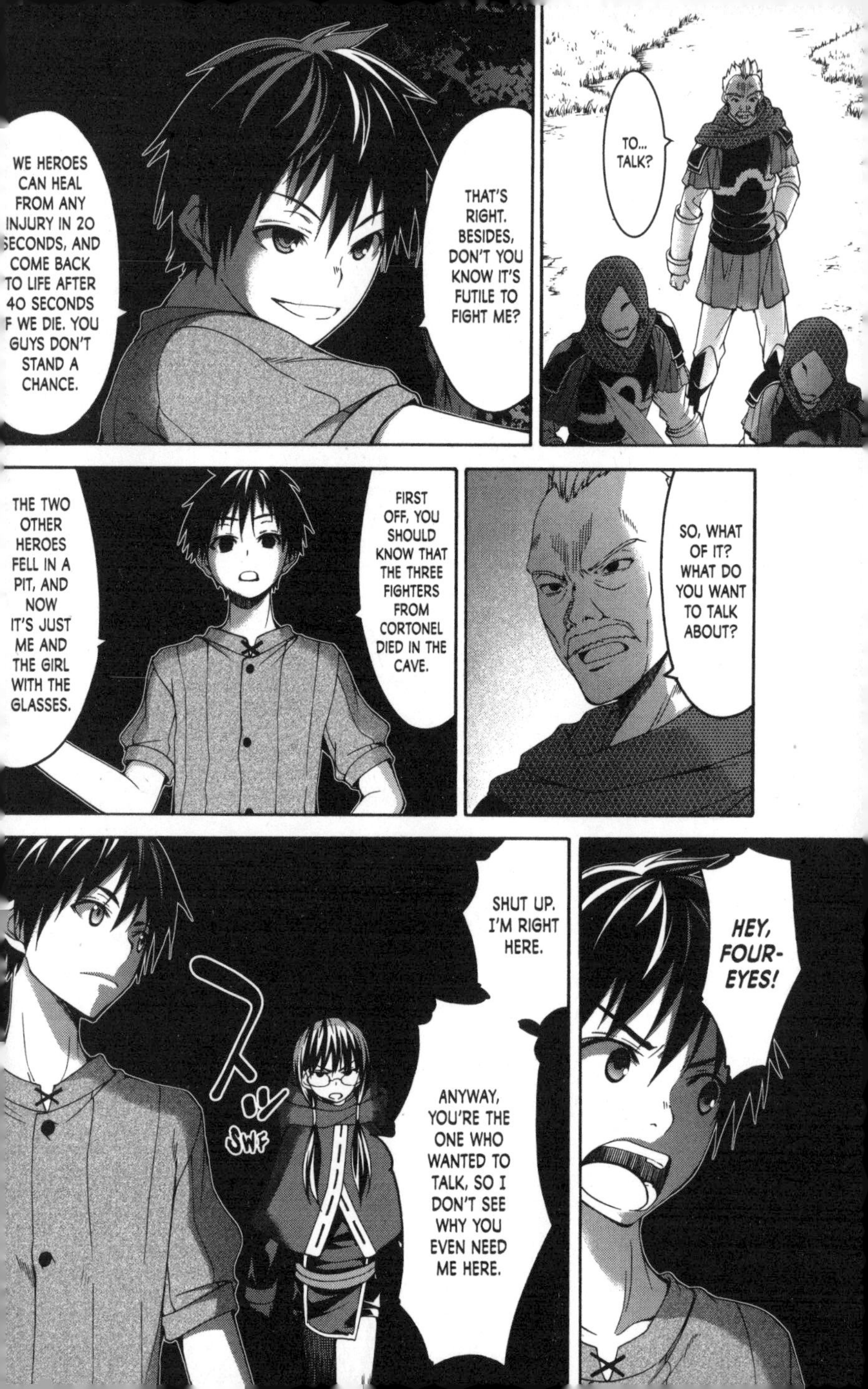
TO... TALK?
THAT'S RIGHT. BESIDES, DON'T YOU KNOW IT'S FUTILE TO FIGHT ME?
WE HEROES CAN HEAL FROM ANY INJURY IN 20 SECONDS, AND COME BACK TO LIFE AFTER 40 SECONDS F WE DIE. YOU GUYS DON'T STAND A CHANCE.
SO, WHAT OF IT? WHAT DO YOU WANT TO TALK ABOUT?
FIRST OFF, YOU SHOULD KNOW THAT THE THREE FIGHTERS FROM CORTONEL DIED IN THE CAVE.
THE TWO OTHER HEROES FELL IN A PIT, AND NOW IT'S JUST ME AND THE GIRL WITH THE GLASSES.
HEY, FOUR-EYES!
SHUT UP. I'M RIGHT HERE.
SWF
ANYWAY, YOU'RE THE ONE WHO WANTED TO TALK, SO I DON'T SEE WHY YOU EVEN NEED ME HERE.

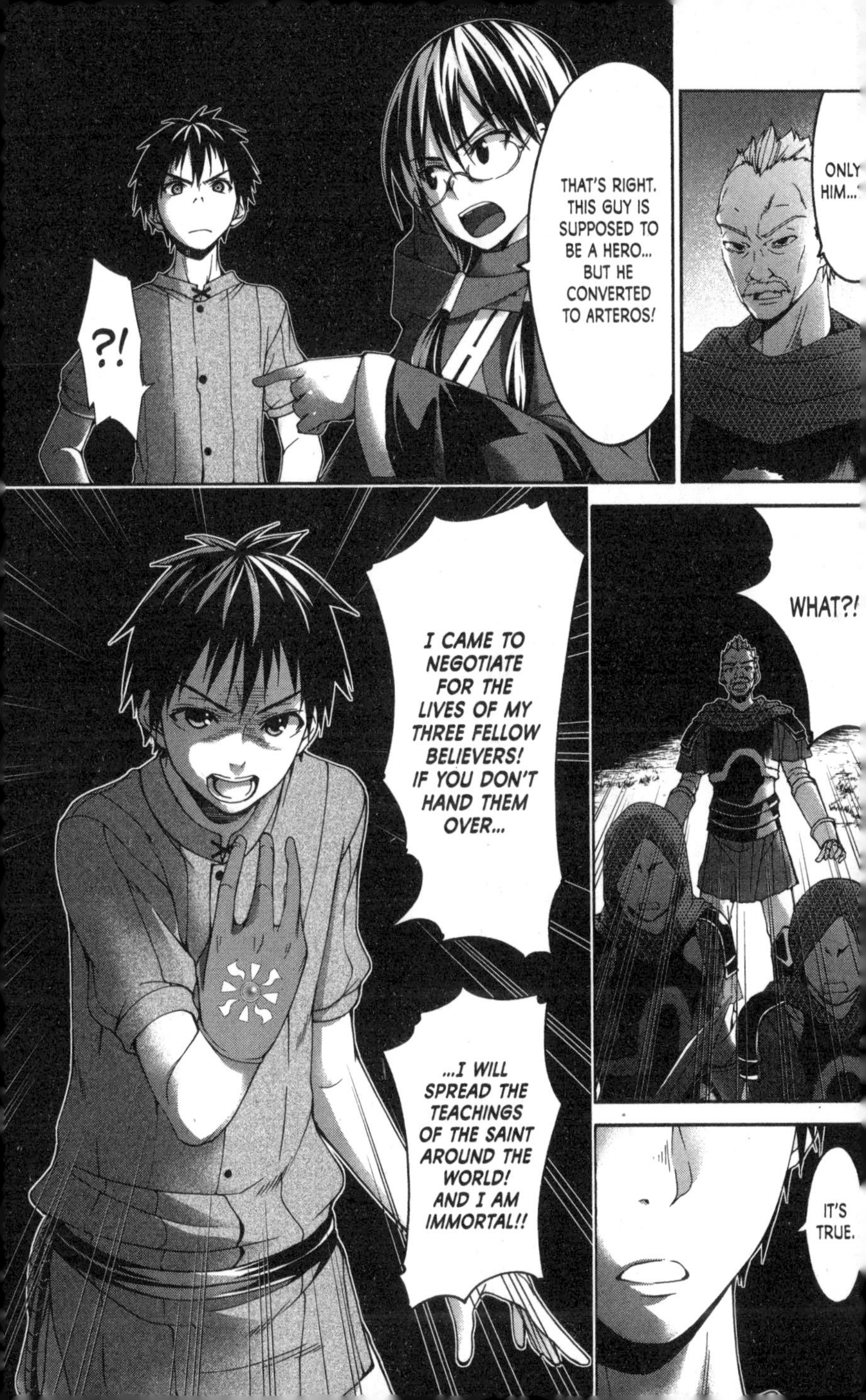
ONLY HIM...?
THAT'S RIGHT. THIS GUY IS SUPPOSED TO BE A HERO... BUT HE CONVERTED TO ARTEROS!
?!
WHAT?!
IT'S TRUE.
I CAME TO NEGOTIATE FOR THE LIVES OF MY THREE FELLOW BELIEVERS! IF YOU DON'T HAND THEM OVER...
...I WILL SPREAD THE TEACHINGS OF THE SAINT AROUND THE WORLD! AND I AM IMMORTAL!!

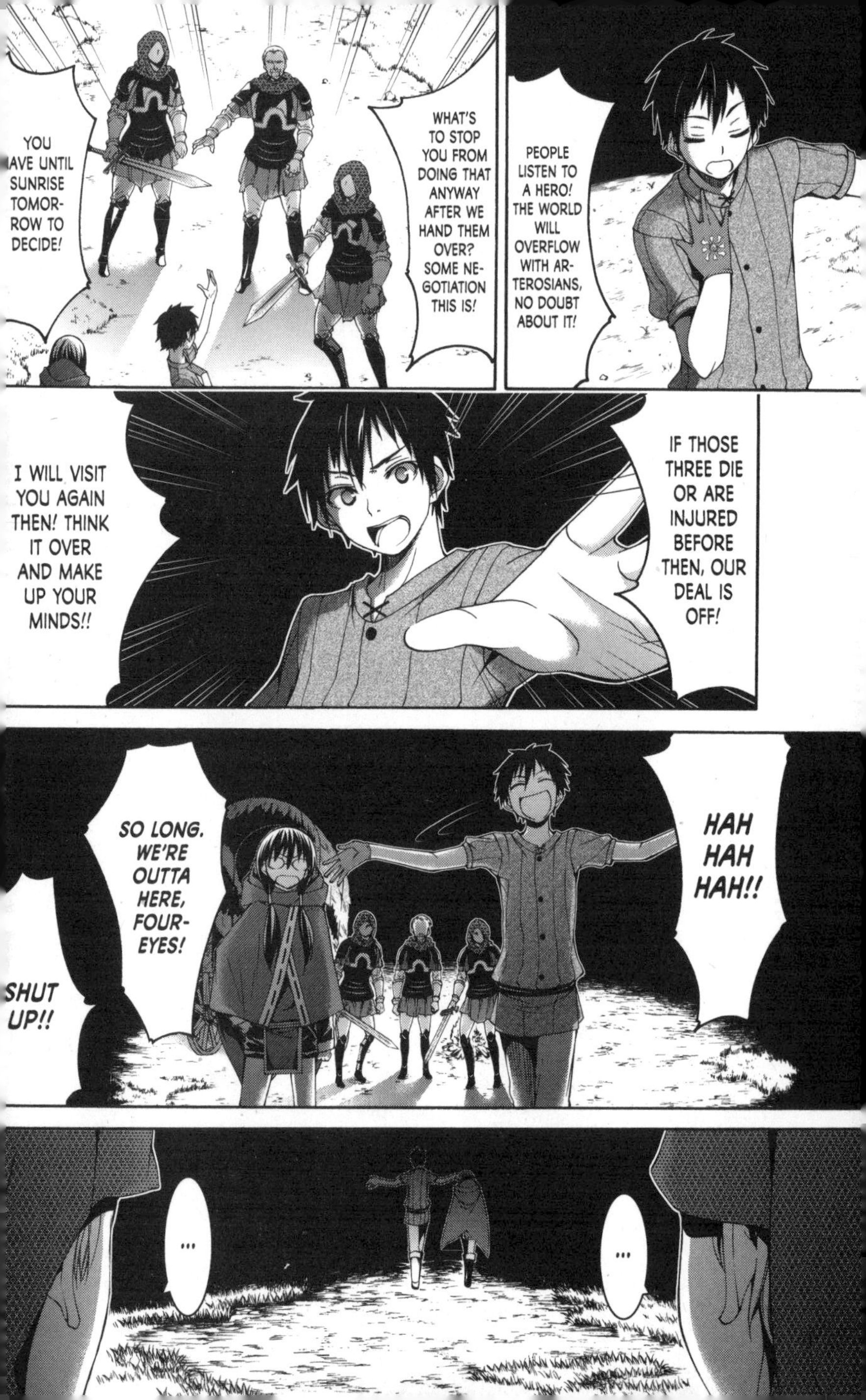
PEOPLE LISTEN TO A HERO! THE WORLD WILL OVERFLOW WITH ARTEROSIANS, NO DOUBT ABOUT IT!
WHAT'S TO STOP YOU FROM DOING THAT ANYWAY AFTER WE HAND THEM OVER? SOME NEGOTIATION THIS IS!
YOU HAVE UNTIL SUNRISE TOMORROW TO DECIDE!
IF THOSE THREE DIE OR ARE INJURED BEFORE THEN, OUR DEAL IS OFF!
I WILL VISIT YOU AGAIN THEN! THINK IT OVER AND MAKE UP YOUR MINDS!!
HAH HAH HAH!!
SO LONG. WE'RE OUTTA HERE, FOUR-EYES!
SHUT UP!!
...
...

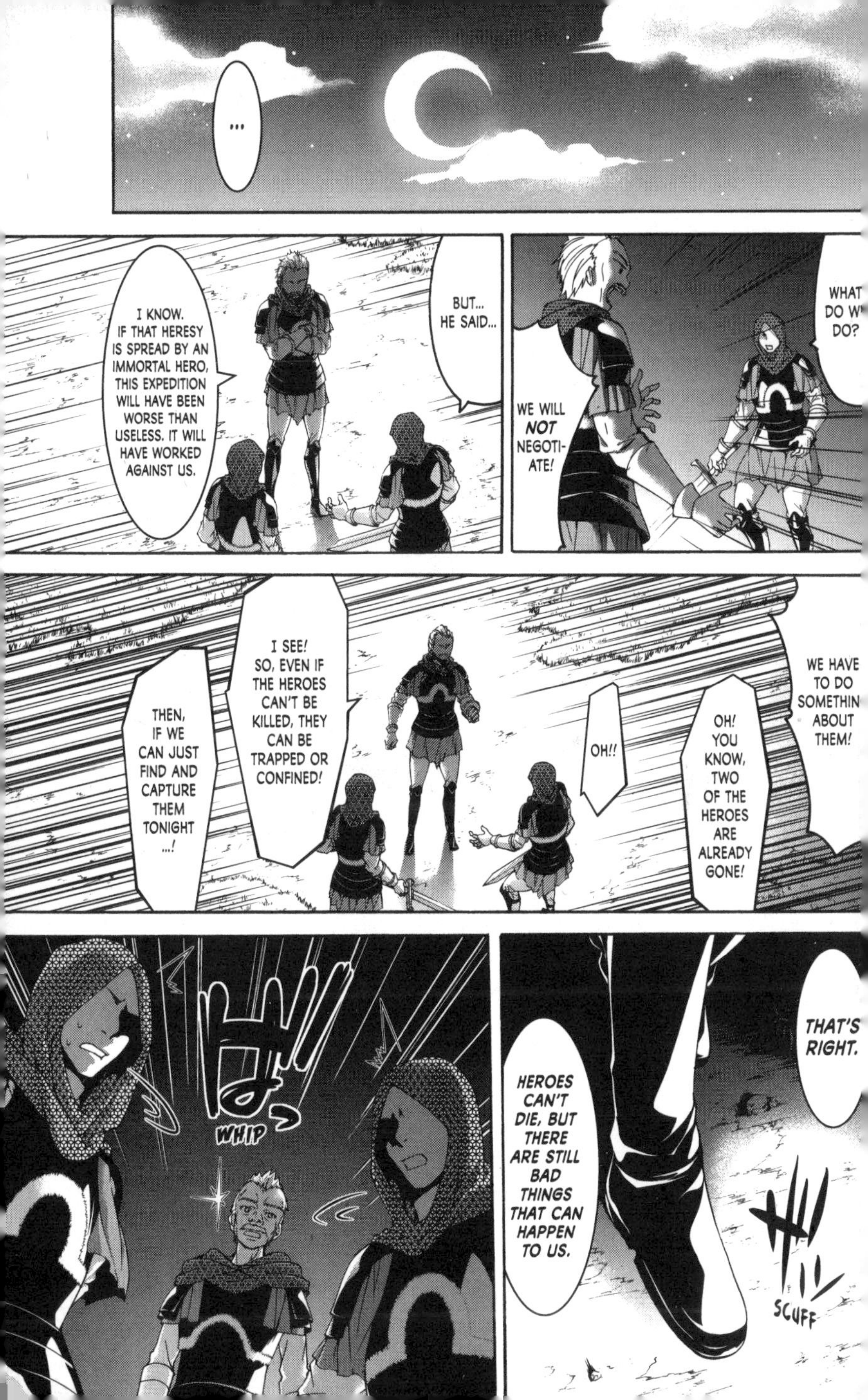
...
WHAT DO W DO?
WE WILL NOT NEGOTIATE!
BUT... HE SAID...
I KNOW. IF THAT HERESY IS SPREAD BY AN IMMORTAL HERO, THIS EXPEDITION WILL HAVE BEEN WORSE THAN USELESS. IT WILL HAVE WORKED AGAINST US.
WE HAVE TO DO SOMETHIN ABOUT THEM!
OH! YOU KNOW, TWO OF THE HEROES ARE ALREADY GONE!
OH!!
I SEE! SO, EVEN IF THE HEROES CAN'T BE KILLED, THEY CAN BE TRAPPED OR CONFINED!
THEN, IF WE CAN JUST FIND AND CAPTURE THEM TONIGHT ...!
THAT'S RIGHT.
HEROES CAN'T DIE, BUT THERE ARE STILL BAD THINGS THAT CAN HAPPEN TO US.
SCUFF
WHIP

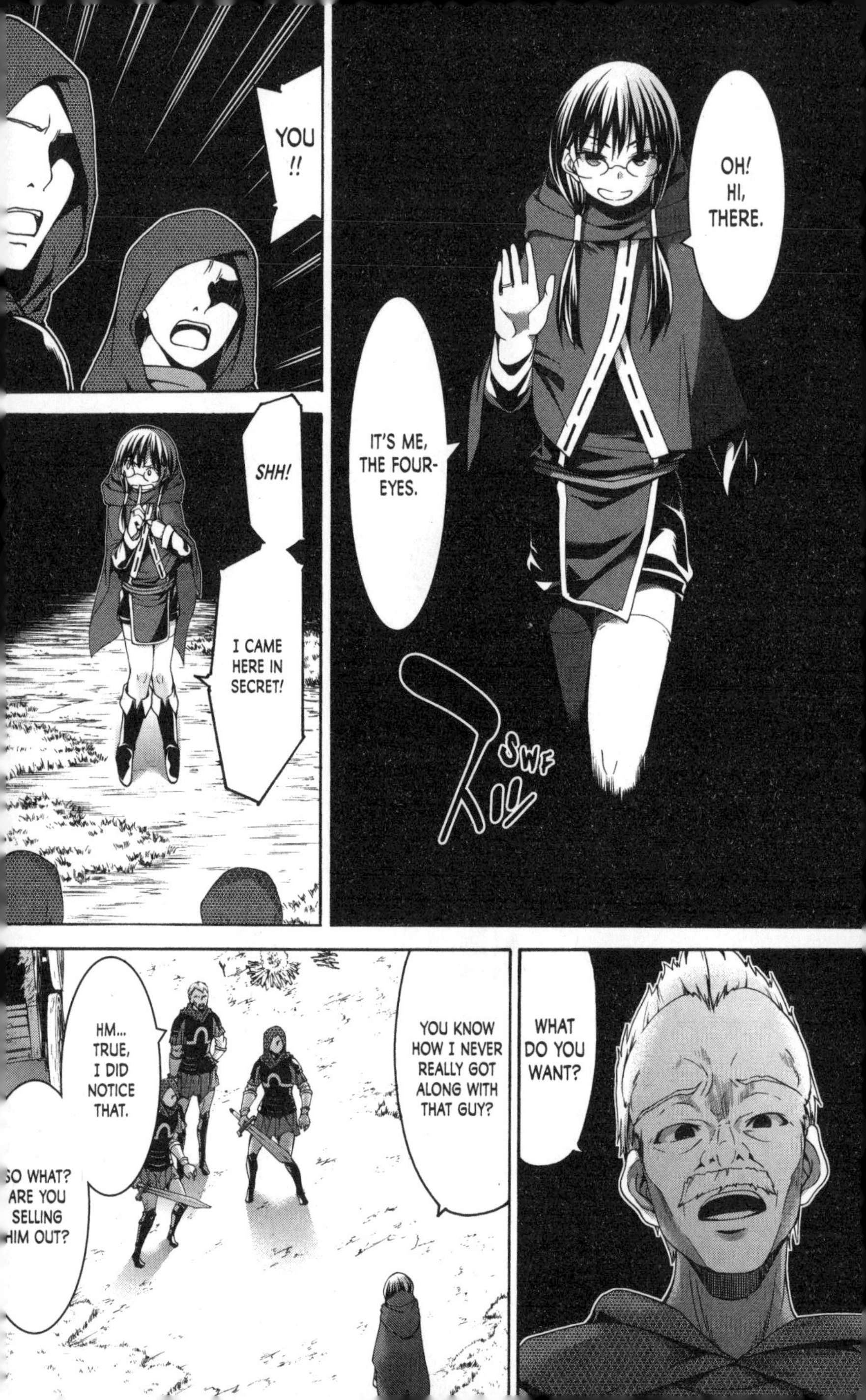
OH! HI, THERE.
IT'S ME, THE FOUR-EYES.
SWF
YOU!!
SHH!
I CAME HERE IN SECRET!
WHAT DO YOU WANT?
YOU KNOW HOW I NEVER REALLY GOT ALONG WITH THAT GUY?
HM... TRUE, I DID NOTICE THAT.
SO WHAT? ARE YOU SELLING HIM OUT?

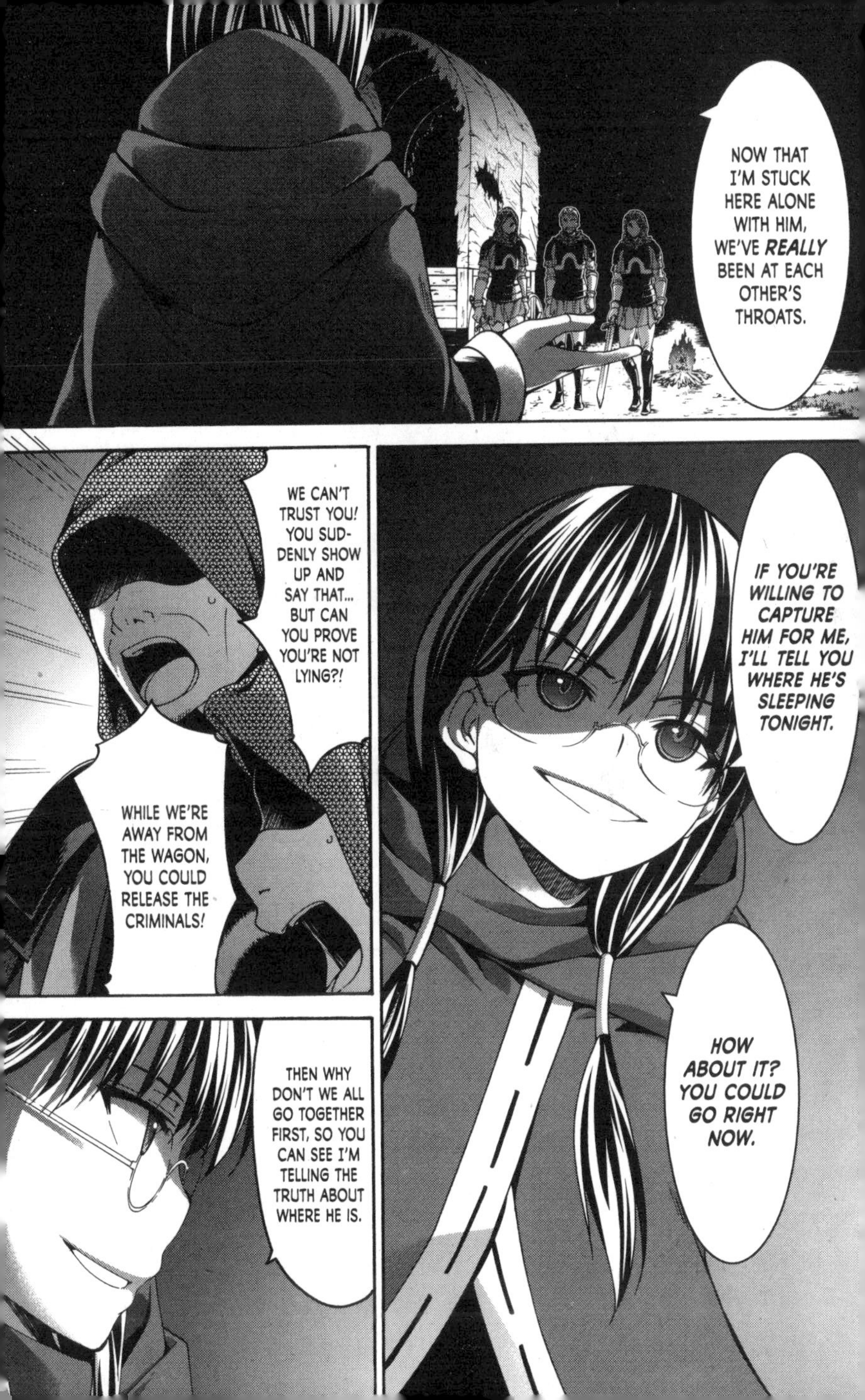
NOW THAT I'M STUCK HERE ALONE WITH HIM, WE'VE *REALLY* BEEN AT EACH OTHER'S THROATS.
IF YOU'RE WILLING TO CAPTURE HIM FOR ME, I'LL TELL YOU WHERE HE'S SLEEPING TONIGHT.
HOW ABOUT IT? YOU COULD GO RIGHT NOW.
WE CAN'T TRUST YOU! YOU SUD-DENLY SHOW UP AND SAY THAT... BUT CAN YOU PROVE YOU'RE NOT LYING?!
WHILE WE'RE AWAY FROM THE WAGON, YOU COULD RELEASE THE CRIMINALS!
THEN WHY DON'T WE ALL GO TOGETHER FIRST, SO YOU CAN SEE I'M TELLING THE TRUTH ABOUT WHERE HE IS.

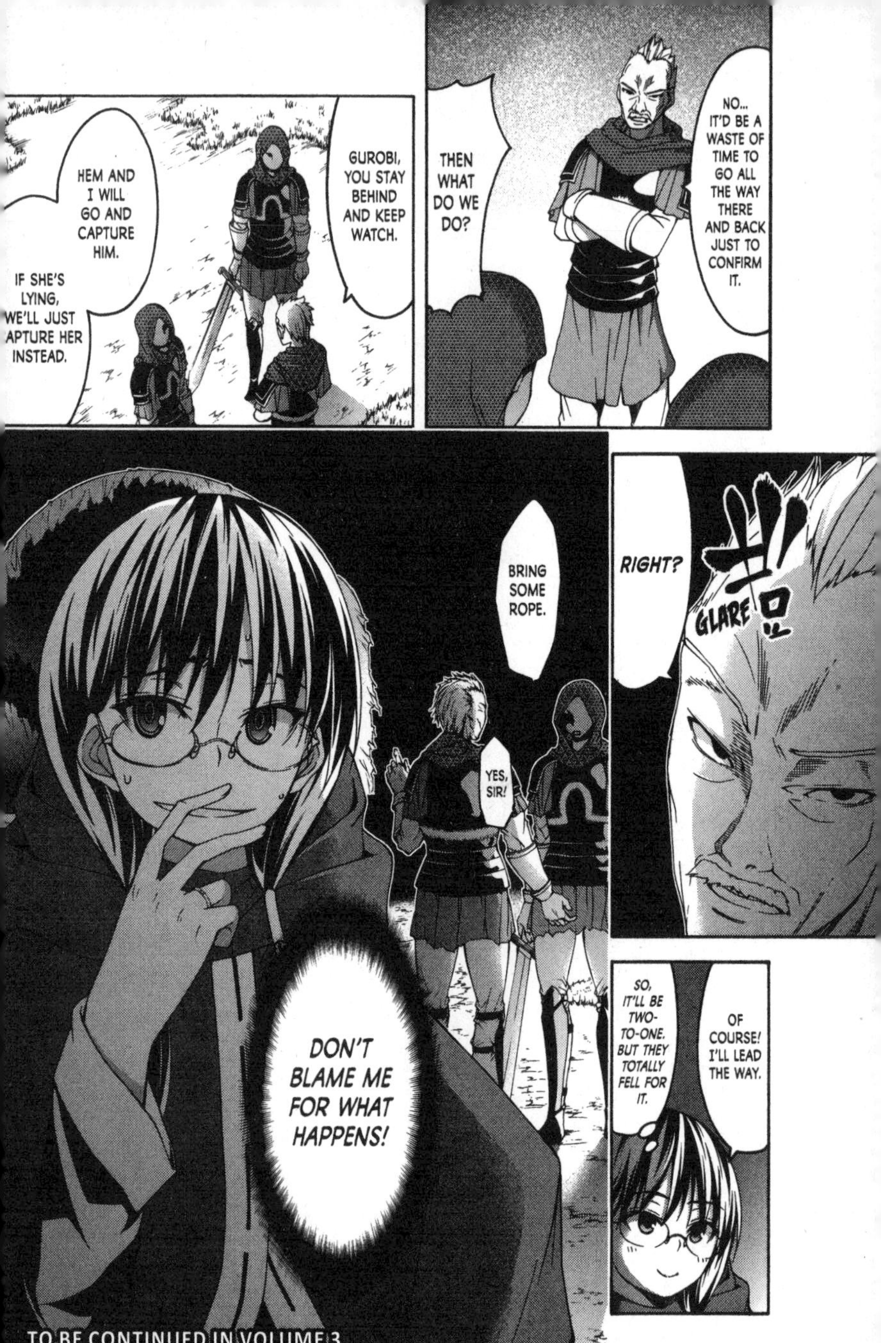
NO... IT'D BE A WASTE OF TIME TO GO ALL THE WAY THERE AND BACK JUST TO CONFIRM IT.
THEN WHAT DO WE DO?
GUROBI, YOU STAY BEHIND AND KEEP WATCH.
HEM AND I WILL GO AND CAPTURE HIM.
IF SHE'S LYING, WE'LL JUST APTURE HER INSTEAD.
RIGHT?
GLARE
OF COURSE! I'LL LEAD THE WAY.
SO, IT'LL BE TWO-TO-ONE. BUT THEY TOTALLY FELL FOR IT.
BRING SOME ROPE.
YES, SIR!
DON'T BLAME ME FOR WHAT HAPPENS!
TO BE CONTINUED IN VOLUME 3

I'M STANDING ON
A MILLION LIVES

A dark and sexy body-horror action manga perfect for fans of _Prison School_ and _High School of the Dead_!

Shuichi Kagaya is a smart kid, and most smart kids his age would be thinking about college. Shuichi is also a monster, and he's smart enough to know that monsters don't go to college. But after he uses his monstrous form to save his classmate Claire Aoki, it doesn't matter what his plans for the future were, because he's not the one making the decisions anymore. Now that the seductive, sadistic Claire knows Shuichi's secret, she's got her own ideas about what a monster is good for—because he's not the first monster she's met...

KC KODANSHA COMICS

GLEIPNIR

nir © Sun Takeda/Kodansha Ltd.

"You and me together...we would be unstoppable."

EDENS ZERO

エデンズゼロ

HIRO MASHIMA IS BACK! JOIN THE CREATOR OF ***FAIRY TAIL*** AS HE TAKES TO THE STARS FOR ANOTHER THRILLING SAGA!

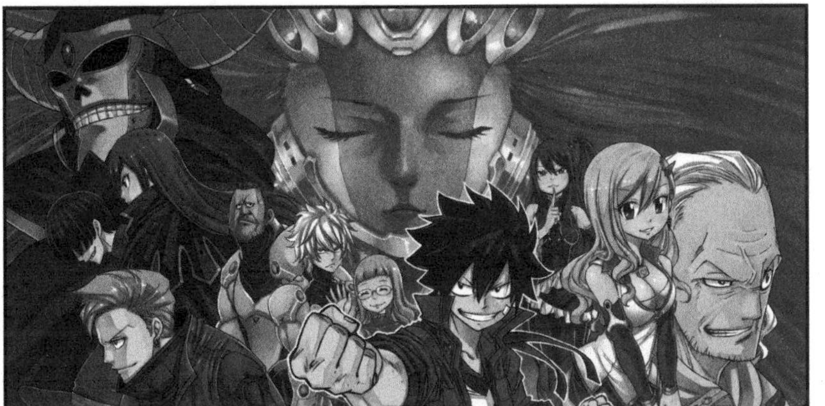

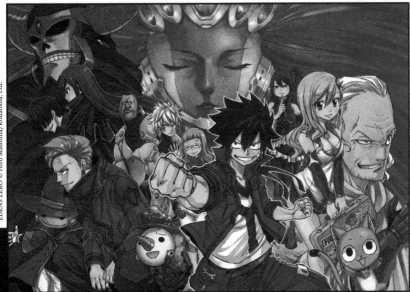

A high-flying space adventure! All the steadfast friendship and wild fighting you've been waiting for...IN SPACE!

At Granbell Kingdom, an abandoned amusement park, Shiki has lived his entire life among machines. But one day, Rebecca and her cat companion Happy appear at the park's front gates. Little do these newcomers know that this is the first human contact Granbell has had in a hundred years! As Shiki stumbles his way into making new friends, his former neighbors stir at an opportunity for a robo-rebellion... And when his old homeland becomes too dangerous, Shiki must join Rebecca and Happy on their spaceship and escape into the boundless cosmos.

KC KODANSHA COMICS

A Kodansha Comics Trade Paperback Original
I'm Standing on a Million Lives volume 2 copyright © 2017 Naoki Yamakawa/Akinari Nao
English translation copyright © 2019 Naoki Yamakawa/Akinari Nao

Published in the United States by Kodansha Comics, an imprint of
Kodansha USA Publishing, LLC, New York.

Publication rights for this English edition arranged through
Kodansha Ltd, Tokyo.

First published in Japan in 2017 by Kodansha Ltd., Tokyo.

ISBN 978-1-63236-822-5

Printed in the United States of America.

www.kodanshacomics.com

9 8 7 6 5 4 3 2 1
Translation: Christine Dashiell
Lettering: Thea Willis
Editing: Erin Subramanian and Tiff Ferentini
Kodansha Comics edition cover design by Phil Balsman